THE BIG BUDDHA BICYCLE RACE

From defilement can come much wisdom.
                                     – Ajahn Po

From defilement can come much defilement.
                             – TSgt Harley Baker

THE BIG BUDDHA
BICYCLE RACE

TERENCE A. HARKIN

 Silkworm Books

ISBN 978-616-215-132-3

First published in 2017 by
Silkworm Books
104/5 M. 7, Chiang Mai–Hot Road, T. Suthep
Chiang Mai 50200 Thailand
P.O. Box 296, Phra Singh Post Office, Chiang Mai 50000
info@silkwormbooks.com
http://www.silkwormbooks.com

5 4 3 2 1

Dedication

To Captain Kenneth Little, a pioneering African-American graduate of the Air Force Academy (Class of 1969). Like far too many veterans of Vietnam, Thailand, Laos and Cambodia, he spent the rest of his life in self-imposed solitude, Missing in America;

To Phil Hawkshead, who flew more than 150 combat missions at night over the Ho Chi Minh Trail and to his fellow air force cameramen, twelve of whom died in combat in Southeast Asia;

And to the people of Laos, who were caught in a crossfire of Western ideologies that proved that war didn't need to be nuclear to be catastrophic.

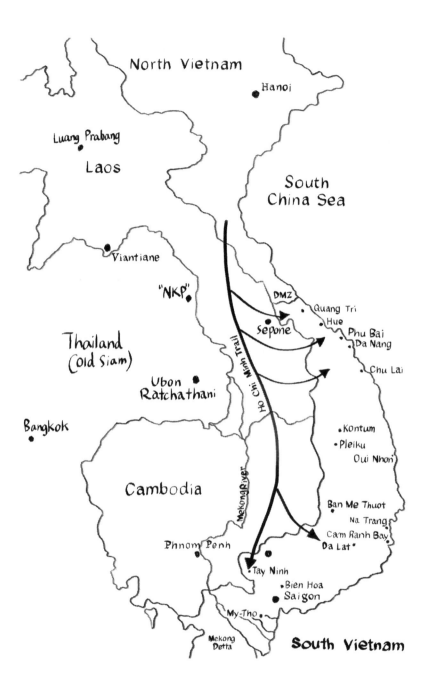

Prologue

When you've been to the mountaintop
     the valleys seem tame
When you've flown through lightning
     Death's just a game
When you've kissed Carly Simon
     other women seem plain
When you've been to Mexico
     you can't come home again

When your back was aching
     she washed away the pain
When the storm was raging
     she knew what song to sing
Lost in the desert
     she brought you the sea
When your mind was sinking
     she fed you tea

When you've been to the mountaintop
     the world seems flat
When you've fought in Cambodia
     peace feels like a trap
When the full moon breaks through the clouds
     the light bursts like flak
When you've flown through the Mu Gia Pass
     you know you can't come back

The waters taste bitter
     when you've sipped on champagne
Your throat becomes scratchy
     despite monsoon rain
Your ears fill with silence
     when the sweet sparrow sings
When you've been to the mountaintop
     you can't come home again

Falling Backwards

It must have been a hallucination. Sitting in a mountain cave along the winding road that led northwest to Luang Prabang, I could smell the incense floating in the air—pure, not burned to hide some weekend hippie's marijuana cigarette—a dusky smoke perfume that had burned in Asia for a thousand centuries. The light was golden, an aura unseen in America since brigantines stopped bringing whale oil back from the Pacific...

How can I trust dream-visions that keep floating up from the murky depths? Hasn't my memory been obliterated by drink and drugs and the passage of time? Why am I afraid to ask, afraid of being mistaken for a rambling derelict on an L.A. street corner?

Alone on New Year's Eve in a bungalow atop Mount Washington, I snort cocaine and chase it down with Jack Daniels when I run out of stale champagne. Mesmerized by blurry car lights floating in the distance up and down the Pasadena Freeway, I can hear the *voice* of Ajahn Po—my first true teacher—calling to me, but I'm not sure I understand his *words*.

Would anyone believe that I was once a Buddhist monk who sat in Noble Silence on the rock floor of that cave, cushioned only by a thin straw mat? Deep in meditation, I recollected the painful days of my Irish Catholic youth when my heart wanted to love Jesus while my mind warred with Pope Pius and Martin Luther, with Saint Thomas Aquinas and Bishop Fulton J. Sheen and would give me no peace. When did my father, my aviator hero, become my oppressor? Why was he angered by questions about race and politics and faith? Why did he offer to help me with drums or flying lessons, but not with both? Was it a test? Did he already know the answer? Why did he never talk about his days in Florida, already a man at age eighteen, who turned English farm boys into the pilots who drove back the mighty Luftwaffe?

While candles and incense were burning on the cave's stone altar I went into a trance so deep that the graceful bronze image of a Sukhothai Buddha, sitting in eternal serenity and wisdom, transformed into a television that droned with an endless loop of John F. Kennedy—young and handsome—giving his inaugural speech with unblinking, granite-chiseled confidence that made me eager to pay any price and bear any burden he asked of us. Deep in dreams and memories, I forgot I was a holy man and drifted in a cloud to those tragic days from high school to college when I lost my innocence but tried to cling to my ideals. I would pay any price and bear any burden to go to *film school*—that was how I would do my part to save the world now that JFK was gone. But when I meditated even deeper I had a troubling vision within my vision: Harley Baker was burning on a funeral pyre, his outlaw-bluesman's heart and mind blown away with amphetamines, his hard, white body and redneck soul wasted with opium-tainted grass and BX booze.

I didn't meet Harley until I stood toe to toe with Death. A warrior, an Air Commando, he taught me how to laugh at it and fear it and quash it away and never quite ignore it. Nothing in my Boston childhood had equipped me for the realities of Southeast Asia—the smooth, cool pages of *National Geographic* magazines stacked in our attic in the outskirts of Boston made Indochina look like Eden. It was Harley who prepared me for combat, accidentally preparing me for monkhood along the way. But in my vision I knew that Tech Sergeant Baker was as doomed as President Kennedy. And I could see my own soul, lost in the void, lost along the sidelines of the Big Buddha Bicycle Race.

My mind skids past fading memories I want to recall and lands in catastrophe on days past I have forgotten just as vividly as days I never lived at all. It must have been the whiskey. Or the red-rock heroin. How did we survive the plane crash? It seemed so real when the North Vietnamese took us prisoner. Why do I still dream of fire and fear a candle burning in the night? Who was Tukada? Baker survived two crashes, but didn't he kill himself shooting up speed? Why aren't I certain? What has happened to my mind?

I too walked away from the burning wreckage. I too survived a SAM missile's direct hit—or was it a Strela? Harley looked off a thousand yards into the tree line when he talked to you, often rambling and unable to make sense. I needed someone to tell me that I had *escaped* the thousand-yard stare, but how did you translate that into Laotian? Had I survived the crash or was I a ghost trapped in my own nightmare, unable to escape even to the Buddhist *samsara* of endless rebirths, never-ending cycles of worldly suffering and delusion? Was I living in hell or purgatory or just the twentieth century?

Sitting in that cave in Laos, I could not erase my memory-visions of

Colonel Strbik and Captain Rooker—the best damned pilots in the unit. I could see them burning, their faces serene like the face of Saint Polycarp, except there would be no miracle—streams of their own blood would not put out the flames. My visions were seared by burning wreckage and smoldering villages and I could no longer distinguish the mangled corpses of war heroes from beauty queens, of Asians from barbarian invaders, of friends from enemies. I was haunted by grunts like Pigpen Sachs, the door gunner, and Jeff Spitzer, my fellow cameraman, who dreamed of being held in the arms of college girls as they died—and called out for their mothers. Reporters said that bodies were being stacked like cordwood in Vietnam, but in Laos nobody was going to that much trouble. Human beings were being chopped down like the weeds the hill-tribe Hmong dried out by the side of the dirt road to make into hand brooms. Only nothing could be made from something so useless as a dead human being. Cremation was merciful in the jungle.

In the distant days between college and monkhood, in the days when I failed as a draft-dodger and failed as a soldier, I would have been satisfied waking up in the boondocks of Thailand with day lilies filling the vase that sat on the rickety rattan table next to my bed at Bungalow Ruam Chon Sawng. I would have been content with flowers that lived a single day, even though waking up with a tiny bar girl's hand on my chest, whispers of "lovely, so lovely" alighting like soft petals, was what I really needed to put my mind at ease. In the boondocks of Thailand along the Lao frontier, Baker, Washington, Wheeler and Shahbazian usually got to the Corsair Club before me and I often went home from the bars alone because even in my days as a lover of whores I maintained certain standards. I had to know her name and where she was from and if her dad was a rice farmer or a sailor in the Royal Thai Navy, because whores were people too, just like GIs.

Vietnamese villagers prayed for us every September, wrapping the sculpted Buddhas that sat inside their pagodas with saffron to appease the souls of the unburied dead—the wandering restless souls of beggars, soldiers and prostitutes. But I fear those prayers were not enough. So many nights on the Lao frontier it was not until the first pink glow of dawn that I finally fell asleep, and even then it was not peace that came but my own private samsara. To this very day I ask: *Will I wake up ten thousand times without awakening? Or will these cycles of rebirth become the path to my redemption?*

I hadn't gone crazy yet when I first went out to California, although I sometimes fear my madness started the day I was born. Sure, I'd been thrown out of the Pentagon. Something about my involvement with the GI contingent that walked at the head of a 250,000-person anti-war march on Washington called the Second Vietnam Moratorium. It might have cost me an automatic promotion from airman first class to sergeant, but it had been part of a *plan*. It got me assigned at last where my recruiter had *guaranteed* I'd be assigned all along—the 1361st Photo Squadron at Norton Air Force Base, California, headquarters of the Aerospace Audio-Visual Service, acronym AAVS (and pronounced "AVIS" in air-force speak).

A year earlier I had been teaching English to Portuguese immigrants at a high school in Bristol, Rhode Island. It kept me out of the draft, but I was miserable. I could have blamed the fact I had no textbooks. Or I could have blamed my students—the boys had barely avoided being sent off to fight colonial wars in Angola and Mozambique only to discover when they got to America that they would be drafted to fight in Vietnam if they learned English. In the end, though, I had to blame myself—a dedicated career teacher or even a dedicated draft-dodger would have made it work. Instead, my heart was three thousand miles away. I had been accepted for a master's program in film production at the University of Southern California. I was ready to go, except Congress changed the rules for the Class of '68 and eliminated draft deferments for grad school. Some of my friends talk-ed bravely about Canada and Sweden, and I gave it some thought, but I couldn't help noticing that none of them left. The head of the AV depart-ment at Bristol High had been a Marine cameraman in Korea. When he got wind of my story, he suggested I pay a visit to an Air Force recruiter he knew—Tech Sergeant Gallipeau.

Gallipeau seemed harmless enough, with a Pillsbury Doughboy body stuffed into his dress blues and a crooked grin that reminded me ever so much of Gomer Pyle's. He enticed me into giving up my teaching gig by promising with great sincerity that I would be spending four years with a motion picture unit an hour from L.A. The son-of-a-bitch had lied, of course. Thanks to something in the fine print about "Needs of the Air Force," I ended up in a converted broom closet in Washington, DC, cranking out certificates of graduation for each and every attendee of DOD-COCS, a semi-boondoggle Department of Defense computer school for field-grade officers. Thanks to its prototype 1937 Xerox machine, I got to singe my fingers in a pint-sized oven, baking the toner on each and every diploma. I shared one other job at DODCOCS with two fellow low-level enlisted men—keeping the massive urns in the officers' lounge filled with enough coffee to make sure the majors and colonels didn't snore during the lectures. I never wanted to see or smell coffee grounds again.

The experience was suffocating—pasting on a phony smile day after day for the powerful, blindly ambitious careerists who surrounded me. At the same time, my mind was being buffeted by what I could only describe as powerful forces of history. It was the summer of 1969 and Richard Milhous Nixon occupied the Oval Office. He promised in June to start bringing troops home, but more than two hundred a week were still coming home in body bags. Even more unsettling, stories started appearing in the GI underground press about an Army lieutenant named Calley being charged with the massacre of hundreds of unarmed women, children and old men in an obscure hamlet called My Lai.

I had never been able to sort out exactly what I believed about the war as a college student, even after the Tet Offensive in January of '68 showed that the Johnson administration had been dead wrong about there being "light at the end of the tunnel." In the spring of '68 we learned at campus teach-ins how General Navarre, the French commander in Vietnam, had said exactly the same thing in *1950*—four years before the Vietnamese crushed the Foreign Legion at Dien Bien Phu. As a college senior, however, large anti-war protests had left me cold. I had been put off by fellow students who came across as spoiled rich kids who couldn't be bothered with the sacrifices our fathers had taken for granted during World War II. I was downright disgusted when these same children of privilege turned into angry mobs shouting nursery rhyme chants like "Ho, Ho, Ho Chi Minh, the Viet Cong are gonna win." Now though, I was being sucked into the anti-war movement by fellow *servicemen* who found My Lai repugnant and by returning combat veterans who were fed up with the senselessness of the whole enterprise, a quagmire that by June had cost 35,000 American lives.

I tried to discuss the situation with my father that summer, but when you begin your aviation career as a World War II flight instructor, you don't question authority any more than you want your own authority questioned. It was right about then that we stopped talking.

DODCOCS was supposed to be a plumb joint-command assignment, but I was just as miserable as when I left Rhode Island. All I had accomplished was trading bedlam for solitary confinement, and I was still three thousand miles from California. Major Elton Toliver III, our Marine personnel officer, sported a throw-back old-school flat-top haircut like my dad used to wear. It reminded me so much of a miniature aircraft carrier that I half-expected to see little fighter-bombers taking off whenever I ran into him, which was often. He seemed to *enjoy* calling me into his office and telling me with a smirk how poorly I was fitting in, never missing a chance to point out infractions only visible to a gung-ho career military man—a mustache hair that had grown an eighth of an inch too long or a runaway sideburn that decided to graze my ear. My freshly shined shoes never seemed to make it to work without getting scuffed, and my belt buckle was forever wanting to slip out of alignment. Colonel Manketude, the Air Force liaison officer, started checking up on me too and was soon harrumphing at the pictures of Woodstock hanging on my broom-closet bulletin board and harrumphing again when he found a GI underground newspaper lying on my desk. A few weeks later he went positively apoplectic when I turned down a slot as a navigator/bombardier at OTS (Air Force shorthand for Officer Training School), pretty much echoing my father's sentiments about wasting a good education when I could be earning my wings.

What Manketude, Toliver and my father failed to understand was that freshly minted navigator/bombardiers were *not* being assigned to the Aerospace Audio Visual Service. Toliver, a third generation Yale graduate, seemed to take it personally that a fellow Ivy-Leaguer would turn down a commission, which in turn seemed to deepen his irritation at my wispy mustache and the Air Force regulation that permitted me to raise one without his permission. A couple of mellower lifers down in the print shop took me under their wing and clued me in that the *real* Air Force wasn't all spit-and-polish and square-your-corners like Headquarters Command. I should go for it, they said, if what I really wanted was to be assigned to a photo outfit. And if it meant risking deployment to Southeast Asia, so be it, I figured, so great was my fear of going brain dead at DODCOCS. The only catch was that I had no idea how to "go for it." I was depressed as hell until it dawned on me that I was just a stone's throw from the office of Ted Kennedy's Air Force caseworker. I was thrilled to hear back from Mrs. Riley that they were looking into my situation, but that didn't keep things from getting dicey.

It was in mid-November, on the Monday morning following the Second Vietnam Moratorium, that Toliver totally blew his stack, stopping in his tracks when he saw me in the hall. "Airman Leary—what the fuck are you doing wearing a black armband?"

"It's in memory of American soldiers killed in Vietnam, sir. Forty thousand so far. Ten thousand this year alone."

"Report to my office in one hour."

And when I did, he and Manketude were waiting for me. "I've done two fucking tours over there in case you forgot. And I'd rather be killing an eight-year-old gook kid in Vietnam than having to protect my own son from a bunch of Commies landing on the shores of California or Connecticut."

I wondered what Vietnamese naval genius Toliver knew about who could lead a fleet of sampans across the Pacific. Before I could ask, however, Manketude stepped in. "You've made *another* big mistake, Leary. You're finished here."

And with that he handed me a set of orders that bounced me out the front door of DODCOCS and on across the Potomac to the Pentagon itself for a temporary duty assignment (how did the Air Force come up with the acronym *TDY*?) at Headquarters Squadron, USAF. While the brass figured out what to do with me, Lieutenant Colonel Wippazetti put me to work painting nail heads visible only to him in the veneer paneling of his temporary office. "The reflections hurt my eyes," he said. And then, miraculously, Senator Kennedy's office got word that AAVS was shorthanded. Mrs. Riley made a couple of phone calls and suddenly my life jumped back on track, kind of like the movie *Easy Rider*—only in reverse, with a *happy* ending—as I headed off across the country, taking the southern route by way of New Orleans and Mardi Gras. Chuck Berry danced in my head singing "Route 66" as I headed out of Austin towards Amarillo, Texas; Gallup, New Mexico; and—on the home stretch for California—Flagstaff, Arizona. Driving my red '64 VW down Interstate 15, winding my way through the Cajon

Pass and on into San Bernardino, I felt sane and brilliant. I had crept out of D.C. in an ice storm—and now it was palm trees in February.

At Norton Air Force Base I remained hallucination-free even when we smoked the very fine Laotian dope Woody Shahbazian had brought back from Danang Air Base, Republic of Vietnam. It was early in 1970, and we were certain it was the *world* that was coming unglued, not our minds. The U.S. had metastasized into a giant dysfunctional family, full of barely controlled chaos, ruled with as much terror and amnesia and charm as Dad and Grandpa Leary had employed to mold our own clan into their image of what a proper Irish-American family should look like. I wasn't crazy, just inquisitive. With a bad habit of trying to ferret out the truth from only the flimsiest of evidence—about Grandpa Leary's drinking and Grandma Shepler's "nervous breakdowns" and about why the U.S. government was *really* sending us to Vietnam. Wanting to be seen and heard was a bad habit when you were a Leary child or an Air Force enlisted man.

No question about it, I was still a bit touchy when I landed in California. Five years going on ten of bad mood. The Revolution was coming, and I hadn't wanted to be caught dead with the squares in D.C. who were going to be standing trial in front of Jerry Rubin and Abbie Hoffman. Deep down inside, though, under my olive-drab fatigues, I was more a Flower Child than a revolutionary. A rock drummer since high school, I wanted to take *my* band, Stonehenge Circus, to India to find a guru of our own and a good electric-sitar player. With the dawning of the Age of Aquarius, I no longer had to be embarrassed by my secret passion to save the world nor tortured by my aching dream of being made love to by a harem of California poster girls. I no longer had to be trapped by the battle that had raged for years deep in my soul between the nuns at Holy Family and the centerfolds in Playboy magazine. In the Age of Peace and Love, I no longer feared Grandpa Leary's drunken tirades. Our main fear as GIs was that the Age of Aquarius would be over by the time we were given our discharge papers.

In the meantime, we tried to be as hip as possible while sporting GI buzz cuts, searching out other hipsters in the ranks who were testing the regs by wearing John Lennon-style granny glasses, prescription sunglasses, wristbands, mustaches, long sideburns, or long hair slicked down with Groom and Clean. At Norton, I soon discovered that mixed in with the GI hipsters were musicians like Sonny Stevens and Woody Shahbazian.

Stevens sported long sideburns and hid his long slick hair under his fatigue cap, day and night, indoors and out. Shahbazian, with the nonchalance of a soldier of fortune, did a full-court press on the regs with sideburns bordering on muttonchops, a bushy mustache, and long, styled hair that he hated to mess up wearing regulation head gear. He did wear regulation aviator sunglasses—despite not being an aviator—and got by on a single contact lens, always managing to misplace the other. His leather wristband commanded a lot of respect from his fellow enlisted men, wearing it as he did in honor of his hootch-mates at Danang who had died from a lucky shot with a shoulder-mounted rocket that had hit his quarters while he was off shaving or shitting, the details changing to fit his audience.

We pursued the hippie lifestyle as best we could by jamming in our barracks and later at the base theater, which finally led to a paying gig at Sarge's, the biker bar across the street from the east gate. At Sarge's, from my perspective behind the drums on the bandstand, I noticed several of the young AAVS production officers pursuing the hipster lifestyle themselves once they were off base and out of uniform. Two in particular stood out— Lieutenant Lisa Sherry and Lieutenant Rick Liscomb. She was statuesque with olive skin and deep, piercing eyes. He was a light-skinned black man, built like a linebacker, with a warm smile and a bone-crushing handshake. It was hard to tell at first if they were an interracial couple keeping it low-key or just good friends. It turned out that they had been both. She was the daughter of a French farm girl and an American fighter pilot who abandoned them soon after they got to the States, leaving her mother distraught and leaving Lisa to eventually scrape her way through the University of Maryland on scholarship. Liscomb had grown up in a comfortable middle-class section of Washington, DC, the son of the principal of a private school for children of diplomats. He had been one of the first black graduates of the Air Force Academy, where we found it easy to believe he had once been the light-heavyweight boxing champion.

Norton Air Force Base turned out to be my first assignment where they actually had airplanes. The flying part of the base was run by the Military Airlift Command (MAC) and was busy seven days a week operating a steady stream of flights full of troops and supplies headed for Vietnam. Every C-141 long-range transport in the MAC inventory was flying, and they still needed to bring in charters from Braniff, Continental, TWA and

Seaboard World. Our third of the base was converted from what had recently been a Strategic Air Command operation assembling and storing intercontinental ballistic missiles. When the Pentagon assigned AAVS primary responsibility for documenting the war in Southeast Asia, the 1361st quickly became a major source of television news footage seen by the American public and the main source of briefing films shown to the Congressional Armed Services Committees responsible for funding the war. They also did plenty of in-house Air Force training films, *Air Force Now!* (the movie newsmagazine shown at monthly commanders' calls worldwide), and a vast amount of still photography. Now that AAVS had consolidated its operations from Orlando, Florida; Wright-Paterson, Ohio; and Lookout Mountain in the Hollywood Hills, its labs were processing more feet of film a day than any movie studio in the world.

I was assigned to the editorial department, with a wisecracking young film editor named Larry Zelinsky as my immediate supervisor. Once he showed me how to thread up a Moviola, I was on my own. The 16mm synchronizer, viewer and splicer were pretty much the same as the 8mm equipment I had used at the Rhode Island School of Design. I felt lucky then that an English major from Brown was able to take film classes next door at RISD. I felt even luckier now to find myself in a spanking-new editing room as spacious and comfortable as anything in Hollywood.

Shahbazian talked me and Tom Wheeler, one of the unit clerk-typists, into going in with him on a mountain chalet in a pine forest high above San Berdoo. First Sergeant Link—"Missing Link," Zelinsky used to call him— was the Non-Commissioned Officer in Charge of all enlisted men in the 1361st. He split a gut when he found out we weren't stuck in the drafty barracks on base with the rest of the guys, but Shahbazian was a retired colonel's son and knew Link couldn't make us move back. Link blamed *me*, figuring as a college graduate I had to have been the brains behind the operation, but in those days I laughed it off, foolishly assuming his glowers were harmless. No one else seemed to mind, however, and soon hipster enlisted men and hipster officers were dropping by regularly, especially on the weekends. Liscomb was learning to play the guitar and was into Peter, Paul and Mary at the time. Woody wasn't a whole lot better on his acoustic guitar, but we enjoyed the change of pace singing folk songs after the din of the blues and Southern rock we were churning out at Sarge's. Somehow the lovely Lieutenant Sherry—Lisa when we were alone—began fraternizing with me after hours, volunteering to help me pack up my drums at Sarge's at the end of the evening and get them home safely. Woody, a firm believer in fraternizing with female officers, gave me his seal of approval, breaking into his Hank Williams imitation and singing, "If you've got the money, honey, I've got the time," whenever he saw me around the cabin.

Lieutenant Sherry might have been a little out of her mind dating an enlisted man, but I was sure my brain was firing on all cylinders when she let me take the wheel of her dazzling white MG convertible and we crossed the border into Mexico for the first time. Maybe we couldn't get to Woodstock, but we could enjoy this little caesura of pleasure and apparent sanity by camping out on a deserted beach on the Gulf of California. It was March, the end of the California rainy season. The rains had been kind that year, and the dusty chaparral and mesquite that covered the hills running south from San Bernardino and Escondido into Baja California had transformed into an emerald veil dotted with poppies, lupine and larkspur in full bloom. We sought out a simple fishing village she had heard of on the mainland side of the Gulf called Puerto Peñasco where we could sleep on the beach under the stars and where the food and drink in the nearby cantinas was plentiful and cheap. I was completely new to sleeping under the stars—the Boy Scouts had always used tents—but after quenching our thirst with cold, dark Mexican beer it seemed to work out fine.

Drinking some more of that cold, dark beer with dinner the following night, the kind WAF lieutenant expounded for me on her theories of free love and open marriage. After a few beers of my own, her logic seemed incontrovertible—in the Age of Aquarius, two people could care about each other deeply without chaining each other down. It didn't bother me at all that an old captain friend from Tan Son Nhut would be coming in TDY in the next few days. Our relationship was going to be chain-free.

Shahbazian had been worried that I had run off to get married that weekend, but any thoughts I might have had of marriage, open or otherwise, vaporized in the hot San Bernardino sun. I didn't hear a word from Lisa the entire week her captain was in town. The cabin seemed empty when I got home from work, and sitting alone out on the deck, I polished off two bottles of bootleg Tequila, one shot at a time, licking the salt off the back of my hand and biting down hard on the lemon chaser. And then the icing on the cake: I was diagnosed with non-specific urethritis. The doctors were concerned it might be one of the nasty new strains coming out of Vietnam, so they shot me full of antibiotics and ordered me to stay off sex and booze for a month. I spent much of my convalescence in a melancholy mood, nursing a broken heart while deprived of alcohol, a substance more precious to the Leary bloodline than oxygen. For four weekends at Sarge's I flailed dutifully at my drums, the only person in the joint who was sober. I swore off women for life and then drove myself crazy watching a parade of tanned San Bernardino townies in tank tops undulating before me on the dance floor. Liscomb sat down next to me at the bar one night while I was on break and noticed that I was sipping a ginger ale. "What's this, Brendan? You aren't in training, are you?"

"I'm afraid I've been burned by our friend, Lieutenant Sherry."

"*Lieutenant Sherry,*" he smiled. "She's great as a friend, even better as a drinking buddy, but when we tried to get serious once upon a time I just couldn't get used to her ideas about free love. Sounded good on paper, but the first time her old captain friend came in TDY from Tan Son Nhut, she had me crawling the walls. Our apartments at the Bachelor Officer Quarters are right across the hall from each other."

"Ah yes, the captain from Tan Son Nhut. I live up in the mountains and she *still* had me crawling the walls."

Before I went back on stage we clinked our glasses nostalgically to Lisa and free love.

Doing on-the-job training as a film editor in the AAVS postproduction department meant Zelinsky had pretty much left me alone to teach myself. I had a hunch work was going to get a lot more interesting when Lieutenant Liscomb asked for me on one of his projects, and, sure enough, he quickly became my favorite production officer, continually coming up with new and crazy ways to make an Air Force documentary while encouraging me to experiment with flashy editing techniques and cut to the beat of the heaviest-metal rock and funkiest funk we could dig up. We drove the civil-service types nuts over in the animation department, throwing new projects at them daily, depriving them of the down time they usually spent counting the hours until they could start collecting their pensions. He brought in a couple of experimental films he did when the Air Force sent him to the University of Rochester, and they turned out to be the only flicks I had ever seen weirder than the stuff my classmates at Rhode Island School of Design used to dream up. The weirdest of all was about a sculptress who had not created anything except genitalia of various shapes and sizes for over two years. Not something we'd be doing for *Air Force Now!* or for a congressional briefing film.

I had gone out of my way to avoid the big, brawling border towns at Mexicali, Tecate, and Tijuana in my travels with Lieutenant Sherry. I had heard too many horror tales about barroom blowjobs and hard-to-imagine debauchery involving smiling young señioritas and their pet donkeys. Naturally, the night I was pronounced cured, Tijuana was precisely where Woody Shahbazian, Tom Wheeler, Frank Lutz and Larry Zelinsky decided to take me, or more precisely, where *I* would take us since I was the one with the '64 V-Dub.

It's unlikely that Shahbazian, a flamboyant Air Force brat, and Zelinsky, a blue-collar wise guy from Detroit, would have ever crossed paths in civilian life, but in the Air Force they shared a powerful unspoken bond—they had already done a tour of Southeast Asia and felt right at home across the border showing us new guys the Third World ropes in case, despite Nixon's promised troop reductions, we too were shipped out. Zelinsky, in fact, had been so at home during the year he spent in Thailand that he had volunteered to go back so he could marry his Thai girlfriend. As he and Woody predicted, we had a roaring, rowdy good time of it that night, starting out at the Long Bar, Shahbazian's favorite, spending *Yanqui* dollars like visiting royalty while he told us about the time on R&R in Hong Kong he'd had a dozen girls sent to his room. "Sounds like love at first sight to me," said Lutz, the elf-like techie who worked on the dubbing stage recording sound.

We wound up at a back-alley hole-in-the-wall called Hernando's and decided around midnight that we had better hit the road while we were all accounted for. We had lost Wheeler for an hour until Zelinsky stumbled upon him sitting in a dark corner booth with a small-but-voluptuous young Mexican girl snuggled in his lap, smooching hungrily and sipping from the salty rim of the same margarita glass. We chattered all the way home, lamenting the night's near misses and bragging about old conquests—real, embellished and imagined—as we rolled down the open highway. Everyone, that is, except Wheeler, who pretended to sleep in the back seat. "Has everybody heard that Wheeler's in love?" asked Zelinsky. His uniforms may have been rumpled and he may have talked with a flat Midwestern twang, but there was a shrewd intelligence behind the Cheshire-cat smile that lit up his pudgy face.

"She's *nice*," protested Tom in those innocent days before he and Zelinsky became my bungalow-mates at Ruam Chon Sawng. He had the look of a blond-haired surfer but was in fact a pioneer pothead from a small town in upstate New York called Wappinger's Falls. "She's an orphan and she's only working the bars in Tijuana to save up for college."

Zelinsky howled with laughter. "Mom, I'd like you to meet my fiancée, Angelina. The entire Pacific Fleet wants to be her best man."

I had lost count at what might have been my eighth Cuba Libré; as we neared San Bernardino, I found myself wondering if Shahbazian's Hong Kong story could be true. With his long Joe Namath sideburns and his Grand Prix race-driver mustache, anything was possible with Woody and women. It was two weeks later that he smuggled a pair of Tijuana hookers back to San Bernardino. Dashing and charming, he was waved through customs at the border and the back gate at the base without a hitch. When he was confined to quarters for a month, he told us it was a small price to pay for becoming a genuine war hero and a legend in his own lifetime. When I asked him why he brought them to the barracks instead of up to the mountains, he said, "What do we need hookers for? We're living in a chalet." And sure enough, a few days after his release he started dating Kristin, the foxiest civilian secretary working at AAVS headquarters. I wasn't surprised to learn her family in Palm Springs had money. Shahbazian mentioned to her early on that his mother's family owned mining interests in Pennsylvania and West Virginia, leaving out the part about going bankrupt.

In the early months of 1970, of course, our only *real* bond at the 1361st Photo Squadron was a quiet determination to save our collective hides. The white contingent at Headquarters Squadron, Aerospace Audio Visual Service, was pathetically pimply-faced and naïve, which may have explained why the chaplain's daughter was willing to gang-bang the entire second floor of Barracks 1247. The Bloods weren't innocent at all, but they weren't clueing us in, preferring to watch from a distance as the pothead draft-dodgers and the beerhead lifers made each other miserable. Rick Liscomb tried to float with both the brothers and the hipsters when we were off-duty, which earned him the nickname "Moonbeam" from his fellow blacks. When he stopped eating meat and got into Zen meditation the hipsters picked up on "Moonbeam" too.

Our crowd was a fluke, crawling as it was with white, suburban dropouts; urban, upwardly mobile soul brothers; and hip, young officers who figured we could hide out in the safety of photo labs, sound stages and editing rooms in San Bernardino until the U.S. and the Vietnamese came to their senses. Nixon's Vietnamization program meant bringing home American ground troops and turning the fighting and dying over to the ARVN—the Army of the Republic of Vietnam. Even if a few of us might still be sent over to Southeast Asia, it would be to another photo squadron—on an Air Force base with bunks and a roof over our heads and, according to Shahbazian, swimming pools and air-conditioned NCO clubs. The certainty that we would never be slugging a gun through leech-infested equatorial jungle brought us all a measure of unspoken cheer. The assumption that many of us were heading for careers in Hollywood added to the warm, fuzzy vibes.

I was especially upbeat because I'd survived a temporary overdose of naïveté, volunteering for cameraman duty and getting turned down. Like a lot of my later problems, it was Ron Cooper's fault. I was impressed that Cooper had connections in Hollywood and had permission to drive in to Disney Studios every Friday afternoon to observe a real, live American Society of Cinematographers cameraman at work on the sound stage of the latest Disney live-action feature. It didn't seem important at the time that he was parlaying his part-time-projectionist gig at the base theater into a film-bootlegging racket. It was his passion for cinematography that rubbed off on me to the point that I volunteered to give up my air-conditioned editing room. Fool that I was, I failed to notice that every cameraman on base *except* Ron Cooper was scheduled to do a tour of Nam—flying combat—or had just come back. It turned out that editors were leaving the Air Force for cushy civil-service jobs faster than the Viet Cong could kill cameramen, however. Colonel Sandstrom, AAVS Director of Production, turned down my request, confining me instead to three years of hard labor hunched over my Moviola editing semi-truthful news clips. The more combat footage I looked at, the luckier I felt.

We were coasting, biding our time. And then, late in that fateful April of 1970, Commander in Chief Nixon, on the advice of his field marshal, Henry Kissinger, ordered the invasion of Cambodia, and everything changed. If you were a grunt in Vietnam, it made perfect sense. The Ho Chi Minh Trail was the North Vietnamese Army's main supply route into South Vietnam, and its southern branches ran through the hills and jungles of northeastern Cambodia. To make things worse, enemy troops often hid there with impunity between forays into South Vietnam. Unfortunately, nobody had explained that to the GIs in a stateside photo unit. We may have had Top Secret security clearances, but we didn't have a *"need-to-know."* And nobody explained it very well to the American public. To millions of Americans, Cambodia was a neutral country we were invading without a Congressional declaration of war and without informing its pro-American prime minister.

On April 30, Nixon went on national television, pointed to Cambodia on a map of Southeast Asia and announced, "This is *not* an invasion." He played it down as "an attack on enemy outposts," but college kids didn't buy it. The next day hundreds of campuses erupted—even apathetic USC, home of the film school I dreamed of attending. Eleven students were shot by police at Jackson State. Two died. The inept Ohio National Guard killed an ROTC cadet and three other students at Kent State, wounding nine more in the process. I had stumbled into the GI anti-war movement back in Washington, DC, when the My Lai story broke, but this was new—this wasn't a rogue unit gone bad, it was an entire administration going *mad*. We had been lulled into believing American troops would be coming home, not invading another country. Nixon's deceit pushed me over the edge, turning me—an active-duty GI—into a full-blown radical. I wasn't alone, but it wasn't comfortable. In rebuking our government we were in some way rebuking our fathers who had served unquestioningly in World War II.

Sonny Stevens, our lead guitar player at Sarge's, took a carful of us down to UC Riverside to see what kind of hot water we could get ourselves into at the office of the Student Mobilization Committee—the SMC for short. "It'll be a great way to meet college chicks," promised Stevens, like Shahbazian a colonel's son who knew how to fly under the brass's radar. He had been spending the war in relative obscurity, a laid-back, natural-born still and motion picture camera technician at the 1361st whose only failure had been trying to re-train Shahbazian as a fellow camera tech when Woody returned from his year of lifeguarding at Danang. Stevens was having better luck upgrading Woody's skills on rhythm guitar, but when college campuses erupted after Kent State, he saw that Woody's greatest potential was as a hell-raiser.

A couple of the SMC leaders at UC Riverside sent us off to a place called the Movement House near the University of Redlands to see some people who wanted to start organizing GIs. With the exception of Zelinsky, who never left the base, they didn't have much trouble molding Woody and the rest of my former Tijuana drinking buddies into the nucleus of Norton GIs for Peace, and soon we were turning out an underground newspaper, the *sNorton Bird*. Woody drew a cartoon for the first cover—a ruffled, cigar-chomping bald eagle wearing aviator's goggles and giving the finger mid-flight. Working stealthily at midnight, we delivered the inaugural issue to every officer and enlisted man living on the base. The next day, to paraphrase standard Air Force terminology, the Shinola hit the fan. The brass would have summarily shipped Stevens to Vietnam, but he didn't have the requisite year left on his enlistment, so they sent him a hundred miles up the coast to the Vandenberg Missile Test Range instead. Two of the brothers, a sound man/still photographer named Gene Blackwell and a lab tech named Lonnie Price, had orders cut the same day for opportunities to participate in what we jokingly called the Southeast Asia War Games, but it was no joke. They were heading for Nam. For Blackwell it was Detachment 13 ("The Lucky Thirteen") of the 600th Photo Squadron at Nha Trang. For Price it was Squadron Headquarters at Tan Son Nhut. Just before they left, their orders were changed to detachments at Korat and Udorn, Thailand, respectively. We speculated that this was a hush-hush part of Nixon's troop reduction plan that only looked like a troop reduction to the American public. Air force units that moved a hundred miles west to Thailand appeared on paper to have gone home, yet remained within easy striking distance of any target in Southeast Asia. Our president, we had to admit, was a tricky bastard.

A few days after the others, Wheeler and his sidekick, Dave Murray, found out they were going to do tours as combat clerk-typists, but at opposite ends of the war zone. Wheeler was being sent to Photo Detachment 2 at Takhli, Thailand, just north of Bangkok, while Murray was going to be squirreled away with the photo outfit at Cam Ranh Bay, Vietnam. Shahbazian got orders to do a surprise second tour at Tan Son Nhut a few weeks later, which didn't seem to make him all that unhappy now that Kristin was pressuring him to get married. Zelinsky was a strange case—he'd avoided our anti-war activities because he *wanted* to go back to his old unit at Ubon, Thailand. He had volunteered so he could marry his Thai girlfriend, and knowing the Air Force, Zelinsky told us, they would have punished him by *not* letting him go. Maybe it was because Lutz was an undersized munchkin, but he was overlooked. His orders didn't come through till the following spring—in plenty of time for the Big Buddha Bicycle Race.

Wheeler, from his vantage point in the orderly room, was keeping an eye on First Sergeant Link for us and reported that Link had figured incorrectly that I was the mastermind behind Norton GIs for Peace. Link made sure my orders for Tan Son Nhut came through with the first batch, but I fought it tooth and nail, applying for discharge as a conscientious objector with the help of Edward Poser, Esquire, an ACLU lawyer from Hollywood, the closest bleeding-heart enclave I could find to San Berdoo. He charged me what for an L.A. lawyer was a bargain fee of $50 an hour—even though I was only making $140 a month—but he offered me an installment plan. I would send him half my paycheck every month until my bills were paid. I accepted, given that I didn't have much choice. He didn't succeed in getting my orders canceled, but he did get them pushed back a month at a time while I met on base with Captain Allen Shelby, a lawyer at the judge advocate's office, and completed a long checklist of paperwork. Along the way I was evaluated by the base chaplain and base psychiatrist, at the same time requesting supporting letters and other documents from friends and family scattered across the country. It was a relief to know that my compadres from GIs for Peace were standing behind me. As Blackwell put it, "We're *all* doing our part for The Revolution, brother—working in different ways, that's all."

Wheeler, in addition to keeping an eye on Link, was using his back-channel contacts to make sure my application didn't get lost in the bowels of the Pentagon. Up at Vandenberg, it hadn't taken Sonny Stevens long to see how the brass was using a divide-and-conquer strategy to destroy Norton GIs for Peace. He resisted in a small way that summer by moving back to the area following his discharge. Going underground, he holed up on a ranch out in the desert near Victorville, growing marijuana to make ends meet. We co-edited the paper, bringing in an old friend of Blackwell and Price's, a hard-as-nails, pissed-off black Air Policeman just back from Pleiku, to give the editorial writing a little Black Panther bite. Still working out of the Movement House, we organized a GI contingent to lead a peace march on Riverside, home of March Air Force Base and the Big Ugly Friggin' "BUF" B-52's of Link and Sandstrom's old 22nd Bomb Wing. Maybe this was when I started to lose my mind, or maybe it was the presence of living, breathing long-haired hippie chicks from the University of Redlands and Cal State Riverside that got the better of my good judgment, but the next thing I knew we were promoting the Riverside peace march—off-duty, wearing civvies—by handing out leaflets at the entrance to George Air Force Base, a fighter base situated not far from Stevens's pot plantation, and at March Field itself. Given that March was a SAC base where Air Policemen in the perimeter guard towers shot to kill, we didn't squawk when they confiscated our fliers and brought us in for questioning. The hippie college girls seemed impressed when I called Captain Shelby at the JAG office at Norton and arranged our release—albeit with orders to stay five hundred feet from the main gate. An Oceanside march—next door to Camp Pendleton and half the Marines in America—soon followed. On both occasions I somehow ended up making speeches in front of thousands of people. Stevens's prediction seemed to come true when I started getting involved with one of the organizers from the Movement House who had been with me the night we were arrested, but she broke it off over some unfathomable breech of hipness at the moment of our greatest triumph—People's Independence Day, a Fourth of July rally that filled up a park in the middle of San Bernardino.

Shahbazian, Wheeler, and Zelinsky, my old Tijuana drinking buddies, stood together in the front row cheering me on, and next to them was my lovely radical organizer. Zelinsky knew he was shipping out the following week, and Wheeler and Shahbazian would be gone by the end of summer. Our hulking Air Policeman/editorial writer and an equally imposing cohort stood behind me on the dais, out of uniform, my volunteer bodyguards. Sonny Stevens, Frank Lutz and a couple of the bigger guys from the Movement House, also ex-GIs, weren't too far away, keeping their eyes out for any local crazies who might decide to rush the podium. I was glad to have them, because the only San Bernardino policemen I could spot were off in a distant parking lot enjoying coffee and doughnuts. The crowd was miniscule after what I had seen in Washington, but by San Bernardino County standards, several thousand people at a political rally was substantial, enough to attract an editor, a couple of reporters, and a photographer from the San Bernardino and Riverside newspapers. In the midst of introducing a lineup of agitprop folksingers, student radicals from the University of Redlands and UC Riverside, and a pair of Farmworkers Union organizers, I spotted Captain Shelby, along with Lieutenant Liscomb, Lieutenant Sherry, and a couple other young production officers, all dressed in civvies, observing the rally from the shade of a gnarly California oak. And then it was my turn to speak.

"Our objectives in Vietnam are illusory and our means of attaining them are barbaric," I said, trying to sound presidential even though I was skinny as a toothpick and in my twenties. I caught an approving smile from my soon-to-be-ex-flame and continued. "Where is this administration taking us? Where will the escalation end? If we are pursuing a failed policy, how can we continue to ask young Americans to die? And how can we ask black and Latino GIs to shed more blood than their white counterparts when they are still fighting for their civil rights at home? *Who will be the last to die in this tragic lost cause? Is there anyone in Washington who would step forward to take their place?*"

I thought I noticed Liscomb standing up a little straighter, straining to hear, but he was too far away for me to be sure. I continued, questioning the wisdom of a peacetime draft, comparing it to slavery, and hoped nobody noticed too many contradictions when I compared the modern U.S. to ancient Rome and Athens and to the Spanish, French and British empires in modern times, asking if we too were in decline and about to fall. I took another glance at the girl from the Movement House and finished up with the best Jack Kennedy imitation I could muster, seeming to inspire the audience when I exhorted, "If this nation is to survive as a beacon of democracy, we must commit ourselves to ending the war *now*! It is we who have taken on the awesome responsibility of leading the way. We must not falter! We must have peace!"

I was still basking in warm applause when we opened up the mike and Lieutenant Barry Romo stepped out of the crowd. Almost as soon as Romo took the podium, I realized that a new day had arrived. Stateside GI speakers were no longer needed. We now had combat veterans like Romo coming back, fresh in from hand-to-hand fighting in the Ashau Valley, who were willing and able to tell it like it was and who had all the strength, intelligence and character that a Lieutenant William Calley lacked. "The valley of the shadow of death," he called it, "a place where even the Lord's rod and staff offered little comfort." As instinctively as he might have taken one of those nameless hills in the Central Highlands, Romo had taken the open mike, pouring out his heart with a true soldier's understated eloquence. "Again and again my men died to take an objective. Whether it was a hilltop or a village, it didn't matter. We never failed. And again and again we were pulled out, giving that hard-earned ground back to the enemy...."

I could see Moonbeam Liscomb in the distance wanting to make a move for the stage. And I think it was his own privileged upbringing that held him back. He'd been raised black-upper-middle-class in Washington, DC, sensing the racism rampant in the country but never really experiencing it overtly except in its most refined forms—like the pressure of being the third black man ever to enter the Air Force Academy. Even from a hundred yards away I could see Moonbeam inching forward, away from his fellow officers and out into the hot sun. I wondered what was running through his mind, sensing that he regretted being trapped in his role as an Air Force support officer and that he realized he would never have his own war stories to tell.

I never really got a chance to talk to him about it, though. His proposal for an *Air Force Now!* series on black fighter pilots was fast-tracked into production in a matter of weeks. It meant he would be on the road the rest of the summer and most of the fall doing interviews, starting with World War II-era Tuskegee Airmen who went on to form the 99th Pursuit Squadron, an all-black fighter unit that had distinguished itself in North Africa and Europe. The plan called for following up with black aviators who had flown in Korea and during the Cold War. He would conclude with black pilots before and after tours of duty in Vietnam. Alas, it was going to involve months of editing. My iffy status—not knowing if I was going to be discharged or sent off to Tan Son Nhut—meant the end of my collaboration with Moonbeam. Instead, I'd be back doing puff-piece news releases while I waited out Poser's legal dogfight with the Air Force.

Just before Zelinsky shipped out we learned that *Link* had requested assignment to Ubon. He joked that it was so he could personally look after Zelinsky and protect him from the rest of us bastards, Wheeler reported, but in reality he had already been stationed there the year before Zelinsky and another tour in a combat zone would give him a shot at making chief master sergeant before he retired. "He's got to do it before the war ends," Zelinsky quipped. "Nobody makes rank in the peacetime Air Force." The whole unit was relieved when Link actually shipped out a few weeks later.

Over the next few months Lieutenant Liscomb was so busy with his *Air Force Now!* series that we scarcely saw him. I worried about my buddies who had been shipped overseas, deeply appreciating the supporting letters they had written for my discharge petition and the thanks they had offered me and Stevens for keeping Norton GIs for Peace going in their absence. Knowing they had been sent off to a war zone motivated me and Stevens to work hard, meeting with what remained of Norton GIs for Peace to plan for the fall and do more organizing with the students at UC Riverside. The brass had known what they were doing, however, and when they scattered the GIs for Peace membership, they successfully knocked a lot of the wind out of our sails. Late in August when Sonny and I went by the Movement House, it was boarded up, giving us a high and dry feeling. I felt a little higher and drier when the FBI called the extension in my editing room at Norton, asking me if I recognized any of the calls made to that number with a stolen telephone-company credit card. I played dumb and they didn't call back.

I didn't get into Sarge's much anymore, and when I did, I never saw Liscomb. Instead, I spent most of what little free time I had at the base theater with Ron Cooper, joining him up in the projection booth. He was on a kick about how you could learn a lot from watching bad movies, which is mostly what we got. I feared that the only thing we were learning was how to make bad movies.

Lieutenant Sherry, now *Captain* Sherry, requested me on a couple of her news releases and kept me up to date on Moonbeam, expressing mild concern that he had entered his Quiet Period, doing long periods of Zen meditation on the carpet of his bachelor officer apartment, only breaking off occasionally to take out his guitar and play along to his favorite soft-core protest songs. I ran into him by chance one day on his way to the dubbing stage at AAVS and asked him how the Tuskegee Airmen piece was coming along. "Would you believe they got *arrested* trying to enter the Officers' Club at Wright-Paterson when they got back to the States after the war?"

That was not an answer I was expecting. I cleared my throat before replying, "I think that got left out of the defeating Hitler part of our U.S. History books. Maybe you can set the record straight." Changing the subject, I asked if the meditation he was doing was anything like what Jack Kerouac had been into.

Moonbeam just smiled. "The Beats didn't quite get it right," he told me. "They were trying to take an easy path into Zen without giving up sex, caffeine and alcohol."

I didn't get to follow up, nor did I especially want to. With Wheeler and Shahbazian exiled to Southeast Asia, I'd had to move from our chalet into a one-bedroom cabin, but a week before Labor Day something miraculous happened: Danielle Haber showed up. We had barely known each other back in Washington, DC, and yet the few hours we had spent together had lingered poignantly in both our memories. We had met by chance during the candlelight march to the White House that opened the Moratorium II weekend. I first noticed her while we were walking along Memorial Bridge, crossing the Potomac from Arlington Cemetery toward the Lincoln Memorial. It was just after sunset, and the November night was crisp but mild. The procession was solemn and dignified, so we didn't talk much, but when we did, I was soothed by the clarity of her voice and her quiet intelligence. It wasn't until afterward when she poured a glass of wine for me up in her apartment that I was struck by her subdued beauty. She looked at me with pure blue eyes that were unafraid to let me see deep inside her when I returned her gaze. When I tried to put my arm around her she was gentle when she pushed me away, putting her hand on my arm in a way that still kept me close. "My husband was killed last summer, just before I was supposed to start my junior year at Drexel. The Army only told us he was killed in action, but a friend wrote later that Craig's M-16 jammed crossing a stream near a village west of Huế. My family tried to console me, but how could they? I dropped out of school and ended up moving in with a girlfriend in D.C. who knew about an opening at a gallery in Georgetown.

So here I am," she said with a sad smile.

Danielle was only supposed to crash with me in San Bernardino for the first few days of a two-week California vacation, but one day led to another and she still hadn't left for San Francisco. On the tenth day she told me she wanted to stay. I told her it was fine with me. She had some money put aside, and we could live together for almost nothing in our little log cabin. With Danielle around, I enjoyed chopping firewood for the old stone fireplace. Whatever food we needed I got cheaply at the base commissary. Soon I was agreeing with her that going back to school in January was a good idea, and after putting in a call to the admissions offices at Cal Arts and the University of Redlands she was encouraged enough to give up her gallery job in D.C., unpack her suitcases, and send in her applications. In the meantime, while she waited to hear back from the colleges, she started dropping me off at the base and heading over to the SDS and SMC offices at UC Riverside. She wasn't fussy—she designed anti-war posters when that was needed but didn't mind handing out leaflets wherever they sent her. She fell in love with our cabin in the mountains and started putting up curtains and decorating it with folksy rugs and rustic furniture we found in the antique shops around Crestline and Big Bear. She fell in love with swimming and hiking up there with me on the weekends and with coming home to cook together in our tiny kitchen. Best of all she started to fall in love with *me*, and I felt the same way about her.

My original orders had been cut for Squadron Headquarters, Tan Son Nhut Air Base, Republic of Vietnam, like Price's. My lawyer's delays might have had something to do with it, but I suspected it had more to do with the fine print in Nixon's troop reduction plan that my orders were changed from Tan Son Nhut to an outpost on the Laotian frontier of Thailand called Ubon. I never would have heard of the place if Zelinsky didn't have a girlfriend there and Link hadn't decided to return for an encore, which got me wondering if *he* had anything to do with my change of orders. I was slated to join them at Detachment 3 of the 601st Photo Squadron as an editor of bomb damage assessment footage—BDA for short. When I found Ubon on a map, I noticed it was smack dab in the middle of Southeast Asia, an hour by fighter-bomber from potential targets all over North Vietnam, South Vietnam, Laos and Cambodia. Zelinsky mentioned that he had never seen a reporter in Ubon the entire year he was there on his first tour, something we were sure the press-hating Nixon found comforting. I did *not* find it comforting to see that Ubon was fewer than fifty miles from either Cambodia or Laos—a two-day march for an enemy infantry unit. It was even less comforting to realize that my old nemesis, First Sergeant Link, was already there waiting for me, but it made *Danielle* happy, at least, that I wasn't going to Vietnam.

We fell even more deeply in love that autumn, and she decided to pass on Cal Arts, despite its great reputation, because it would mean moving two hours away. We were still in love when she started at Redlands in January. It was tricky, but we managed to juggle our schedules and get by with my aging Bug. Thank God she was still in love with me when I phoned my Hollywood ACLU lawyer one chilly Thursday in March and learned that I was shipping out the following Monday. "Sorry, I haven't had a chance to call you," he said in a nasally voice. "You lost the restraining order and the writ of *habeas corpus*, but I'll keep working on it from this end. In the meantime, when you get over there, just follow lawful orders."

I would have asked about *un*lawful orders, except I was speechless. He'd already won a case like mine, which gave me both confidence he could win mine and doubts he'd bother to try. Danielle and I spent the next day packing and making love and putting things into storage and making love a little more. We decided to drive down to Mexico for our last weekend together and camp along the Baja coast where the cactus-filled desert ran down to the sea at San Felipe. We zipped our sleeping bags together and slept under the stars, making love with the sea breeze lapping at our faces, and in the morning we had breakfast in a little cantina on the edge of town that served fresh ceviche, warm tortillas and hot, black coffee.

We got back late Sunday night, exhausted. The next morning I gave Danielle the keys to the V-Dub and she drove me and my duffle bag to the base passenger terminal. She cried hard and I forgot for a moment about being afraid and alone, kissing her and comforting her and promising that I'd write to her every day and that a year would go by in no time. Walking down the aisle of the chartered 707, I didn't see a single face I recognized, not a soul to warn me that I was going to get to be a combat cameraman after all.

Klong Airlines

I spent my first night in Thailand just outside Bangkok at a small hotel near the Don Muang International Airport / Royal Thai Air Force Base. There, within an hour after disembarking from that cramped Continental Airlines charter, I was greeted warmly at the hotel bar by a "tour guide" who guaranteed the young virgins in the picture albums he showed me were eager to meet GIs. My roommate, an aspiring American goodwill ambassador, succumbed, but I stayed behind, choosing to remain faithful to Danielle. Although we weren't officially engaged, our intentions were clear. My biggest concern was how I'd break it to my parents that I was marrying an Episcopalian.

Early the next morning I boarded a C-130 trash-hauler flown by a branch of the Military Airlift Command affectionately known as Klong Airlines and headed up-country. To a large degree, Vietnam was supposed to be a conventional *guerilla* war, which made it a bit puzzling to me why we even had air bases in Thailand. Thanks to the Air Force's "need-to-know" policy, I hadn't been told a damn thing to clear that up, only that Ubon was "up-country" along the Laotian frontier. Thanks to the horror stories that had been filtering back to us from Vietnam, I took my virgin flight full of apprehension about jeeps with bombs rigged to their ignition switches, shoeshine boys with hand grenades, and base barbers who traded in their straight razors at night for handheld shoulder-launched rockets like the one that hit Shahbazian's barracks.

The moment my boots hit the tarmac at Ubon, I knew something big was up, something way bigger than shoeshine boys with hand grenades. Two F-4 Phantom fighter-bombers were taking off in tandem just beyond the flight line, rumbling down the runway and then shaking me to my depths when their afterburners kicked in and their noses shot straight up like a couple of rockets. The smell of JP-4 fumes filled the air, mixed with a lot of testosterone. *Holy shit!* I thought. Larry Zelinsky, my sponsor and official tour guide, was there to meet me, grinning and shouting, "Brendan Leary! Welcome to the Rat Pack!"

He shook my hand and snatched up my garment bag. "Follow me!"

I slung my duffle bag over my shoulder and followed him into the aeroport terminal. Zelinsky didn't waste a moment diving into my orientation. "The 8th Tactical Fighter Wing runs the show here. They call themselves the Wolf Pack and they're the largest, MiG-killingest fighter wing in all of Southeast Asia."

"Why have I never heard of them?"

"Because you didn't have a 'need-to-know.' Now you do. We call *our* little sixty-man photo detachment the *Rat* Pack, but even if we're small, we play an active role here. We do awards ceremonies and passport photos and the usual bullshit, but our main mission is combat documentation—Com-Doc—in real time and with after-action reconnaissance. We do a lot of it using gun cameras and camera pods installed on select aircraft. They record 16mm motion picture footage whenever the F-4 jocks squeeze their trigger finger. Our technicians mount the camera systems and service them and reload film between sorties. The rest is done by living, breathing motion picture cameramen and still photographers."

"I imagine *that* could get a little intense," I replied as we stepped outside. My head was already starting to spin.

Four F-4s were taking off, two flights of two—a lead and a wingman each—that rattled our bones and momentarily drowned out Zelinsky's briefing. Finally he continued, "*Everything* in Ubon is intense. There's an official war and a couple of secret wars going on twenty-four hours a day, seven days a week, although we try to cut back on Sundays."

He led me to a jeep with the Det 3 mascot painted on the door—a rat dressed in fatigues with a question mark over its head staring in confusion through a tripod handle. The motto read: "We kill 'em with fillum." We threw my bags in back and climbed in. As we pulled out, he handed me a little pamphlet, *Welcome to the Wolf Pack*. "Don't worry about remembering everything I'm telling you—this booklet's pretty good. It's got a little bit on Thai culture and some stuff on the history of American operations here. These days the 8th Tactical Fighter Wing is made up of four fighter squadrons totaling more than eighty F-4 Phantoms and ten B-57 Canberra light bombers."

"And that's just *one* base?"

"That's not all. The wing also includes a special operations squadron that's expanding this year from twelve to eighteen Spectre gunships—C-130 transports all tricked up for night operations. And of course there's a detachment of Jolly Green search and rescue helicopters to pick up downed air crews."

Jesus Christ, I thought. "How often do *they* go out?"

"We've been lucky. Haven't lost a plane in almost a year. The main thing you'll be interested in right now is the map—kind of a screwed-up map to confuse spies, I think—but good enough that you'll be able to find your way around after we finish your tour of the base."

"Thanks," I said, trying to hold onto my hat as we roared past a mile of barbed-wire fencing and some serious-looking guard towers.

When we reached the main part of the base Larry pulled to a halt. "How about a cup of coffee at our twenty-four-hour-a-day chow hall? You must be beat."

"Sounds fine by me." I *was* beat from all the traveling. Inside, it felt good to sit down for a moment on something that wasn't moving and have enough room to stretch out my legs. It didn't matter that it was a hard bench.

Zelinsky continued his briefing, switching now to the history and geopolitics of the region. "Bangkok Thais think of Northeast Thailand—the *Issan*—the way Russians think of Siberia and Americans think of North Dakota. The American *government*, however, likes it just fine. South Vietnam's a mess—and the enemy's main supply route in is the Ho Chi Minh Trail. It runs through Cambodia and Laos, which have Communist revolutions of their own going on. We're supposed to stay out of Laos because Kennedy signed the Geneva Accords banning military operations there. The North Vietnamese signed the accords too, but the ink hadn't dried when they started building the Trail. We need to stop them, but since we actually care about world opinion, we have to run a secret war and make the guns we're shipping to the Hmong counterrevolutionaries look like humanitarian aid. We *know* what the American public thinks about sending troops into Cambodia, so once again it's secret-war time. It's starting to look like the American public is getting pretty sick of the whole damn war effort—and that's where Ubon comes in. Nixon figured out that from here the *Air Force* can operate all over Indochina without the press or the public having a clue. All that and no Arctic blizzards."

"Should I really be hearing all of this? They really did talk a lot about 'need-to-know' back at Norton."

"That's the great thing about having a Top Secret security clearance and editing Battle Damage Assessment footage from all over Southeast Asia. We 'need to know' a *lot* to put together briefing clips that make sense when they're sent back to the Pentagon and the Armed Services committees and sometimes even the White House."

"How can you be so *into* this? I thought you hated the war like the rest of us—"

"Like I said, the war's a mess, but this is a free trip back to be with the *woman* I love. When you meet Pueng, you'll understand."

"For someone who really didn't want to be here, I have to admit you've made it sound pretty exciting. *Intense*, as you say."

"Well, you're here," Zelinsky said with a smile. "Might as well make the best of it."

He continued talking as we finished our java and walked out to the jeep. "Part of the intensity around here might be pure logistics—everything that every man on this base needs is squeezed into a few square miles. Let me show you around."

We drove off, and soon Zelinsky was pointing out revetments where long rows of fighter-bombers were parked between missions, maintenance sheds and hangars, the motor pool, engine test areas, Quonset huts housing squadron operations, and finally the control tower. Then came the fun stuff— the post office, storefront branches of Bank of America and Chase Manhattan, the Officers' Club, the NCO and Airmen's Club-Casino complex, the swimming pool and patio, the bowling alley, the hobby shop (and music-pirating club), the movie theater, the library and the gym. The *un*-fun chapel, hospital, and Wing Headquarters—what the men called the Little Pentagon—were also nearby.

Altogether, according to Zelinsky, it took more than six thousand American airmen to keep the Wolf Pack flying, not to mention the hundreds of Thai nationals who cleaned our quarters, staffed the officers' and enlisted-men's clubs, and worked elsewhere on base. Zelinsky clued me in that Ubon was technically a *Royal Thai* Air Force Base with a nominal Thai commander, Thai trainees in the control tower, Thai air policemen, and two token A-37 fighter squadrons made up of slow-moving jet trainers that had been reconfigured for combat. In reality, like pretty much everywhere else in the Southeast Asia theater, the U.S. had taken over.

"The Thai commander *has* worked it out so that token Thai concessionaires run the barber shop, the tailor shop, a little jewelry store, the base laundry operation and a few snack bars. In a way the concessions are your gateway to downtown Ubon. They'll give you a little taste of the goodies you'll find when you get off the base, even if you only make it to the shops and restaurants clustered outside the front gate. The Thais have taken it upon themselves to provide you with all the things you *don't* need or *think* you don't need but will soon find you can't live without. Life's pretty intense for them too. Ubon used to be a sleepy little provincial capital until the Americans turned it into a boomtown. Now Issan shopkeepers and rice farmers are getting richer than they ever imagined possible. Even the restaurants and shops and theaters in the old sections of town are booming. But behind all the courtesy and warmth they lavish on us Americans, I suspect, is the fear that the gravy train will end even faster than it began."

"What's that big building across from the Little Pentagon?"

"Ah—the Base Exchange!" Zelinsky answered with another smile.

"Why is it so *huge*?"

"Because the BX has the goodies they *don't* sell downtown—shoes big enough to fit American feet, electric appliances, TVs, stereo equipment and record albums, and especially American booze and cigarettes. To put it more accurately, they've got it downtown, but the Thai government charges very heavy duty on imports—400% is routine on things like cigarettes."

After checking me in at CBPO, the Consolidated Base Personnel Office, Zelinsky brought me by Payroll, Bank of America and the post office to do a little more processing in before he finally showed me to my hootch and gave me the rest of the day to sleep off my jet lag.

I knew before I shipped out that Larry was going to be my supervisor at Ubon and that Link was going to be spreading gloom as the Detachment 3 first sergeant. What I was *not* expecting was the little surprise Larry sprang on me the next morning when he led me over to the ComDoc command trailer to report in. Damn if it wasn't *Tom Wheeler* pecking away on an IBM Selectric in the outer office of the orderly room. We quickly exchanged low fives and agreed to meet for lunch—before Zelinsky ruined the mood, reminding me that First Sergeant Link was in his office waiting. Link growled something like "welcome aboard," dismissed Zelinsky, and picked up his direct line to Captain English, the detachment commander. "Leary's here. Yes sir, he's the one." Link gave me one of his dark lifer smirks and said, "The captain's expecting you."

Later, over at the chow hall, I learned that Wheeler was living off base with Zelinsky and a motion picture lab tech named Groendyke. The three of them filled me in a little more about life in Ubon. "I suppose you've noticed," said Wheeler, "that a wartime fighter base is a little more intense than a place like Norton."

"I've noticed," I replied.

"Wait'll you see downtown at night," said Zelinsky.

Wheeler jumped in. "It can be quite a scene when the combat crews are on the prowl. The officers mostly come down for a massage—a 'scrub and rub' they call it—and do most of their hell-raising back at the O Club. The ones you gotta watch out for are the Spectre and Jolly Green door gunners. They're seeing a lot of combat—"

"And none of them have been to finishing school," laughed Zelinsky.

"Makes 'em pretty wild when they're off duty," Tom warned.

"Something else about downtown," said Groendyke. "The girls over here have never been taught about sin and guilt. Right and wrong, maybe, but not sin and guilt, and it makes them *very* easy to get along with, if you know what I mean. Free enterprise at its finest, you might say."

"Which reminds me," said Tom. "How much has Zelinsky told you about the BX?"

"They've got stuff that's hard to find downtown?" I offered.

Tom smiled. "There's *way* more to it than that. It's the GI's bargaining chip. A first-term enlistee can virtually double his one- or two-hundred-dollar-a-month salary by buying his electronic toys carefully—it's 50 to 70% cheaper than in the States."

"Maybe even more important," added Groendyke, "he can deliver goods to the people of Ubon that cost four to ten times more on the outside. Seems to make it a lot easier to find a girlfriend—except Zelinsky, of course, who has done it with animal magnetism."

Zelinsky grinned. "The locals who work at the BX and know how to game the system have risen fast in Ubon society."

Last but not least, they brought me up to date on the latest AAVS scuttlebutt, which Tom had a talent for cultivating through his contacts at

CBPO. He had gotten word that the inscrutable Moonbeam Liscomb had something to do with the switcheroos that brought us to Ubon. Wheeler's old buddy Dave Murray was due in the following week from Cam Ranh Bay, and a few others—all *cool guys* like Blackwell and Price—had already rotated in. Link was pissed at first, then a little mystified, but now seemed to be getting a perverse joy from having his old problem children from Norton working under his watchful eye, never catching on that *he* was working under the watchful eye of Tom Wheeler.

Once I finished reporting in it was eight hours a day, five days a week editing gun-camera footage that the Wolf Pack's F-4s and B-57s brought back from all over Southeast Asia. I may not have understood the tactics or rules of engagement yet, but those planes had definitely been to war and I knew from the first reel I looked at that the war was far nastier than anyone could have ever imagined from watching the evening news at home. I watched cluster bomb after cluster bomb cutting through the jungle, butchering any enemy soldiers trying to hide there. Along the rivers, sampan after sampan was strafed and sunk. Napalm engulfed village after village in flame, forcing me to ponder how the Air Force could do in seconds with a single canister from Dow Chemical what it took Calley's platoon a full day to accomplish. Rockets were generally saved for bridges, larger buildings, and once a week or so, to shoot down a MiG up around Hanoi. Clearly the civil war between the North and South Vietnamese was still raging, which made me happier by the day that my orders had been changed from Tan Son Nhut to Ubon and that I had been taken under the wing of an old friend like Staff Sergeant Larry Zelinsky, who was blessed with a special kind of glibness that allowed him to look at bomb damage assessment footage as flat strips of 16mm celluloid, just pigment on acetate, not the three-dimensional depiction of devastation that my eyes took in.

It only took me a few weeks to confirm that Ubon Royal Thai Air Force Base and Det 3 of the 601st Photo Squadron were indeed a stealthy part of Nixon's Vietnamization program. American foot soldiers were going home. By reducing American casualties, Nixon won over enough *American* hearts and minds to keep the war going. He may have talked about downsizing, but like every American president before him he was damned if he was going to be the first to lose a war. The U.S. Air Force was sticking around at full strength, moving to Ubon, several other locations in Northeast Thailand and, according to Wheeler and Zelinsky, a couple of secret bases in Laos where Air America may or may not have been operating. It was about this time that a lean, ramrod-straight stranger with dark, piercing eyes showed up and spent a week working quietly with Zelinsky in the corner editing cubicle. I guessed from his military bearing that his civilian clothes were a cover and that he worked for the CIA. From what I gathered, you could only get to *his* secret base by helicopter and then mule train, and it could have been located in Northern Thailand, the Burmese Shan States, Northern Laos, or even South China, seeing as how the private thousand-man army he was training hailed from all those regions. Clearly Nixon wasn't limiting his stealth to Thailand, but Zelinsky refused to talk much about the project other than to show off the flintlock musket the CIA man had given him as a little thank-you. The musket looked like something out of the Revolutionary War, but a Hmong militiaman had only turned it in a week earlier in exchange for an M-16.

When Colonel Grimsley, the base commander, announced proudly at my first monthly Commander's Call that the U.S. Air Force had now dropped more tonnage of bombs on the Ho Chi Minh Trail than the Allies had dropped on all of Germany in World War II, I realized from the loud applause that I was deep in the heart of lifer territory. With my application for discharge still rumbling around somewhere in the labyrinthine USAF bureaucracy, I was glad to know Wheeler again had my back, keeping tabs on my case the way he had at Norton. It seemed like a good time to take Poser, Esquire's advice and maintain a low profile following lawful orders while I waited for my hearing.

The first weekend after I arrived, Zelinsky took me on a tour of Ubon proper. With it came a great riddle: as much as the war turned out to be far worse than I imagined, Thailand turned out to be just the opposite. It didn't matter that I was still a little woozy with jet lag—I was immediately intrigued by the lively Third World economy that swirled around us downtown—in the bustling shops of the business district and a few blocks away along the river at the open-air Noy Market. There, bartering playfully was as routine as it would have been unimaginable in a Boston supermarket or department store. When Zelinsky led me into air-conditioned Raja Tailors ("just to window shop," he told me), the smiling salesgirl handed us each an ice-cold Coca Cola, and before I knew what hit me, a tailor in a turban had taken measurements for two silk shirts and a pair of dress bell-bottoms, to be ready in three days. Zelinsky had a good laugh, as usual, and sipped his Coke while I was left scratching my head.

Stepping back outside, I smiled, soothed by the buzz of activity that drowned out the sounds of fighter-bombers taking off and landing just a few miles away. About the only thing that didn't win me over that day was the stench of stagnant sewers and canals (what the Thais called *klongs*) mixed with the pungent aroma of pork, chicken, river fish and dried squid that were hanging in the market stalls.

A little before noon Zelinsky suggested we break for lunch. It was hot season and it had been hours since the blistering sun had burned off the morning haze. He led me to a noodle shop that looked out across the Noy Market. Like noodle shops throughout Thailand, it had an open front, a steel grate that was shut at night when they closed and a shiny cement floor that was at the same time depressing and spotlessly clean. The tables were well-worn Formica, the stools an almost elegant hand-lacquered bentwood. In front of me was a glass and steel pantry displaying the day's menu and next to it several charcoal braziers that kept an array of woks sizzling. In the rear was an industrial-grade, glass-fronted refrigerator chock-full of frosty Cokes, Fantas, Green Spot sodas, bean-curd milk and Thai beer.

Zelinsky was grinning when we stepped inside. "I know you won't believe me," he said, "but you'll be used to the fragrance of klong water and dried squid by the time you come back tomorrow. Amazing organism, the human body."

"Speak for yourself. I'm sticking with sorry-assed chow-hall food."

A petite young woman in her early twenties wearing aviator sunglasses, a faded, loose-fitting navy work shirt and torn bellbottom jeans was making her way out of the noodle shop carrying two plastic satchels full of the morning's groceries. I hadn't noticed her until I pulled out my chair to sit down and managed to put it directly in her path, nearly jarring loose one of her shopping bags. She recovered gracefully and gave me the special condescendingly friendly smile that Thais trotted out for clumsy *farang*. I only caught a glimpse of her before she disappeared into the steamy late-morning sunlight, but as a serious student of photography she struck me as a particularly photogenic representative of a country noted for an abundance of beautiful women. Zelinsky snapped his fingers, bringing me out of my momentary trance.

"Maybe you're right after all about that human-body-being-an-amazing-organism stuff," I muttered.

"I was talking about your nose adjusting to the smell of dried squid," replied Larry with a twinkle in his eye.

The waiter, an old friend of Zelinsky's, picked up on the subject of our conversation. "*Pu-ying suay mahk*, Sergeant Lar-ry. She very beautiful."

Zelinsky exchanged a few Thai pleasantries before ordering us two Singha beers and some mildly spicy duck soup. The soup was delicious, and the beers did such a fine job washing away the dryness in our throats that we decided to have one more for dessert. Outside, we shook hands, soul-brother style, and Zelinsky headed home to spend the afternoon with Pueng, his reason for returning to Thailand. Given that this was my first trip downtown, I wanted to stay and take some pictures.

I meandered along Prommahtehp Road as it followed the Mun River toward the Warin Bridge. A block from the bridge I saw her again. Among hundreds of people thronging from jewelry shop to tailor shop to dry goods store to stationer, the lovely stranger in the teardrop sunglasses and oversized denim shirt somehow stood out by radiating just a tiny bit more grace and sensuality than the many other attractive young people around her. Her hair was just a fraction longer and silkier as it bounced to the cadence of her gentle footsteps. Her golden skin glistened ever so slightly brighter in the midday sun. Intrigued, I put on the longest telephoto lens I could successfully hand-hold and stole a few shots of this lovely stranger, mixed in with pictures of the shops and the many exotic products they sold. Even the cheap notebooks in the windows of the stationery stores captivated me, bound as they were in various patterns of silk landscapes.

After battling so hard to avoid being shipped overseas, I wondered that day why fate was turning out to be so kind, and I smiled to myself at how much I was enjoying my first day off. On a lark, I continued following my accidental model from the opposite side of the street even though I couldn't frame her closer than a waist shot. As attractive as she might have appeared in close-up through my lens, this was a comfortable distance. I expected to marry Danielle when my tour was up and didn't need any complications. Besides, I was fundamentally shy; without being able to speak Thai, it would have been hard to accomplish anything other than to scare her away if I had moved closer.

And so I kept following her, taking pictures from across the bustling *thanon*. A couple of times I lost her and was surprised to find myself feeling *sad*, for Christ's sake! And then I'd spot her again. I'd feel a little surge of joy and have to laugh at myself. I followed her around the traffic circle that fed the bridge to Warin and the depot for the Bangkok train. Before I realized it we were at a dead end on the outskirts of town among rat-infested shacks that clung to the muddy embankment of the Mun River. The denim work shirt and bell-bottom jeans that belonged on a San Francisco hippie-panhandler suddenly looked like the silk robes of royalty when she was surrounded by a horde of tiny street urchins dressed in rags. Patiently she gave each one of them a piece of fruit and let them reach their tiny hands into a bamboo tube of sticky rice and scoop out enough to form into a riceball. When she opened a can of tuna, they eagerly dipped in their little balls of rice and ate voraciously. When the tuna was gone she passed out at least twenty more unopened cans until her shopping bag was empty.

As the children started to drift back down the embankment into the maze of hovels built out of sheet metal and packing crates salvaged from the base garbage dump, I noticed I had attracted a throng of my own. They seemed to have never seen a 35mm Pentax camera before, so I bent over to let the ragtag leader take a look through the eyepiece. In an instant I was swarmed with tiny dirt-encrusted hands and found myself staring into the large, dull eyes of children who had eaten too little too long. The camera was being torn from my neck and I had to brace myself with my left hand on the rough, broken sidewalk to keep from being pulled over and trampled. Barely able to hang on to the camera with my right hand, I took a deep breath, grunted, and broke free, staggering to my feet, stunned at how many kids had appeared out of thin air and how these scrawny, underfed waifs could so easily take down a six-foot American. Hugging my camera tightly to my body, I dug deep into my front pocket with my free hand and pulled out a handful of coins, flinging them as far as I could toward the shacks at the side of the river. As quickly as it had appeared, the miniature mob disbursed in a cacophony of chatter. Choking a little in the hot, dusty air, I looked around and finally caught a glimpse of my mystery woman as she disappeared up See Tong Street into some sort of hospital compound.

I lived on the base in a tin-roofed hootch with only a ceiling fan for air conditioning, sleeping in a squeaky bunk, keeping myself clean in hopes that Danielle still wanted a proper church wedding when my time came to go back to what black GIs called "the World" and what I still called home. I quickly settled into a mind-numbing routine at work, cutting combat film day after day, bearing witness to endless miles of South Vietnam as beautiful as the Thai countryside being laid waste with napalm, rockets and cluster bombs originating from Ubon Royal Thai Air Force Base. The enemy was firing back with anti-aircraft artillery ("triple-A")—we saw plenty on the Night Operations footage—and sending up MiG interceptors *and* triple-A over North Vietnam, but it had been eerie—not one plane flying out of Ubon had been shot down for ten months. Sure, we had recently lost two of our cameramen, Spinelli and Nevers, but they had been on TDY out of Danang. And it was during Lam Son 719, the screwed-up South Vietnamese attempt at invading Laos that got bogged down along Route 9. They shouldn't have even been on the helicopter that crashed; they were supposed to be on a flight back to Ubon, but they couldn't pass up a chance to cover the operation with Larry Burrows, the famous *Life* photographer who went down with them. I slipped into a kind of trance as I spliced together scenes of extraordinary violence, acquiescing in silence the way Richard Poser, Esquire, had instructed me to and wishing I could quit thinking altogether.

I couldn't stop thinking, though, and soon understood the rules of engagement well enough to know that our light observation planes were being shot at by real snipers using real bullets and were spotting real guerillas disappearing into the hamlets and jungles of Vietnam, Laos and Cambodia when they called in air strikes, but I couldn't for the life of me figure out how our pilots knew beyond the shadow of a doubt that every sampan we sank and every village we bombed and burned belonged to the enemy. I found myself wondering how many times it only took sighting a single flash from an enemy rifle down below to entice our fighter-bombers into destroying an entire village built with the calloused hands of peasants who had lived among the same patchquilt rice paddies for a hundred generations.

Colonel Grimsley, the base commander, and Captain English, our commander at ComDoc, made it clear that those were the kinds of questions they did not want asked. At Ubon Royal Thai Air Force Base, at Commander's Call and posted on bulletin boards everywhere, "loyalty" was the buzzword. "Loyalty" meant keeping your mouth shut. Lifers and apprentice lifers knew the drill. *Loyal* soldiers did not make waves that would keep captains and colonels from getting anything less than perfect efficiency reports and their tickets to advancement punched properly. So I did my job and kept my mouth shut and spoke only in whispers to Tom Wheeler and Larry Zelinsky.

One concession to convention at Ubon that came easy was getting myself a basic five-speed no-name aluminum road bike when Wheeler got his. The base was crawling with bicycles, which I found comforting; it reminded me of a pleasant college campus back home, except that the birds chirping in the distance at Ubon were a little bigger, noisier, and more carnivorous than the pigeons that nibbled at breadcrumbs on a college green. For the entire month of March and most of April, while other guys were heading off base to go nightclubbing and visit massage parlors, drinking and doing some of the purest drugs money could buy, I rode my bicycle over to the base library and holed up reading the *American Cinematographer*. I wrote to Danielle every day, telling her that I missed her and how even though American foot soldiers were truly going home, things were tougher than anyone could imagine for the Vietnamese. I put it off for a few weeks, but I finally started getting ready for my discharge hearing, motivated by a hunch they would be springing it on me unexpectedly. It wasn't long before I was reading about the brutal, tragic history of the French in Indochina in books like Bernard Fall's *Hell in a Very Small Place* and finding myself obsessed with how we were repeating so many of their mistakes. When I tried to figure out where Thailand fit in, I didn't get past the *Encyclopedia Britannica* for the answers to be disturbing—our ally was a constitutional monarchy that had had more coups than elections since the current king's grandfather gave up absolute power in 1932. The entire World War II era was murky, with factions overseas seeming to be pro-Ally while Thailand itself was ruled by a Franco-like character who hadn't put up any resistance to the Japanese occupation worth writing about. Unions were illegal even though per-capita income in the Issan region that included Ubon wasn't much more than fifty dollars a year, which might have explained the history of leftist insurgency in the Northeast. Equally disturbing to me, Thailand received plenty of U.S. aid to put it down.

Tom Wheeler and Larry Zelinsky worried about me. They weren't readers—Wheeler pretty well stayed with *Rolling Stone* and Zelinsky confessed he hadn't touched a book since elementary school. They didn't go in much for letter writing, either. Instead, they kept twisting my arm, telling me I needed to get off the base—to get some exercise, if nothing else, and to keep the lifers from messing with my head twenty-four hours a day—but I passed.

The war sucked and the work sucked, but something miraculous was going on with the staffing at ComDoc. Almost as if the by the hand of God, *cool guys* from Norton kept turning up at Ubon. Two of the first came from the Soul Brother division of Norton GIs for Peace—Blackwell, the soundman/still photographer who had been stationed at Korat, and Price, the lab technician who came down from Udorn. And of course there was Wheeler, who had never even made it to his original assignment at Takhli, and his sidekick Murray. Some were cool guys I didn't even know about like Ernie Perez, another lab tech. As a novice film editor at Norton I rarely left my editing room and rarely spoke to anyone besides the writer-producers and the directors assigned to my projects. The motion picture laboratory might as well have been on another planet. And given that Perez was from Spanish Harlem and a devotee of Tito Puente's, he had never turned up at Sarge's, where it was strictly country rock for the young dudes and a little rockabilly for the lifers.

It was similar with Jamal Washington, the very cool motion picture cameraman. I had hung out with Ron Cooper, but he had the single next door to my room in the barracks at Norton. Washington was in a different barracks and was more a habitué of Jerry's Velvet Lounge, an elegant jazz and blues club on the north side of San Berdoo, than a biker bar like Sarge's. I did know his work, though. His footage was consistently good—as good as Ron Cooper's—and he hadn't gone to Bob Jones University or Disney Studios to learn it. I started bumping into him regularly once we got to Ubon and noticed that he usually had Otis Redding or Big Mama Thornton going on the tape deck he'd set up in the cameramen's ready room at ComDoc. He seemed pleasantly amused when I told him they were two of my favorite singers.

Maybe the strangest, coolest move of all was when my old cabin mate, Woody Shahbazian, the Air Force's worst camera technician, got reassigned from Tan Son Nhut to Ubon. He had become the Air Force's worst camera technician because he had flunked out of missile school and the Air Force couldn't think of anything better to do with the two and a half years left on his enlistment after he returned from his first stint in Vietnam. He tried to make his tour sound like a lark—lifeguarding at the Officers' Club swimming pool and renting out inflatable rafts for the beach—except he wore that leather wristband in honor of his dead hootch-mates. The wristband drove the lifers crazy, but it was legal. Much of what Woody did was legal but maddening to lifers, a legacy of his childhood as an Air Force brat. B-58 pilots like his dad had a tradition of thumbing their noses at rear-echelon types, and that tradition had been passed on to Woody even though Woody himself *was* a rear-echelon type. His bad eyes had prevented him from becoming a pilot, but he knew the regs better than the NCOs who tried to rein him in.

While we were still at Norton, Woody had managed to run up some serious gambling debts in Las Vegas with his new gal pal, Kristin, who had been unable to dissuade him from booking penthouse suites that cost per weekend what he was making in a month. The tab he and Kristin had amassed at Sarge's would take a couple more months' paychecks to clear up, and for a coup de grâce, he had managed to put an expensive ding in his restored Porsche showing off for Kristin out at the L.A. County fairgrounds trying to pretend he knew how to run time trials. Woody had made a nifty profit on his first tour shipping home a case of Johnson Baby Powder filled with Laotian grass that had fallen out of the back of a visiting Air America "rice supply" flight. He confessed to me later that he had gladly gotten caught passing out the *sNorton Bird*, knowing that the war couldn't last forever and thinking it might be a good time for a final business trip to Southeast Asia. With a little luck he'd be able to pay Kristin back the cash she'd lent him and get taken into the family business before she caught on that his trust fund had dried up long ago.

He showed up at Ubon driving a dusty red Fiat convertible and still sported a scruffy goatee when he reported in. Speaking with the trace of a French accent, he claimed to have *driven* over to Thailand, which should have been impossible since it meant passing through parts of Cambodia we had invaded and abandoned less than a year earlier. When he said he had no trouble taking the ferry over from Pakse, Laos, we cringed to think he had stumbled onto a western branch of the Ho Chi Minh Trail for the last leg of the trip. "The trick is to only travel by day," he said with an insouciant grin, "and insist you are French or Canadian...or French Canadian. A forged passport helps." Our only complaint about Woody was that he had hung out with the "Proud to Be an Okie from Muskogee" crowd over in Saigon and was more into country and western now than ever. We weren't sure *what* to make of the white Grand Prix jump suit he'd had custom-made in a Saigon tailor shop .

Wheeler pricked our interest when he told us that according to his reliable source over at CBPO, the rumor was true that Moonbeam Liscomb was behind the moves. The story was especially intriguing because, according to the latest scuttlebutt, Moonbeam himself was slotted to be coming in once his black fighter pilot series was wrapped up. Rumor *also* had it that he had completely flipped out, joining a couple of crazy California cults for a month or two and then turning right around and getting involved with some Black Nationalist group in South Central L.A.

None of this seemed to make much difference at first. Despite the colorful new cast of characters that was reporting in, I continued to live a monk-like existence, holing up in my editing cubicle by day and the library by night before climbing into my lumpy bunk for a bad night's sleep. Sainthood began to get a lot more difficult, however, when I heard from Ernie Perez about Talent Night, held every Monday at the Ubon Hotel. I had left my drums with Danielle, never imagining they had rock bands in a war zone. Ernie told me about a place downtown on Prommaraj Road not too far from the Noy Market called Woodstock Music where I was able to pick out a pair of drumsticks. I drove the guys in the hootch crazy while I practiced on a couple of coffee cans and a pretzel tin I was able to scrounge from the base dumpsters, but when Talent Night came I was able to do a pretty decent drum solo, given that I was playing a *cappella* on the house drum set without a band or a song for context other than humming "Topsy, Part II" in my head. Perez, Wheeler, Zelinsky and a few other guys from the detachment were there to egg me on, buying me a few rounds of Mekong whiskey and soda, and it even looked for a while like I might win. My hopes were dashed, though, when Woody Shahbazian, who used to torment me back at Norton with country music, showed up with his battered guitar case, pulled out his vintage Martin D-28, and tormented me once again with "Your Cheatin' Heart" to win the twenty-dollar first prize. He sewed it up with a yodeling finale that drove the lifer contingent wild and forced Zelinsky to howl along in agony. But in the end it worked out fine because Brother Brian Golson, lead singer for the Band of Brothers, and Sugie Bear Suggs, his bass player, introduced themselves and told me that their drummer was rotating back to the World.

That Saturday night I hopped on my five-speed and headed downtown to sit in for a couple of numbers at the Soul Sister, located just across a potholed street from the Club Miami and not far from an iffy part of town that was full of Vietnamese refugees and Off Limits. They seemed to like my rimshots on "Knock on Wood" and when they "gave the drummer some" on a James Brown number, they must have kept on liking what they heard. I was in and accepted a chance to buy the old drummer's made-in-Japan drum kit cheap. I also agreed to a Monday rehearsal at the base chapel annex, a large multi-purpose room where we stored our equipment. Did I know any guitar players? They were still looking for a lead guitar to take the pressure off "the Reverend," as they affectionately called Golson, so he could play rhythm and concentrate on his vocals. I briefly thought of Shahbazian but didn't think a Merle Haggard sound was what they were looking for.

The day after my audition, I rode my bike downtown again, this time back to Woodstock Music. I was trying to decide between some Ludwig and Slingerland drumsticks when I struck up a conversation with Sommit and Vrisnei, the friendly young brother and sister who ran the music part of Yoon On Store for their eternally middle-aged Thai-Chinese parents. Sommit, the brother, wore casual Western clothes, spoke exceptionally good English and was crazy about American music. In a hushed voice, he promised top dollar for any jazz or rock albums I could bring him from the BX. It sounded good to me—a chance to make some spare change for doing musical missionary work. Vrisnei was a year or two younger than her brother. Wearing little makeup and keeping her hair pulled back simply under a bandanna, she was wholesomely attractive. It was while she was ringing up my purchase that Harley Baker came in looking for guitar strings. Sommit introduced us and told me, "Khun Harley play guitar very good!"

Baker was a twenty-three-year-old lifer in training, a hatchet-faced gunner with the 16th Special Operations Squadron, but it didn't take much chatting to learn that he also played a mean, bluesy Les Paul guitar. And it didn't take much more chatting to find out he was game to come to the Monday rehearsal and take a crack at joining the Band of Brothers. He was hired on the spot. And so it was that within two days a couple of jive white dudes joined an otherwise all-black soul band.

Wheeler and Zelinsky were finally able to talk me into dropping by their off-base bungalow once I started performing downtown with the band, enticing me at first with an invitation to join their merry crew for Thai food. Whether it was home-cooked or from a street vendor, it was a big improvement over chow-hall grub. *Khaopaht gung*, a simple, mildly spicy shrimp fried rice, cost twenty-five cents from a mama-sahn on the street and was more delicious than anything I had ever eaten in Boston, with the possible exception of Lobster Newberg. Soon I was spending a lot of my free evenings with Wheeler, Groendyke, Zelinsky and his fiancée, Pueng, hoping Lek, Wheeler's new girlfriend, would show up with fresh fruit for dessert.

Before long, I was also stopping by to smoke a little weed, which didn't seem to be anywhere near as dangerous to our bodies or souls as Sister Susan, Father Boyle, and the federal government had warned us. It wasn't much later that Baker stopped in with me one night after a gig. When they heard he was from Fresno, Zelinsky and Wheeler, stoned, started reminiscing about California, which led to Norton GIs for Peace and the *sNorton Bird*.

"So you guys are fuckin' *Peaceniks*?" The mellow mood was over for Harley. "Let me explain something just once: our main job here at Ubon is to stop convoys coming down the Ho Chi Minh Trail. Fuck the Geneva Accords and fuck politics—American or Vietnamese. If we don't kill trucks, American soldiers get killed."

Tom, the mellowest of the mellow, calmed things down. "Why don't *we* call a truce?" And with that he lit up his bong, passed it over to Harley, and put on some Johnny Winters.

Late that night, lying on my bunk back at my hootch, it hit me—I was halfway around the world from everything I had ever known. Even on a base crawling with six thousand American airmen, I was lonely as hell without Danielle.

14 May 1971
The Ghetto

The sun looked like a juicy apricot floating in the thick syrup of tropical evening air. Tom Wheeler and I sat regally in a pair of high-backed wicker throne chairs on the second floor porch of Unit #4, Bungalow Ruam Chon Sawng, passing some especially smooth and potent Laotian weed between us and chasing it down with Mekong and soda. Lek, Tom's part-time girlfriend, was cutting up fruit on a chopping block nearby, squatting on the floor as naturally as Tom and I were sitting in our chairs. As we neared the end of the joint, I watched Tom pull out his roach clip and take a drag, and I recalled how in the past year the Pentagon brass had denied there was any drug use among GIs in Southeast Asia. I remembered how a month or two later, after the press had proved them wrong, the same brass claimed their drug *eradication* programs were a great success. Neither the press nor the brass had ever visited the GI denizens of Bungalow Ruam Chon Sawng, a motley assortment of hippies and soul brothers who called their dead-end alleyway the Ghetto.

Unit #4 was one of five newly constructed stilt-shacks that ran down the left side of the alley. We called the bungalows stilt-shacks because like traditional village huts all over Thailand and Laos, they were elevated on teakwood pillars that for centuries had provided protection from flooding in monsoon season and, the rest of the year, a source of shade from the scorching sun. Wheeler lived there along with Zelinsky, my boss, and Phil Groendyke, the Det 3 lab tech. I was just visiting.

For the average GI, Bungalow Ruam Chon Sawng was an adequate place to hang your hat if you were sentenced to a year in Thailand. Wheeler, Zelinsky and Groendyke considered it a bargain. Sixty bucks a month bought them a stilt-shack made up of four slat-walled rooms with ceiling fans, a bathroom, and a wide, shaded front porch. The bathroom, or *hong nam*, featured cold running water for shaving and lukecold water stored in a large klong jar that you dipped a plastic bowl into for something like a shower. Zelinsky explained to me how in the tropics this was pleasantly refreshing—*most* of the year. Electricity was relatively new in upcountry Thailand and brownouts were not uncommon, but enough juice reached

Ruam Chon Sawng to run a stereo and a mini-refrigerator twelve hours a day, more or less. A Thai with half a brain would not have paid more than twenty dollars American to move his entire family in, but Wheeler, Groendyke and Zelinsky didn't mind splitting their sixty a month three ways.

A long, *un*elevated structure ran down the opposite side of the Bungalow Ruam Chon Sawng complex. It might have passed for a barracks, more easily for a chicken coop, but it was in reality a row of one-room apartments. Each unit on the long, squat barracks side had a bed-sitting-room, a private bath and a little area outside, boxed in with a cement wall and containing a cement bench, that passed for a patio. The chicken coops ran ten or twenty-five dollars a month, depending on whether you were getting the Thai or the American price.

There was nothing Tom and I enjoyed more when we were stoned than perusing the little world below us from our second floor perch. The two Thai national policemen who squeezed their families into the studio apartments closest to the gate often spent the late afternoon relaxing with their wives and children outside on their little patios. On our side of the alley across from the policemen, Mama-sahn, the brains behind Ruam Chon Sawng, often sat out in front of her two-story cottage with her son and a covey of half-naked grandchildren. Mama-sahn's little palace had once been a stilt-shack like Tom's, but the first floor was now finished off and the interior pine-paneled, a sign that she had done well in the war. She had done so well, in fact, that Bungalow *Ruam Chon Sawng* literally meant "Bungalow People Come Together *Two*." Number One, the original, was located downtown near the post-telegraph office.

Tom and I especially enjoyed gazing across his little cul-de-sac in the late afternoon and watching the most beautiful woman in Ruam Chon Sawng sitting out on her patio dressed in a silk kimono drying and brushing out her hair. Water was abundant in Thailand and taking two or three showers a day was not uncommon. She spoke no English and was once visited every day at noon by a Thai soldier who was married and could not leave his wife. At one o'clock she helped him button up the shirt to his uniform and returned to her job giving manicures in a nearby beauty shop.

The most beautiful woman in Ruam Chon Sawng was proud of the fact that she spoke no English, but that did not mean she was not ambitious. She had carefully saved her money so that she could attend the really good beauticians' school near the Chinese quarter in Bangkok. After she returned, she started saving money to open her own salon. She also made a change—a business decision really—in the boyfriend department, even though the Thai soldier had been very handsome.

Now a Thai kickboxer lived with the most beautiful woman in Ruam Chon Sawng. He got to smell the sweet, soothing incense that burned each night from the spirit house, a miniature temple that sat on a pedestal in front of the cinderblock wall that closed off the alley. I suspected that it had been a long time since the boxer had been surrounded with so much beauty. He was scarred and bruised and pasty-skinned from spending much of his life under the artificial light of gyms and indoor arenas. His wire-straight, close-cropped hair was thinning on top, his body seemed rough-hewn and gangly on his five-foot six-inch frame, and his flat face had been rendered flatter still by countless kicks and punches in the ring.

But now the most beautiful woman in Ruam Chon Sawng had a lover who might marry her someday and who promised to set her up in business when he won his next fight. Tom and I secretly admired how uncomplicated she had kept her life by never learning English. At the same time we were glad we had Lek and Pueng around to keep us up-to-date on Ghetto gossip.

Ruam Chon Sawng might have been considered a blight back in the States, but in May of 1971, young GI potheads and soul brothers lived in harmony there because it was cheap and far from the base—and because girls and drugs were plentiful. Thais lived there because, for bar girls and masseuses, for soldiers and policemen and petty civil servants, for musicians and the kickboxer and the beautician, for all these people the bungalows and studio apartments of the Ghetto were a great luxury after growing up in the thatched huts of rural villages. They now had tin roofs that never leaked, electricity instead of kerosene lanterns, and they no longer had to haul water in buckets from a well—they could fill their klong jars by turning a handle.

"Happy Happy Hour, dudes," said Lek, who had finished slicing up a *sapparoht*, magically turning the ungainly fruit into a bowlful of sweet, watery pineapple chunks that she carried over to her boys. Lek always surprised me, looking and acting more Puerto Rican than Thai. She was petite, attractive, but the spit curls, the glossy lipstick and especially the intensity she radiated from her eyes brought to mind one of the sexy dancers in the chorus of West Side *Story*, if not Rita Moreno herself.

Tom took a pineapple chunk for himself and then put one into Lek's waiting mouth, letting her lick his fingers before he slowly pulled them away. His eyes twinkled at hers, and hers twinkled back. We had started calling Tom Wheeler "the unenlightened Buddha" long before we left California for Southeast Asia. No matter where he lived, he wore a perpetual smile of gentle bliss unperturbed by the world that swirled around him. He wasn't movie-star handsome, perhaps because he had brown eyes instead of blue to go with his long, straight blond hair, but his mellow good cheer and his endless supply of grass seemed to attract a steady stream of women. "What do you mean 'unenlightened'?" he used to ask with a bemused smile.

Zelinsky and Pueng, the unabashedly plump Thai girl he had returned to marry, never let food sit around uneaten for long and soon came out of their room to join us. Pueng's round face and sparkling eyes radiated warmth and naughtiness and gave her the kind of beauty that would age well into a Thai version of Mrs. Santa Claus. It was the kind of beauty that a guy like Zelinsky, who had been too shy to find a date for his senior prom, could feel secure with. No high rollers would be hitting on her back in the World. The two of them would keep it to themselves how great she was in bed. "Did we hear something about Happy Hour?" Zelinsky asked.

"Count us in," said Groendyke, who came out of the third bedroom followed by a smiling, somewhat embarrassed young bar girl who looked from her disheveled hair and squinting eyes like she had just woken up. He was apparently on hiatus from his engagement to his high-school sweetheart back home.

The elevated porch began to rumble pleasantly. Tom looked off in the general direction of the base. "Here they come," he said.

Silhouetted by the copper sky, a Spectre AC-130 gunship, an ominous black version of a Klong Airlines troop transport, took off over the south end of the base, droning as it floated past us, climbing out slowly for the hills of Laos. A few seconds later another appeared. "Ghost Riders in the Sky" wafted down the alley on somebody's portable cassette player. It grew louder as footsteps began banging their way up the wooden stairway.

A third Spectre bird floated past as the song filled up the porch with twangy guitar, paused, and then disintegrated into the kind of acid country that Jimi Hendrix might have played had he transferred from the 101st Airborne into the Air Commandos instead of running off to England. "What the *hell* is that?" I asked, taking a long toke and finally looking up to see Harley Baker and his girlfriend, Mali.

"My brother got it from a bar band called the Outlaws that was playing around the Florida panhandle. He thought I might dig their arrangement of the Spectre theme song and sent it along." Baker's chalky white complexion and pink-rimmed eyes gave him the appearance of someone who'd spent some time in Transylvania. Between night operations with the 16th Special Operations Squadron and his off-nights spent in bars, he saw less daylight than the Thai kickboxer across the alley. Baker was the kind of walking bundle of contradictions who had no trouble blowing up trucks on the Ho Chi Minh Trail one night and playing soulful blues guitar the next. I admired his guitar playing and his fearless approach to life. At the same time he scared me, constantly walking a fine line between fearlessness and recklessness. We figured out early on to not talk politics.

Mali's skin was as golden brown as Harley's was pallid. Her face was as soft and sensuous as his was hard and angular. Her coal-black hair was as long and soft and wavy as the patch of straw that covered Harley's head was greasy and straight. While Harley carried himself as aggressively as his gold prospector grandfather had swung a pickaxe, Mali carried herself with the grace of a village girl, even though her father was in fact a petty official in the provincial capital at Roi Et. I liked Harley's music, but the Air Commando part made me uneasy, both the hawkish politics and the macho attitude. If he'd been a Thai guitar player and wasn't earning flight pay and combat pay, I wondered if Mali would have given him the time of day.

"Let's crank it up," said Tom, opening up the chintzy leatherette case of Baker's Norelco portable and taking the cassette inside to the music room. He pushed his system, the finest mixture of Sansui, Teac, Pioneer and Dual components the BX had to offer, to the limits of semi-fidelity, shaking the entire alleyway with *nair nair nair nair*'s shrieking out of the lead guitar and *duga duga duga duga*'s cascading down from the bass into explosions of cymbal crashes. Satisfied with the ear-splitting volume, Tom came out and sat back down, smiling blissfully as Lek rested her hands on his shoulder and nuzzled him from behind and they watched gunship after gunship take off that night. Zelinsky and Groendyke and their companions had settled in to watch the show from the chairs and pillows they had brought out with them. When I offered my seat to Harley and Mali, she slid into his lap and they leaned back comfortably in the high-backed chair. I drifted over to the porch railing and rested my hand high up on the wooden support post, soaking in the pleasant blend of music, Mekong whiskey, juicy pineapple and weed while watching a few more slow-moving Spectre birds pass us by. When "Ghost Riders" ended I went inside to turn down the stereo and came back out. I was by myself, but I wasn't alone and I didn't mind.

Finally, the last of the sixteen Spectre gunships taking off that evening turned right over downtown Ubon and lumbered off to the secret war in Laos that no one back in the World was seeing televised on the evening news. The sky had quickly turned indigo. Six forty-three p.m.—twenty minutes after sunset. Right on time in the tropics.

Tom finally broke the spell. "Hey, Baker, why aren't you flying tonight? Isn't that a lot of planes going out?"

"I had to rearrange my schedule. Didn't Brendan tell you we've got a gig at the Soul Sister?"

"It's the bass player's birthday," I explained. "You oughta catch it."

"*Tommm*," purred Lek, "can we go?"

"Should be a good show," Harley said as he and Mali got up to go. "See you later."

"See you there," I replied.

"Later," said Tom and Lek.

"Mai Pen Rai," OR: The Show Must Go On

At quarter of nine down at the Soul Sister, the band had almost finished setting up. I had already put my cases backstage and checked that the stands and other hardware on my kit were ready to take a pounding. I gave the bass drum, tom-toms and snare drum one last thunk, decided the tuning sounded good, and made my way over to the bar to relax a few minutes before the show began. Ackerman, the sax man from New Orleans, was warming up, running through some staccato arpeggios and scales. Angel, the Thai-Filipino trumpet player on loan from Jay and the Ugly Americans, had been smoking grass with Ackerman all afternoon, looking for inspiration. He was still looking, unable to play more than a series of soft, long tones on his horn while he stared blankly at the wall, the faint smile on his face alternating between perplexed and mellow.

Sugie Bear, the birthday boy, was sitting in a corner booth with Oi, who had just moved in with him and officially become his *tii-rahk*. It had taken me two months in-country to learn that *tii-rahk* literally meant "loved one." I had been surprised because I had heard it used so much in other contexts that it never occurred to me that it meant anything other than "shack up" as either a verb or noun. Sugie Bear was a gangly, homely eighteen-going-on-nineteen-year-old from the streets of Brooklyn. Oi, a frequently zonked twenty-seven-year-old, sported a bright orange Afro that was hard to miss even when the lights were dim and the place was crowded. They were deeply in love, Sugie because he didn't know any better and Oi because she was close to retirement and realized that Sugar *Bear* might be her last chance to find a Sugar *Daddy* who could whisk her off to America and a life of ease. He was especially looking forward to tonight's performance because her name meant Sugar *Cane* in English and he'd be singing lead on a soul version of "Sugar, Sugar" that the band had worked up as a little surprise serenade. While Sugie Bear and Oi waited for the show to begin, they slid a little closer together and continued sweet-talking.

Harley banged through the door, nearly dropping his guitar case, and lumbered in. Everyone stopped what they were doing and stared, the room growing almost silent. I could make out a couple of the bartenders and waitresses in the distance saying, "Farang khii mao *mahk mahk*" ("foreigner very, very shit-faced"). Brian Golson, "the Reverend," our leader who never worried about anything, looked worried. "Where you been?" he asked.

"Nowhere. Just a little Spectre farewell party."

"Where's Mali?" I asked.

"Sent her home," Harley replied.

"You look like hell," I said, giving up my comfy bar stool and walking over. "What's wrong?"

"*Mai pen rai*," answered Harley, plugging in his Les Paul but having a hard time tuning it. "There's nothing wrong with me that a large bottle of Singha won't cure." He grabbed a beer off the tray of a passing waitress and took a swig, setting it down precariously on his amplifier. "*Mai pen fuckin' rai*," said Harley a little too loudly. "The show's gotta go on."

I would have liked to take him off stage, but he was right—it was show time. Despite being the first time the band had played in public in over a week and despite having only had an hour of rehearsal in between, we sounded pretty good—except for Harley, who missed a couple of cues and was still out of tune. "Sugar, Sugar" was an in-joke for the Thai waitresses and bartenders who knew Oi and got us a round of laughter and applause that went over the heads of the GIs in the audience. We were in the middle of the Otis Redding version of "Satisfaction" when Tom Wheeler and Lek came in with Larry Zelinsky and Pueng. Dave Murray trailed behind them, accompanied by a girl I didn't recognize in the smoky haze. When they danced up close to the bandstand, though, Murray's mystery girl looked vaguely familiar in the swaths of reflected spotlight that occasionally hit the dance floor. She reminded me of the girl I took pictures of my first weekend in Ubon, but she kept disappearing into the crowd of dancers before I could be sure. It didn't help that the night was extremely hot and this girl was wearing a vermilion tank top instead of a navy work shirt and her hair was pulled up in a twist.

I gave my full attention to the cymbal crashes that I matched to the three loud opening chords on "That's How Strong My Love Is," but once we settled in for a fairly conventional ballad, my mind started drifting, wondering at first whether I liked the Otis Redding or Mick Jagger version better and then smiling to myself, realizing that I liked *our* version best of all. Nobody sang soul better than the Reverend, his North Carolina voice both clear and resonant as it wrapped itself around notes in a way that nobody with a recording contract back in the World was doing any better, a quality equal to Joe Tex at his best on a song like "Hold On to What You've Got." Even though the drumming demands on "That's How Strong My Love Is" were simple, I tried to make every beat count, timing my fills on the tom-toms to dig deep into a listener's heart. As if by mental telepathy, Brian called for the Joe Tex song next. It had a similar gospel-ballad feel and it sounded *so* good that I wasn't surprised at all when I caught Dave Murray's mystery lady staring up at me and smiling a couple of times, even while she was dancing with her body pressed close to his. I tried to smile back but she kept disappearing into the darkness. Now that I had gotten a couple of good looks at her, though, I had no doubt that she *was* the girl I had seen that first weekend in Ubon at the market down by the River Mun.

I didn't know much about Murray's personal life other than that he shared a place off base with a strange dude named Mole and that they were serious potheads. If she was Murray's *tii-rahk*, he was a lucky guy. If he was only with her for the night, I figured he was *still* a lucky guy. It was right about then that I was snapped out of my reverie by the neck of Baker's guitar crashing into my big ride cymbal.

Golson quickly wrapped up the song and stepped up to the mike. "It's break time, folks. Don't forget to tip your waitress." Baker had already picked up his beer and was about to head for the bar when Golson caught his arm and guided him backstage. The Reverend was calm, but he wasn't happy. "What's *with* you tonight?"

"I'll be fine," said Harley. "I just need a little fresh air." He lurched toward the stage door and put his shoulder to it, forcing it open with an ugly thud. He stepped outside, not having spilled a drop from his bottle of Singha.

The Reverend looked at me regretfully. "We gotta send him home."

"I'll take care of it," I said, packing up the Les Paul.

"You might need some help," said Sugie Bear as he and Ackerman followed me outside. We surrounded Baker, grabbed him by the elbows, and guided him around the corner to a waiting three-wheeled, bicycle-powered rickshaw called a *sahmlaw*. I overpaid the driver and asked him to take Harley back to his bungalow, but Baker wasn't in a cooperative mood and broke away from us. "Fuck you, Leary. Fuck all of you."

He was too wobbly to walk, however. We took hold of him again, forcefully this time, and maneuvered him into the back seat, where I handed him his guitar case. "Go," I told the driver.

"I oughta come back and *shoot* you bastards!" Harley screamed as they drove away. "Watch your back, Leary—you're gonna be first!"

By the time we got onstage for our next set, Wheeler's group was gone. The mystery girl would remain a mystery. A bigger concern was how capable Harley was of actually carrying out his threat. Pissed-off troops over in Nam were fragging second lieutenants, but this would have been ridiculous. We slogged on through the night's performance, grinding it out. Harley didn't need to kill anybody for his tirade to have put a damper on Sugie Bear's birthday celebration. When the last set was finished, everybody threw their equipment into their cases and skedaddled, leaving me to pack up the drums alone. By the time I was finished, the manager had emptied out the cash registers and turned out all the lights except one. It was creepy stepping outside and finding the streets deserted, not a cab in sight. Turning my bass drum case on its side, I sat down and waited. A trash can fell over in the alley behind me, making a sharp crack that I mistook for a gunshot. I dived behind my drum cases, my heart racing, and I hoped like hell it had been a hungry cat raising the ruckus and not Harley with his Ruger Blackhawk.

When I got back to the hootch, my bunkmates were already sound asleep. Leaving the lights off and walking on tip toes, I wearily peeled off my clothes. Reaching into the shadows to pull back my covers, I put my hand on a *body*! "Jesus Christ!" I shouted, instinctively jumping back from the bed.

"Shaddup, Leary!" one of my unsympathetic hootchmates grumbled.

I flipped on the light and what did I see but Harley Baker passed out on my bunk holding his guitar case in his arms like a long-lost teddy bear. "Baker," I said warily, trying to shake him awake, "I thought you wanted to kill me."

"I *love* you, man." Opening his eyes, he rolled out of the bed unsteadily and put his arm on my shoulder. "Let'sh go to th'NCO Club. We need a *drink*."

"Sure that's a good idea? You're a scarier drunk than my kid brother."

"I'm *shupposed* to be scarier, ashshole." He started pushing me toward the door. "We *Scotch* Irish're way scarier'n you *Irish* Irish. Le'sh go—or I really will have to kill you." Harley could be a hard guy to say no to.

"Would you bastards turn out the light and let us get some sleep!" came another groan.

We slowly made our way over to the NCO Club, which was kept open twenty-four hours a day on account of the several secret and not-so-secret wars and non-wars in the area that were flaring up twenty-four hours a day. "You sure it's okay bringing a two-stripe airman in here?" I asked.

"*Mai pen* fuckin' *rai*—" Harley answered, "we're in shivvies an' I'm acshully fighting in thish goddamn war. Any Rear Echelon Motherfucker who wansh to complain can try takin' it up wi' my commander. 'Grouchy Bear' Della Rippa'sh been hating REMFs for *three* wars now."

The place was crowded and smoky but eerily silent. Nothing on the juke box. Just a low hum of men's voices and the occasional whirring of a blender, a somber bartender making a pitcher of margaritas. We found Pigpen Sachs, one of Harley's fellow gunners, sitting alone nursing a beer in a quiet corner booth and plopped our tired bodies down next to him. Their faces were gaunt and their eyes dull, but their expressions were different. Sach's jaw was slack and his thick lips slobbery under his overgrown mustache. Harley's jaw was clinched tight, the muscles occasionally twitching. Wordlessly, they exchanged soul-brother handshakes. The lovely Thai waitress didn't smile when she took our order. "What's going on?" I asked. "It's like a wake in here."

"Something big went down tonight before I got to the Soul Sister."

"Didn't Harley tell you?" Sachs asked.

"He said something about a Spectre farewell—" Suddenly I got it. Part of growing up as an airline pilot's son was the shock, rare but devastating, when another pilot—a fellow *god*, really—went down in flames.

"When I shtopped by the chapel annex to pick up my guitar thish evening, Kirkgartner, that young assistant chaplain pulled me ashide and tol' me tha' one of our gunships wush coming in wi' battle damage."

"A bunch of us had already gathered around the radio at Spectre operations," said Sachs.

"When I got there," Harley continued, "We could hear Major Brishtow, the pilot, requeshting an emergency landing."

"The flight engineer wuzh reporting more'n a foota JP-4 fuel sloshing around the cabin, down with all those NiCad batteries an' all that other electronic shit," Sachs added.

Harley finished the story. "We could hear other voices screaming in the background. I wushn't positive, but I thought I heard Booty Simms, the gunner who had taken my place. They were all lined up for an emergency landing on Runway 2-3, jush eighteen minutes out. And then *poof*. Nada. Vaporized."

We sat quietly for a moment, our eyes lowered, staring into our beers. The ten-month lucky streak was over. My chest had seized up, and it was a long time before I could let out a breath. "Here's to Booty Simms," I said, clinking bottles with my melancholy bandmate and his friend.

"An' here's to the rest o' the crew," added Sachs. We clinked again.

Harley kept his bottle raised. His face looked bloodless and waxy, like it had been embalmed. "But here's *eshpecially* to Booty. I've seen some bad shit over in Nam. Some very bad shit. But thish is the firsht time somebody's died when it shoulda been me." We sat there in silence for a while, and then out of nowhere Harley said in a quiet monotone, "Le'sh go down to the Ubon Hotel."

"Isn't Mali going to be waiting up for you?"

"I just can't go home right now. I need to go somewhere bright."

"I need to stay somewhere dark," said Sachs. And with that he curled up in his corner of the booth and went to sleep.

I often saw a procession of *sahmlaws* and taxis heading for the Ubon Hotel when I packed up after our gigs at the Soul Sister. The GI and bargirl passengers could be boisterous or they could be deep in thought, but they were all headed for the same destination—the after-hours restaurant perched on the ninth floor of the tallest building in Ubon. Sugie Bear and Ackerman sometimes asked me to join them there for a nightcap, but I had never felt a desire to do anything more than get home to my bunk and write my nightly letter to Danielle. Tonight was different, though. Tonight I could cut my grieving bandmate some slack.

Long before we arrived, the night's losers had started gathering around the rooftop bar and out on a gigantic revolving dance floor. The tired-out bar girls and besotted GIs were going through the motions of dancing to a live band when Harley and I made our entrance, but nobody seemed to be having much fun. Cramming ourselves into a couple of seats at an undersized cocktail table and looking around for a waitress, we wouldn't have admitted it, but we fit right in. "How the hell do they get enough electricity up here to budge that thing?" I asked Harley as I gawked at the dance floor for the first time. There hadn't been a night when this backwater boomtown had not endured a brownout or blackout shortly after dark when thousands of GIs returned to their off-base bungalows and fired up their stereos.

"They wait till everyone else in Ubon has turned off their lights. An' then they put some food in that spirit house back by the kitchen and pray like hell the friggin' cosmos is in alignment. What are you drinking?"

We polished off a big platter of *paht thai* while we drank a couple more Singhas and nibbled on some chicken *saté* in peanut sauce. "What are they going to do with that oversized lazy Susan after the war?" I asked, still fixated on the revolving circle of parquet. It would have been impressive in a rooftop restaurant in L.A. or Boston, but I was mostly fixating on it because I was too numb to think of anything meaningful to say to Harley.

"Mali says the mayor of Ubon wants to move it into his auto showroom, but Pigpen figures they'll turn it into a new-fangled way to grind rice— and turn the whole damned hotel into a grain elevator when there are no American contractors or GIs left to fill it up." He tried to smile and gave up.

The music was making it hard to converse. Glancing out over the dance floor, I pitied the washed-up whores who were still trying to sell themselves to the bottom of the GI barrel. I wondered why they didn't return home to the simple dignity of their childhood villages or their family rice farms. *Hadn't they already done their share for the war effort?* I asked myself. *When did they finally know they had enough?*

BOOM! Harley's head hit the table with a jolt. He sat up in slow motion and checked that his jaw still worked.

"You okay?" It was Woody Shahbazian stepping out of the crowd. He'd brought his drink and an aging bar girl with him from the bar. She looked familiar, one of the regulars who hung out at Mama-sahn's café at Ruam Chon Sawng. "This is Bun-lii everybody. I've hired her to be my 'Thai teacher.'"

"An' Khun Woody teach me how to drive race car!" added Bun-lii happily.

"I can't remember if I've ever told you," I said to Woody, "but Harley here's from Spectre—"

"And I shoulda been on the bird that went down tonight. 'Cept I traded trips so me an' Leary could play downtown at the Soul Sister."

"Wow, man, I'm so fuckin' sorry," Shahbazian muttered. "Sorrier'n you could imagine. I knew Major Bristow, the pilot in command. His son and I went to school together when our fathers were both instructing down at Randolph."

"Small fuckin' Air Force," said Harley. He checked out his jaw again and then something caught his eye. "What's that wrishband for? You some kinda hippie or what?"

"It's for some friends. On my first tour over at Danang a lucky VC rocket hit our hootch while they were sleeping. Here," he said, starting to unlace it. "You just lost an AC-130 with a crew of fifteen on board."

"No, no, no, no," Harley responded, fumbling to fasten it back on Woody's wrist.

They were both tired and inebriated and depressed and made a half-hearted attempt to wrestle the wristband onto each other's arm. Finally, Woody gave up, lacing it back up. "Okay! Uncle! But I'm gonna make one for you over at the base hobby shop."

"Leary here won' be needin' one." Harley turned to me with jaundiced eyes. "I don' think you have a clue how lucky you are to be a shupport troop here in Thailand."

"I have a clue, Baker. I wouldn't want to be your shoes for a minute flying combat."

"Only shometimes Fate does the deshiding for you. When I firs' got to Nam we were flying night opsh with AC-47s—friggin' *Puffs*. Flyin' at much lower altitudes wi' nowhere near the kind of instruments we have on AC-130s. And one night it wush really bad—real rainy, cloudy— but we were TIC—Troops in Contact. A company of Marines wush surrounded and gettin' itsh ass kicked, so we hadda go out. And damn if we didn' get hit by the Puff that wush comin' in to relieve us. I woke up lyin' in the mud with a massive headache and looked up and what little ish lef' of the plane ish on fire. Gasholine an' ammo burnin' ash far ash you could see acrosh the rice paddies. Everybody dead excep' me. *That* wush fuckin' Fate," said Harley, slowly standing.

"I'm makin' you *two* wristbands," Woody called as Harley and I made our way to the elevator.

Ubon may have been the capital of the largest province in Thailand, but the first thing we heard when Harley and I stepped outside was the crowing of a neighborhood rooster. We found a sleepy cabby willing to take one more fare and headed home. Along the way I wondered if a ComDoc cameraman had been on board the flight with Booty Simms. "What'll happen now?" I asked.

Harley was staring at the back of the cab driver's head. "There *will* be payback. You can count of that."

Back at my hootch I undressed in the dark and climbed wearily into my bunk—not surprised this time when I bumped into the Harley's vintage Les Paul. I slid the case under the bunk and settled in, but I couldn't sleep, lying there instead with my eyes wide open, staring at the sagging springs above me. I started thinking about the uncomfortable intensity of life at Ubon Royal Thai Air Force Base that Zelinsky and Wheeler had warned me about and how simple things had been in my mountain cabin with Danielle. It seemed as if ten years were being pressed into one. The war wasn't turning out at all like I expected. It was worse. On one hand, it seemed like an absolute massacre. Indochina was being laid waste while North Vietnamese and Viet Cong units were taking staggering losses. But when fifteen American airmen go down at once, the enemy's ability to inflict random, instant death hit close to home. I began to toss and turn and was surprised to find myself pitying the next North Vietnamese convoys that tried to make it down the Trail—tonight and tomorrow night and the night after that. Spectre would be shooting to kill. The North Vietnamese would be shooting back. My mind was racing. I shivered at the thought of the next Spectre bird shot out of the sky by North Vietnamese triple-A. I didn't see it ever ending, and I wanted out. I tossed and turned some more and wondered why my case was taking so damned long. At last, trying to figure out how much of this to tell Danielle, I drifted off to sleep.

Monday at lunch in the chow hall Tom Wheeler asked me if I had heard what had been coming down in Washington the last few weeks.

"Nixon and Kissinger have decided to suit up and come fight the war?"

"Not quite. But they might have to the way things are going in the Senate. Stennis and the Armed Services Committee will always say the military's doing a great job, but people like Fulbright and Church are pushing to investigate Laos and Cambodia. They want to know why we've got spooks operating there and how the CIA got involved in drug-running. They're cutting night ops over the Ho Chi Minh Trail a little slack—probably because there's so much intelligence verifying North Vietnamese truck kills. As far as Cambodia, though, we were supposed to go a few miles in last year, kick some butt, and get out. The word around Saigon is that there is still *a lot* of Air Force activity there, what Nixon is calling "armed reconnaissance" and "protective reaction strikes"—firing only when fired upon. That might apply to F-4 and Spectre sorties. But what do you call fuckin' *B-52s* out of Guam and U-Tapao, Thailand, saturation-bombing the jungle? A group of want to cut off the funding altogether, but Nixon's stonewalling them and keeping a tight leash on the Pentagon and the State Department. Commanders may be filing false reports—saying they're operating in Vietnam when in reality they're going anywhere in Southeast Asia that they're sent."

"Jesus, Mary and Joseph…. What's to keep a president who goes off the deep end from bombing anywhere he pleases—anywhere in the *world*?"

"Eventually we'd run out of money, I suppose. Or have the whole damn world turn against us."

"Holy shit."

"There's another inquiry *you'd* be especially interested in, Leary—about why the Pentagon is foot-dragging on CO applications. Turns out they're swamped with new requests and too understaffed to catch up. So you're not alone. Which ties into the latest *really* big development: a bunch of combat veterans threw away their medals on the Capitol steps. There were so many it took 'em a whole day."

"I wouldn't mention that to Harley any time soon. That coulda shoulda been him that bought the farm Friday night."

"But it's connected in a weird sort of way," Tom said. "Some of the guys in D.C. had been up at the DMZ within a few miles of North Vietnam *and* Laos—take your pick—during a secret invasion of Laos early in '69 called Dewey Canyon. A few of them have just left units that were involved with something recent called Dewey Canyon II—the operation the South Vietnamese called Lam Son 719. This time no GIs went in, they just babysat the South Vietnamese Army right up to the border and then let *them* get slaughtered on the Ho Chi Minh Trail. Trouble is, they took a bunch of our choppers down with them."

He had caught my interest. "And that fiasco is what Larry Burrows was photographing when Spinelli and Nevers went down for the count."

"You're a smart boy."

"And that's probably where the Spectre bird got hit before it vaporized on Friday. You gotta figure that by the time the NVA got done wiping the ARVN's ass, that part of the Trail was more heavily defended than ever."

"Pretty good chance," said Tom.

"This is reminding me of a term paper I did in high school for Modern History. Seems the Air Force did a big study after World War II and found that short of nuking Hiroshima and Nagasaki, bombing seemed to *increase* a people's will to resist—be it England, Germany or even Madrid during the Spanish Civil War. Bombing a ball-bearing factory might hurt an enemy's capacity to hurt *us*—"

"'Cept there ain't no ball bearing factories in Laos," said Tom, taking a pregnant pause.

"Yes?" I asked.

"Remember your old buddy, Lieutenant Barry Romo, the dude just back from the Ashau Valley who spoke at our Fourth of July rally in San Bernardino? He was the leader of the California medal-tossing contingent."

"What a mess," I replied. "Combat veterans throwing away medals. Barry Romo's supposed to be going to law school on the GI Bill. You sure Lewis Carroll didn't write this?"

"Not even Lewis Carroll could think *this* shit up. And Washington's not the only capital under siege—a Buddhist monk and nun just set themselves on fire over in Saigon, and that's got students taking to the streets in Bangkok protesting American troops in *Thailand*! Compared to the Vietnam War, I'm afraid *Alice in Wonderland* makes way too much sense."

Lieutenant Rick "Moonbeam" Liscomb

Scuttlebutt in the Air Force was funny. It could be true or false. It could *come* true in minutes or it could take a year. Moonbeam Liscomb could generate all kinds of the stuff, which might have explained why I felt a mixture of happiness and concern at reports circulating around the detachment that the good lieutenant was finally done with the first two installments of his black pilot series and was due to rotate in. On one hand, a glorious ray of sunshine was heading our way just as we were hunkering down for the dreary monotony of rainy season. On the other hand—if only *half* the rumors were true—Moonbeam was on a personal journey that would *not* be endearing him to the Air Force commanders who would make or break his career. Few of his friends understood. I had a hunch that I did understand, that we were both in a spiritual crisis, no longer accepting the dogma of our childhood, and I had a hunch we were in turmoil over the war for similar reasons. But I also heard the voice of Father Boyle whispering in my ear, asking if Moonbeam and I weren't surely on a parallel road to perdition.

The monsoon rains were falling now, sometimes for a few hours and sometimes all day long, but they fell every day with no letup in sight. The roar of jet engines still filled the air, but many of the F-4 Phantoms returned with a full load of undelivered ordnance, using up the entire runway before their drag shoots could bring them to a halt. Even so, another flight of two or three F-4s would soon be rumbling down the runway, climbing out and kicking in their afterburners as they disappeared into the cloudy sky. There always seemed to be a spot someplace in Southeast Asia where the clouds thinned out enough for the Wolf Pack to hunt.

With the arrival of monsoon season I'd begun wearing a rubberized nylon rain suit with the hood pulled up, resolutely riding my bike between my hootch and ComDoc with a stripe of mud splattered down my back. At night I found it soothing to ride my bike through a light drizzle over to the chapel annex to rehearse with the band or over to the base library to do some reading. And as long as it wasn't a heavy downpour, I didn't mind riding downtown to see Tom, Lek, Larry and Pueng, who often rewarded me with home-style Thai cooking and Khon Kaen grass.

But now Lieutenant Rick "Moonbeam" Liscomb was rotating in. Back in California we had shared an unspoken faith that we were warming up for the day when we would make our mark on Hollywood as fresh, brash New Faces. That great rapport we once shared made it hard for me to believe that Moonbeam—with the help of Ron Cooper—would soon be responsible for getting me locked out of my cozy editing cubicle at Ubon Royal Thai Air Base and sent off to a life of abject terror.

Then again, in all fairness, I may have helped set the good lieutenant on the path that nearly landed him in Long Binh Jail. It was shocking to realize how far Moonbeam could fall from his days as an intercollegiate boxing champion and trailblazing Afro-American graduate of the United States Air Force Academy. All because somewhere along the line he had begun questioning the war. I felt a mixture of pride and concern that People's Independence Day might have been the catalyst that set him off.

Captain Sherry and I had kept it hush-hush, but word had gotten out long ago that Moonbeam was a vegetarian. It was about the same time that he became known as the first Academy graduate to admit publicly that he practiced Zen Buddhism and was a great admirer of the poet Allen Ginsberg. By fall, though, when all my free time was devoted to Danielle, further reports of Liscomb's worrisome descent into major flakiness kept coming in. The black fighter pilot project was getting good word-of-mouth, but off-duty, where Moonbeam had once been discreet dating Lisa Sherry, he started openly, defiantly dating white women, sometimes bringing them into Sarge's Café where he'd mess with the heads of the rednecks and the bikers sitting next to him at the bar by agreeing that integration would never work.

In the months that followed my deployment to Ubon, rumors continued to trickle in that Moonbeam had flipped out even further. At first, word had it that he had joined a cult. A few weeks later Washington and Blackwell got me especially worried when I overheard them arguing whether it was the Black Panthers that Moonbeam was running with or the Nation of Islam.

Liscomb had been on the short list for assignment to Southeast Asia for some time, but his *Air Force Now!* series kept taking longer than planned. In the meantime, a new rumor was circulating that he and Captain Sherry had been unwinding on the weekends at a nudist colony in Topanga Canyon. The base commander at Norton and Colonel Sandstrom at AAVS decided

Lisa had been a very bad girl and disappeared her in the middle of the night to the ComDoc detachment at Danang. They couldn't do anything with Moonbeam until Part 2 was edited, but once it was, according to Wheeler, they were relieved to find that he had long ago put in for an open billet at Ubon with the 601st.

I was over at the chapel annex putting away my drums after a band rehearsal, the last one to leave as always, and was looking forward to a free cup of coffee next door at Chaplain Kirkgartner's House of Free Expression when behind me I heard the sound of powerful, purposeful bootsteps on the polished linoleum floor. "Nice looking set of drums."

I looked up to see Lieutenant Rick "Moonbeam" Liscomb, in the flesh, striding through the open double door. "So Wheeler was right! Welcome to Ubon, sir!"

"Cut that 'sir' shit. What's this I hear about you joining a soul band?"

"Blame it all on Hank Ballard and Bo Didley. I've been hooked on rhythm and blues since eighth grade. I wanted to put a blues band together back at Norton, but history didn't cooperate—it was a country-rock kind of town."

"History does seem to have a mind of its own," Liscomb replied with a warm grin. I was dying to know if any or all of the rumors about him were true, but I had no idea how to broach the subject. Instead, I studied his face carefully. Moonbeam had changed since I'd last seen him, but the changes were subtle. He didn't have that born-again Christian lobotomized look he used to share with the well-intentioned innocents who listened to "Puff, the Magic Dragon" a few too many times. But neither was he in spaced-out Zen mode, nor did he appear to be a mad-as-hell Black Nationalist like our old editorial writer at the *sNorton Bird*. He just seemed *cool*, the way he was when we first hung out at AAVS editorial and across the street at Sarge's.

"Come on over to the coffee house next door, Lieutenant, and I'll buy you a coffee." He followed me through another double door and over to a dented, not-too-sparkling coffee urn. We poured ourselves some java and found ourselves a seat.

"This is kinda nice," said Moonbeam, looking around at walls covered with posters of Jimi Hendrix, Janis Joplin, Marvin Gaye and other present and future dead cultural icons.

"This is our junior chaplain's bright idea after the race riots at Korat and

Takhli. So far the guys at Ubon have preferred free Cokes, coffee and endless bullshitting to beating the crap out of each other."

"Sounds good," he replied, taking a sip from the Styrofoam cup. "Anybody come up with any answers?"

"I think everyone's a little frustrated. The career guys want to kick some enemy butt, except the enemy's been hiding lately. The young guys don't want to be here at all, except they've discovered nightlife that beats spring break in Fort Lauderdale. I don't know how much you've been shown around, Lieutenant, but for a basic briefing, we use an audiotape interview with a fed-up old-time fighter pilot called 'It's a Fucked-up War.' The Rat Pack itself, though, is full of some pretty far-out dudes."

He leaned in conspiratorially. "I of all people should know *that*."

"How so?"

"You don't think an Air Force Academy graduate is going to get stuck for a year in the boondocks of Southeast Asia without hand-picking some of the coolest guys in the entire Aerospace Audio-Visual Service to suffer along with him, do you?"

"You mean—"

"I kinda picture our own little sub-unit here at the 601st. How does Bitchin' Guys Productions sound? Code name: Bravo Golf Papa. I'll need a couple of you for the last segment of the black fighter pilot series—interviews with the dudes flying over here now. Once that's in the can, we start slipping in some boondoggle projects in Bangkok, Chiang Mai and Pattaya Beach."

"I just hope I'm one of the Bitchin' Guys—"

"One of the bitchingest!" he answered with a smile and a wink. "About my only disappointment was not being able to get your old buddy Lutz over here full-time. Captain Sherry wanted to keep him at Danang, so we compromised and put him at Tan Son Nhut. We get first dibs when we need a sound guy up here on temporary duty, and it looks like I'm going to use him right away when I hop around Vietnam finishing up those interviews."

"You're not responsible for Shahbazian, are you? He breaks more cameras than he fixes."

"We've got crates of spare cameras down in Saigon. What I really wanted was a personal driver who can play a little rhythm guitar and who's also had experience lifeguarding, bingo-calling and generally raising hell. Woody's our man. It keeps our options open. It was Woody's idea, by the way, to do an *Air Force Now!* special on surfing Southeast Asia. It'll give us a chance to visit China Beach over in Nam and the new R&R center down in Pattaya. If we play it right, we might even be able to swing through Okinawa, the Philippines and the Great Barrier Reef."

Liscomb continued, "Rounding up the Bitchin' Guys gives us one other possibility—I thought we might be able to stir up some political action like the old days back at Norton."

I nearly spit out a mouthful of coffee. "With all due respect, sir, I don't think you'll be able to do much political hell-raising around here. Take a look outside—there's a war going on, and our old crew from Norton is keeping its collective head down."

"Relax, Leary, I was just playing with you. I've still got plenty to do on that final segment for my *Air Force Now!* series. I'm heading out tomorrow to do some interviews at Bien Hoa. I'll be meeting Lutz and a crazy Polack from Boston you might have heard of named Sliviak. Sherry is sending him down from Danang to do the camerawork. I wish I could get you in on the editing, but I've got to send all the footage back to Norton on this one." He started to get up.

"Can I ask you something before you take off?"

He sat back down and said, "Shoot, Leary."

"What were you up to back in California after I left? We've been hearing all kinds of rumors."

"Such as?"

"Heard you'd joined a couple of *cults*. Then it was the *Panthers*."

He cocked his head back and thought a moment before asking me, "What were *you* doing with all that anti-war stuff?"

"I was trying to make peace with my conscience—make some noise while I still had a platform. Everything I believed in was being turned upside down."

"*Well*?" he asked, giving me one of his dumb-like-a-fox-smiles.

"Well *what*? What's with this cult business?"

"I guess I was on some sort of spiritual quest. Someone at the Los Angeles Zen Center said I should check out the Theosophy library near Griffith Park if I was really interested in world peace and racial harmony, but they were a little too much into ESP and séances for my tastes. But that led me to Krishnamurti, who had been selected as a child over in India to be the prophet-guru for the entire Theosophy movement until he abdicated and retired to the hills outside Ojai. He was brilliant, but Ojai is a four-hour haul from San Bernardino. I had to fly commercial up to San Francisco at one point and ended up sitting next to a very foxy producer from Argentina. She told me that if I was interested in world peace and harmony with a little meditation thrown in, I should check out the gardens and meditation centers built throughout California in the Twenties by an Indian guru named Yogananda. She was right about the temples and gardens being lovely, and I liked their belief that Christianity and Hinduism could coexist, but the Hindu part of the program had too many gods and gurus for me to keep track of. One of her friends invited me to a Baha'i service, and they seemed like lovely people believing as they did in world peace and equality for men and women, but they met in private homes and I was on the road too much to follow up. It was almost like I was wearing a sign saying 'recruit me,' because I was invited to check out a bunch of other groups like Science of Mind and Nichiren Shoshu and Scientology and even a group that believed Jesus was coming to pick us up in a space ship in the year 2000. At which point I said, 'Whoa! Why don't I stay focused on a single path and work on *inner* peace before I try to save the whole world?' The ritual at the Zen Center was complicated, but the meditation itself was something I could do the rest of my life.

"Unfortunately, I had trouble applying my spiritual practice to the racism I kept hearing about putting the Tuskegee Airmen piece together. I think I told you about how they were denied admission to the Officers' Club at Wright-Pat when they got back from Germany. The court-martial that followed played a major role in Truman's decision to integrate the entire armed forces and gave the story a happy ending, but they never would have left Alabama if Eleanor Roosevelt hadn't interceded for them. They were getting busted *on the way* to flight training because redneck MPs couldn't believe Negroes were capable of flying airplanes. And so on.

"And then, while I was back in California editing that segment, I got a strange request to drive in to L.A. to interview some Vietnam infantry veterans. They had gotten wind of the project and wanted to clue me in that they had all been sent out on highly dangerous LRRP missions doing long-range reconnaissance in the mountains and jungles along the Laotian border after committing minor infractions with their home units along the coast of Vietnam. They took terrible casualties and promised each other they'd meet up again as members of a Black Panther assassination squad when they got 'back to the World.' I couldn't use the material, but they clued me in that the Panthers really did have a bunch of Vietnam combat veterans in their ranks. It sounded impressive—except what they were talking about was suicidal. One of them turned me on to a Black Muslim minister who was very convincing talking to me about Black Pride and the need for black men to step up, but he lost me with stuff about white men being blue-eyed devils and how their prophet Elijah Muhammad never died, how he's flying around the earth in some kind of spaceship called the Mother Wheel. Another former LRRP turned me on to traditional Islam and the absence of racism in the teachings of Muhammad, but the world peace part seemed to be missing when I looked through the Koran he gave me. Long story short, I returned to my Zen meditation practice. And then it was time for me to go back out on the road for the Korean and Cold War segment of the series.

"The more active-duty black pilots I talked to, the more I was bugged about lingering discrimination in the military, but I began losing interest in black nationalism when I started investigating Martin Luther King's perspective—seeing the Vietnam War as a distraction from solving social problems at home and seeing passive resistance as a way to elevate black *and* white Americans the way Gandhi liberated India and Britain by waging peace instead of war. Is there anything else you wanted to ask about?" he asked.

"Was there any truth to the stories about you and Captain Sherry at Elysium?"

"We checked it out. But the base commander was a lot more upset when we tried to get an integrated bowling league going off-base. 'Blacks don't bowl in San Bernardino,' he told me."

The Black Power Squadron

I worried how Moonbeam would handle the culture shock of exotic Ubon, where killing and partying seemed to go hand in hand, but he had no sooner unpacked his bags than he took off for location shoots over in Vietnam. Reports we got over the next two weeks, however, hinted that his metamorphosing wasn't letting up. After only a few days in Nam, Bitchin' Guys Productions was put on the back burner. We knew Moonbeam was going through some major changes when he swapped out Sliviak and Lutz, his hand-picked Vietnam-based crew, for Washington and Blackwell, his hand-picked Afro-American crew, even though Washington wasn't nearly as experienced as Sliviak and Blackwell wasn't even working in his primary job classification. We got word that off duty Moonbeam was now on a Black Power kick, hanging out with black officers and enlisted men only, avoiding white dudes and other minorities.

The day of Liscomb's return to Ubon, he was named Deputy Chief of Combat Documentation for the 601st and became my supervising officer on *Hits of the Week*. I didn't know quite what to expect the first time he stopped by to see me at the editorial section of the ComDoc lab trailer, so I gave him a warm smile and played dumb. "Welcome back, Lieutenant. How'd the interviews go?"

He returned my smile, but I had a sense he was sizing me up. "It was strange, Leary. This time the pilots were interviewing *me*. 'Who is it down there we're killing?' they asked. 'Are Thieu and Ky *really* our friends or are they just ripping us off while we do the heavy lifting?' And then they asked why a higher percentage of black pilots than white are being sent out on high-risk missions—softening up hot landing zones, for instance, or dodging walls of triple-A up near Hanoi. I said I'd look into it, but when I put in a call to Seventh Air Force in Saigon, all I got from General Gong's staff was, 'We don't have time for bean counting, Liscomb. In case you didn't hear, there's a goddamn *war* going on!'"

I switched off the Moviola and looked up. "Sounds like you had an intense couple of weeks, Lieutenant."

"Unless they're called in by troops-in-contact on the ground, how *do* these pilots know for sure who they're killing? We're fighting a ruthless enemy that's badly outgunned and has to make up for it with guile. Several of the pilots I talked to think they've been set up: a lone sniper hides in a friendly village and fires at a Forward Air Controller. The FAC calls in an air strike, napalms the friendly village—men, women, children, grandparents—and *voila!* we've turned the survivors into hard-core Viet Cong. The pilots I talked to don't like this 'Free-fire Zone' business, either—shooting at anything that moves over big stretches of countryside. They've heard about too many ground troops who thought they were firing at Viet Cong and ended up finding the bodies of women and kids."

"I've been asking myself a lot of the same questions, Lieutenant. It's comforting to know I'm not alone. But it still leaves me wondering who's nuts around here, you and me or the other five thousand nine hundred and ninety-eight people on this base?"

Moonbeam paused a moment and glanced around, giving Zelinsky a little smile at the editing bench behind us. He leaned down and whispered, "You better start running that machine. I don't know who else should be hearing us."

I cranked some film through the Moviola, pretending I was paying attention and pantomiming marking usable scenes with my grease pencil. "Tell me again," he asked me softly. "What were you trying to accomplish with all that rabble-rousing back in San Bernardino?"

"I was trying to waltz my way out of the Air Force. When Nixon invaded Cambodia, we were sure the war would never end. When I got orders for Nam, I didn't want any part of it."

"And did you mean what you said at that July Fourth rally about how 'our objectives in Vietnam are illusory and our means of attaining them are barbaric'?" He looked around and saw that Zelinsky was busy canning up out-takes and trims to store away in the department safe. He put his head back down close to mine, asking, "That was *you*, wasn't it, who spoke out against asking more Americans to die while we're pursuing a failed policy in Southeast Asia? That was *you*, wasn't it, who asked why black and Latino GIs are shedding more blood than their white counterparts when they're still fighting for their civil rights at home? And wasn't that *you* who finished to a rousing ovation when you cried out, 'We must not falter! We must have peace!'?"

I laughed uneasily. "I said that? I think there might have been a UC Riverside co-ed in the front row who got me carried away."

"From what I could see, you had her spellbound—"

"That wasn't all," I blurted. "We had our heads all puffed up because the San Bernardino *Sun* had given us some good press, never thinking it was just to sell newspapers. When a couple of local limousine-liberal lawyers gave us their business cards, we thought it meant they had our backs, never figuring they were just looking for work. But the Air Force brass has pretty well had their way with us. We hadn't stopped to figure that being a colonel was what some very tough cookies did for a career. My personal attorney came highly recommended by the ACLU in L.A.—but he turned out to be dripping behind the ears, and he didn't work for free. So now I'm sending half my paycheck home each month to a bleeding-hearted bozo who forgot to call when he got blown out of the water on every motion he made to keep me stateside."

"I got a call through last night to the guys at the Movement House. They gave me some good ideas and said you'd be able to help me."

"The Movement House was boarded up when I left."

"Had a little trouble paying their rent. We got that straightened out."

"The guys at the Movement House are down in Santiago, Cuba, getting ready for the fall sugar cane harvest for all I know. They can't think for themselves and they're going to volunteer my services, eh? I love you, Rick, but read my lips: I have absolutely no desire to be a martyr. My support group in California was as paper-thin as a cutout movie set. I'm sure as hell not sticking my neck out over here alone."

"How about if I had a few hundred brothers lined up?"

"We're living in Lifer Heaven. And they can feed you all the crap in the world about 'parliamentary democracy,' but the fact is we're guests of a military dictatorship. The lifer brass is right at home here. I'm a half-lapsed pacifist making $127 a month. I just want to keep my nose clean, do as good a job as I can stomach and get back to the friendly smog of San Bernardino. Headquarters Squadron. Home. The government already paid for you to go study film at the University of Rochester. USC cinema has promised me I'll still have a spot when I get out, but the only way I'll ever afford it is with my GI Bill intact."

"What about your father? Heard he's an airline pilot making the big bucks—"

"He's old school—when you turn twenty-one, you're on your own in his book." I hated to disappoint Liscomb, but I was damned if I was going to take a fall for *his* noble cause. "Come on Rick, give me a break. Right now I'm off the Air Force shit list—I'm eccentric instead of radical, the white dude who plays soul music—"

"But I need your help right now. You've had experience organizing and we've got something big coming up. Doesn't it bother you that the racial harmony you've helped create ends up making the Air Force a better killing machine?"

I couldn't help thinking about Moonbeam at People's Independence Day and couldn't help squirming at the thought that he was about to end his career—and it was my fault. "The war I can't do a damned thing about. You and me, black and white, red and brown, *blue* and *green*, for chrissakes—that's different. With a little luck we're all going to be living together for a long time back in the World."

"We got something really big coming up."

"I'm not interested. Shahbazian's the natural-born hell-raiser. Wheeler may keep it to himself, but he hates the war as much as he hates Nixon and his War on Drugs. How about Perez and Washington? *You* brought them in. And Blackwell and Price. They go back to the *sNorton Bird* days and they always came through—always cool under pressure even when the Air Police were grilling us."

"I've already been talking to them. Shahbazian and Wheeler let me down. Woody of all people is suddenly afraid of making waves. 'Nobody's rocketing the base here,' he told me. 'I've been happy pretending to repair cameras. I'll be happy to be your part-time driver—just don't get me sent back to Nam.' Meanwhile, Wheeler rambled on and on about how he's got this Thai girlfriend who's supposed to move in and how the dope here is so mellow—I should try some. And they both talked about working on business deals. Perez only agreed after I promised there would be five hundred people marching. As far as Washington, Blackwell and Price—they'll march, along with every soul brother on base. But we still want *you*."

My butt was beginning to ache. I wanted to escape, but Moonbeam had me trapped. "If you've got five hundred people rounded up, what do you need me for?" I asked.

"Because like I said, this has got to be *really* big. We'd like to get *another* five hundred brothers and sisters to come over from Korat, NKP, Udorn, Takhli. Make it an even thousand. Callin' it *People's Independence Day II*, so you *gotta* be in on it, sucker. Remember that Army lieutenant, Barry Romo, who spoke at your little get-together back in San Bernardino? He was one of the *main men* at Dewey Canyon III in Washington back in April."

"So I heard."

"Head of the California delegation. Got some serious attention from Walter Cronkite. Maybe they didn't change the world, but it wasn't another piss-assed protest by a bunch of spoiled college kids. And maybe *this* ain't gonna change the world. Maybe we ain't gonna change jack. But we sho' nuff gonna ruffle the Air Force's tail feathers, and sleepy l'il Ubon's gonna wake up and take notice.

"I've got Washington and Blackwell doing lots of photography, so that when we get the story to CBS, they'll have plenty of pictures of active-duty GIs raising hell *in theater*. We could really use your help. We've got to print five thousand flyers without a soul knowing about it. And I need a speechwriter. Why reinvent the wheel, Leary? This is your thing. *sNorton Bird* revisited. And that rag you helped turn out back in D.C. Didn't think anybody knew it was *you*? It's in your master file, bro—the one only we officers get to look at. You were *born* to turn out this trash. A regular twentieth-century Thomas Paine. You're part of history, man. Can't fight history, so go with the flow. You know in your heart of hearts and soul of souls this is why you were called into the Air Force. This is your gift, your talent. It's in your Irish blood. It's your true Air Force Specialty. It's right up your alley, Brendan, and you know it."

"Maybe it *used* to be up my alley. But *damn*, Rick, I've got to cool it right now. I've finally got my discharge hearing next week. I might be going home. Why do you have to show up *here* of all places *now* and try to mess it up?" I took a deep breath and wished for once that I smoked cigarettes. I needed a hit of nicotine. A shot of Mekong would have helped. "Alright," I said, "this is the deal. I happen to know a fellow-traveler pacifist named Greg Quam who happens to be working the night shift in the base printing plant. Sort of a quasi-legal way of putting him in solitary. He's been turning out some mildly disrespectful underground GI stationery on his coffee breaks. He's your man. I'll make arrangements for you to meet him, and then I go *back into retirement*, sir. Got it?"

"You're hooked, sucker, and you know it."

"I'm hooked on cheap dope and Mekong whiskey. Maybe you didn't hear me a moment ago: I've got my *discharge hearing* coming up next week. Martyrdom is all yours, Rick. Sorry."

The next night Shahbazian dropped us off in the shadows behind the print shop. I led Moonbeam in through the back door to meet Quam, a new friend because by some kind of mysterious hunch he had figured out I was a fellow conscientious objector when we chatted in the chow hall on a rainy night at the start of monsoon season. Quam had been a sergeant back in San Antonio, Texas. The day before he was scheduled to ship out for Thailand, he went downtown to check with his lawyer on the status of their request for a restraining order. The base commander trumped it up to make it look like he had gone AWOL and busted him back to airman first class. I hated to imagine what Quam's commander would have done to *me* for leading People's Independence Day.

Lieutenant Liscomb showed Quam a mock-up of the flyer he wanted printed. "Can do," Quam said simply. "But isn't September a little late for an Independence Day march?"

I saw Liscomb pause for the first time since he arrived in Ubon. "You've got a point."

"How about *March* against *Racism—March* for *the Dream*?" I piped in.

Rick's face lit back up. "Thomas Paine has come through again!"

"It's your lucky night, Lieutenant. It's a little slow. Can you come back around two?"

"I'll be in the Rat Pack pickup with the funny-looking mouse on the door," Liscomb answered enthusiastically and strode out to rendezvous with Shahbazian.

I hung back, needing to catch up on some unfinished business of my own. "Did your lawyer ever send you copies of his filings?" Quam asked, wizened by his own experience. "You'll need them if you don't get a favorable ruling and need to resubmit your claim later. It also lets you keep an eye on the quality of his work."

"I haven't heard from him. But his office manager keeps sending out billings every month."

"Hate to say this, but he might not be doing a thing. You're low priority now that they've already won a few of these."

"And he's billing me?"

"He's a lawyer, isn't he? He might just figure you're a spoiled rich kid."

"And maybe he's right," I winced. "What do you think of Liscomb's peace march, by the way?"

"What peace march? I'm printing the fliers on local Thai newsprint with Thai printer's ink that Lieutenant Moonbeam takes with him. And then I disappear back into the woodwork while my case is on appeal."

"My sentiments exactly."

Hearing in Wonderland

Edward Poser, Esquire, had advised me to waive my hearing, telling me it would only delay my request for discharge as a conscientious objector. But since this was the same guy who bungled my case in federal court and left me with seventy-two hours to pack up my life at Norton and ship out for Southeast Asia, I decided to see if ignoring his advice wouldn't work better. The *catch* was that *Air Force* Regulation 35-24 was full of booby traps that made it easy for the Air Force to keep its troops around for their full enlistment—unless the Air Force decided to get rid of them. Unlike a civilian applying for CO status, I had to prove my beliefs "crystallized" in a specific period *after* I had joined the military but that they had *roots* in my civilian life. The other trap facing all conscientious objectors was having to prove you were opposed to *all* wars. That was where I felt uncomfortable. Playing by their rules, I couldn't admit I was glad Lincoln ended slavery or that the Allies brought down fascism.

It didn't matter. I wanted *out*, period. It started with the Tet Offensive and the My Lai Massacre. The invasion of Cambodia and the killing of American college students while I was on active duty had "crystallized" it for me. When I first enlisted I thought I could ride out the war in silence, but the war kept butting in. I may have been keeping my head down and my mouth shut at Ubon, but the devastation I saw every day in the editing room at ComDoc only deepened my aversion and reminded me how aerial warfare throughout the twentieth century had either strengthened an enemy's will to resist or led to nuclear annihilation. The crash of the Spectre gunship showed me how powerful the desire for revenge could be and how easily two avenging armies could fight a war without end. I had come to see the Vietnam War—and by extension, all war—as futile. The time had come for me when the end—getting out—justified the means, and if I had to contort the truth, so be it.

The hearing room was typical Air Force: new, clean, modern and sterile, capable of being packed up and shipped to the next war faster than I had packed for Thailand. Colonel Della Rippa, Harley's commander at the 16th Special Operations Squadron, was the lead hearing officer. It didn't take me long to discover why they called him "Grouchy Bear." He had the sandpaper voice and leathery skin of someone who smoked too much and drank his whiskey neat and would rather be out fighting a war than sitting at a long table in a meeting room with wall-to-wall carpet discoursing on *philosophy*. Oh yes, that was another complication. Halfway through college I had lost my faith in Catholicism and was using existentialism as the basis of my claim. An awful lot of the officers I bumped into in the Air Force spoke in the cadence of war-loving, hellfire-and-brimstone TV evangelists, and I suspected a few eye-for-an-eye Baptists would be ruling on my case before all the dust settled.

Colonel Della Rippa, two junior administrative officers and Chief Master Sergeant Sturbutzel from CBPO sat at the far end of the table. I felt a little lonely down at my end. After running through the rudimentary facts of my application, I watched the colonel squint painfully at the seventy-some pages of documentation I had submitted. A lot of it was letters of support from old friends, teachers and professors and one awfully milquetoasty missive from my old priest, Father Boyle, who probably didn't care much for the *existential* approach I took, the result of four semesters of French filled with way too much Sartre and Camus and enough Hemingway, Salinger and Wilfred Owen in my English lit classes to make the French writers plausible.

"Aren't you concerned about what will happen if Communism takes over the Free World?" asked Della Rippa.

I sat up confidently. This seemed too easy. "By the Free World, sir, do you mean places like Thailand?"

"That's right," said the colonel.

"And we should defend the Free World at all cost, sir?"

"That's right."

"And is Thailand a kingdom, a constitutional monarchy, a democratic republic, a military dictatorship, or some sort of a medieval theocracy?"

Della Rippa's neck seemed to swell up and his leathery skin turned a little red. "I don't pretend to be a politician, Airman Leary. I don't know much more than it's an American ally, but that's plenty good in my book." He cleared his throat and re-gathered his thoughts before glaring back at me. "Let's not lose sight of the fact that this is *your* hearing, Airman, not mine and certainly not the American government's."

"Do you think it's okay for American kids to kill and be killed defending a government we don't know a thing about?" I was surprised to find I was enjoying this.

"Airman Leary, I won't remind you again—*I'm* supposed to be asking the questions here."

"I would just like it on the record that like many of you here, I used to think that war was a necessary evil, an ugly fact of the human condition. We were trained since elementary school to believe that every American war was justified and divinely blessed. But I had trouble for a long time fitting this with the Old Testament commandment not to kill and Christian teachings to forgive and love our neighbors. My thinking was still confused and muddled, however. Some wars in the past *did* seem to be justified, but my college ROTC class in modern warfare taught only about nuclear war and wars of counterinsurgency. Wars of counterinsurgency are offensive wars, and you've got a 50% chance of picking the wrong side.

"As far as a nuclear war is concerned, we had a young Japanese girl living with us when I was a kid who had survived Hiroshima and was getting her face rebuilt at Mass General. They did reconstructive surgery on her for a year and still she would never marry. Nuclear war to me is unthinkable, and yet there we were in class thinking about it. And I'm afraid there are respected American generals today who are thinking about it in Vietnam—*without* worrying about getting into World War III with China or the Soviet Union.

"Vietnam is supposed to be a limited, conventional war, and yet from my perspective here at Ubon editing raw gun-camera footage, the war has been devastating, especially for rural civilians. All I have seen is escalating levels of violence on both sides—war producing more war with no end in sight.

"I've spent many nights in the base library reading about the tragic history of the French in Indochina. I've been trying to make sense out of Asian culture and history and where we fit into it other than as barbarians. I can only conclude that war as the United States fights it is an *unnecessary* evil."

The captain whispered something in Grouchy Bear's ear.

"Was fighting *Hitler* unnecessary? Who else was going to close down the concentration camps?"

There it was, one of the sticky wickets that Edward Poser, Esquire, feared would trap me. Suddenly, my counsel's strategy seemed brilliant, whereas *I* had simply *hoped* they wouldn't ask about Hitler. "That was a different war, sir, the one that gave us the atomic bomb. The stakes are too high now. The chance someone pushes the button by mistake is too great."

The pasty-pale lieutenant had the look of someone who had successfully carried out his plan to spend his entire tour hiding out in a windowless cubicle. "If Abraham Lincoln hadn't ended slavery," he asked stiffly, "would white and black musicians be playing together in that soul band of yours?"

"With all respect, sir, it's been a hundred years since Lincoln was around. Slavery has ended everywhere on the planet and it didn't take General Sherman scorching the earth to do it."

Sturbutzel was perplexed. "Let me get this straight. Did I understand you to say you think rock'n'roll music is a *good* thing?"

Colonel Della Rippa rumbled through his thick stack of papers. "What does this letter from your old priest mean? 'While I don't concur with Brendan's devotion to existentialism, I know him to be a young man who other than coming to a few CYO dances drunk and being a little girl-crazy, was generally of good character.' Is Father Boyle saying you don't believe in God?"

My heart sank. I knew I was dealing with a man who'd never read my full application. The kind that Edward Poser, Esquire, had warned me about with his little joke about how it would be good practice for dealing with Hollywood production executives who never read a script. "The regulations don't require that I hold a conventional belief in an established religion as long as my beliefs are deeply held and fixed," I replied.

I was starting to see how lifers like Della Rippa and Sturbutzel didn't get upset when they disagreed with some low-level pipsqueak, they just turned into human bulldozers. Della Rippa pressed on. "How can you be sure that war is wrong and not believe in God?"

"Because that is the same thing concluded by existential philosophy— that we are alone in the universe and our only hope is in acting out of human compassion."

Grouchy Bear Della Rippa's attention span had screeched to a halt. It was time to get back to the war. "Let me get this straight. You don't believe in God?"

"I've lost my faith somewhere along the line, sir."

Sturbutzel looked over at the colonel sympathetically. Colonel Della Rippa stretched his neck, which seemed to be choking from an imaginary tie. "And you're requesting discharge from the United States Air Force based on the teachings of a couple of *French* philosophers?"

My own imaginary tie seemed to be getting a little tighter. "That would be correct, sir."

"That will be all, Airman Leary."

I stood up and gave the snappiest salute I could muster for someone who was supposed to be a pacifist. Della Rippa gave back one of those swatting-fly-type dismissive salutes that did not fill me with confidence. Just as I was turning to leave he pretended to remember something that had nearly slipped his mind. "Oh, Airman Leary," he said, clearing his throat, "There's one last question I almost forgot." I felt a trap closing in on me as he paused—dramatically, I noticed—before asking, "What would you do if you saw a couple of thugs beating your mother?"

"I don't know, sir."

He had me, he thought, squinting at me and giving me a crusty smile.

"But I know I *wouldn't* call in a B-52 strike."

The pasty-faced lieutenant snorted, trying to suppress a laugh.

"Will that be all, sir?" My salute was a little sharper this time, and I left feeling that I had held my own, but in the world of the Little Pentagon, holding your own wasn't enough. Before I got out the door I felt pretty hopeless.

By nightfall the hopelessness turned to despair. Perez and Shahbazian stopped by the hootch to offer their condolences about my discharge petition being shot down. "It hasn't been shot down yet," I protested.

"The word around CBPO wasn't good," said Perez.

With near-incontrovertible logic, they urged me to come downtown for a massage at Niko's, a Turkish bathhouse they had recently discovered. "Face it, Leary, you're gonna be stuck around here for seven more months," said Shahbazian. "You might as well make the best of it."

Despite the soundness of their logic, I controverted them anyway and walked over to the library to write some letters. Danielle had sent along a clipping from the L.A. *Times* reporting how happy General Abrams had been with the Army's new drug eradication program in the Mekong Delta region. I wrote back that Abrams might not be so chipper if he visited Thailand. I tried to think of a funny way to describe my CO hearing but finally gave up and told her simply that I wasn't feeling too hopeful about getting home early. At least we would finally know one way or the other. I tried to write to my parents but quickly got stuck. I kept hearing my father's voice asking, "What's your problem?" And the answer was that I was lost. I was disgusted with the devastation of Southeast Asia that I witnessed every day and which seemed to be accomplishing nothing. But as much as I wanted nothing more to do with Nixon and Kissinger's war, I was haunted by Della Rippa's last question. In my heart of hearts I didn't know what I would do if I saw my mother, or any old woman, being mugged. I couldn't honestly tell myself whether I believed in non-violence, or minimum necessary force, or if I was just a coward.

"Insufficient Documentation"

A week and a day after my hearing, I was sent over to see Lieutenant Billy Hill at the ComDoc orderly room. Hill was a freckle-faced, red-headed, perpetually sunburned good ole boy who gladly filled the dual slots of deputy commander and chief of combat documentation for Detachment 3 in the hopes it would look good on his next efficiency report. Looking at him, I couldn't help thinking of a Gomer Pyle who had miraculously made it through college ROTC. With his jutting jaw, wispy crew cut and premature beer belly, he was hard to take seriously as a symbol of authority, but when he called me into his office, I saluted. He handed me a large packet in a manila envelope that had come from Air Force Headquarters, Washington, DC. "It looks important, Leary. You might want to open it."

It contained a thick photostatic copy of my request for discharge along with several pages of comments from officers who approved and disapproved it along the way up the chain of command. I didn't need to look beyond the cover letter, however. My seventy-page application had been duly processed by the Directorate of Personnel at Randolph Air Force Base in Texas and turned down—for *"insufficient* documentation."

I was stunned when I closed Hill's office door behind me even though I realized that I shouldn't have been surprised. Link sat in his office pretending to ignore me, but from his vindictive smile, I knew that he knew. Out in the orderly room, Dave Murray was napping, using his typewriter as a pillow. Tom Wheeler, sitting at the opposite desk, stopped typing and looked up. "Not good, eh?"

I didn't try to hide my disappointment. I had put months into this, providing a stack of supporting letters from teachers and professors and friends like Tom attesting to my integrity and the depth of my conviction, not to mention over fifty pages I had written myself describing my beliefs, their sources, and how they evolved. "I gave them over seventy freaking pages of material, Tom, and they called it 'insufficient documentation.'"

Wheeler laughed, not exactly the emotion I was looking for. "That's what they do on all these cases, hoping they'll just go away. Why don't you bring your copy down to Ruam Chon Sawng tonight and I'll take a look before we get wasted."

I rode through a monsoon drizzle that night on my way to Wheeler's bungalow. When I pulled the manila envelope from under my rain jacket and handed it to Tom, he just held it in his hand, weighing it. "I can tell you already, you got way too much stuff here."

"But they shot me down for 'insufficient documentation.'"

He sat down, and while I looked over his shoulder, he started flipping through my application. "That's their standard excuse. I talked to one of my contacts over in CBPO who works for Sturbutzel. The whole system's swamped right now. If you want the brass to actually read it, make it *a page or two* with lots of strong supporting letters." He paused a moment. "All this Camus and Sartre and Wilfred Owens stuff—get rid of it."

"But…"

He wasn't paying any attention to me, instead leafing through the letters. "What the hell is this letter from Father Boyle doing in here?"

"He was the last priest I confessed to."

"Throw that out and go see Chaplain Kirkgartner. He's cool. He's the dude who came up with the House of Free Expression, right? Have him write something about how your existentialism shit *developed* out of your wonderful Catholic upbringing."

"Kinda smooth out my rough edges, huh?"

"What the hell is this Appendix!" He almost fell out of his wicker chair, scaring the hell out of me in the process. "You've got twenty pages of poetry and speeches in here. How could you send a bunch of colonels *poetry*! You're cutting into their drinking time at the O Club."

I was feeling more than a little sheepish. Tom was completely right. I was so full of my own angst that I completely failed to consider my audience. "I thought that's what they wanted in item 4, subsection F: 'have you ever made public expression of your beliefs?'"

"For a bright guy, you sure can be stupid, Leary. Throw out the appendix. You can answer it in a sentence—something about going to peace marches and prayer vigils. Lie and say you've even started praying to God lately."

"Thanks," I said, taking out a pack of Blue Moon cigarettes and offering one to Tom. "So you think it's worth resubmitting, eh?"

"Not in the shape it's in right now. You've got a lot of work ahead of you."

I pulled out my little Ronson and lit up before giving Tom a light. Taking a deep, relaxing drag on the Blue Moon, I thanked Papa-sahn that somehow, somewhere in Ubon Province one of his little elves was removing the tobacco from these commercial Thai cigarettes and replacing it with some of the old man's very potent Khon Kaen grass.

I sleepwalked through work the next day. When I stopped by the base post office at lunch time, I found a special-delivery letter from Edward Poser, Esquire, saying he had received a copy of my CO rejection. He pointed out something that Tom and I had missed: the Air Force had called the application "opportunistic"—inferring I had simply been trying to avoid service in a war zone. He advised *not* trying to appeal, given that I was serving in a non-combat role and given that Air Force regs required new facts or some other substantial change to justify a second application. He was kind enough to include a bill for over a thousand dollars. My head felt spongy, but somehow that afternoon a murky thought popped up that maybe—*just in case*—I should look into a foreign passport. I remembered my backpacking brother telling me about reading on the bulletin board in a youth hostel in County Donegal that we qualified for an Irish passport. All we needed to trace our lineage back to the Ould Sod was our father's and grandfather's birth certificates, which my father said he would give me over his dead body. Back at my hootch I wrote my brother a short note asking if there was another way of proving Grandpa Leary had been born in Ireland and how long it might take. I wrote another to Danielle telling her I wouldn't be coming home early but that I loved her and looked forward to the day we *could* be together.

After mailing the letters, I bicycled in a daze over to the base library and tried to read a *Newsweek*, an *American Cinematographer* and a *Rolling Stone*. Unable to concentrate on any of them, I nodded off for I don't know how long and then sat up with a start, filled with a need to get downtown. I stopped off at the BX and picked out a stack of albums to bring down to Woodstock Music, where I studied Sommit carefully while he inspected my goods and I decided which albums I wanted duped back onto tape. I might not have been dealing with a hard-core black marketeer, but he *was* a businessman. I couldn't say if it was inspiration or desperation, but in any case I asked him if I needed to go to Bangkok to obtain a Canadian passport or if it could be arranged around Ubon. Sommit took me to a dingy office in back of an old warehouse to meet Indian Joe, the blue-eyed Sikh who *was* a black marketeer and had expanded his operation effortlessly into a consortium of small businesses catering to GIs. Khun Joe told me not to sweat it if I didn't have passport pictures and said he'd take me to arrange my spare identity the next night.

It was the same kind of little shack run by a wiry, energetic papa-sahn that many of my fellow GIs visited across the river to score dope, only this establishment was not far from Prommaraj Road, in VC town, the off-limits Vietnamese ghetto. *This* papa-sahn didn't have any dope for sale, but he took a Polaroid and said he'd have my passport in two days.

Ron Cooper Isn't Coming, OR:
The Day I Donned My Plastic Wings

I don't know how he pulled it all together in two weeks. Perhaps he *was* the radical messiah that militant blacks had been waiting for. In any case it was an awesome sight watching Lieutenant Liscomb lead his Black Power Squadron, over five hundred strong, down Ubon's main drag toward city hall on what was supposed to be a quiet Saturday morning in a backwater provincial capital. With great dignity, Brian Golson—"the Reverend"—marched in the front of the procession only a few feet from Liscomb. I could make out Sugie Bear and Ackerman walking confidently, not far behind. Mixed in with the Afro-American majority was a sprinkling of Latinos, including Perez, who had disguised himself in dark sunglasses and a Yankee cap. Further back, Price, Blackwell and Washington strode past in a festive mood, striking up a chant of "Say it loud! I'm black and I'm proud!" A few potheads including Dave Murray and his friend Mole tagged along, taking up the rear.

"Fuck it," I said to Wheeler as we locked up our bikes and joined in. "What are they gonna do—"

"Send us to *Vietnam*?" we mouthed derisively.

From the top of the granite stairway at the front of the provincial government building, the lieutenant gazed happily at his motley multitude and began speaking, using a bullhorn that echoed for blocks. "Eight years ago," he extolled, "Dr. Martin Luther King told the world he had a dream, a dream of tolerance and equality and opportunity for all, a dream that even an assassin's bullet could not kill. Today, even as the struggle for racial equality continues at home, we have a new dream here in Ubon—to stop this racist war. Fat-cat Washington politicians and the lobbyists and contractors they are in bed with have *profited* whether we *lived* or *died!* The Thai elite has been bought while Thai *soldiers* have paid in blood. But today we dream of peace. We dream of a new day when American soldiers lay down their arms and *demand* to be sent home so that our Thai brothers and their Vietnamese cousins can live in harmony. We have a dream that powerful White Anglo-Saxon politicians back in Washington will never again be able to put a gun to our heads and make us pawns on their global chessboard. But our struggle is just beginning. Whether we are black, white, Latino, or Native American, mark my words—"

"I think he's starting to get warmed up," said Tom.

"As long as the military-industrial complex continues to profit—as President Eisenhower warned us—*this war will continue!*" The crowd gave him a few shouts of "*Right on! Right on!*"

"As long as the military-industrial complex continues to own our elected representatives in the U.S. Congress—" He paused this time so the crowd could join him: "this war will *continue!*"

"As long as the Silent Majority of American voters believe this is a fight of Freedom against Tyranny—"

"*This war will continue!*" chanted the crowd.

"Until we hold up the racist underbelly of this war to the light of day—"

"*This war will continue!*" shouted the crowd, picking up Liscomb's cadence.

"If it is truly Communism that we are fighting, why are we fighting here among the brown-skinned people of Southeast Asia instead of against the *white-skinned* Communist regimes of Hungary, Czechoslovakia, or Russia itself?"

"Fuck racism!" somebody shouted.

Liscomb held up one hand and smiled, calming the crowd—but just a little. "Our objectives in Vietnam are illusory and our means of attaining them are barbaric! Where is this administration taking us? Where will the escalation end? When will our brothers and sisters at home learn that the devastation we are wreaking in Southeast Asia is far more cataclysmic than anything they have seen on the evening news!

"How can we continue to ask young Americans to die while we blindly pursue a failed policy? How can we continue to ask *Blacks and Latinos* to take 50% higher casualties than their white counterparts!

"Has a peacetime draft made it far too easy to go to war? Isn't an army of draftees in reality an army of slaves? And wasn't slavery supposed to *end* with the Emancipation Proclamation?"

Someone shouted, "Fuck slavery! Fuck the draft!" and it was taken up by the crowd and repeated a few times. The speech was rambling, but the audience was following closely enough to respond energetically.

"A nation's greatness must be measured by more than wealth and power! Shouldn't a great nation be a land of opportunity for all? And shouldn't a great nation be a beacon of liberty that reaches every corner of the world?"

Another sprinkling of voices shouted, "*Right on! Right on!*"

"I fear instead that the beacon of American liberty has grown dim of late. America's experiment in democracy is less than two hundred years old. How can we expect to *impose* that system on a culture as ancient and proud as Vietnam's?

"Thousands of active-duty GIs around the world are signing petitions calling for immediate withdrawal from Vietnam. I urge you to join them and sign the petitions that your brothers are circulating."

Tom and I spotted Sugie Bear, Price, and Ackerman walking through the crowd gathering signatures while Washington and Blackwell took stills with Rat Pack Nikons. Liscomb began to wrap things up, perhaps hoping to leave some time for an open megaphone. "We who have gathered here today know that withdrawal from Vietnam is a most *difficult* course of action. It is a course we must take, however. We, as soldiers of color, must lay down our arms in Southeast Asia and join the fight for social justice that is still being waged in the United States of America! We, as soldiers of color, must stop the senseless killing that has spread like a cancer over two thirds of the Indochinese Peninsula! The war must end *now*, and it is *we* who have taken on that awesome responsibility of leading the way..."

It was eerie hearing an evocation of my own words—words I could only half remember—being comingled with those of a black martyr and saint. It was eerier still watching Ubon Thais look on with bewilderment, waiting for Liscomb and his little army to be sprayed with machine gun fire. By the time a caravan of Air Policemen showed up and confiscated his bullhorn, it occurred to me that no one had briefed Moonbeam on how badly the Thais and the Vietnamese had hated each other for the last thousand years—long before the French *or* Americans showed up. "We must not falter!" Liscomb boomed, his voice filling the square even without a bullhorn. A couple of APs spotted Washington and Blackwell, took their cameras, and exposed their film before shoving it all back into their hands. "We must have peace!" Liscomb cried as he was handcuffed and whisked away in the back of an open AP jeep.

Wheeler and I disappeared into the shadowy back alleys of the business district. Behind us, the APs carted away a hundred marchers and American bystanders. The Thai national police did their part by rounding up a group of local street hustlers and a few off-duty Laotian *sahmlaw* drivers. We decided to worry about our bikes later and found a cab to take us to the Soul Sister. As we bounced along, Tom asked, "Did you notice a couple of lifer types mixing in with the crowd?"

"I'm afraid I missed them," I confessed.

"They were dressed in civvies and taking plenty of their own pictures."

"Why do I get the feeling they got the cameras from Link?" I sighed.

When we walked into the Soul Sister, the liveliest club in Ubon, the quiet was creepy. We nursed a beer, and finally word came in that the arrested marchers had all been released—except Moonbeam. He had been put under house arrest.

The next day, before I had a chance to plant a muddy foot in the Rat Pack editorial trailer, Zelinsky sent me over to the orderly room to see Captain English. The orderly room was bustling when I straggled in as invisibly as possible. Several of the camera technicians and drivers were picking up their instructions on which planes were to be fitted and unfitted with gun cameras and which of the cameras already fitted needed to be reloaded. A trio of civilian contractors was coming out of Captain English's office discussing a newly modified 70mm reconnaissance camera that was tucked proudly under the arm of the lead contractor. First Sergeant Link sat in his side office nursing a cup of coffee, warming up his arm for the afternoon he would be spending at the NCO Club drinking lunch. He threw me a snarling smile that looked more Neanderthal than Homo sapiens.

Tom Wheeler and Dave Murray were tip-tapping at their typewriters, Murray's eyes seemingly focused on his work while he blissfully listened to acid rock on shiny white Pioneer headphones. I flipped off the toggle switch on Tom's typewriter and leaned into whispering distance. "What the hell does English want? Performance reports don't come out for another month."

"Something about Ron Cooper. He's due in tomorrow and there's some kind of SNAFU. I think Link's up to something—he's been in and out of English's office a lot this morn—"

"Leary, get your butt in here!"

I hadn't felt comfortable in an officer's lair since Major Toliver started calling me in back at DODCOCS. Stepping into English's office, I couldn't help feeling that a bad dream was about to begin again. "Airman First Class Leary reports as ordered, sir," I said, throwing him a nervous salute.

I felt like a virgin auditioning for a porn film every time I had to go through this ritual. For someone who for years had thought of himself first and foremost as a rock drummer, there might have been nothing in the world harder to do than saluting. Captain English gave me a look with beady eyes that reminded me of a cross between a shark and a pit bull. The thick chest hair that sprang from the open collar of his khaki shirt was longer than the shaved hair on his head. It scared me. "Sit down, Leary."

I didn't want to sit down. Being called in by a commanding officer could only mean trouble. At least Toliver used to let me stand when he delivered bad news. Sure enough, the moment my butt touched the chair, the booby trap went off.

"You're flying tomorrow."

My heart lodged itself squarely in my throat. "What!" I gasped. "I'm a goddamn film editor, Captain English. Excuse the French, but what in hell are they going to do with a film editor inside an airplane?"

"Cooper's been delayed. He's going through a psych evaluation right now. Seems he's got an uncontrollable fear of flying. They figure they can use him better back at Norton, anyway, working on the sound stage. He's a helluva lighting cameraman, you know."

"Sir, I was *with* him back at Norton. He's a helluva lighting cameraman all right. But sir, he *is* a cameraman and we do send cameramen off in airplanes in the Air Force. What does Cooper being held up with late-onset fear of flying—two-and-a-half years into his enlistment—have to do with putting a *film editor* up in the sky? We've got perfectly good Moviolas and editing benches right here at ComDoc."

"You've been in a lot of hot water from the day you left Basic Training, Leary. With your education and test scores you might have made a good officer. Instead you've spent two years in deep Shinola. This could be your chance to clean up your record and get back with the program."

"Don't take it personally, Captain. I just can't seem to stop myself from being a freethinker. Back when I was a kid, I was thrown out of catechism class for doubting the Immaculate Conception. I guess being a freethinker had something to do with why I passed on OTS—all the production officer slots had already been filled by ROTC graduates like yourself or Academy grads like Lieutenant Liscomb. The only way to get assigned to a photo unit was as an enlisted man. But somehow along the way, far from becoming a production officer, I've been unfairly labeled as the Resident Radical wherever I've been sent."

"Leary, you're not the Resident Radical—I think the Village Idiot is more like it. Only a village idiot would print these." He held up several copies of Liscomb's *Black Manifesto* with short, squat fingers attached to a hand and body of similar proportions.

I stared hard at the fistful of pamphlets Captain English had thrust in my face. I felt a warm and secret glow in my heart for my newfound ability to delegate surreptitiously and defer martyrdom. "Never saw them before," I said.

English opened the tattered brown folder that held my accumulation of near-perfect test scores, Article 15 convictions, and highly contradictory performance reports. He pulled out a page buried in the back, written on civilian letterhead stationery. "We checked through your records and it turned out Cooper was right. Your professor at Rhode Island School of Design gave you rave recommendations in editing *and* cinematography."

My armpits were beginning to slosh like the bellies of a pair of first-night honeymooners. "What would some professor know, back there in his ivory tower? He was probably so whacked out on drugs that he couldn't tell a pan from a tilt."

The balding bulldog turned over another page in my record folder. "It says here the Air Force paid for you to take a few photography classes when you were back in Washington—"

"They only paid *half*, sir—and it was *still* photography. I mean we all know that still photography is nothing like motion picture photography."

"Photography is photography, Leary. Quit the B.S. Cooper recommended you. You should be flattered." He flipped the cover shut and tossed the folder into the OUT basket. Matter closed. And then a little of the warmth that they taught him the last semester of ROTC. "You should look at this as a hell of an opportunity, Airman. If you do manage to live long enough to get to Hollywood, you're going to find that motion picture cameramen make a pile more money than editors."

Lieutenant Hill came from I don't know where and scared the bejesus out of me. "Shee-it, son, a *girl* can be an editor. We're giving you a chance to be a camera*man*."

My blood was boiling. *I* was the one who had been terrified of flying. Goddamned Cooper had stolen my story. Could I sue for plagiarism? I'd probably never live to find out. "Sirs—*I'm* terrified of flying. My dad trained British cadets for the Battle of Britain. Barrel rolls fifty feet off the deck, that sort of insanity. And my uncle was a crop duster. Nothing made them happier when I was a little kid than to take me up in his Stearman and do outside loops until *I* dusted crops with my sick stomach. To this day there are pieces of my fingernails embedded in the bottom of that back seat. And then in high school two of my classmates lost their dads on the same training flight over Buzzard's Bay. I still have nightmares about that 707 snapping off an engine and doing its own uncontrolled barrel rolls until it smacked the water. In college there was the day we lost our right engine returning from a track meet and the co-pilot came back and stood right next to me while he tried to lower the flaps by hand. He couldn't even get the damned crank into its slot above his head—this was some oddball high-winged propeller-powered *French* airplane that only *had* two engines—"

"Let's cut the crap, Leary." English had lost the smile he had pasted on a few minutes earlier. I didn't get a chance to tell them how when we touched down we must have still been doing close to two hundred miles an hour. And how it wasn't until we ran off the end of the runway and ground-looped to a screeching halt that the bumbling co-pilot finally got the flaps down. I especially needed to tell them how I didn't go near an airplane for years without downing three stiff belts of Southern Comfort.

"I hope you realize that this is exactly the same story that Cooper told to Colonel Sandstrom back at Norton." The captain's short, squat bulldog neck was puffing out and turning violet. "You're damned lucky we don't have regs against plagiarizing in the Air Force."

Hill was bemused. "If what you're telling us *is* true, Leary, what the hell did you enlist in the Air Force for in the first place?"

"The head of the AV department at the school where I was teaching knew this Air Force recruiter who *guaranteed* that I'd be a film editor until my OTS class for film directors opened up...."

I had been too embarrassed to tell this to anyone since the day I got on the faded blue school bus that took us out to Logan Airport for the flight down to basic training in San Antonio and fifty raw recruits split their guts howling at the guy who actually believed his recruiter's spiel and brought along his golf clubs. *Sergeant Gallipeau*—I prayed for months that a horrible, incurable disease would bring a slow and painful death to the man who baited the trap that got me into my current, seemingly unending conundrum. And now I had Ron Cooper to add to my incantations.

Lieutenant Hill was wearing one of his patented ear-to-ear shit-eaters. "Goddamn, Leary, any man dumb enough to believe a recruiter *deserves* to fly combat! Report in here tomorrow at 0800."

Cherry Popping Time

I showed up as ordered. Hill asked me to close the door. "Don't think of this as punishment, Leary. Think of it as an *opportunity*. You'll be picking up flight pay and combat pay starting today."

"What about training?"

"That's why we're sending you out on a routine F-4 orientation flight. It's a milk run—a new pilot getting his feet wet cruising along the Mekong and then doing a systems check at the bomb dump on the way back in."

"I thought our camera guys all went to tech school and survival school and jungle school before they got over here."

"You'll pick that up on the job. With guys like you and Lieutenant Liscomb who already did photography in college, tech school would have been a waste of time."

"I thought Liscomb was under house arrest."

"He will be, except when he's out doing reconnaissance photography for us. Turns out the RF-4 recce birds that just came in, *loaded* with high-tech camera pods, can't operate in the mountains of Laos. They fly so damn fast it takes a pilot a week to get his butt unpuckered. Liscomb'll get better stuff handheld hanging out of a prop-driven OV-10.

"You've lucked out, by the way. Your friend Baker over at Spectre says he'll keep an eye on you when you start flying for real over the Ho Chi Minh Trail. Now get on over to the camera trailer and they'll set you up with an Arriflex and a light meter before they drive you over to the Wolf Pack."

Hill took me warmly under his wing and led me out past Tom Wheeler, who looked up from his typewriter and threw me a little salute-wink combo. Dave Murray, oblivious to everything but the music blaring in his headphones, sat nearby typing at the speed of a Chinese water torture.

In another of my many waking bad dreams of 1971, I was fitted far too easily with a flight suit and a helmet and whisked through a pre-flight briefing that I completely failed to understand. Most of the pilots at the Wolf Pack walked with the swagger of their flamboyant commander, Robin Olds, who would have taken Air Marshall Ky's place as Vice President of Vietnam in a heartbeat if anyone had been brilliant enough to ask. My pilot,

Lieutenant Kyle Glotfelty, a new guy from West Virginia, did not possess that swagger, a relief to me as a budding pacifist but a source of fatalistic terror to me as a passenger.

"Tower to White Lightning, you're cleared for takeoff on Runway 5. Climb to one thousand feet and hold, over."

It was garbled and muffled and scratchy, but I could hear traffic control chatter over my headset. I wasn't sure if I felt more like Lucille Ball or Ethel Mertz.

"White Lightnin' takin' off Runway 5," replied Glotfelty. "Climbin' upta one thousand feet, over."

He jammed forward the throttle and the two thundering engines hurtled the F-4 down the runway. Squished against the back seat, I remembered the old joke about there being no such thing as "only *minor* surgery" if you're the one being sliced open. I prayed fervently to whatever god answered the prayers of existentialists that this *first* flight would miraculously be my *last*, not in the "bought-the-farm," "crash-and-burn" sense, but rather in the "war-is-over-and-the-Armistice-signed" sense of last. My eyes felt like they were going to burst. We lifted off, I swallowed a mouthful of oxygen, and I began to relax. At the sound of a large explosion my eyes popped open again.

"*Shii-itt*," I heard over the headphone, the last thing you want to hear your surgeon mutter in the middle of minor surgery. "I guess this is a Mayday, damn it. I'm shutting down the starboard engine and RTB'ing to base." *RTB* was Air Force shorthand for "*returning to base*," so that "*RTB'ing to base*" literally meant "*returning to base to base*." Air Force lingo could be a mystery to an English major.

Glotfelty looked back at me with a kind of Charlie Brown fathead stoicism. "Looks like we don't make it to the practice range today. What do you think we oughta do with these bombs, Airman?"

That was not really the kind of question I had been trained to answer in my Air Force assignments as a diploma-maker/coffee-maker at the Pentagon nor as a film editor/apprentice cameraman with the Rat Pack. It was all I could do to figure out how to read a light meter and set an f-stop while wearing flight gloves. The tower radioed back that it looked like the exploding engine might have damaged the landing gear and instructed Glotfelty to dump his ordnance in the Mun River east of Ubon on his way back to the base. "Emergency clearance for Runway 2-3. Foam on its way, over."

On the turn I awkwardly pressed my camera against the canopy and began rolling film on the view below. I watched several cluster bombs rather gracefully open up and begin spinning just before they hit the water. Except that when we ran out of river they kept falling. First a long canoe along the shore and then a whole village full of fishing shanties began to explode. "You're missing the river!" I cried.

"They're just shacks. Legal can handle it."

The giant fighter strained mightily to reach the runway. Far off in the distance the fire crew looked like it was making artificial snow at Killington, shooting foam out on the runway that would supposedly keep us from burning up. Resigned to the fact I might be filming my own cremation, I put the camera back to my eye and began rolling. My jaw hung limp when buildings and trees began passing a few feet below us and then streaked by at our side. At touchdown the camera jostled hard and then smoothed out a few seconds before we plowed into the foam. I shut off the camera and collapsed in relief, only to bolt upright when I heard the lieutenant begin cursing the drag chute for not opening. "Dah-yamn!" he shouted. He had read my mind.

Dejectedly I put the camera back to my eye and began shooting as the plane careened on down the runway, barely slowing as we plowed through half a mile of what seemed like shaving cream. Apparently the landing gear was fine, but I began to really miss that drag chute when we cleared the last of the foam, ran off the runway, and continued at high speed onto a taxiway, across a muddy field, and up onto a perimeter road that took us through the main gate, barely missing a pink baht-bus heading for town full of off-duty GIs. We finally came to rest across the street from the base in the parking lot of Maharaj Massage, the F-4's nose poking impolitely at the back door. Sitting there in a daze, I let the camera run.

Glotfelty and I got the Rat Pack's finest One Hour Service when we arrived with the film at the 601st lab. While I put my equipment away, Billy Hill invited Glotfelty over to his office for a cup of—wink, wink—coffee. I checked in with Homer Harwell, the NCO in charge of motion picture photography, who seemed to take it in stride the day before when he was told he'd be training an editor as his new cameraman. He'd been short-handed since Nevers and Spinelli went missing in action, and now that Ron Cooper was being held up back at Norton, any warm body would help. Setting down my cases, I asked, "Anything I can do about the door on this Arri? Seems like that landing loosened it up a little."

"At least you've still got a camera. We didn't know what to expect when we heard them calling out the crash team. Take it over to Shahbazian. That's what he's here for."

"Have you seen any of his work?" I asked, a bit puzzled at Harwell's confidence.

"He just needs a little practice. Nobody can screw up the door on an Arri St."

Shahbazian's workshop was just off the editorial room. He looked awfully comfortable sipping bad coffee and browsing through the *Pacific Stars and Stripes* while Armed Forces Thailand Network Radio played Grateful Dead in the background. He'd shaved off his goatee the day he drove in from Saigon, but the mutton chops and bushy mustache that he left in place were something he could only get away with working in obscurity at the Com-Doc camera repair shop. "Why if it isn't Brendan, me lad! Bringing me a camera instead of a Moviola. I *told* you to lay low while Moonbeam was losing his marbles."

"Can you cut the crap and do something with the door on this thing?"

Woody seemed thankful to have something to do now that most of the men in the Rat Pack had started doing their own maintenance. "No problem!"

He had a little trouble getting the door off, even though I had barely been able to keep it *on*. Once he got it off, he held it up at a strange angle, trying to get some light on the clips inside the door that held it in place when they were adjusted properly. He kept twisting it around at strange angles and then I remembered. "You still wearing just one contact?"

"The other one'll turn up sooner or later."

He was as industrious as I had seen him in the year or so I had known him, studying the piece carefully and finally getting an idea. He set the door down on his workbench and rummaged through his oversized tool box, finally pulling out a rubber mallet that would have been right at home in a Roadrunner cartoon.

"Hold on a second!" I called as I ran out the door and headed for Harwell's cubicle in the camera trailer. Before I could catch my breath to speak, we heard a loud BAM coming from the trailer I had just left. "I'm afraid that was Shahbazian," I told Harwell. "I was about to ask you if it was okay for him to use a mallet on those little tin prongs that hold on the camera door."

"Tell him to put a salvage tag on it and swap it out for a new camera from the warehouse at Tan Son Nhut." Harwell was unperturbed, apparently secure in the knowledge we had plenty of ammo and movie cameras to see us through the war.

I did as I was told and then stopped over to chew the fat with Zelinsky in his editorial cubicle next to the lab. "Heard you had quite a ride today, Leary."

"I'll let you decide for yourself," I replied.

"Here it is!" announced Jack Wu, stepping in with a large reel of film in his hand. Wu was a ruggedly handsome Taiwanese-American tech sergeant who ran the motion picture lab and who, like many of us, had come from Norton. Zelinsky and I had talked it over, however, and decided that he was a little too Boy Scout to have been one of Liscomb's "bitchin' guys."

Zelinsky threaded up the Moviola, then changed his mind. Word had gotten around fast and we were attracting a crowd. "Let's put this on the big screen."

Billy Hill had brought Lieutenant Glotfelty back over from the orderly room, along with Tom and Dave. Now Homer Harwell, my new boss, brought in his protégés, Jamal Washington, Leo Guttchock and Jeff Spitzer. He wrapped his arm around me and said, "Leary here's the airman I told you boys about who's gonna be filling in for Ron Cooper—if he didn't fuck up his audition. Today we're gonna see how he handles landing on one engine."

Shahbazian brought over the unit's best analyzer projector and plugged it in. Wu and his lab techs crowded in while Zelinsky put on the reel of film and threaded it up. "I heard your Fourth of July speech back at Norton," Wu said to me as Shahbazian dimmed the lights. "You ought to think about politics when you get out."

"That's kind of you, Jack, but I think I like it better behind a camera than in front of one, although you might not know it from looking at *this* crap." I wasn't sure if I was squirming more from Jack's comment or from the embarrassing footage on the screen that went on way too long of the back of

Glotfelty's bobbing helmet. Finally a little air-to-ground stuff came on and I was relieved to see that it was in focus with the correct f-stop set on the lens. Things got a lot more exciting at the sight of the fishing village going up in flames, and Zelinsky cried out, "I want to use *that* to lead off *Hits of the Week*."

"But they're *Thais*," I protested.

"Stennis and the Joint Chiefs just want to see things burning prettily," said Hill. "Makes 'em feel like we got us a real war going on."

The emergency landing came up next, which made me cringe again. I had blanked out on what ran through the camera after we came to a complete stop a mile past the terminal gate. I had no recollection whatsoever of filming the massage girls running out in their little smocks and their customers, if they were lucky, wrapped up in towels or whatever articles of clothing were within arm's reach. Before the camera ran completely out of film I had involuntarily panned back across Maharaj Massage just moments after most of the east wall collapsed in a dusty cloud, leaving an entire VIP section of distinguished older men sitting in bathtubs or lying half-naked on massage tables. "Whoa!" called Hill. "Zelinsky, back that last shot up and run it slow motion."

"Damn!" Spitzer yelled. "That's Colonel Strbik and Major Horney from Spectre!"

"And that's Colonel Grimsley, the base commander," shouted Shahbazian. "Way to go, Brass!"

"Who are the two Thais?" I asked wearily.

"The thin one would be the Thai base commander and the dirigible-shaped gentleman would be the provincial governor," said Wu, who often amazed us with a vast store of useful knowledge.

"Zelinsky," barked Captain English, "splice some Top Secret leader on that last footage and send it over to my office." English possessed an uncanny instinct for showing up just when we were starting to have fun. First Sergeant Link followed in his wake, giving us one of his evil smirks that Zelinsky insisted was a cover for total cluelessness.

As the lights came up, I noticed that Lieutenant Liscomb had come in quietly with Link and English, but before I could say anything, Harwell stepped up and shook my hand. "Looks like you'll be bunking with the cameramen," he said. "Hope you enjoy air conditioning."

Washington, Guttchock and Spitzer followed him with more handshakes and a few "Way to go's." "It's more like semi-air conditioning," Washington said. "It's a converted hootch that still lets in hot air and mosquitos. At least they left up the ceiling fan."

"Take your pick of the open bunks," said Spitzer.

"Spinelli and Nevers are going to be proud to have you with us," said Guttchock enigmatically, his eyes darting around, unable to make contact with mine. It was rumored that Guttchock was a graduate of the USC film school, but I decided to save that for a later conversation. Instead, I walked over to Liscomb. "Where'd they send you?" I whispered.

"Outside of Paksong, up into the Boulevans Plateau."

"What're you filming?"

"70mm stills. Reconnaissance. Lots of after-action battle damage assessment."

"I think they got me going to Laos with Spectre tomorrow night."

"Welcome to the club."

"Lieutenant Liscomb, don't we have a meeting with Captain English?" Hill interrupted. On their way out Hill flashed me a thumbs-up. "Good shit, Leary. Keep it up."

I followed them out, heading over to the ComDoc ready room, a spartan lounge where the Rat Pack cameramen hung out when they weren't in the field. I plopped onto the old bus seat that served as a sofa and settled into my own private oblivion. My body had turned to lead, my muscles too weak to lift a finger or an eyelid. Through the usual mix of Johnny Cash, Black Sabbath, and Sly and the Family Stone on Armed Forces Thailand Radio, I dimly perceived a couple of announcements for Special Services tours (not to be confused with Special *Forces* tours, I had to remind myself) to Tadtohn Falls, to the Big Buddha and to the two-color river where the Mun met the Mekong out near the Royalist, pro-American part of Laos around Pakse. October, if I lived through it, promised the end of monsoon season. For Thailand, unlike the rest of Southeast Asia, it meant the beginning of major festival season. The Phichit boat races came early in the month. The Kluai Khai banana festival was especially dear to GIs who were burned out on chow-hall food. Sergeant Wu, I noticed, never missed a tour, being both an avid amateur photographer and a technician at a lab that processed all his film for free.

I had just dozed off when Harley Baker arrived. "Wake up, draft dodger. Just saw the roster and tomorrow's your lucky day. Your first Spectre mission is gonna be with *me*. If you're *real* lucky, I'll make you part of our hard crew, which means you'll fly permanently with the best damn truck-killers in the squadron and you'll have me as your personal guardian angel."

"I'm wiped, Baker. Can't you let a man sleep?"

"Captain English asked me to give you a little 'chalk talk.' Don't want you puking all over my nice new airplane. Come on," he said, "I'll buy you a beer over at the patio."

I still hadn't figured out quite what to make of Baker other than loving his music when he was sober enough to play it—and now my life was going to depend on him. My on-the-job survival training began the minute we stepped out the door. I was no longer one of the ninety percent who would spend the war in the rear echelons, and Harley was determined to drum it into my head that survival depended on understanding the true nature of a very fucked-up war. He started out by telling me about being assigned to Qu Son, on the border between Vietnam and Laos, as an FO—a forward observer—for a Green Beret outfit in the middle of his first tour in '65. He was all of eighteen at the time, a lowly two-striper with the Air Commandos.

"Didn't you tell me you joined the Air Force because they promised you'd be stationed in England?"

"That's what my recruiter told me. *Guaranteed* I'd be stationed in the United Kingdom, jamming with the Beatles—it sounded so good I passed on my scholarship to the University of Southern California and signed the dotted line. But then there was that fine print about 'Needs of the Air Force.'"

"You gave up a *scholarship* to USC? And I'm spending four years in the friggin' Air Force to earn enough GI Bill just to make a *dent* in my tuition! Next thing you'll be telling me you would have been pre-med—"

"It was a *football* scholarship. I still hold the California record for total yards for a high school quarterback."

"You gave up USC *cheerleaders*?"

"Once they sent me to weapons school and told me I was going to Vietnam, I figured what the hell, I'm joining Special Forces, I'm gonna be an Air Commando. I'm gonna be a hero. I'm going all the way!"

I was having a hard time relating. I had been a draft-dodger, a bookworm, so scrawny as a kid that I never made a Little League team. The only varsity I made was in chess and cross-country. "So how'd you end up being assigned to *Army* Special Forces?"

"Because the Army had run out of lieutenants who knew how to call in air strikes. But here's the part of this story where you've got to pay attention: I never got to call in any close air support the night we were attacked, thanks to a double-agent South Vietnamese general in charge of Pleiku Tactical Control Center who ignored our calls. I finally went through back channels to order a dust-off chopper to evacuate our wounded, which was everyone. My feet were still hanging out the door of the Slick when we lifted off. We couldn't take the Montagnards we'd been training—there wasn't enough room. We had to kick a couple of them off the skids to take off. Captain Richards, an awesome West Point grad, and First Sergeant Minor, the dude who gave me my first bottle of Jack Daniels, stayed behind to blow up the ammunition bunker and disable the Howitzers."

"How'd they get out?" I asked.

"They didn't. Richards and Minor were still inside the bunker when the ammunition blew sky high. We had to fly right through all that dust and smoke to keep from flying into the mountain behind us. It wasn't until we were halfway home that I realized I had shit my pants. It wasn't exactly what I had pictured when I volunteered to be a hero with the Air Force Special Forces." Harley gave me one of his piercing stares. "Qu Son turned out to be the very first Green Beret outpost to be overrun by the enemy. And that was pretty much the end of calling in close air support through the ARVN chain of command. The highest levels of the Army of the Republic of Vietnam were either incompetent, corrupt, or infiltrated with people working for Ho Chi Minh."

When we got to the patio next to the base swimming pool, we each grabbed a pop-top Budweiser at the snack bar and settled in at a picnic table that was partly shaded by a couple of scrawny palm trees. "The ARVN general shouldn't have surprised me," Harley explained, "after what had happened at Bien Hoa before I'd been in-country two months. Our interpreter, Vinh, is part of our hard crew there—we fly together all the time. And he takes us home to mama for fug *thai bouton*, her Vietnamese chicken specialty. And when the whole town is put off limits, he goes, 'No sweat,' and takes us the back way down to Turkey Alley so we can go whoring together. He helps us load ammo, he's the cream of the crop, and one night ground control asks, 'Any of you fuckin' idiots up there speak French?'

"And our pilot radios back, 'I'm in command of this aircraft and I can assure you we barely speak English.'

"'Well, your interpreter does, and he's giving away all your coordinates. You might want to do something about it.'

"The Viet Cong were so desperate they had been shooting mortar rounds up at us, and everybody knows you don't shoot mortars at airplanes, but these were star shells which were lighting us up enough somebody might get lucky with an AK, which, again, everybody but the fuckin' VC knows you don't shoot at airplanes. Except that at A or B altitude, the altitudes we usually worked at between a quarter- and a half-mile up, we were in range of a lucky shot, a Golden BB that couldn't bring down a plane but could pick off one of the crew. So here's our good buddy Vinh giving away our coordinates and we can't just throw him out of the airplane—his mother's just cooked dinner for us. So we put him under arrest and high-tailed it back to base. And when we land, we taxi our C-47 right up to the hangar and there's about thirty trucks and jeeps standing there and recovery lights turning night into day practically, and as I helped Vinh down the gangway, I ask him, 'What the hell were you doing up there?'

"And he says, 'No sweat. Somebody's bullshitting you.'

"And an ARVN colonel walks over to him and puts a gun to his head and goes BAM. Blows his fuckin' brains out all over the tarmac right in front of us."

Harley crumpled up his empty beer can and tossed it into the trash. "Now what do you think about *that* shit?" he asked, seeming to stare right through me.

"I think you just got my full attention."

He plunked down another couple of beers and, whether I was ready for it or not, began preparing me to operate at night at ten thousand feet, where our bodies would be dragging from oxygen deprivation. Much of the time we'd be circling in a thirty-degree bank, pulling extra G's while I tried to operate a movie camera, with or without gloves depending on how well I could stand the cold. Contrary to what I'd told Hill and English, I had pretty well conquered my childhood fear of flying, or at least learned to ignore it, a must in a family full of pilots. That was the good news. The bad news came from editing combat footage. I had observed the enemy getting ever more skillful firing ever more impressive kinds of anti-aircraft at the Spectre birds engaged in night operations. It had already been giving me nightmares. Now I was going to get to experience it first-hand. Harley got the Thai cashier working behind the counter to find him a paper plate and a pencil. We polished off the second beer while he diagrammed the inside of the gunship for me and showed me the spots back by the illumination operator and forward with the NOD operator where the cameramen usually hung out, filming live action, and up in the fire-control booth, where they filmed close-up stuff off of the various sensors.

"Cool," I said, attempting to exude confidence. "What's a NOD?"

"Night Observation Device. A starlight scope, so you can see like a cat." He leaned in, uncomfortably eyeball to eyeball, and said, "You're aware that this is highly sensitive information, I assume."

"I can see that it is."

"I'm a highly sensitive guy."

"You learn something new every day," I joked weakly, wiping drops of his spittle off my forehead and cheek.

We began working on a third beer while he extolled the virtues of the AC-130. "The first one we lost, back in '69, made it all the way back to Ubon before it burned up on the runway. Most of the crew bailed out the instant they crossed the Mekong into Thailand. Only lost two dudes. The illumination operator—the IO, who these days is mostly the rear spotter— got hit right after he warned the pilot to take evasive action. Seems that spotlights make pretty good targets. Watch out back around the IO if we're ever supporting troops-in-contact and he's got that damned thing turned on. But even when he's lying out on the rear platform watching for incoming, make sure you don't trip over him and fall out. You wouldn't be the first."

I felt a little lump welled up in my throat. "If you *do* fall out," he continued, "make sure you've got your safety harness snapped on so we can reel you back in."

He gave me a comforting smile that didn't give me much comfort. "What happened to the second guy back in '69?" I asked.

Harley lowered his eyes and talked to the table. "That was the flight engineer who was handling the radio for the skeleton crew that stayed on board. They had landed and were parked on the runway, but he couldn't get his damned seat belt unbuckled before the fire reached the cockpit."

He took a long tug on his beer. Reluctantly, I asked, "What about the one that went down the night of Sugie Bear's birthday party?"

"Those guys were shit out of luck—S.O.L. Fuel leaked into the electrical system. But that was a fluke. We come in all the time with battle damage. Stick a little duct tape over it and off you go. You don't know how lucky you are to have four big Allison turboprops over your head."

A fourth beer had appeared and we were halfway through when some unseen wizard turned on the sodium-vapor lights overhead. The sky seemed to have skipped from sunset to total darkness. I glanced at my watch. "Holy shit! Don't we have a gig tonight?"

The band had finished setting up by the time Harley and I blew in. Brian "Rev" Golson was a maintenance chief down on the flight line. "Heard that was you in the back of the F-4 that crash-landed today."

"I'm afraid the grapevine got that one right," I answered.

"Come on guys," said the Reverend, "let's give Leary a hand. We're lucky to have a drummer tonight." And to my amazement, instead of getting chewed out, I got all the help I could have dreamed of unloading my drum kit from the cab and hauling the cases up on stage. The rest of the evening at the Soul Sister was routine, with just two exceptions. First, after way too many Budweisers at the patio, I let Harley talk me into trying a pint glass of Singha with a shot of Mekong whiskey dropped in, shot glass and all, something Spectre crews called a "Dive Bomber." Second, in the midst of my second Dive Bomber, an incredibly tall and gorgeous *Vogue* cover girl stepped out of the smoky shadows and started giving me the eye when I got back up on the bandstand to play. Mali came in for the last couple of sets and ended up at a table just off to the side of the stage. To my amazement, the *Vogue* model sat down with her just before we took our last break. The juke box was blaring when Harley and I joined them, but I could make out Mali's gentle voice saying something to the effect of "Her name *Gung*. She think you play drum very good! And she think you handsome *mahk mahk*."

I was still ripped from the afternoon chalk talk and further ripped by two or three or four Dive Bombers, I wasn't quite sure which, but Harley felt strongly that we needed a "safety" Dive Bomber to make sure we stayed ripped. "Maybe we should all go down to the Ubon Hotel after the show," I suggested blearily.

Everybody agreed, but when I hit the stage I started dragging and wondered if I could make it. Too little adrenaline and too much beer and whiskey made the last forty-five minutes an agony. Fortunately, we finished up playing Sam Cooke's version of "Good Times," with the whole audience singing along on the chorus of:

> Come on and let the good times roll,
> we're gonna stay here till we sooth our soul—
> if it takes all ni-ight long.

It was nice to end on a high note, but Harley and I couldn't get off the bandstand fast enough. We cleared it with the manager, stashed our equipment backstage and rounded up the girls. The four of us seemed to float outside and into a cab headed for the Ubon Hotel, my impaired moral fiber no match for a majestic *Vogue* cover girl in stiletto heels and an Annette Funicello bouffant.

Soaring heavenward on the elevator ride up to the ninth floor, I felt like a wobbly version of the wing-footed Greek god that was painted on the side of trucks delivering flowers for FTD, only stumbling once on the way to our table. Mali and Gung ordered a small banquet of appetizers, curries, and platters of stir-fried beef, chicken and shrimp. On the way in I had estimated Gung's height at five foot eight. Between the crowd noise and loud music it was hard to converse, but by the time we had passed all the food around I managed to ask her how she got the name Gung, which means "shrimp." She answered in a mixture of English and Thai that it was partly a joke, but, she confessed, she was also considered an ugly duckling when she was a scrawny young farm girl.

"Looks like you get the last laugh," I said, gazing sympathetically into her sad eyes. "You might be the most beautiful girl in all of Thailand."

Without saying a thing, she put her hand on mine. We sat there like that a few minutes while the band played. The song finished and I was about to ask her for the next dance when she leaned in and said, "Let's go." After perfunctory *wais* of goodbye, she led me to the elevator, leaving Harley and Mali behind, gorging themselves contentedly on heaps of steaming rice and spicy side dishes.

"You have bungalow?" she asked on the elevator down.

"Do you?" I asked back, unable to take my eyes off her long *Vogue* body. Soon we were climbing out of a cab in a part of town I had never been to. I happily gave the driver a ten-dollar tip for a one-dollar ride and floated off with Gung down a narrow alley and into her one-room cottage. "Stay here," she ordered cheerfully, "I be right back." Something started going dreadfully wrong, though, when she stepped down from her dangerously high heels, stripped off her false eyelashes, wiped the paint from her eyes and cheeks, pulled off her wig, her silk dress and her padded bra, and transformed herself back into the plain little country-girl daughter of a rice farmer that she was and had been all along. The transformation was powerfully sobering, and when she wrapped herself in a large bath towel and stepped into the *hong nam* for a shower, I left another ten dollars on the dresser and fled in silent terror out her front door, preserving myself one more night for Danielle.

Lying in my bunk that night, my head spun before I finally fell asleep. *Who are your true friends in Southeast Asia?* I wondered. *Vinh of Bien Hoa takes you home for dinner and then tries to shoot down his own plane with you on it. South Vietnamese generals work for both sides. Even* Vogue *cover girls can't be trusted. Besides Wheeler, do I have any true friends on this side of the Pacific?*

I got an answer the next time I visited Woodstock Music. Sommit and Vrisnei smiled sympathetically as they rang up a new pair of drumsticks for me. "Harley say you fly with him now," said Vrisnei as she reached below the counter, pulling out a small plastic container, red on the bottom and clear on top, about the right size to hold a ring.

"I don't know if I'm allowed to answer that."

Vrisnei handed me the little box. "For good luck," she said.

"Just in case," said Sommit with a knowing glimmer in his eye.

Inside was a tiny Buddha, a size that could be strung on a gold chain and worn around my neck. "Just in case," I said, smiling and putting it carefully in my shirt pocket.

Gunship
(OR: "Ghost Riders in the Sky")

The monsoons were supposed to have been winding down for the year and the serious hunting season about to begin, but the monsoons—a little like the North Vietnamese Army, the Viet Cong, the Pathet Lao and the Khmer Rouge—refused to follow the schedule mapped out by the Seventh Air Force. The NVA's 559th Transportation Group continued to expand the Ho Chi Minh Trail, which was actually a constellation of dirt paths, much of it hidden from the air by thick jungle canopy, and hardcore NVA combat units continued oozing through into South Vietnam. The Viet Cong ("VC" or "Victor Charlie" to American combatants) had spearheaded the Tet Offensive in '68 and sustained horrendous casualties all over South Vietnam, but they were continuing to hang around. Their Pathet Lao cousins were holding their own against Neutralist and Royalist factions in Laos, and the Khmer Rouge were beginning to stir in Cambodia, aroused by wayward American B-52 strikes intended for NVA units operating within their borders. We weren't sure who was taking pot shots at us in Thailand.

I left out the story of the *Vogue* cover girl in my next letter to Danielle, but I did mention that there had been some interesting developments on the work front—the good news being that I was going to get some valuable experience as a cameraman, the bad news being that it might mean flying combat. Danielle was distraught in her next few letters, reliving the death of her husband and begging me to come home alive. I decided to spare her the story of Lieutenant Glotfelty's crash landing, instead assuring her that the war was winding down and that things weren't bad so far and that this experience could really pay off shooting aerials for car commercials back in California. Of course it was easy to take on the nonchalance of Snoopy about to face the Red Baron—I had been flying for weeks and had yet to see action. There had been a break in the weather the day of my training flight with Lieutenant Glotfelty, but the next day the rains resumed.

I was now assigned to Spectre, but for almost a month it continued to rain night after night, and we often sat. When we did take off, we hunted for hours on end, but the clouds obscured our view and Laos seemed quiet beneath us. We cruised over Steel Tiger East and West in the well-defended panhandle of Laos, and we took a few side trips up to what the crews called "the Pan" (code name Barrel Roll—northern Laos northeast of the Plain of Jars). To break up the monotony, we occasionally headed south to Commando Basket (code name for Cambodia). I continued to be surprised at how little activity we saw. Tom Wheeler passed along some interesting rumors from In-tell, Air Force shorthand for Intelligence, about why NVA convoys weren't being trapped by the muddy roads and flooded rivers for our gunships and fighter-bombers to chew up from the air. Instead of trucks this time of year, they were using elephants and water buffalo—and bicycles—to travel by land. On the water they used a mixture of hollowed-out logs, rafts, and small boats, some of which were rigged as ferries on lines running under the old French bridges. It was enough to keep a steady trickle of supplies flowing on nights that we were flying blind.

Harley and I played as much as we could with the Band of Brothers, knowing that rehearsal time was going to be scarce when the weather cleared and we might be flying four, five and even six missions a week by the time we got into November and December. I kept going back to the Ubon Hotel—on auto-pilot, a perverse sort of built-in gyroscope, a directionless direction finder that pulled me along as powerfully as an eighty-pound Thai farm boy could pull along a two-thousand-pound water buffalo by its nose ring. I didn't go every night. At first it was just nights that the band played at the Soul Sister and then it was nights when Spectre got in before two. Some nights Harley and I went together, some nights we brought Mali along, and some nights I went alone. I liked it especially on nights that it kept raining, when it hadn't just been a brief afternoon cloudburst. I could sit on a bar stool for an hour or two people-watching, pretending I could read the minds of the GIs and the girls, writing little stories for them of love and deception, of loss and redemption. In the end, though, when my imagination quit on me and my true feelings started percolating, I was miserable and alone, afraid I would never see Danielle again. That might have been why I liked it best when the city lights outside were blurred by the rivulets of rain that streaked the picture window. The Ubon Hotel could do my crying for me.

115

And then one night the sky cleared. I watched my moonshadow racing ahead of me as I bicycled to the ComDoc ready room, and there was no wet clay on the pavement spraying a muddy stripe down the back of my rain suit. We were going to fly and we were going to hunt. My jittery stomach and I said a little prayer, thanking whatever spirits guarded combat cameramen that we were flying with Spectre and not on one of Harley's old twin-engine Puffs.

Like the rest of the crew, I had started wearing my flight suit to work under my rain gear, and like the rest of the crew, I'd had it dyed black to match our gunship. At ComDoc I picked up my motion picture equipment and loaded it into the Rat Pack delivery van, a big blue milk truck that shuttled between the 601st and the flight line. Washington and Spitzer had been clueing me in for weeks to travel light. There was no need for a sound blimp or a zoom lens, or even a light meter—photographing at night, the Law of Reciprocity broke down. With three high-speed lenses on a turret, we shot with the irises taped wide open. Some charged-up belt-batteries, a shoulder brace, and three four-hundred-foot magazines were going to be about all I needed, most of it fitting into one case.

I dropped the camera gear off at the Spectre equipment room and joined the crew for a short briefing. We were waiting for Colonel Strbik, the aircraft commander, to return with the other Spectre pilots from the In-tell briefing. Strbik was a pilot among pilots—gravelly voiced and square-jawed—who looked like he stepped right off the pages of a *Terry and the Pirates* comic strip. In reality, he *had* flown C-47's over the Hump into South China during World War II and word had it that Terry's Dragon Lady was based on Strbik's first or third wife or both. When Strbik arrived, we were called to attention, which he quickly waved off, telling us to be seated. "We'll be the first off tonight and should arrive on target with first darkness."

"Gonna be a long wait if we're shot down," whispered Harley.

"The Word of the Day is *Ping Pong*," Strbik announced. I let it slide that the Word of the Day was two words. You were supposed to use it in a sentence if you were shot down and a rescue helicopter wanted to make sure you were a Good Guy. According to Harley, they used to use a Number of the Day, but it required some basic algebra and after getting more "*What the fucks*?" than correct answers when downed airmen were being shot at by Bad Guys, the system was switched.

116

The navigator was a small guy who wore thick glasses and reminded me of a weatherman on a small-town TV station. "You want to tell us about the location, Major?" asked Strbik.

With a crooked little smile, the navigator replied, "We're doing something a little different tonight, ladies and gentlemen. Instead of Steel Tiger West, it's gonna be Hotel."

Harley winced. "Might be pucker time," he whispered to me. He was talking about the area around Sepone where Lam Son 719 turned into a rout.

Colonel Strbik turned to the rear spotter, another crusty veteran of three wars who came to work every day in starched fatigues and wore strong aftershave to cover the smell of whiskey on his breath. "Sergeant Vodvarka, you'll be the jumpmaster tonight in the unlikely event we have to bail out."

Bail out? My head started reeling. Vodvarka might have said something about bailout procedures and proper form for parachute landings, but I couldn't concentrate because I was already preoccupied worrying about equipment. Would I be able to wear a flak helmet and still fit the camera to my eye? Would my eyepiece fog up? Should I wear a flak *jacket*, or would it weigh me down? Should I wear the quilted flight jacket, or would I be too hot? Shooting out of the open doors at ten thousand feet, would I need to wear my Nomex flight gloves, or would the silk liners keep my hands warm enough? The answer to almost all my questions was that I wouldn't know until I was on the job—in pitch-blackness, breathing thin air, and pulling G's. As best I could, I'd try to follow Harley's lead.

After the briefing, Harley and I moseyed over with the rest of the crew to the equipment room. I had a two-foot by two-foot locker not far from Harley's, where we left our fatigue caps, our Air Force ID cards, and all of our cash that was in Thai baht—taking along a few American dollars for mad money. Like the rest of the crew, I had been issued a Geneva Convention card saying I *was* a GI and a piece of silk they called a Blood Chit that said in many local dialects that I *wasn't* an American—but that the American government would pay them handsomely if they helped me return to a U.S. military installation. We hung our headsets over our necks and pulled out our helmet bags, which contained our flak helmets, quilted jackets and gloves. Harley put on his survival vest and picked up a couple of radios and a .38 caliber Smith and Wesson handgun from the duty sergeant at the controlled-items cage. He stuffed the radios into the front pockets of the vest and then swapped out the government-issue .38 ("a peashooter," he complained) for the .357 Magnum Ruger Blackhawk that he kept stashed in his locker. "I guess the government doesn't want us to hurt ourselves—or anyone else, for that matter," he said to me under his breath. "Well, fuck that shit."

I had followed Harley back from the controlled-items cage and, without making a big deal about it, stuffed my radios into my survival vest but left my .38 behind in my locker. I had made a promise to myself to get through the war without killing or being killed. Carrying a weapon would have made it too easy to do either, intentionally or by accident. I mentioned it in a letter to Danielle shortly after I told her I'd be doing some flying. When she wrote back she said that this was all worrying her sick, she'd already lost a husband, but that she respected the difficult choice I had made. Tom Wheeler was the only person I told in Ubon, and I appreciated it when he promised to do the same thing—he'd turn in his gun card if we were ever put on alert and issued weapons. The difference was that I'd be flying combat three or four nights a week, whereas the base hadn't been on red alert in a year. I hadn't gotten around to picking up a chain for my little Buddha, but I did permit myself one little good-luck charm—my grandfather's old two-inch penknife. Grandpa Shepler—my mom's dad—had used it to sharpen his pencils since he had been in grammar school and had given it to me on my last visit to Pittsburgh before he died. I mentioned it to Danielle, but I don't think she had much faith in good-luck charms.

I stuffed my survival vest into the bag with my helmet. I'd bring it along but I had no intention of wearing it. I didn't want any extra weight when I was handling the Arriflex, and despite my stomach being knotted in fear, I liked to think we weren't going to crash. I *did* follow Harley's lead and strapped on my parachute harness, just in case, before carrying my equipment out to the Spectre crew bus.

We flew a modified C-130 transport, a trash-hauler whose guts had been ripped out and re-configured with lots of guns, ammunition and night-vision electronics. The crews affectionately called it the Big Turkey, but painted black for night ops, it looked ominous. The nightmarish squadron logo was painted on the nose, just under the cockpit—a skeleton with a winged skull trailing a torn green shroud and firing a blazing Gatling gun in front of a large crescent moon. It wasn't going to scare the North

Vietnamese Army from ten thousand feet, but it scared *me* every time I walked past and I suspected it helped get the crew into a proper truck-killing mood.

Four massive turboprop engines were mounted on large overhanging wings that for me had the look of vulture wings. The high wings kept the huge propellers clear of the guns below, which lined the entire left side of what was once a cargo bay and now looked like the gun deck of a pirate frigate. It was an imposing arsenal of weapons that poked out of the aircraft's many doorways and ports. Two six-thousand-round-per-minute mini-Gatlings could spray a football field in seconds from five thousand feet, but only against ground troops because the North Vietnamese now had 23-mm anti-aircraft along the Trail effective to *six thousand* feet. Two truck-killing four-thousand-round-per-minute 20-mm M-61 Vulcans were just as nasty and were effective at seventy-five hundred feet, which the pilots considered a fair trade-off against new NVA 37-mm guns that were accurate to *eighty-two hundred* feet. Spectre's ace-in-the-hole was the twin-mounted tank-busting 40-mm Bofors, the kind the Navy had used to shoot down Zeroes during World War II, guaranteed by R&D to kill trucks from ten thousand feet. When the North Vietnamese introduced 57-mm triple-A, effective to thirteen thousand feet, the crews said, "Fuck it." They could only operate for short periods above ten thousand feet, so they would stand and fight. Or go lower so they could kill trucks quickly and clear the area.

The only way we could get on board was from the rear cargo ramp, lowered almost to the tarmac. While the co-pilot did a walk-around of the plane and Harley and his buddy, Pigpen Sachs, did a walk-around of the guns, I brought my equipment on board, shot a test burst with the camera and got ready for takeoff. Once everyone was on board, the cargo ramp was retracted to horizontal, and I joined the gunners and spotters on the rear-facing jump seats that pulled up from the floor. One by one the engines fired up, emitting a shriek that penetrated the thin skin of our stripped-down bird. We taxied slowly to the end of the runway where the engines were revved up to full throttle, the brakes were released, and off we went, watching Ubon disappear behind us. It was almost pretty.

Shortly before we crossed the Mekong the navigator told us it was time to suit up, which meant closing up the jump seats and taking our battle stations. I felt a mixture of fear and adrenaline that was something like stage fright. Figuring I would be dividing my time in the cabin between filming off the ramp, shooting over the guns, and recording a monitor hard-wired to the Night Observation Device, I set up on the right side of the plane beside the mysterious booth where I would occasionally film the monitors used by the Black Crow and Infrared sensor-operators who worked under the guidance of Major Horney, Strbik's regular fire-control officer. I tried on the flak helmet and soon discovered my eyepiece fogged up as I feared it might when I looked through the camera, so it was back to headphones only. I followed the gunners' lead and spread out my flak jacket under the camera cases, giving my butt part-time protection, anyway. I decided to put on the quilted flight jacket to provide some padding for the camera, and I figured from my experience with spring skiing in Vermont that the glove liners would suffice to keep my hands warm while still being able to operate the camera. The fireproof quality of the Nomex gloves never crossed my mind.

We had passed the last of the lowland rice paddies and had just started climbing over the jagged foothills when we turned sharply in a thirty-degree bank and went into orbit. "Holy shit!" I cried, my voice lost in a howling mix of wind and engine noise. I was confused. It was still dusk and there was nothing visible below us except the intersection of two muddy roads. Suddenly I heard *"Boresighting!"* over the headsets and the Big Turkey rattled from one end to the other as each gun was tested and aligned with what the scanners were seeing in the booth. *Damn!* I thought, watching the intersection turn into an Olympic-pool-sized crater. We hadn't bothered to boresight on my previous missions because it wasn't worth wasting the ammunition with no trucks on the road. In-tell must have picked up something that they passed on to Strbik. The Air Force had dropped electronic sensors along the Trail that sometimes picked up nothing more than the sounds of NVA soldiers pissing on them. The sensors were often dead on arrival, picking up nothing at all. But when they did pick up the rumblings of trucks, something was definitely happening. Harley came back to pay me a visit. "First time you heard us fire off the guns, isn't it? That was to get Strbik's testosterone flowing—get him back in kill mode after all that flying in the rain."

"Definitely got my adrenaline flowing," I shouted as my eyeballs returned to their sockets.

We flew deeper over what were now five-thousand-foot mountains and the gray skies soon turned indigo. In the cabin where I would be working, the only illumination came from a few recessed light fixtures whose tiny bulbs produced a dim ruby glow. The gunners had permission in an emergency to use a penlight when they cleared a jam, but they prided themselves on being able to work by touch alone. Washington and Spitzer had trained me to be equally proficient loading and unloading my Arri. The nights we had flown without making contact had given me plenty of time to practice.

By the time we reached our target area forty-five minutes after crossing the Mekong, our eyes had adjusted to the darkness as well as they were going to. We began cruising over long stretches of dirt highway, but after prowling for what seemed like an hour there had been no sign of enemy activity. I sat down on my camera case, put the Arri in my lap, and tried to relax. Harley squatted down next to me and said, "Still pretty muddy down there. Probably won't be many trucks out for a few more days."

No sooner had he spoken than I started hearing a subdued, tense excitement in the crew's voices on the intercom. The Black Crow had picked up truck ignition. The hunt was on. "I'd better get back," said Harley.

My heart racing, I climbed up into the booth to film the Black Crow and infrared monitors while the sensor operators tracked down the convoy to begin the kill sequence. They soon located several trucks, and it was time to leave Major Horney's electronic nest, continuing forward to where Captain Rush was manning the NOD. Figuring Strbik would be using Rush's sensor when he started firing on targets, I re-checked the magazine on my Arriflex and double-checked the connection between my battery belt and the back of the camera. My hands were shaking, but I couldn't tell if it was caused by engine vibration, the cold breeze blowing through the open ports and doorways of the unpressurized cabin, or my own nerves. The Spectre gunship turned into a thirty-degree bank and began circling. Taking a deep breath, I surrendered to whatever fate was awaiting me. I didn't have time to think about my hands when, as expected, Colonel Strbik switched from IR to the NOD to finish lining up the target, the rear spotter in illumination-operator mode dropped a few flares, and the crew started blasting down a thunderstorm of twenty- and forty-millimeter shells. Horney, the fire-control officer, yelled ecstatically, "We got us a burner!"

"Shit hot!" called the co-pilot.

They burst hundreds of rounds into the wounded lead truck in just seconds, then noted there were four other trucks that had gotten trapped behind it. It was a little blurry filming the video tap from Rush's NOD, but I could see clearly enough that the drivers of the first two trucks were jumping out and scrambling north to get away from the action. I caught myself rooting for the drivers to make it to safety, thinking they had already surrendered their trucks and the supplies they were carrying. The 20-mm guns obliterated the running blurs. "Night Owl Lead, Night Owl Lead, this is Spec One. Got four targets for you, north northwest of the burning truck, over."

"This is Night Owl Lead. We read you, Spec One. Target is acquired. Ordnance up and armed. Night Owl Two, Night Owl Two, follow me in, over."

"Roger that, Lead. This is Night Owl Two on your wing. Up and armed and following you in. Over."

With the lead truck destroyed and burning, it seemed like a good time to head back to the ramp to get a wider-angle shot of the Night Owl F-4 Phantoms making their run. I stretched out on the tailgate next to the spotter and counted my mixed blessings when he reverted to his role as illumination operator and decided to help out my photography by lighting up the scene with a few extra flares. It made the photography easier but made it more difficult to stay alive by also lighting *us* up. No sooner had I filmed the trailing trucks aflame with napalm than the fun began. "Triple-A. Five rounds. Hold your course," the IO reported coolly, back in spotter mode.

Colonel Strbik decided to circle one more time so that I could verify on film that all trucks were destroyed. I personally wished we'd get the hell out of orbit and head on down the road.

"Triple-A! Accurate! Break right!" The anti-aircraft site had opened fire on us for the second time from a place in Laos where the Defense Department assured us there was no triple-A. The IO/spotter, hanging out the open cargo ramp at the rear of the plane, didn't waste a syllable on military formalities like "sir." We pitched hard, forcing me to grab hold of the tailgate with one hand and the camera with the other, terrorized, barely able to keep myself on board, cursing myself for forgetting to hook on to a safety cable.

And then I cursed Strbik for going back into his thirty-degree bank.

Below me I could see the F-4 fighter-bombers alter their course to go after the anti-aircraft emplacement. The sky glowed with burning napalm before they leisurely peeled off to finish dealing with the doomed, immobile convoy. By the time they completed the next pass every truck was burning. "The Night Owl gang is Bingo and Winchester, over," said the lead pilot— they were out of fuel and ammo and were heading home.

"We're returning to base too," Colonel Strbik informed his crew as we leveled off and headed south.

Relaxing for the first time since we had engaged the convoy, I made my way forward to stow my camera and look for Harley. I thought I could hear him not too far away shoveling up shell casings, a chore the gunners performed to keep the scrap from reaching the North Vietnamese, who reputedly could repack the shells and fire them back at us. Before I could set my camera down, though, I sensed in the dimness that something was wrong with the plane and wondered if it was somehow connected to the near miss with the anti-aircraft and the harsh maneuver we took to avoid it. Working my way in the direction of the flight deck, my nostrils picked up an acrid scent of smoke and my tired heart started racing again. The crew may have called the AC-130 a big turkey, but in the blackness it seemed like I was groping my way through the belly of a whale—and the scent kept getting stronger. Blinded by darkness, I ran forward in a panic, sliding over loose shell casings, fighting my way past two mini-guns and nearly dumping my camera when I bumped into something padded but big in the shadows near the Night Observation Device. It was Captain Rush, the NOD operator, inhaling a bowlful of grass from a hand-carved ivory opium pipe. He grinned euphorically, illuminated by the glow of the bowl. "Have a hit, cameraman. The old man's cool, as long as we wait till we're heading back to Ubon."

Before I could answer, though, we got word that our plans had changed and Rush had to put out his pipe, wasting some of his finest stash. The hunting was so good over in Steel Tiger East that we were requested to go have a look. And like a cat hunting mice, we took out eight more trucks on that fateful night that I flew my first true combat mission. The last eight mice were defenseless, however. Maybe I'd seen too many cartoons growing up, but I couldn't help feeling bad for them. At the same time I worried like hell about my own crew and my own butt. The triple-A we encountered earlier that night fit the pattern I'd been watching for months—the sites were moving steadily south and the return fire was getting heavier. We touched down a little after ten, and as I rode the crew bus in to operations, I reflected back on the evening as best I could. There was no ambiguity at night on the Ho Chi Minh Trail—those were definitely Bad Guys, not rice farmers, livestock, or unarmed women and children. And that was definitely triple-A they were firing back at us.

Back at the equipment room, I cornered Harley. "You've been to Survival School. What the hell do we do if we're actually shot down over Laos?"

Pigpen Sachs brought us each a cold bottle of Singha beer. The Spectre door gunner rented one of the bungalows down at Harley's compound and, other than the night I saw him passed out at the NCO club, was a tall, imposing ex-Hells Angel. His muscular arms were covered with tattoos, mostly about his mom and a small United Nations of ex-girlfriends mixed in with a few skulls and crossbones, but his face was kind, with a jaded glint in his eyes and a faint smile behind his bushy mustache. "Don't get him started on that," said Pigpen.

Harley started in anyway. "Some efficiency expert decided to combine Survival School with the Escape and Evasion course—POW School—up at Fairchild in Washington State. So we prepared for Southeast Asia in fuckin' *snowshoes*. Gave us five days to cover fifty miles with nothing but a friggin' onion and a pemmican bar while we're ass deep in snow, being chased through mountain forests by pretend Bad Guys who capture us and put us through the POW segment. Lesson there? You'll be hungry if you ever get shot down, but at least you won't be wearing snowshoes."

Pigpen joined in. "Seriously, don't know more than you need to know and you won't have to worry about being a hero if you're ever tortured."

I didn't like the thought of being tortured, I hadn't signed up to be tortured, and so I made up my mind to follow Pigpen's advice and remain in a high state of ignorance.

Harley remembered something important. "Three days later we were in Snake School in the Philippines. And there we did learn one cold, hard truth: any path or creek or back road you'd really like to be traveling on is exactly where you'll find the Bad Guys, moving twice as fast as you because it's their fuckin' terrain and you're a surprise visitor."

"Here's to your first real combat mission," said Sachs. We clinked our bottles together, chugged down the ice-cold beer, and headed home.

13 October 1971 (2300)
Perfect Lady

I was bone-tired when I got back to the hootch, my legs still rubbery from pulling G's at an altitude where we could have used some oxygen. In the dim glow of the street light that leaked in from outside, I peeled off my uniform and pulled my lanky body into the upper bunk I learned to prefer after banging my head a few too many times in the berth below. Even with a row of lockers separating me from Leo Guttchock, I could hear him talking to his invisible wife. "Yes, dear, the boys'll all be home for Christmas, the President *says* so.... Yes, that's right. Nevers and Spinelli are back flying. You just can't keep some guys down on the ground.... Same here, honey. Can't wait to see you. I'll be coming in on the midnight train...."

Leo was about thirty, pale and paunchy, and with thinning, tangerine-yellow hair looked at least forty. I remembered how when I shipped out for Ubon, everyone who knew I had been dreaming of going to film school at USC had told me Leo was a guy I was going to love hanging out with. He had gotten his bachelor's degree there in cinema production before he headed off to Air Force Officer Training School. He ended up as an enlisted cameraman when he was thrown out of OTS for refusing to run or do pushups, although he insisted it was Self-Initiated Elimination. "I like the Orson Welles, Francis Ford Coppola look," he had grown famous for saying, "and no one ever made *them* do pushups or run in combat boots." He was also famous for having played a dead body in a student gangster film that actually won some obscure prize at Cannes. I suspected Leo had spent a few days too many out in the California desert locked in the trunk of the gangster's black Cadillac, because now he was spending way too much of his spare time peeling labels off Singha bottles. Just the same, I couldn't help being a little jealous of Leo, because even though he was slowly going nuts, he was still receiving real letters from a real wife.

Thanks Leo, I thought as I lay there listening to his babbling, tired as hell but unable to sleep. Week after week I had tried to be a good boy, preserving my moral purity for Danielle and for the review board that would be considering my application for discharge as a conscientious objector. Now that the board had turned me down, however, my deeply

125

held but non-traditional moral grounds deemed insufficient, I felt myself sinking into a moral and spiritual limbo. I hadn't lived in a cloister, I'd been performing with the Band of Brothers and been downtown plenty to visit Tom and his buddies, but even when I started dabbling in Thai and Laotian weed and paid my occasional visits to the rooftop restaurant at the Ubon Hotel, I came home every night to my modest bunk. My alcohol consumption was not noticeably high for a GI, a little below average for a Leary. But even when I was still a photo interpreter of sorts, staring eight hours a day at raw combat footage, I often lay in my bunk at night, mentally drained but not able to fall asleep, wondering how many civilians were getting killed by mistake. I agonized over my doubts about the war and ached to my depths with attacks of loneliness I couldn't control or understand. I was disgusted with myself for feeling alone when I had a girl waiting for me back in the States, but I had heard enough gut-wrenching stories about Dear John letters to not completely trust that Danielle would stick this out.

I felt crappy knowing that Danielle's late husband had spent his final nights humping the boonies a hundred and fifty miles away in I Corps with only the here and now to worry about and that my kind of inner whining could have gotten somebody killed. Grunts like Danielle's husband were too busy filling sandbags and digging foxholes (their salvation and their own shallow graves) to have time for whining at the end of each day's march to nowhere. They were too exhausted from boredom and gushing adrenaline, from unrelenting heat and humidity so heavy it seemed to push them into the spongy ground, from hour upon hour of breaking trail through jungle that was not meant to be penetrated by man, from day upon day of walking across moonscapes where life as we knew it had ended, from thoughts forever unspoken of death that had burst upon them like a thunderstorm and would explode again. With a hundred incarnations of Death as their companion, ground pounders never had a chance to be lonely, especially in the hot and spicy nighttime when they were caressed by their desperate mistress, Fear.

Fear and death for the infantryman. Loneliness and self-destruction for Air Force flyboys and their support troops. It was embarrassing. But for fate we airmen could have been battling hard-core North Vietnamese regulars crashing through our perimeter, coming at us with fixed bayonets the way they once came at the French at Dien Bien Phu. Instead, we killed ourselves slowly with cheap BX booze and cigarettes, with opium-laced grass and amphetamines smuggled from the infirmary, and if the rumors were true, with pure Laotian heroin.

In the limbo-land between worried thought and troubled dreams, I feared these loneliness attacks would keep worsening until one day I would lose my mind completely. I grew ever more certain of my impending madness when I started flying and my memories grew more confused—were those old *dreams* that tormented me as I lay there, or were those *remembrances* of real parties and places and friends and lovers that were mixing together like bad chemicals at the photo lab, incapable of bringing up a clear image? Once-critical pieces of reality were fading away into the dark sludge at the bottom of the developing tank.

Most troubling of all for me was the Perfect Lady. I might have met her on a weekend at the Cape during my two years at Holy Cross. Or it could have been anywhere in New England during the junior and senior years I spent at Brown playing drums on the weekends in a drunken haze and taking film classes on the side at Rhode Island School of Design. I could barely picture her—she was more like a shadow and a feeling—but a certainty lurked within me that we had once had a brief, perfect love affair. How could this faint memory of a college girl from Boston fill me with dread that my engagement to Danielle was a mistake? How could I doubt Danielle's commitment when I had her letters and her picture in my locker just a few feet away? What was happening to my mind after the lights went out?

Tonight, while Leo snored, I drifted off and once again saw the familiar dreamscape. *I'm home from the war and searching every corner of a strange Northeastern city for her, my perfect backup, my ace in the hole now that Danielle has finally called it off. I can almost remember her golden summer skin and her Swedish international movie star lips. Still in my jungle fatigues, I am desperately certain that she has been real and wonderful. I ache at the memory of losing her phone number forever in the back pocket of a pair of jeans in some forgotten Laundromat. I keep finding what looks like her old apartment building—a gray three-story wood-frame townhouse that has been divided into flats. But when I wander up the stairs and through the hallways inside, I can't find her. Further down the street I find another building, exactly the same, another old home turned into student slum apartments, and I go inside and again find nothing. The night grows colder and a thin film of ice and snow begins to cover the letters on the street signs. I am about to give up when out of the corner of my eye I find her blurred name on a mailbox outside a decrepit tenement house. I go inside, feeling a rush of excitement as I climb the stairs, a smile forcing itself upon my pursed lips. The door to her flat is open, and as I approach, it seems like I am floating, drawn inside by a powerful magnetic force. A warm, contented feeling is beginning to wrap itself around me: instinctively I know where my slippers and robe are waiting, and I can hear the crackling of the hot embers in the fireplace. Inside, it is dark and empty. The Perfect Lady has vanished again.*

The scene dissolves into a party full of student artists in a shabby apartment near Rhode Island School of Design, full of dope and half-finished bottles of Scotch and men and women in black turtlenecks talking seriously between puffs of cigarette smoke about Larry Rivers and Jasper Johns and how it all means so much, how the emptiness is the message, and through it all a Dark Woman in a black leather overcoat keeps appearing in the labyrinth doorways and finally I stumble upon her alone in the kitchen, a kitchen strewn with the refuse of a hundred post-modernist, post-pubescent desperadoes but which has been abruptly evacuated, a miniature Dunkirk left for the bomb squad to defuse. I sweep her into my arms and she melts into me and devours me with kisses that are deeper and softer than any I have known or dreamed were possible—deeper and softer than the Perfect Lady's unless she is the Perfect Lady—except, too like a zephyr, her warm kisses disappear. At the very moment my heart opens, gaping and vulnerable to this mysterious ac-tion-painter, this flinger of pigment and palette-knife slasher of canvas, my aorta is severed. Fatally wounded, I try to follow her home through the foggy New England night, staggering as a trail of blood streams behind me. But on that cruel Halloween night the Belle Dame Sans Merci disappears, leav-ing only the echoes of her knee-length jackboots to torment me and lead me dumbly into an alley behind the Faculty Club where I shiver, lost and con-fused, until morning when I wake up in my own proper bed on a tranquil street in divine Providence, my body unscarred.

My sun-filled bedroom pleasantly dissolves into a dormitory lounge at Wellesley on a snowy night. The Perfect Lady is sitting there, leaning back regally in a wing chair, obscured in the highlights and shadows thrown by the flickering light of the fireplace, reading War and Peace. *My heart pounding, I can smell the perfume on her neck and in her hair as I touch her perfect* shoulder. "Thank God I've found you," I cry. "I was afraid I would never find you again." And I see in her eyes that our torrential love will never end—and at the precise moment she says, "I love you," I am back in Boston, certain that I'm wide-awake, traipsing in bare feet through the filthy slush along streets that are gray as Death. My jungle fatigues are soaked through and my flesh is numb, so chilled and wet that the sleet feels hot when it hits my face.

Tossing and turning in a moment of sleepy wakefulness, my T-shirt soaked with perspiration, I asked, *Who was this Perfect Lady that I try so hard to remember? Who was the Dark Woman I want to forget?* My dream began to slip away, and I remembered Danielle's plans for a large family wedding in her hometown Episcopal church. A mosquito buzzed around my ear, ignoring the smoke from the green mosquito coil. After several misses I slapped the intruder and dozed off, only to be awakened again by three New Guys from the lab who turned on the lights, took a few beers out of the refrigerator and snapped open the tops, realized they were in the wrong hootch, and left without switching off the lights.

I climbed down, turned out the lights and no sooner got settled back in bed than Washington, my bunk-mate, came in with one of the waitresses from the NCO Club. The waitress was an uncontrollable giggler. Just as exhaustion finally overcame the sound of her soft gurgles and I fell back asleep, she woke me up again with her moaning. I was wiped out, but the shaking of the bunk and the cries of ecstasy coming from below now kept me wide awake, staring again at the ceiling. I climbed down in a trance, trying not to glance into the wriggling darkness, and swapped my sweaty T-shirt for a clean cotton short-sleeve shirt, pulled on some jeans, and slipped on my finest shower shoes. Through my aching eyes I could make out midnight on my tick-tocking Baby Ben. As I closed the creaky door to the hootch, I heard the girl give one last high-pitched tickly giggle, followed by bellowing from Washington that shook the flimsy quarters like the mating call of a lovesick water buffalo.

Everybody Comes to Niko's

A little after midnight I climbed on board a cramped, pink, three-quarter-scale *baht*-bus, paid my Thai nickel and rode out to the main gate. The usual line of Datsun and Toyota taxicabs and the horde of *sahmlaws* that waited across the street had thinned to a handful now that the action had moved downtown. Two motorbikes and drivers were standing by in front of Maharaj Massage, waiting for midnight ramblers in a hurry. I climbed into the closest cab. It would be the last time I rode a late-night *baht*-bus out to the gate, but my late-night rambling was just beginning.

The driver stopped at the Soul Sister and the Club Miami, but the first was in brothers-only mode that night and the other was too noisy and crowded to lure me in. Ubon was a small, dusty provincial capital. It didn't take long to backtrack to the west side of town to check out the Corsair and the New Playboy Club, except the New Playboy was in the midst of an eerie lull, quiet as a crypt. Finally, at the Corsair I took an empty seat at the bar and looked around. Among the girls who were left, one looked stunning from a distance, but when she passed me on her way out with a tipsy GI, my mind's eye flashed back to the night my booze-damaged eyeballs mistook a scrawny farm girl for a *Vogue* cover girl. The memory chilled me, but I continued to sit, fascinated, watching the hardest, most worn-out, most jaded of the girls go through the motions of their craft. The GIs out at midnight were generally the drunkest, most miserably married or most hopelessly single of a crowd that was suspect when it left the base. The nightly dance of death had begun, a last chance for an aging village girl to pay her rent, a last call for a rough-hewn farm boy on flight status to hold a human being close. I lied to myself that I was not a part of it, that I could watch dispassionately, gaining valuable life experience, that I was a future auteur taking mental notes for an anthropological documentary I might use for my PhD thesis.

At two the last of the bars would start closing, the trickle of *sahmlaws* and taxis to the Ubon Hotel would turn into a steady stream, and for three more hours the standoff would continue. I was already hungry, though, and the kitchen at the Corsair had closed, so I crossed the street, got into one of the cabs in front of the New Playboy Club, and headed off for the penthouse restaurant at the Ubon Hotel. On this, the night of my first real combat mission over Laos, I decided to treat myself to something a little better than street food.

I had grown to like the Ubon Hotel because it was pleasantly noisy and modern and bright, and the food was good. Even sitting there after-hours by myself, surrounded by wilting bar girls and tipsy GIs, I felt the same way I used to feel at home when the relatives were visiting at Christmas and the Fourth of July. I might have felt alienated and vaguely irritated at the small talk, the excessive drinking, the reactionary politics and the thinly veiled racism, but I never felt that worst of all feelings—I never felt alone.

And so it was that on the fateful night of my first genuine butt-puckering, truck-killing combat mission over the Ho Chi Minh Trail, I sat down at what had become my personal bar stool at the furthest end of the imitation-marble bar and ordered a *somtom* salad. Service from the kitchen was slow, however, and suddenly I was seized with a need to split, fearing for no good reason that I might be fooled again by a desperate teenager made up to look twice her age when what I really wanted was to be a good boy and return pristine to Danielle and the sanctity of marriage. The bartender brought me a beer, which seemed to calm me down. And as I continued waiting for my order, I slipped deep into one of my semi-hypnotic reflections, this time on the slowly revolving dance floor and its whirling patrons, wondering how the G's they were pulling compared to the G's we felt on an AC-130 gunship. And as my mind continued to drift, I laughed to myself when I realized that there was one other similarity between after-hours at the *Rongraem Ubon* and being home for the holidays: they were both places where I would never ever find my Perfect Lady. My trance was broken by the plate of papaya salad clanking down on the bar in front of me, and I began to wonder what kind of tricks my mind was playing on me. Wasn't *Danielle* my Perfect Lady after all? Wasn't she a Good Girl whom I could take home for a family dinner, but who could, back in our mountain cabin, make torrid love to me in countless ways and then hold me tenderly, sleeping until the sun came up and we made love again?

Washing down my *somtom* salad with a second bottle of Singha, I noticed an old knee injury flaring up, and soon the rest of my body joined in. My butt went numb, my back ached, and my neck throbbed with a pinching burn. When my legs started to cramp up, I knew it was time to get moving, even if it meant leaving half my salad. On the elevator ride down, every jolting start and stop gave me a shot of pain. I had been flying for a month, but tonight had been the real thing, combat photography, looking through a flickering eyepiece while in contact with the enemy. For a handheld movie camera, an Arri St with a four-hundred-foot magazine wasn't all that light when you first picked it up. After five hours of flying, it felt like a forty-pound bag of cement.

I spotted an old Laotian *sahmlaw* driver not far from the hotel entrance. Using a lot of sign language, I asked him if he knew where I could get a good hard *nuat* for my aching shoulder muscles.

"*Sahp, khrab*," he answered and off he went, peddling steadily with thick, muscular legs.

I felt a strange kinship with the *sahmlaw* drivers, which might have had something to do with my own family's peasant roots. Some of the hill-tribe villages the drivers came from didn't yet have the wheel, and here they were wrangling around three of them at a time. I suspected the level streets of Issan Thailand were a welcome respite for the Laotians after clambering up and down mountain footpaths that tired us out *flying* over. I hated to hear that some of them were suspected of collecting intelligence for the Pathet Lao, counting up takeoffs and landings from our base, something pretty simple to do since there was only a single runway to keep track of.

In any case, whether or not he was working part-time for the Pathet Lao, my driver was soon turning down an alleyway not far from the New Playboy Club. He stopped at a massage parlor that, judging from its faded, mold-streaked exterior, had been around since the Japanese Army was in town a war earlier. The name, Niko's, seemed vaguely familiar, and then I remembered Perez raving about it a few weeks back.

Inside Niko's was plush red, a little frayed, the seediness hidden in the shadows of the subdued lighting. My eyes were drawn to the girls who were still working at one in the morning, brightly lit, sitting like Kewpie dolls, scattered in three rows behind a one-way window. I stood there, looking them over in a daze, feeling for a moment like I had slipped back into a dream. The manager greeted me like a long-lost cousin and offered me a beer. After politely declining, I asked if any of the girls spoke English. He began to rave about the academic accomplishments of Number 18, but I was distracted by a girl curled up in the back row, half-watching the television. She was lovely in a quiet way, but what I noticed most was that she was wearing *no* makeup. Her hair fell over her shoulders in too much disarray to be a wig. And instead of wearing a small apron like the others, she had on a man's navy work shirt. The manager assured me she too spoke excellent English. Her one concession to house convention was the badge she wore on her shirt pocket, Number 25.

As I followed Number 25 down the hall, admiring the rhythmic swaying of her hips, little bubbles of memory began floating up. Could she have been the girl I bumped into at the open-air market the day Zelinsky showed me around Ubon for the first time? Would that make her the girl with Dave Murray at the Soul Sister the night Harley's buddies crashed and burned? I wished Dave and the gang had stayed longer and that whoever was with him spent less time lost in cigarette smoke and shadows.

Closing the door to our cubicle, Number 25 asked, "You want bath first, or massage?"

"I could use a good hot back and neck scrub. I worked late tonight."

"You can get undressed while I run water." She handed me a large white terry-cloth towel.

"What's your name?" I asked, kicking off my flip-flops.

"Tukada. In English, it mean 'Doll.'"

"Your parents named you well. A beautiful name for a beautiful woman."

She gave me a jaded smile while she adjusted the temperature of the bath water. "My frien' jus' call me Dah."

"*Yindii tii dai rujak, Khun Dah,*" I said, trying to get the tones right.

"*Arai na?*" she replied, confused by my terrible pronunciation.

"Pleased to meet you," I translated as I took off my shirt.

"Oh. Pleased to meet you too," she answered with an amused half smile. "*Khun chu arai, kha?*"

"*Phom chu* Brendan. I've seen you before, you know."

"*Jing ru*—really?"

"Giving food to street kids begging down by the bridge."

She looked up at me coolly, expressionless. "Oh zat. Zat is nos-sing."

I hung up my jeans, wrapped myself in the towel and sat on the massage table, admiring the graceful way she moved while she finished running the bath. "I've got some pretty good pictures of you."

"Did you get some at VD clinic?"

"VD clinic?" I replied, caught off guard by her directness. "No, I lost track of you."

"Zat where I go next. Every week, get checked to keep my work permit."

"I'm afraid I still have a lot to learn about Thailand."

She led me to the oversized tub, took my towel, and helped me in. The warm soapy washcloth felt good against my neck and back. While she scrubbed me, she asked, "Are you GI or Peace Corps?"

"I'm afraid I'm a GI."

"Zen how you get to grow your hair so long?"

"Lots of Groom and Clean," I laughed. "And I mostly work nights."

"You smoke pot?"

"Sometimes," I answered, wondering if I was somehow being set up.

After rinsing off my back and chest, she helped me up and handed me my towel. While I dried myself off, she picked out a bottle of scented oil from a nearby wall cabinet and set it under the table. Wrapping me in a fresh towel, she led me over to the table and had me stretch out on my stomach. "Thai girls don' smoke ganja," she said condescendingly.

I expected her to tell me why. Instead she poured some oil into her palms and rubbed them together to warm it. "You look like a hippie freak to me," I said. "Are you sure you never smoked?"

"*Maybe,*" Dah answered with an enigmatical smile. She began working on neck muscles that I didn't know existed, and I began to relax. "Are you hip-pie?" she asked.

"Are you?" I replied.

"When I'm with hip-pies, I'm hip-pie." She pressed her hands deep into my aching back muscles. "And when I'm with li-fers, I'm li-fer."

"How'd you learn to speak such good English?"

"I finish high school," she answered, somehow insulted. "We had very good *ajahn* from Peace Corps, Khun Bill. I was going to be tea-cher like my aunt." She hesitated. "You know how much Thai teacher make? In coun-try my aunt make twenty dollar a month, for her and two kids. Zat not enough. So I do zis."

She pressed deeply into my shoulders and worked down each side of my spine, seeming to know where my body was aching better than I knew myself. She loosened the towel but kept it draped over my buttocks as she worked on those large, tired muscles and then kneaded the backs of my arms and legs. When she reached my feet, I winced in pain but soon surrendered to Tukada's skillful manipulations. Politely holding the towel for me, she asked me to turn over and began working on my biceps and forearms, lifting them lightly and stretching out the tendons of my aching hands, wrists, and fingers. She was good, always seeming to have one hand touching me while at the same time managing to warm the oil before applying it to my body. When she pressed her hands into my chest muscles, I closed my eyes and transported myself back to Cleopatra's palace, trying to decide whether I felt more like Caesar or Mark Antony. Her hands moved down to my stomach and loins and I felt a pleasant stirring that got me wondering if Roman emperors had harems. "Thai girls don' like mustache," she said out of the blue.

"What?"

"Thai girls don' like *mustache*."

"Well, *I* like my mustache. Gotta have *some* way of telling the freaks from the lifers."

She opened the cabinet and took out a tube of Brylcreem. "You want hand job?"

I gulped, caught off guard again. Hand jobs had never come up in catechism class. Matter-of-factly, she put the tube back. "You want to stay another hour?"

I laughed. "I want *you*."

"Not while you have mustache," she teased.

A chime sounded and she started handing me my clothes. Helping me on with my shirt, she slowed down. "I see you before too."

"Really?"

"*Jing-jing*. I see you play drum at Soul Sis-ter. Your band very good. You have to be good drum-mer to play with black dudes, *chai mai*?"

"I was lucky. Their old drummer shipped out, that's all."

"I want to hear you again sometime." The jaded look in her eyes softened.

"I *want* you to hear us." She was buttoning my shirt, just inches away, her hair giving off a faint scent of orange blossoms. I looked into her eyes and smiled. She smiled back and I pulled her close, kissing her softly. She surprised me, kissing me back with warm, full lips that parted like the Red Sea. "I thought Thai girls don't kiss," I gasped.

"I'm not Thai girl," she replied, her eyes sparkling. "I'm hip-pie,

135

remember?"

"When you're with *me*," I chuckled. I held her and worried about Danielle and didn't want to let go of Tukada anyway. I was in a real war now. Any day could be my last. And yet Danielle was part of the world that I'd be returning to in a few months. She was out in California, three thousand miles from her friends and family, and I knew from her letters that she missed me and worried about me. Confused, I suggested to Tukada that we go find an after-hours food stand and have a bite to eat.

"Sorry," she said. "Boyfrien' coming for me."

I wanted to ask her if she had been with a dude named Dave Murray when she saw me at the Soul Sister, but there was a polite rap at the door.

"Time is up, sir," said the manager with a sympathetic smile.

"Sorry," said Dah as she slipped past me, leaving her boss to walk me out.

14 October 1971
Moving on Down

The next morning I dragged myself over to the lab to watch my dailies. The daytime footage from the F-4 gun cameras—the kind I used to edit— had been processed first, and Larry Zelinsky was cutting out extraneous footage and cutting in titles. "13 OCT 1971, Suspected VC Command Post Destroyed" described a village of thatch-roofed huts indistinguishable from any other hamlet in Southeast Asia—other than the fact that someone there had fired at an observation plane, and as a result, an air strike had wiped it off the map. "13 OCT 1971, Suspected NVA Supply Ship Sunk on Lower Mekong" wasn't exactly describing the Bismarck going down—it was an old wooden Chinese junk that had been blasted to match sticks because someone either on board the boat or hidden on shore had taken a potshot at whatever spotter plane happened to be cruising by. I watched for a while, transfixed, unable as usual to discern any sign of enemy activity, but then again, by the time O-2s or OV-10s marked a target and called in an air strike, the sappers were long gone.

When I found out my footage wasn't coming out of the soup for another hour, I decided to push on to the ComDoc ready-room and catch some shut-eye. Sprawled out uncomfortably on the bus-seat sofa, it didn't seem like I had been asleep a minute when Zelinsky came barging in shouting, "Ten-hut!" With a phony smile, he intoned, "Your footage is ready."

I staggered over to the coffee urn, grabbed a cup and began pouring. "I'm afraid you're right—I gotta get out of that hootch. I haven't had a good night's sleep since they made me a cameraman."

I started to put some creamer in the coffee but noticed I had dumped most of the java on my boots. I managed to fill the cup on my second try and followed Larry back to the lab. Along the way, he said, "You scare me, man. You're going to pour yourself out of an airplane one night if you keep this up."

"I almost did last night."

"That settles it," he said as we stepped inside. He continued talking while he threaded up the Moviola. "Groendyke moved back on base. Says he'll never cure his chancroids in time for his wedding if he keeps living downtown. But you're different, Leary. You've got moral fiber. That's why you're taking his old room down at Ruam Chon Sawng."

"I'd love to, but I blew every cent I had downtown last night. And don't forget my lawyer in L.A. Gotta keep *him* in furs."

"Make it up to me on payday. Once you square things with me you can worry about your lawyer, but you're not staying in that hootch another night. Tom and I'll meet you over there at four to help you with your stuff."

He turned on the Moviola and we started watching my footage. The sensor stuff was pretty good for being hand-held—even a bit mysterious. The footage I shot of the NOD was blurred at first, and then, just when the quality got good, I wished it hadn't. Two drivers scrambled out their trucks and were starting to run away. Suddenly vaporized. They were real North Vietnamese soldiers moving supplies for the 559th Transportation Group, not anonymous rice farmers, but I was stunned anyway. And then the footage of the trapped convoy came up. It was a grainy at first, but you got the idea. When the F-4s began their bomb and napalm runs, I somehow snapped back into combat cameraman mode, objectively analyzing my work. The fire was nasty but it photographed well. The burning jelly filled up the screen and my Arriflex recorded it with near-perfect resolution in clean shades of blacks and grays and whites, something that would have blown out the picture on a video camera. The five rounds of triple-A were almost beautiful floating towards us and gracefully veering away. And then the plane broke violently right. The camera was still running as I flailed to stay on board, and I was stunned again. Watching the second convoy being shot up, I felt drained, exhausted, thankful to have Baker looking after me in the air and Zelinsky looking after me back on the ground.

That afternoon I made up my bunk with perfectly squared corners and put a pair of spit-shined dress shoes under the bed in case the lunatic assistant base commander actually carried out one of his regularly threatened inspections. Picking up my duffle bag, I began to have second thoughts—about the drugs, about needing to save money for grad school, and about how this fit in with being engaged to Danielle. Groendyke was engaged officially, with a wedding day set, and he couldn't keep himself away from the bar girls. On the other hand, I was going to have my own bedroom in a quiet corner of the bungalow—I'd finally get the sleep that I had craved for weeks. Besides, Zelinsky was right. I had moral fiber. If there was anything Father Boyle drummed into me, it was moral fiber.

Wheeler and Zelinsky showed up at the stroke of four to pick up my bags and several cases containing my still photo equipment and my old spring-wound 16mm Bolex movie camera. Thirty minutes later, Tom Wheeler and I pulled up to Ruam Chon Sawng on our bicycles, followed by Zelinsky in a cab that crept along behind us. Unloading my bags from the cab and balancing them on the bikes, we made our way through a labyrinth of taxis and *sahmlaws* parked in front of the gate. Inside, off to the right, several Thai national policemen and uniformed civil servants sat together at one of the tables in Mama-sahn's little courtyard café. Several off-duty bar girls, dressed casually for the afternoon, sat nearby. Walking up the alley we passed Mama-sahn, the proprietress herself, sitting outside her two-story pine-paneled bungalow. She was old-school, sitting there bare-breasted, smiling flirtatiously, zonked on betel nut that had long ago stained her teeth magenta. *Thank God the GIs did one thing right and brought the current generation chewing gum*, I thought.

Bun-lii, an aging bar girl who depended on lifers for her livelihood, called playfully after Tom, "*Phom Daeng! Phom Daeng!*"

"Those Thai beauties just can't resist that yellow hair," Zelinsky ribbed Wheeler.

I had learned just enough Thai to start getting lost in translation. "Why is she calling Tom's blond hair *red*?"

Wheeler just smiled his laid-back Buddha smile as we carried my luggage up the wooden steps to Bungalow #4 and dropped it off in the empty bedroom adjacent to the music room. Across the alley from us the Thai kickboxer skipped rope awhile and then began shadowboxing. One of the Thai soldiers who usually hung out at Mama-sahn's restaurant joked with the boxer from a cement bench next to the bungalow. The soldier, who I later learned was named Sergeant Prasert, was a pleasant-looking young man with features a little more angular than most Thais. The boxer's girl-friend, pale and delicate, lit incense in the spirit house at the end of the alley and came back to the patio to begin cutting meat and vegetables to stir-fry for dinner.

I did enough unpacking to change out of my uniform and join Wheeler in the music room, where he was perusing the cases that held his hi-fi tape collection. "Looks like Lek might finally be leaving Mole, Dave Murray's housemate, and moving in here." Pulling out a seven-inch reel, he started threading up his tape deck. "I should warn you—she likes to make things complicated. Don't be surprised if she makes a pass at you sooner or later. That's how *we* met. I'd be hanging out over there and she'd bat her eyes and start lamenting how Mole was blowing all their money on drugs. She didn't know what to do—"

"Except mess around with 'Phom Daeng'? Does she know how much *you're* spending on drugs?"

Tom set the music room shaking with a Buddy Miles tune. The speakers could have filled up Shea Stadium. Even with the volume turned down low, the entire bungalow was vibrating to the pulsating bass. I lit up a Blue Moon, choking on the tobacco plug before taking a deep drag on the grass packed inside and passing it to Tom. "As far as making things complicated," I said. "There's no way a chick is going to screw up *our* friendship. Not after all we went through with Norton GIs for Peace. And now here, living off base together. No matter what she pulls, we can handle it."

There was a knock at the door. Tom took a quick drag and handed me the joint. "I guess we're going to find out." He lifted the latch and froze. "Murray! Tukada! You haven't seen Lek, have you?"

My stomach did something like a back flip, but I managed to force a little smile, laughing to myself that it *figured*—I'd be infatuated with a Thai hippie who was involved with Dave Murray, my hangdog colleague. Maybe there *was* a God up there messing with us after all. I inhaled deeply on the ganja. Ubon suddenly seemed like a very small town.

Murray settled onto a floor cushion next to one of Tom's mammoth speakers while Tukada kept standing. On a fifteen-second delay, Murray answered, "Yeah, man. She was fighting with Mole about some money she lent him. Is she coming over?" He nodded off before Tom could answer.

Tom turned to me. "Have you met Tukada?"

Dah and I glanced at each other, but she addressed Tom, stoned but still functioning. "We going to get mar-ried. And when Dave get out of Air Force, we going to get Wee-W van and drive all over America."

Dave's eyes opened. "We've really thought about it...." His brain locked up a moment. He tried again. "We really thought about it—an' we're getting married next week. Dah's already quit at Niko's."

Tom and I took another puff of our cigarette and waited for Dave to continue. "Well, you gonna kiss my bride-to-be?"

Tom kissed her and she responded a little too ardently for a future housewife, about as warmly as she had kissed me in private the night before. "Congratulations, both of you," he said.

And then she kissed me the same way, to my mild astonishment. "Yeah," I said, "congratulations." *What's going on?* I wondered. I loved Dave in a brotherly sort of way, but I couldn't see him as husband material.

Dave didn't seem to notice. He was busy fishing through his pocket, finally pulling out a packet, about one-inch-square, of something wrapped in newsprint. Opening it, he scooped up some kind of coarse red powder with a key and snorted it. I took a drag on what was left of my Blue Moon, inserted it in a roach clip, and passed it to Tom. Dah sat down with Dave and took a snort of the red powder. "What the hell is that?" I asked. My moral fiber was already feeling shaky.

Tom passed the roach to Dave, who with bleary eyes took a deep drag and held it in. "They call it red rock," Tom answered. "B.J. next door sold it to Dave the other night. Said it's some kind of cocaine."

"And you're sure it's not scag?" I asked.

"No way," Dave mumbled in a cloud of smoke. "Otherwise I'd be really strung out by now."

He passed the roach to Dah, who took a final puff and tugged at his arm. "Come on, let's go tell Lar-ry and Pueng."

They shuffled off to Larry's room in the back of the bungalow. "Poor fool," Tom reflected. "Knows a girl a couple of weeks and he's getting married."

We could hear footsteps thumping up the wooden stairway. "Tom!" called Lek. She swept into the room and grabbed a knife to cut up the mango and pineapple she had brought along. On her way out to the porch, she bumped into Larry, Pueng, Dave and Tukada, who were on their way in. Tom stayed behind and took out his bamboo bong, pouring in some wine, filling the bowl with grass and firing it up, taking in a long, cool, bubbling drag and then passing it around. Quicksilver Messenger Service was playing in the background when Lek returned with a platter of fresh fruit, some of it sculpted into small works of art too beautiful to eat, but we passed it around anyway. Eating and smoking together happily, we sang along when we heard the hippie national anthem: *Have another hit—of fresh air!* As we burst into woozy laughter, I noticed an unspoken aloofness between Lek and Dah, but the vibes were too good for me to give it much thought.

Lingering monsoon rains began falling and for a while it grew quiet while we listened to the rain drops tapping on our tin roof, lost in our private thoughts or dozing pleasantly like Dave. Tom finally broke our collective trance. "Welcome to Ruam Chon Sawng, Brendan."

Playing bartender, he made us Mekongs mixed with Coke or soda water that had been chilling in his little refrigerator. He even threw in some tiny ice cubes. When we all had a drink in our hand, Lek made a little toast. "*Sabaidii*, Khun Brendan."

The rest joined in with a mixture of "*Sabaidii*'s," "*Sawatdii*'s," "To your health's" and "Welcome's," followed by a couple of playful pecks on my cheek from Pueng and Lek. Things were just starting to quiet down when Lek whispered something to Tom, who tapped his glass and announced, "Next week Lek will also be moving in—once and for all!"

"Welcome, Khun Lek!" said Larry, followed by another round of cheers and toasts. "You know," he mused, "it's hard to imagine anything better than a night like this together at Ruam Chon Sawng."

Tukada had an idea. "I know one sing even bet-ter. We can go togezzer to Tadtohn Falls, have picnic. It's beautiful place to cool off in hot season, but end of rainy season bet-ter—not too crowded."

None of the guys had been there. The group agreed to get together the following weekend if the weather was good. "You mind if I come along and take a few pictures?" I asked.

Lek's face lit up. "Maybe we find a Thai girl frien' for you."

"Thanks, but I have an American girlfriend, remember?"

"You don' like Thai women?" Lek teased.

I caught a glimpse from Dah. "That's the trouble. Thai women are too beautiful. I better stick with taking pictures."

Later, after the others had gone and Tom was in the *hong nam* taking a quick shower, Lek stretched out on the sofa, undulating to the music and nibbling mango off a large pit. I sat on the floor nearby, leaning back against the wall, my legs sprawled out in front of me. I could not help watching her move, and when she offered me a bite of mango, I could not help sensing she was tempting me to kiss her. Intoxicated, I noted uncomfortably that my memory of Danielle was fading. On my first night at Ruam Chon Sawng, were my moral bearings already coming completely unhinged?

What's happening? I wondered.

I chuckled to myself when I noticed Mick Jagger singing in the background, "*It was just my 'magination—running away with me.*" Tom came back in, and I wasn't quite sure, but I thought I caught a flash of peevishness in his Buddha-smile when he glanced at Lek and me. Not wanting to ruin a perfect evening, I gathered myself up from what seemed like half the room and said, "You know, if there weren't a goddamn war going on, this place wouldn't be half-bad."

Only one small detail dampened my mellow mood. When I got back to my room, I noticed that my wallet was lying on the floor beneath my fatigues. In my rush to change, I had left it in the back pocket when I hung them up. Checking the contents, I was pretty certain that two one-hundred-baht notes were missing, which didn't make sense because there were still five notes left. *Maybe the booze and grass and a long day have fogged my memory*, I thought, climbing into bed. I drifted off to sleep, smiling wryly as "Just My Imagination" kept playing in my head.

Missing Lek, OR: Grounded

For four straight days a storm front from somewhere on the Indian subcontinent had been passing through, turning three hundred miles of Thai-Laotian border into a dark mud hole during what was supposed to be the cool, dry part of the year. I was stuck, not wanting to fly, but not wanting to be sitting in the Photo Squadron ready room doing nothing, either. I found myself daydreaming about the American Northeast and the blizzards that used to paralyze Boston and New York. I recollected the ice storm that locked Washington, DC, in its grip the day I shipped out for California, and I tried to remember what it felt like to be cold. For four straight days somebody wanted a mission flown into Laos, and so it was that for four straight nights we stood by, on alert, ready to scramble the moment the cloud cover broke, but even Spectre, ghost riders of the night sky, had its minimums.

The country is going to the dogs. The dogs are going to the country, I daydreamed. I tapped my fingers on the Formica table where other, more socially adjusted airmen played poker when they had time to kill. I had been studying optics and film exposure charts and other technical stuff in the *American Cinematographer Manual* the last couple of nights, but now my eyes glazed over when I tried to read and I kept hearing "In-A-Gadda-Da-Vida" pounding in my head. I had been stuck and bored, grounded for three days and four nights—a perfect length of time for a run down to Pattaya Beach, except even Pattaya Beach got a little boring in the rain.

Harley Baker stopped by to rub it in that Strbik's crew was being sent home early. I had to stick around in case another Spectre bird went out. When word finally came down from Seventh Air Force to scrub all Spectre missions, I couldn't wait to get home. On the ride out to the main gate the road ran parallel to the runway. A solitary F-4 began its takeoff roll, so close that the roar of its mighty engines rattled through my body. Bundled up in my rain suit with the hood drawn shut over my ears, I felt for a moment like a cosmonaut on a dangerous assignment in a distant galaxy. I couldn't explain why, but it was a moment like this when I loved that rubberized nylon rain suit. I didn't care that it wasn't watertight, nor that I was probably as wet from perspiration as I would have been riding along shirtless. The feeling of being wrapped in my own private cocoon made it worth it. Close to Ruam Chon Sawng, gliding down back streets that had turned into shallow, muddy rivers, I could feel the mud splattering my back and loved that rain suit even more.

Even with the hood covering my ears, I could make out the rumble of two cargo planes feeling their way through the weather. *Must be Air America,* I thought. Only Air America had situations to straighten out that were so desperate they had to go up on a night like this. Only in the parts of Laos that were further north than some of China did men get so hopelessly pinned down and cut off. Only in Laos did things get so bad that regular Air Force fliers couldn't figure out a way to get in. It took soldiers of fortune, men who had nothing left to prove and men who had so much to prove they had to look Death in the eye every day just to know they were alive.

I myself was glad to be safe inside the cozy confines of Bungalow #4, where I could unlace my nylon-mesh jungle boots and pull them off. They were worthless protecting us from rain or mud but were supposed to dry out quickly and resist rotting like leather. It felt good swapping out my damp uniform for dry jeans and a T-shirt. The rain was still drumming monotonously on the tin roof when I crossed over to the music room, where I was happy to see Dave Murray separating marijuana stems from the leaves in a large wooden salad bowl. Harley was using a cutting board to chop up the best of the leaves for Tom Wheeler to pack into the brass bowl of his well-worn bamboo bong. I picked up a bottle of jug-grade French Colombard and poured some into the depths of the water pipe to tame the kicking, scratching, she-devil weed. After reaching the level needed to produce a gentle bubbling when I drew a breath, I screwed on the cap and put the bottle back into our little refrigerator. I passed the bong back to Tom and noticed there was a trace of melancholy on my friend's face. Tom was *usually* quiet and calm, but it was usually a peaceful quiet. Tonight he was not wearing his serene Buddha smile. "You missing Lek, Tom-bear?"

"Ah, she'll be back in a couple of days. She just wanted to see her little boy and her father and bring a few things back to her village before she moved in." He took a long drag and passed on the water pipe.

Harley's raspy voice broke the mood. "Cool Tom getting pussy-whipped."

"Actually, I was thinking more about the girl back in Wappinger's Falls I was going with before I got busted. The judge gave me a choice of the Air Force or jail, and she told me she'd wait for me either way."

Dave, the earnest son of a Nebraska accountant, smiled, premature wrinkles fanning out from the corners of his eyes. "A judge made *you* enlist too?" he asked, giving Tom a stoned attempt at a soul-brother handshake.

"Don't worry about her still being there when you get out," said Baker.

"Actually, I do worry. Been experimenting with mailing her small packages of grass disguised as thick love letters. If hers and the stuff I'm sending to my old business partner keep making it through, I'll have a nice stash waiting—provided they don't smoke it up."

"Unless you got a saint for a partner, you better kiss her *and* the grass goodbye."

"Buzz off, Harley." I couldn't help looking out for Tom when he was down. "Aren't you the one who's had to find a new wife every time you've shipped over here?"

"I take that back. Tom, I'd start worrying a lot if I were you, because if that pretty little thing in Wappinger's Falls ever gets wind of what you been up to over here, she'll stick around all right—to cut your balls off." By now it was pretty obvious Harley had popped some whites, which he normally saved for combat. He had been primed for some truck killing and was irritated to be sitting around in the rain chit-chatting. "We're all animals, man. We'll screw whoever we can whenever we can. You'll be next, Leary."

"I'm sort of engaged, remember?"

"And that was your fiancée you took home from the Ubon Hotel that night you were out with me and Mali?"

"Gave her a cab ride home and went back to the base."

"*Ri-ight.* The same as your young widow-lady is sitting on her hands back in San Bernardino."

Tom's mind had returned from its sojourn to Wappinger's Falls. "Sounds like somebody burned you bad."

"Who asked you, Wheeler? You were fooling around with Lek a month after you got here, even though she was supposed to be *tii-rahking* Dave's buddy, Mole. And before that, there was that black fox back at Norton. I heard about that. You think she and Miss Wappinger's Falls are pining away for you tonight while they're sleeping in someone else's arms?"

"Linda pined away for two or three days." Tom gave Harley one of his twinkly-eyed Buddha smiles.

"Who the hell is Linda?"

"She was Tom's *tii-rahk* for a week before he met Lek," Dave answered, unfolding another of his little papers of powdered red rock. He used his key to take a snort before passing the key and paper over to Tom, who repeated the ritual.

Harley shook his head. "This guy gets more ass than a toilet seat and you guys give *me* crap for figuring out the bitter truth. Now just maybe Lek *did* go home to visit her daddy and her baby before she moves in with Tom. But don't be surprised if she's doing a little Tom-catting of her own before she has to settle in here."

Dave looked at Harley innocently. "How many old ladies have you had?"

Harley rolled his eyes and sighed. "Gimme a hit on that bong."

I passed it over. Letting out a long, long stream of killer smoke, I asked, "You and Mali have a spat tonight?" He didn't answer. "I thought this was it. Wasn't she supposed to be the love of your life—your *neua koo*?" Harley drew deeply on the bong, intent on not answering. "Are you still seeing that bar maid on the side down at the Corsair?" I asked.

"What of it? We're all a bunch of whores. At least I'll admit it. I'll fuck anything in a skirt, dead or alive."

"Does that include kilts?" asked Zelinsky with his Cheshire-cat smirk. He stepped in and found an empty cushion in the corner to plant his corpulence on.

Harley ignored the interruption, "If any of you would look into your rotten souls you'd admit you'd do the same thing."

Tom shook his head slowly. "So Mali caught you red-handed—let me guess—at the Corsair?"

"She was supposed to be at her sister's in Roi Et."

"What the hell are you doing *here*?" I asked.

"Locked out and cut off, man."

I pried Harley's calloused fingers off the bong and passed it to Zelinsky. Pulling Harley up and walking him to the door, I told him, "Go find some old mama-sahn selling flowers, you idiot, buy the most beautiful bouquet she's got, and go home and grovel."

"Tomorrow, man. I was kinda hoping I could crash here until she cools off."

I propped my reprobate friend against the door frame and said, "Listen, Harley, you've been through half the women in the world and the results aren't encouraging. The odds of anybody putting up with a boozing, amphetamine-eating, ignorant son of a bitch like you are zilch. And who do you end up with?"

Baker, Wheeler, Murray and Zelinsky answered in unison: "*The greatest goddamn woman in the world!*"

"You stay here tonight and there's no way you'll ever convince her you weren't doing the hoochie-coochie with Suzie the Barmaid."

Tom and Dave pulled open the faded teakwood door, a wet chill oozing into the room, and I nudged Harley outside. "Where the hell am I gonna find flowers at 10:00 PM?" he muttered as he disappeared down the stairs and into the evening mist.

With Harley's crisis hopefully averted, we closed the door, found our old spots, and settled back. Dave took a last toot of his red rock and burned the paper with his lighter, barely able to keep his eyes open. "I'm glad Tukada and I have our act together. Sure, we had some other people in our lives before we met. But it's amazing. We were just looking for each other all along. We knew that the minute we laid eyes on each other."

Tom and I didn't have the heart to look at Dave. Tom fondled the water pipe and stared blankly at his feet before turning to me. "Do you think Harley's right—that we're just a bunch of slobbering pigs?"

"I always thought we were making the best of a tough situation. '*Don't be angry,* don't be sad,' the song says. '*Love the one your with.*'"

"You ever wonder how *cool* straight arrows like Chaplain Kirkgartner can go for a year or even two years away from their wives and remain faithful?" Tom asked.

"We pretty much know how the *uncool* straight dudes do it—by being assholes," said Zelinsky.

"I don't think we'll ever know how conventional straight arrows make it, will we?" I asked whimsically. "Aren't we past the point of no return on that?"

"Letters," came a disjointed voice. We looked at the half-sleeping Dave, who continued, "My dad was away from Mom for nearly three years during World War II. They wrote to each other every day. Whether there was any chance mail could get through or not. Dad only missed once—I think he was pinned down that night on Omaha Beach."

"Yeah," said Zelinsky, "but that was a real war. No massage parlors on Omaha Beach. No Club Miami to duck into during the Battle of the Bulge."

"My dad wasn't the letter-writing type," I said. "He met my mom at a bar in Kansas City where TWA and Capital flight crews hung out and they've been together ever since."

"At least your fathers could write," replied Zelinsky.

"Yeah, but I've only gotten two letters from mine in my life," I continued. "One chewed me out for switching from engineering to English lit. Said I was going to ruin my eyes for flying. The other was when I dropped out of Air Force ROTC. 'How the hell are you ever gonna get your flight training?' he wanted to know—even though he got all his ratings as a civilian. He was awfully damned eager for me to go off to war for a son of a bitch who spent most of *his* war flying DC-3s between Kansas City and Pittsburgh."

"At least you guys had fathers," said Tom.

"Doesn't do much good if your dad's a boozer and you're busted with a little pot," said Dave. "Mine didn't know the difference between smoking grass and shooting up heroin. Might as well have been doing the hard stuff."

The gate shut at the end of the alley. The moisture in the evening air muffled the husky love talk of Leclerc, one of the brothers who lived next door. Laughter from his young female companion and a few words of melodic Thai barely floated as far as our bungalow.

Tom pursed his lips, blowing high-octane smoke rings. "Maybe we read too much Playboy Philosophy. Maybe we're *too* free. 'No jealousy.' 'No more women as chattel.' It sounds good, but where does that lead? Are we going to be a bunch of wandering nomads 'loving the ones we're with' until we're old and decrepit and no one wants us? It took something out of me leaving Gwen back in California. It's gonna take a little something out of me leaving Lek here. Harley's got a point—I don't know what I'm going to find when I get back to Wappinger's Falls."

"At least when Lek moves in you won't be lonely," I replied. "My college girlfriend hooked up with one of my fraternity brothers while I was going through basic training. Man, that hurt. For a year I was lonely as hell until Miss Free Love came along. When she gave me an STD I swore I wouldn't get close to a woman again until I got out of the service and back to Boston. And then along came Danielle. I knew she was special the night I met her, but I never dreamed she'd come all the way to California to see me. And we just clicked—whether it was politics or hiking or doing nothing on a Sunday afternoon, we always seemed to want to do the same thing. And if we didn't, we found something else to do, no sweat. Almost from the get-go, I kept thinking 'this is someone I can spend my life with.' I'd found *my* 'neua koo.' And I end up here, lonely as hell and scared out of my mind every time I've got to fly. Perez and Shahbazian are always saying, 'Come on, man, loosen up. Come on downtown with us. It's only a one-night stand with a goddamn hooker.' But even when I was sure I was doomed to die a virgin, I couldn't imagine myself sleeping with a prostitute. I don't want to start now. But God, I get lonely. She must get lonely too. I wonder sometimes if she'll still be waiting for me when I get back to the World. I guess I wouldn't blame her if she splits, I'd understand, but still it would sting."

"I can't stand being alone," Tom said dolefully. "Even for a minute."

"And here I thought you were so cool that *nothing* bothered you," I responded.

A solitary C-130 circled in the night above. I wondered if it was one of the two that I had heard earlier and if only one was coming back. I wondered where it had been—and if it been over Laos, how it found its way home through the low, thick clouds and the jagged mountains.

"You guys are depressing the hell out of me," said Zelinsky, pulling himself up and easing out the door. "I gotta go brush my teeth in case Pueng gets off work early."

"Got to write Dah a letter," Dave mumbled in his sleep. Tom and I picked him up and threw his arms over our shoulders, squeezing through the door Zelinsky hadn't bothered to latch and stumbling down the slippery stairway to a *sahmlaw* that had pulled up for the night under Leclerc's bungalow next door. We gave the Laotian driver directions to Dave's house and haggled over the price. The wily old man wanted to charge extra for having been wakened.

"It's early," I replied. "You only sleep because tonight nobody goes out in the rain."

"Okay, okay. Twenty baht." "What!" said Tom. "We can put him on a bus for *one* baht."

"Twenty baht."

"How about eight baht?" I asked.

"Weather very bad. Twenty baht."

"Ten baht," said Tom.

"Twenty baht."

"Okay, this is it," I said. "Twelve baht. Otherwise he takes bus." We started walking toward the gate.

"Okay, okay. Fifteen baht."

"*Toklong*," I agreed, helping Tom get Dave into the back seat.

With slow, powerful strokes, the driver wheeled the carriage into the drizzly night. Dave was protected from the wetness by the canvas top. The driver had only his small straw hat and a scrap of pink plastic over his back to keep him dry. I could make out rivulets of rain running down his sinewy bronze legs.

"*Yut! Yut!*" I called. The *sahmlaw* stopped and the driver looked back, amused. I ran down to him, feeling ridiculous every time reflex forced me to duck a raindrop. When I reached the *sahmlaw*, I gave the ancient Laotian driver a hundred-baht note. "Promise you'll buy a poncho for the rain? Do you understand?"

"Buy taxi better," the old man laughed as he pedaled away, throwing a contrail of fine mist into the air and leaving three long tracks behind him on the glistening macadam.

Red Rock Candy Mountain

On the tenth night of my new Humpty-Dumpty life, I got to fly the midnight shift with Spectre, which, according to Harley, was actually the most desirable time to be going out. If you did get shot down, it would only be a few hours of hunkering in the elephant grass before you heard the whirling blades of a Jolly Green coming out to find you.

Leaving for work around half past ten, I was surprised to hear a girl's voice and some strange pounding coming from the music room, mixed in with music from Armed Forces Radio. The Thai sergeant named Prasert was sitting quietly nearby, almost invisible on the dark porch. Strange— he was one of the regulars at Mama-sahn's café and across the alley at the kickboxer's place, but I wasn't aware of him knowing anyone at Bungalow #4. "*Wadii na, khrab,*" I said, trying not to pay him much attention as I knocked on the door. "Hey, Lek," I called, "I thought you weren't moving in till tomorrow."

When the door opened, I started to ask, "Did you bring some more mang—"

Looking over Tom's shoulder, I saw Tukada sitting on the floor, a sheet of butcher paper spread in front of her, pulverizing a chip of red rock with an empty Coke bottle. She stopped and looked up. "Dave go to base hos-pi-tal."

While she coaxed the powder onto a scrap of newsprint, Tom filled me in. "We were working in the orderly room as usual this morning and— BOOM!—Dave collapsed at his desk."

"Doc-tor say he do too much red-rock hero-in. Tell me no visitor for a week while Dave go through de-tox." Dah scooped up some of the red powder with her house key and inhaled.

I was filled with a nauseating sense of helplessness. I *liked* Dave Murray the way I liked our family Labrador back in Boston. I was confused by the attraction and repulsion I was feeling towards Dah and confused even further by the spark of jealousy I was feeling towards Tom. Back in the days when I thought my mind was an asset, confusion pissed me off. "Goddamn it, Tom—can't you make her stop!"

He looked up sheepishly. "Gotta figure out how to quit myself first."

"You told me this stuff was *cocaine*. Non-addictive. I thought you were strictly a grass-head."

"Nothing is forever, I guess. How much worse can it be than all that Mekong you're drinking?"

"I'm just drinking enough to steady my hands. No sweat."

"Whatever you say, man."

The nauseating helplessness was dragging me down. "Are we still going out to Tadtohn Falls tomorrow?" I was grasping at straws, looking for some way to influence the situation, hoping that a day in the sun, away from the ghetto, might do us all some good. Tom didn't answer. "Dah," I said, "you should do it. It was your idea, remember? Take your mind off Dave."

"Okay," she said softly. "*Toklong.*"

"I've gotta to go fly. I'll be back in the morning around six, ready to go at noon."

I slipped quietly to the door, feeling better, but I didn't know why. Tom and Dah snorted the rest of the rock and then took a breath on a Vick's inhaler to ease the discomfort in their nostrils. Dah must have felt a rush, because her eyes closed and her head fell back on Tom's shoulder. I stole a glance at the inhaler—it had a heavy red residue on the tip. Someone had been doing a lot of grams, and it didn't start yesterday. As I stepped outside, Tom turned out the light.

No Mistaking "Rookie"

We were flying with a different pilot, Captain Rooker, a young hotshot the crew called "Rookie," but it was turning out to be a routine mission for the 1971-72 hunting season, which meant two trucks killed and four damaged over the first hour and a half before we finished up with a bang. We trapped a convoy of twelve by taking out the lead and trailing trucks with our twin Bofors, which were Harley's responsibility, and damaging the middle ten with our Vulcans, which were handled by a New Guy just in from Eglin, and the mini-guns, which were Pigpen Sach's pride and joy, before Rooker called in a flight of F-4 Phantoms to mop up. Night Hawk 1 and 2 lit up the valley floor with napalm, which meant twelve more official truck kills. "Looks like we got us some Crispy Critters," radioed Night Hawk 1. I wished I could laugh, but I had learned early on to play the combat game with a poker face.

"Roger that," replied Rooker. We leveled out and headed for home. I re-minded myself to start breathing again. The new wrinkle for me was getting my own personal camera mount on Rush's old NOD—one of Billy Hill's innovations—now that Rush was up in the fire control booth with a TV monitor. It gave me my best footage yet of the F-4s' finale of molten flame. In near-darkness, I read the camera's footage counter and stepped back, resting against the booth exterior, trying to enjoy the lull in the action. Soon it was like every other lull that night—I drifted off thinking about Dave and Tom and Tukada and Danielle and wishing like hell I could have a hit from Tom's bong. *Where's my moral fiber?* I asked myself. *Dad would know what to do. But Dad would make it easy—he wouldn't leave the base. Or would he just keep his mouth shut?*

North Vietnamese gunners decided meditation time was over. "Break left, sir," commanded the right scanner, looking through a port behind the cockpit. "Triple-A, twelve o'clock."

"Hold on!" barked the spotter from the aft ramp, "Triple-A, accurate, *seven* o'clock, break right! BREAK RIGHT AND CLIMB! PRONTO! WE'RE HIT! LEFT INBOARD ENGINE!"

Sachs, the crazy ex-Hells Angel who enjoyed blowing up trucks the way young boys enjoyed throwing water balloons, laughed as Rookie, the youngest pilot in Spectre, tried to bark bail-out procedures without his voice cracking. The three remaining engines were given full throttle and the bird actually managed a slow climb. "Looks like we'll be RTB-ing to base right on time tonight," Sachs shouted to me cheerfully as the plane settled down and he leaned back next to me against the booth. "Cold Singha beer is sure gonna taste good!"

I could only give Sachs an incredulous stare.

The spotter burst back on line, shouting, "Crossfire! Crossfire! Take evasive action!" But the crippled plane wasn't very frisky trying to maneuver on three engines. The interior of the plane exploded in a bright flash, the concussion pounding at my chest and knocking me backwards towards the ramp. Triple-A had hit the 20-mm gun position, ripping a big enough hole in the side of the plane to vaporize the gun and leave smoldering shreds of cloth and flesh where the New Guy gunner's chest and thighs used to be. The half of the gunner that was still standing slid to the floor only a few feet from Sachs. Which meant a few feet from *me*. The stench was awful, but the terror I felt was worse. At least it was a fucking New Guy, a stranger. Sachs stayed cool and got back to his battle station, linking together belts of ammo for his six-thousand-round-per-minute mini-gun, at the same time looking like he wished he could rip it loose from its mount with his huge Hells Angels arms and spray the countryside. I picked up my hand-held Arri St and began filming the destruction. I was about to point it at what was left of the New Guy but stopped. Instead, I watched through my viewfinder as a small fire in the left inboard engine suddenly flared up and spread outward to number one. The prop on number two was feathered and started slowing down. The prop on number one soon did the same. Shutting down the engines put out the fire completely in number one, but number two kept flaring up. Only three and four were keeping us airborne.

When I fully realized what I had seen, I dropped the camera to my side and started working my way back to the ramp, where I had stowed my parachute, panicking that in darkness and confusion I wouldn't be able to find it. The Law of Reciprocity might have broken down for f-stops and photography over the Ho Chi Minh Trail, but they were still in full force for North Vietnamese gunners—we shot and they shot back. I *really* wished I had gone to parachute school. Then again, there were so many schools I wished I had gone to. Snake School in the Philippines suddenly seemed charming. By the time I located my parachute and started clipping it on, Harley was already tightening his harness straps from his position near the Bofors, truck-killing guns that were now ballast. From the rear of the gunship the sky was still being lit up with tracers. Gradually, though, they began falling short.

The co-pilot came on the intercom. "This is the flight deck with some good news. We're on just the right heading with just enough altitude to actually make it home tonight. Cinch up your parachutes and stand by. We're going to drop most of you off when we get across the Mekong. Over."

We crossed the *Mae Nam Kong* half an hour later and most of the crew prepared to bail out as instructed. I had been "volunteered" to stick around. Giving Sachs, Baker and Rush a fist bump as they headed out the rear of the plane, I was happy to see all three chutes open, followed by seven others.

The sky was turning a pre-dawn gray at the base, where fire trucks were again covering the length of Runway 2-3 with foam. The headlights and flashers of ambulances, fire trucks, and Air Police vehicles filled the air with a pink glow. A couple of auxiliary floodlights were turned on, which, I learned later from Jamal Washington, Billy Hill had requisitioned to make it easier to photograph the pending disaster. First Lieutenant Billy Hill, Detachment 3's director of combat documentation, confided in Washington that he wanted to set the standard for the photography of nighttime crash landings. According to Washington, Hill was out there wearing full battle gear and a shit-eating grin, pacing excitedly next to the Rat Pack pickup when the AC-130 gunship came dimly into view, one of its two dead engines still trailing smoke and flame. He jumped in and revved up the engine. Washington shot a test burst on his camera, resigned once again to being part of one of Hill's moments of lunacy or inspiration, he was never sure which.

In the cockpit of the AC-130, Rookie, his co-pilot and his flight engineer laughed tensely as they fought yawing and uneven lift to get their bird lined up for final. The bill on Rookie's Spectre baseball cap was turned up, which gave him the look of a Little Leaguer hoping for a ninth-inning rally. "You wanted me, sir?" I asked as I climbed up behind them on the flight deck.

"Yes, we do, Airman. Can you get us a good shot of this landing?"

"Might be a little bumpy, but it looks like we'll have plenty of light. That's quite a welcoming party they're giving us."

The crew prepared for landing. "Give me half flaps," Rookie told his co-pilot, keeping his hand on his two good throttles.

"Half flaps."

"Good. Give me full flaps," he said, blowing a little bubble with his gum. "That's it. We're still a little hot. Let's lower the landing gear."

"Left gear is red-lighting," said the co-pilot.

"Gear up." Rooker glanced back at his master-sergeant flight engineer. "Better go have a look"

The flight engineer squeezed past me with a big flashlight and a crank. *A crank!* I thought, remembering my emergency landing in college. I heard some banging and a moment later he popped back up onto the flight deck. "I think I loosened it up, sir. You got a big hole where that twenty used to be."

"Can you handle the radio for me?" Rooker asked.

"Roger that," said the sergeant, strapping himself back in.

"Let's try the landing gear," Rooker told his co-pilot as they cleared the outer marker.

"We've got a green light."

"Let 'er down slow."

The co-pilot eased down the gear, but the yawing turned into a violent oscillation.

"Abort," said Rooker.

"Aborting," said his co-pilot, retracting the gear. The plane settled down—a little.

"Tell the tower it's going to be a belly landing."

"Roger that," said the flight engineer.

The runway lights and a mass of headlights and flashers came into view through a light morning ground fog. "That's a pretty sight," I said, thinking I saw foam being sprayed on the runway.

Rooker glanced up at me. "You ready to roll some film? Why don't you go ahead."

"We're a little low," said the co-pilot.

Rooker goosed the throttle, slowing our descent but increasing our air speed. Bracing myself as best I could against the navigation table and somehow wrapping my right foot around the seat, I rolled the camera, already knowing what the captain was going to say next.

"Gonna be a hard landing, boys. Give me flat props the second we touch down. And stand by to cut the engines." We were down to treetop level, palm trees whizzing by in a blur. "What the hell's that pickup truck doing out on the runway!"

It had Billy Hill's name written all over it, but I wasn't telling.

"Screw 'im," said the co-pilot.

"Yeah, screw 'im," said the flight engineer.

"Spectre 5-7-0," called the tower, "you're cleared to land on Runway 2-3, if the idiot in the pickup truck pulls off. If he doesn't, though—sir, you better just screw 'im."

As we bore down on the end of the runway, flying above normal approach speed with our landing gear retracted, I could see my Rat Pack colleagues doing a wild one eighty and then accelerating desperately, trying to match their speed with ours. When we hit I thought I broke my jaw at first, but a rush of adrenaline blocked the pain. Once I got my eye back into the eyepiece, sliding like a hockey puck at a hundred and fifty miles per hour turned out to be a curiously pleasant sensation. My mind went into slow motion and my workhorse Arriflex kept grinding away in real time. When we hit the runway, Hill was well ahead of us doing a very jittery eighty miles an hour while letting out a humungous rebel yell that had Washington seriously worrying about the lieutenant's present and future sanity. He hit a patch of foam and began skidding along with us. I panned over in time to see Washington stoically pointing his camera up toward our cockpit, and then, mercifully, we skidded on by. It looked like Billy was still whooping.

In the cockpit, Captain Rooker, his co-pilot, and their flight engineer began flipping switches, shutting the engines down, braced but ready to evacuate the second the big, banged-up bird came to a rest. I had on a four-hundred-foot magazine that would run for over ten minutes, so I kept it rolling. I panned over to the damaged left wing. It was bad, and for the first time I got a deep-sinking feeling how this plane should have stopped flying long before we reached the Mekong. We were slowing down, rescue equipment already circling towards us. The Maharaj Massage Parlor and the girls and officers inside were going to be safe tonight. Rooker was releasing his seat belt before we had come to a complete stop, which led me to believe that the terminal gate rule was waived on this trip. Through all the din I could hear his voice calling out, "You gettin' it, Leary, you gettin' it?"

Dailies, ComDoc-style

An hour later, even at six in the morning, the ComDoc lab/editorial trailer was humming. Billy Hill and several lab technicians crowded around the Moviola as Jack Wu started running my footage. Rookie, his co-pilot, and the flight engineer had just arrived from Spectre Operations with the welcome news that the rest of the crew had gotten down safely and were being picked up by a couple of Jolly Greens. My eyes were aching and my brain was fried, but that didn't prevent me from enjoying the crowd's *oohs* and *aahs*. It was when Wu began threading up Jamal Washington's reel that I noticed Washington and Lieutenant Liscomb hanging in the background. Jamal's footage was as steady as a human being could film while careening down a runway in the fishtailing, bouncing back end of a beat-up pickup truck. The moments just after the plane touched down were especially frightening when sparks flashed like a welder's torch through the foam. "Smooth, Jamal," I called out in the darkness.

The lights came up. "You had some great stuff yourself, Brendan," said Wu with a warm smile. I was appreciative despite my dazed state, but when he reached out to shake hands, I had to yank mine out of his reach.

"Sorry, I'm a little banged up," I said, showing him my bruised hand, which was swelling up and turning a Jackson Pollock mix of blue, green, purple and black.

Wu gave me a sympathetic look and disappeared into his darkroom. "Good shit there, Leary!" Hill gave me a bone-bruising handshake exactly where my hand was most swollen. "If that don't make a segment of *Air Force Now!* I'll eat your Arriflex."

"Ahh!" I groaned, yanking away my tender hand. "Sorry, sir, but I think I banged up most of my body when we landed. Nobody offered me a seat belt—or a seat."

"Sorry about that," said Rookie.

"Great photography," said his co-pilot.

"Enjoy your day off," said Lieutenant Hill, slapping my back precisely where it was most tender.

The harsh tropical sun was already beginning its swift ascent when

Washington and I, both bleary-eyed, walked outside together. Liscomb followed close behind. "That really was some good footage, gentlemen, shot under some trying conditions."

He had aged since I saw him last, mostly in his haunted eyes. "How are you doing, sir?"

"If you want to know the truth, I think they're breaking me. Hanging out the side door of an OV-10 wrangling a 70mm camera while we fly around unarmed at low altitude in broad daylight—*none* of that's good for my nerves."

"How about stopping by my hootch for a beer?" Washington asked.

"I really shouldn't," I replied. "We're going out to Tadtohn Falls in a couple of hours."

"Sleep in the taxicab!" he chided.

"What the hell," I said. "What about you, Lieutenant?"

"I really can't," Liscomb answered, avoiding our eyes. "If I'm going to *not* let them break me, I've got to keep my head straight. Maybe do a little meditation back at my trailer. Catch you later, guys."

Back at the old hootch, Washington flicked on the light. There was Leo Guttchock, sprawled out in his bunk, semi-conscious. A six-pack of empty beer bottles lay next to him on the floor, their labels peeled off neatly as usual. Even in the poor light shining down from the bulb overhead we could see that Leo's skin had turned green and his eyes yellow.

We started carrying him to the base hospital with his arms slung over our shoulders when I heard what I would have sworn was a jeepful of giggling angels approaching. Sagittarius Smith, the towering black NCOIC of the Airmen's and NCO Club complex, pulled up alongside us. Tiger, his blowzy, pint-sized "talent coordinator," sat like Cleopatra in the front passenger seat. The Chirping Sparrows, a melodically challenged Korean girl group that Tiger managed for Smith when she wasn't booking strippers for Officers' Club farewell parties, sat in back, unable to stop giggling. "Where you guys headed?" Smith asked magnanimously.

"Our friend needs to get to the infirmary," I said.

"Hop in," he told us. Tiger squeezed her tiny body in next to Sagittarius. Two of the Korean girls moved up front and we dragged Guttchock into the back seat. As we drove off, Leo began singing, "*A band of angels coming after me, coming for to carry me home....*"

"Looks like jaundice," said the medic who was checking him in.

"But I'm supposed to fly on Monday," Leo muttered.

"You're going to be grounded for at least a week," the medic told him.

"Spinelli and Nevers are going to have to cover for me."

"Spinelli and Nevers are dead, Leo." Washington had the same resigned look he had when he rode with Lieutenant Hill. "Leary and I will cover for you. Best I can tell, we're still alive."

Kaeng Sapue Rapids and Tadtohn Falls

I crawled out of bed shortly before noon and checked in on Tom. Lek was in the process of moving in, singing in Thai while she hung up her dresses next to Tom's uniforms on a wooden rail that ran along the back wall of his room. The shelves of the closet were already stacked neatly with towels, underwear, and a few of Lek's sarongs. Next to the closet sat a small dressing table whose top was filled with Lek's jewelry and makeup, everywhere except the back corner where a small stand held her finest wig, made of real human hair. Tom was lying on the bed, next to Lek's small open pasteboard suitcase, smoking a joint and reading *Rolling Stone* when I came in. I could usually get by on five hours' sleep, but that morning I had done a lot of tossing and turning—awakened repeatedly by the sounds of distant roosters crowing, underpowered motor scooters putt-putting past the gate, or voices echoing in the alley. It didn't help that I could never quite find a part of my body to lie on that didn't hurt.

"You look like hell," Tom said kindly.

"I feel like hell. We had a bad flight, a bad landing, and I'm banged up all over."

"You want to go check in at the dispensary?"

"And miss an afternoon off? Hell, no. Jamal and I were already there this morning helping Leo check himself in. I didn't like the looks of the place."

"Was Leo flying with you?"

"I wish. We found him passed out in his bunk. He's drunk himself into a case of jaundice and gotten himself grounded."

"Which means—"

"You guessed it. Now I get to fly missions to cover Ron Cooper *and* Leo Guttchock."

We heard footsteps coming up the plank stairs outside. Tukada entered and made a small *wai* toward Tom and me. "*Sawatdii*, Tom. *Sawatdii*, Brendan."

Lek stared at her for a moment and went back to her work. "You're still going on picnic while Dave in hospi-tal?" she hissed. Dah took a puff of Tom's reefer without answering.

"How *is* Dave?" I asked pointedly.

"I don' know," she replied. "Zey won' let me see him, but I worry about him too much."

"I'll go let Larry and Pueng know we're ready," said Tom.

"Let me grab my cameras—"

Lek rushed past me out of the room. "Where are you going?" Tom called.

"I too busy for picnic. Have to go get rest of my stuff before Mole come home and start begging me not to leave him. Bet-ter you go wit-out me." Before we could say a word, she disappeared down the steps. Tom and I looked at each other and shrugged.

Dah sat down on the floor and began pounding rock to take along. "You mind if my broz-zer come wis us?" she asked.

"I guess if Lek's not coming we can squeeze him in," I replied, feeling a tinge of irritation. It might have been my exhaustion from the night before, but I had an uncomfortable feeling that Tom would be pairing up with Dah. I continued brooding back in my room while I gathered up my cameras. I didn't like it that Lek had decided to disappear, but what was really sending my head spinning was Tukada herself. She and Tom were being powerfully pulled together by what I now knew was red-rock *heroin*. Every day I seemed to learn something new about her flaws of character. In anyone else they would have repulsed me. In *her*, my interest seemed to grow. Why was I experiencing a powerful need to help her even though I realized full well she was showing no reciprocal interest in being helped? Was I being a fool to think an addict who walked a fine line between being a masseuse and a prostitute wouldn't drag me down into the kind of moral abyss that Father Boyle had warned us about and from which there was no return? If I *really* cared about Dah, if I *really* had moral fiber, why wasn't I giving a damn about Dave, who was suffering through detox alone and who, for better or worse, was her intended?

Hanging the Pentax from my neck, slinging my gadget bag over my shoulder, and grabbing the 16mm Bolex by the handle of its leather case, I headed out to the porch, where I was mystified to see the Thai soldier from the night before climbing the last couple of stairs. "Khun Bren-dan," said Tukada, "I like you to meet my broz-zer, Sergeant Prasert."

The young sergeant had somehow known to show up out of uniform and was wearing a white polo shirt, neatly pressed brown slacks, and loafers. I was skeptical about the whole setup, but I *waied* anyway. Larry and Pueng came out hand in hand, smooching and glomming on to each other, oblivious to Thai taboos against public displays of affection. "If Lek isn't coming," I asked, "what are we going to do about our picnic? Has anyone else been to the market?"

Tukada touched my forearm. The warmth and softness of her hand startled me with a fleeting memory of Niko's.

"In Thailand, zere always plenty to eat. We can buy food when we get to riv-er."

Prasert and Dah walked ahead of us down the alley and began bargaining with several cab drivers. Tom and I lingered behind, letting Larry and Pueng slip past. "Isn't Prasert one of the Thai soldiers who hangs out at Mama-sahn's café?" I asked Tom quietly.

"Yeah, I think so."

"You think he's really her brother?"

"Dave used to wonder the same thing when Prasert showed up over at his place."

"Tom, Bren-dan, Lar-ry!" Dah called softly from one of the cabs. "He say ten dollar to Tadtohn Fall—both way."

We squeezed ourselves into the Toyota Corona. Larry sat up front with Pueng in his lap. Prasert and I climbed in behind the driver while Tom and Tukada slid into the back seat from the other side. We headed downtown, away from the base on what the GIs called "Route 66," crossed the bridge into Warin and turned left, heading east along the south side of the River Mun in the general direction of Pakse, Air America's hub for southern Laos.

No sooner had we left the cramped quarters of Warin and headed for the sprawling countryside than I was smitten with the beauty of rural Thailand—emerald rice fields, thick stands of palm trees and bamboo, the serenity of the River Mun where fishermen threw out their nets from dugout canoes with effortless agility. Tom and Tukada didn't notice. They could barely wait to open up one of the packets of crimson powder they had made up back in Tom's room and begin snorting. They followed an unspoken ritual when they finished off the packet, carefully holding the paper wrapper with its incriminating red residue in a roach clip while they lit it, opened the window, and threw out the ashes. It made perfect sense that Tom and Dah wouldn't flout chance and leave evidence tucked in their pockets. Who knew when the brass might start doing drug busts on base the way they did stateside? And while the Thai government seemed lax, when it did make a drug arrest, it had a reputation for being brutal.

The taxi was new but the road was old. Bouncing along soon put Tom to sleep, and another couple of rattly miles down the minefield of potholes, Dah surrendered her head to his shoulder. My grogginess, strangely, kept me half-awake and got me wondering how long it would take to pay off a $2,000 car charging ten dollars per hundred-mile trip. Where did Zelinsky hear about drivers having deals worked out with concessionaires along the way? I would have asked him, but he and Pueng were having too good a time laughing it up in the front seat

Fortunately, Prasert ignored Tukada and Tom, disarming me instead with a mixture of genuine friendliness and a seriousness that I figured was a reflection of his military training. Like Larry, he was a sergeant, but he possessed more military bearing off-duty in civvies than my loosey-goosey American compadres managed to show on base dressed for business. In a country where every schoolteacher and ticket-taker wore snappy uniforms, Prasert wasn't especially unusual, but his military bearing gave him an aura of maturity well beyond his twenty years.

"What beautiful country!" I exclaimed.

"The Thai countryside is beautiful," said Prasert, "but Issan farmers very poor. Only make one or two hundred American dollar a year. Too much drought. No irrigation like around Chiang Mai and Bangkok."

Larry laughed. "Drought or no drought, this sure beats the view commuting to work on Route 66."

"Countryside around my family home in Uttaradit even better," Prasert said proudly. "Beyond the rice field are mountain filled with wild animal. You must come with me some time so I can take you hunting for boar. Do you enjoy hunting?"

"Never did much more than shoot at tin cans back in the States," I answered, "but I'd like to go with you very much. Will your sister come with us?"

Dah had wakened up. "Thai women don' hunt," she said.

Pueng found the concept uproariously funny. "Find Lao girl if you want a girl who go hunting. Thai girl are civilized."

"Which makes Laotian girls?"

"*Un*civilized," answered Pueng and Tukada, which got me hoping I didn't run into one of those uncivilized Laotian lady hunters manning a dual-mounted 12.7-mm anti-aircraft gun up near Sepone or Saravan.

About twenty miles east out of Warin Chamrap, we crossed back to the north side of the Mun River and made a right turn a few miles further that took us down a pleasant dirt road to the Kaeng Sapue Rapids, our lunch stop on the way to the Tadtohn Falls. Not far from the rapids, the driver parked the cab in a shady grove. The place was crawling not only with the usual crowd of Thai visitors but also with two busloads of GIs on a Special Services sightseeing expedition.

"Thai people have expression for when we go out and walk around, have fun, eat picnic, look at other people walking around," Pueng explained as we climbed out of the cab and stretched our legs. "We call it *bai tiao sanuk*."

She and Tukada went over to a little spirit house and lit two sticks of incense before leading us to the riverbank that took us down to the rapids. Prasert hung back, but the rest of us slipped off our flip-flops and waded in. The cool water felt good on our feet as we made our way carefully from one flat-topped boulder to another. "Of course Thais also use *bai tiao* when they're actually going out on business," Larry laughed over the rushing of the water. "And businessmen say they *bai tura*—go out on business—when they're visiting their mistresses."

"*Thanks*, Lar. I'm still trying to get the tones down. Right now 'soft hands' sounds like 'young pig' and 'horse in your field' comes out like 'dog on your face.' Thai's not easy for a tone-deaf drummer."

About halfway across, we found some rocks large enough to stretch out on and sun ourselves. "Larry can *bai tiao* and *bai tura* all he want," said Pueng with a friendly smile. "It just better be with *me*." Larry's girlfriend had a good set of ears on her.

After a few minutes of sunning, I sat up and soaked my feet before splashing some cool water on my aching eyes. Refreshed, we made our way to shore and headed off to an outdoor *rahn-ahahn* where we ordered several spicy Thai dishes and some Thai iced tea to wash it down. We carried it over to a table in a quiet corner of the wooded park and settled in for lunch. Secluded by foliage, Tom and Dah did another pack of rock while the rest of us ate. I shot a few stills and then dug out my old second-hand, spring-wound Bolex. It helped that I got free 16mm film and processing from ComDoc for training purposes, which meant I could pretty well film anything I wanted. Prasert had a way of disappearing, but Tom, Dah, Larry and Pueng didn't mind mugging for me any time the lens was on them. When I was done, Dah scooped up the last crumbs from one of her packets of red rock, snorted it, and burned the paper.

"*Sawatdii.*"

We looked up and were *un*pleasantly surprised to see Jack Wu standing at the table, a Nikon camera with a huge 200-600mm zoom lens hanging from his neck. Jack came across as truly one of the nicest guys in the world, but rumor had it back in California that his job in the motion picture lab was just a front for working undercover for the Office of Special Investigations.

"Out spying for the OSI again, eh Jack?" chided Zelinsky.

"They gave me the day off," he laughed. "Actually, I'm on the Special Services tour. I just had to come over and see what you were filming with, Brendan. Don't think I've seen a non-reflex Bolex in ten years. Doesn't that side viewfinder and all the parallax correction drive you crazy?"

"Back in the States, that was the best I could do on $110 a month. If I ever become a bachelor tech sergeant like you, Jack, I'll think about an upgrade."

"How did you guys get out here?" he asked.

"We found a cab that doesn't charge *farang* prices. How much is your tour?"

"Two bucks—you can't beat it! When you're a 'bachelor tech sergeant' you don't really need a taxi." He took a glance behind him. "Looks like the bus is loading up. See you guys on Monday."

Wu was no sooner out of earshot than Pueng whined, "Lar-ry, it's too crowded here. Let's go to the falls."

"Wu gives me a case of claustrophobia all by his lonesome," Larry said to Tom and me. "He comes across as a great guy and all, but sometimes he's just *too* damn nice, if you know what I mean."

Wu's bus was still waiting for stragglers when we shot past. At Khong Chiam we doubled back across the river to the south. "Next time," said Tukada, "we stay here and go see the Two-Color River—"

"Where the blue River Mun meet with the red Mekong," added Prasert, happy to be our tour guide.

The Tadtohn Falls were quite a bit higher than the Kaeng Sapue Rapids, but the unbroken cascade of water still fell serenely. We took out some blankets and settled in to enjoy the scenery. It was cooler than at the rapids and late enough in the afternoon that the crowd had thinned out to a few couples lost in their own sweet talk.

Zelinsky took out a pack of loaded Blue Moon cigarettes and lit one up. He offered it to Prasert who politely begged off. I took a puff and had it snatched out my hand by Pueng.

"I thought Thai girls didn't smoke ganja."

"Bull shit," she replied.

Tom and Dah broke out another packet of rock. I wanted to say something, but before I could string the words together they folded up the paper and stuffed it in Tom's pocket. I heard a loud rumble behind me and turned around in time to see the two Special Services tour buses pulling in. Jack Wu climbed off, waved, and came over.

"I was *hoping* I might see you guys again!" he said with a shy exuberance. "I was going to take another one of these tours to the Surin Elephant Festival in a few weeks. But I got thinking how it might be a lot more enjoyable to get our own group together and go by train."

"Where's Surin?" I asked.

"About a hundred miles west of here, about halfway to Korat, right along the train line that runs to Bangkok."

"Hey," Tom interjected, "isn't that where the VC pulled off all those train robberies?"

"We don't have Viet Cong in Thailand," Prasert corrected him. "Viet Cong are in South Viet Nam. We have robbery, same as any other country."

"Except I don't think we've had a train robbery in the U.S. since the 1880s," said Zelinsky with a smirk.

"I'm not going to worry about train robberies on a big holiday in Surin," Wu said. "Especially if I'm traveling with a bunch of GIs."

"When exactly is the festival?" I asked.

"Not till the end of November. Loy Kratong up in Chiang Mai is more beautiful—lots of candles floating at night in banana-leaf boats—but that's four days of traveling. Surin's do-able as a day trip. I'm still trying to get the hang of this new lens, though."

"Maybe you can buy a small elephant at the festival to help you carry that thing," said Zelinsky. "You ever think about using a tripod?"

"Might have to," Wu answered, smiling modestly. "That's why I'm taking some test shots today. Mind if I take a few of you guys?"

"Thought you already had, back at the rapids," said Tom.

"Let me see how I do on some close-ups." Our hearts weren't really in it, but thanks to his power drive, it only took seconds to burn through a roll of film. He lowered the camera, letting it hang from his neck without bothering to reload. "Looks like the buses are heading back to the base," he said, giving us another shy smile. "Thanks for being my guinea pigs."

We all waved cordially, but nobody said a word until he was out of earshot. "You remember Jack back at Norton?" I asked Tom and Larry. "He was always lurking around there too. Except I don't remember the telephoto and the power drive."

Tom pondered a moment. "His records said he had been in the Army Signal Corps before he transferred over to the Air Force, but rumor had it he'd been an MP. Somebody asked him when he first came to Norton if he was some sort of OSI agent. All he did was hold up his hands and say, 'Drat, my cover is blown!'"

"Wouldn't it be a bummer," grinned Zelinsky, "if he really *is* a great guy but that he goes around busting dudes like us anyway?"

"I think he just shy," said Pueng. "Not brave with Thai and American women like you guys."

"You think he's seen you and Dah snorting rock?" I asked Tom.

"He a li-fer. He too straight to know what we doing before," Tukada said coolly.

Tom was beginning to nod off. He waved his hand, trying to hold court. "She's right. *Mai pen rai.*"

Tukada watched the tour buses driving off. "Prasert and I know better waterfall," she said. "Nobody know about except us."

We packed up and got back on the main road, heading east a few miles before turning south when we reached the Mekong River. "What's it called?" I asked.

"Huay Sai Yai Falls," answered Prasert. "It close to the border, so people afraid to go because of war in Laos. But don't worry. My unit patrol there."

Passing through the village of Ban Kaeng Tana, Pueng spotted an old woman selling pineapples. "Dessert!" she cried, stopping the cab. The woman sliced one up, put it in a couple of small plastic bags, and soon we were back on the road, bouncing along happily, picking out fresh-cut chunks of *sapparoht* with long toothpicks. When we got to our final stop of the afternoon, Dah and Prasert led us down to the bank of a stream, where we finished up the fruit and rinsed off our hands before walking a little further down the trail. The falls were small by Niagara or Victoria standards, but they were the largest we had seen all day. The action of the falling water cooled the air around it, and we again felt refreshed and at peace on what would have been a hot, muggy day back in Ubon.

We found a spot to spread our blanket and sat there quietly, enjoying the view. Tom and Tukada opened their last pack of rock, snorted it, and fell back to enjoy the rush. A moment later Dah whispered in Tom's ear, and they went off into the jungle together.

I got up to join Prasert, who was sitting nearby on the trunk of a fallen tree. "I'm worried about Tom and Dah," I said quietly.

"I'm wor-ry too, Bren-dan. Once before, at Takhli, not too long after the American build their first base there, Dah take this hero-in with her American boyfrien' and soon they cannot stop. One day she shoot with needle and almost die. She went to hospital and they make her better. But now she start again."

"Do you blame the American?" I asked.

"Lots of people to blame. The French trade heroin in Indochine since before World War I. An' before that the British bring opium from India to China and stop in Bangkok along the way. The Chinese and the Indian— who know how long they smoke opium? Now communi't propaganda say CIA bringing heroin from Prathet Lao by plane."

"I hope they're wrong, Prasert, but who knows? What I do know is that Tukada needs to stop, even if she's only snorting right now. I haven't known your sister very long, but I can't help thinking Dave is a lucky guy. I hope they can learn how to stay off drugs and have a good life together. Your sister has a beautiful style, like a village girl. Quiet and graceful. Not like a lot of Thai girls who spend time with Americans."

"Many people love Tukada," Prasert reflected sadly. "Love her in many different way. But she run free—like water in this stream."

"Maybe that's why she's so fond of waterfalls," I replied.

"The people in her village very poor. Too many drought. Too little irrigation. That why our father sell farm and join Thai Navy. She tell me she never want to go back there an' be an old woman at forty."

"Water can't flow uphill, Prasert. She can't go back now, even if she wanted to."

"I want to say something to her about this red rock, Khun Brendan, but she is so difficult. If I say too little, she pretend not to hear me. If I say too much, she will do more."

Pueng and Larry came over and sat down with us. I lit up a Blue Moon and offered it to Prasert. He again waved me off politely, instead lighting up a black-market Camel. I passed the Blue Moon to Pueng, who took a long drag.

"Now that Dave is in the hospital," I asked Prasert, "will you be able to look after her?"

"As much as she will let me."

"Will she go back to Niko's?"

"Not right away. She still get some money from her American captain. Maybe you should take her to a movie, help take her mind off Dave. She like American movie."

"I'd like that," I said, not following up on the American captain. It was not uncommon for Thai girls to get money from old boyfriends who had finished their tours. Instead, I picked up my Bolex and looked around for Tom and Dah.

"I will speak to her," Prasert said in a subdued voice. "Tom and Dave are both nice guy, but they can't help her get better."

"I don't know if I can help her either," I said. "But maybe I can at least help her get a job on the base if she quits doing rock."

"Maybe we can help her together," he replied.

"I like how you think, Prasert." I started filming a random panorama of the forest flowers. As I turned far to my left I caught Tom and Dah in the corner of my viewfinder, almost hidden among the reeds along a ledge of sandstone that lined the riverbank. I tried a traveling shot, walking toward them on my toes, Indian-style, as smoothly as I could manage. Dah was squatting at first with Tom standing behind her. I changed to a longer lens and started moving closer again, hoping to finish in a tight two-shot. It was magical, one of the movie accidents that happens once in a while when filming free-form. Just as I was settling into my final position, Tukada stood up, resting her back against Tom's chest and letting her head tilt back against his shoulder as he gently encircled her waist with his arms.

25 October 1971
"Cadillac" Gunships, Blue Movies, and a Bicycle Race

Monday morning, the same scene of Dah and Tom ran on the Moviola at the lab. "A little shaky on that zoom, Leary," taunted Zelinsky as he rewound my film. "Why don't you try using a tripod like mortal cameramen?"

"If you weren't so busy playing kissy-face with Pueng, you might have noticed I don't own a zoom *or* a tripod. I have to make do with my own two feet and the three lenses that came with the camera."

The door opened and in came Colonel Strbik and Major Horney, dressed as usual in their black, non-regulation Spectre flight suits. "Good morning, gentlemen," said Strbik enthusiastically. "Well, Sergeant Zelinsky, have you got any more of that new videotape footage transferred to film for us?"

"Yes, sir. Let me put it on for you." Zelinsky handed me the picnic footage and started threading up a large reel on the table viewer. He glanced up at Colonel Strbik, mildly embarrassed. "We've got a little problem, Colonel, now that we've got live sound recorded on this stuff—"

"What's that?"

"Well, sir, it's come down through In-tell from the Pentagon by way of the base commander that film ain't allowed to go out of here with your crews yelling 'Shit hot!' and 'That bastard's got balls—he's tearing along like a bat out of hell!' and things like that. I guess Seventh Air Force and Command Post are scared what'll happen if Congress and President Nixon hear pilots talking dirty. I've been using up so much blooping tape that Lieutenant Hill's afraid we might run out."

"I'll be sure to talk to the boys," Strbik promised.

The talk of blooping tape pricked my curiosity. "I seemed to have missed something flying with Captain Rooker Friday. What's this about sync sound?" I asked.

"We're testing out a prototype bird rigged up to record BDA footage right off the sensors. Don't worry, Leary, there are still lots of bugs to work out. Your job is secure."

I didn't quite know how to tell him I was sorry to hear that. "I'd give up the glamour of gunship cinematography in a nanosecond if I could come back here and work with a master film cutter like Zelinsky again." Everyone chuckled, thinking I was joking.

"These new AC-130 E-models have so many electronic bells and whistles on them they're calling them 'Cadillac' gunships," added Horney proudly.

Before Zelinsky could start running the transfers, Jack Wu came through the revolving door from the darkroom. "Anybody want to see the slides from Kaeng Sapue Rapids and Tadtohn Falls?"

Zelinsky had something new to worry about—protocol. "Sergeant Wu, I think our guests from Spectre might need to look at their *combat* footage first—"

"Nonsense," said Strbik magnanimously. "We've got all day. Let's take a look."

Larry shut down the table viewer and we gathered around the light box on the other bench. Wu laid out the slides and Zelinsky passed around a couple of viewing glasses.

"These are good!" said Strbik.

"Let me get the slide projector," said Shahbazian, who had been bored and come in from the repair shop next door.

"Where'd you learn to shoot like this?" I asked.

"Oh," Wu laughed, "I was a crime scene photographer for the MPs before I left the Army to join the Air Force." Zelinsky and I shot each other a quick glance.

Shahbazian set up the projector and Zelinsky pulled down the overhead screen. Wu dropped a box of slides into the stack loader and began clicking the remote, showing us postcard-quality shots of the Thai countryside and the Mun River. Suddenly Zelinsky and I about gagged. There on the big screen was a shot of Tom and Dah on the bank of a stream snorting red-rock heroin. Fortunately Wu couldn't handle the 600mm end of the telephoto zoom and the pictures were blurred.

"What the hell are *they* up to?" asked Strbik.

"Ask Zelinsky and Leary," Wu suggested innocently. "They were out there with them."

Zelinsky shrugged. "I was busy with my girlfriend. Leary was filming it."

Everyone turned to me. My mouth was so dry that my tongue stuck to the roof. "Nosebleed," I lied badly. "She was right in the middle of giving Wheeler a blow job when damn if she didn't get a nosebleed. That last slide—see he's giving her his handkerchief."

Strbik winked. "And we thought chivalry was dead."

Zelinsky, soon to be marrying Pueng, was impressed. They had never varied from the missionary position—not that he was complaining—but it had taken him most of his first one-year tour to teach her how to French kiss. "How'd that devil Tom get a Thai girl to give him blow job?"

"Might be his blond hair," I suggested.

"Maybe Pueng's saving it for your wedding night," Shahbazian added.

"*Next slide*," said Zelinsky, and I breathed a sigh of relief as we looked through the rest of Wu's pictures, agreeing it was a beautiful area out there. Strbik and Horney lamented that they'd never gotten out of Ubon except by air, mostly at night.

"There's another Special Services trip in a couple of weeks," Wu replied, "out to Big Buddha. Up north about an hour. It's supposed to be just as beautiful. Why don't we get our own group together and go out there in style?"

I shot Zelinsky a pained look. This wasn't exactly the group I wanted to be touring with. Strbik and Horney were colorful, but they were *officers* and they were past thirty. Jack Wu was a peach of a guy, but he had done nothing to dispel rumors he was working undercover for the OSI. And then I had a funny idea. Half-joking, I said, "If the countryside is as beautiful as the ride to the falls, why don't we ride our bikes out?"

"Cool," said Shahbazian.

"I'm afraid I'd have to hire a *sahmlaw* for Pueng," laughed Zelinsky.

"Isn't that road kind of bad?" Strbik asked.

"From what Special Services told me, the entire road to Mukdahan has been repaved recently. Some kind of big USAID project," said Wu.

Zelinsky was almost as out of shape as Guttchock and started to worry this might really happen. "A couple-hour bus trip—can you really ride that on a bicycle in a day?"

"It's only forty kilometers," Wu replied. "That's only about twenty-five miles each way. You guys could almost *walk* that."

"How about riding our bikes out and having a few trucks and buses there to give us a lift home?" Zelinsky asked, looking around hopefully for support.

"How 'bout if we made it a *race*?" I asked him. "Would *that* get you motivated?"

"I'd be motivated a little more if we could set up a little squadron-to-squadron wager," he replied with a smile.

"Let me take this under advisement," said Colonel Strbik. "We've got some pilots who don't *walk* further than from a jeep to an airplane or from a taxi to a bar. A long-distance bicycle ride to nowhere might be a hard sell."

Horney perked up. "But if we can get just *two* guys racing you'd get some betting action."

I turned to Sergeant Wu. "You're the one who suggested going out there on our own. Are you in, Jack?"

Wu confessed sheepishly, "I can't ride a bike. I'm a great organizer, though, and you're going to need plenty of that."

I was in favor of anything that took my mind off night missions over the Ho Chi Minh Trail. I turned to the others. "If you decide you really want to stage a race, I've got a name for you. How about the 'Big Buddha Bicycle Race?'"

"Not bad," said Wu. It didn't take long for the rest of the group to agree.

"Now that we got that settled, should we look at a little of Colonel Strbik's bomb damage assessment footage?" asked Zelinsky. "Woody, what do you say we put this on the big screen too?"

"I'd better get back to the darkroom," Wu said. The red light came on, meaning he was going to be in there awhile developing and printing the previous day's still photography.

Shahbazian brought in a projector and Zelinsky threaded it up. I was curious to see what a videotape-to-film transfer from a "Cadillac" gunship looked like. Shot in what Zelinsky called "dying black-and-white," much of it was grainy at first, just a lot of late-monsoon clouds blowing by. But when the sky cleared and the moon came out, the detail was amazing. "God *damn*," I cried. "You can practically see that driver's eyeballs! How'd you get that footage?"

"They've put a big two-inch broadcast-quality videotape recorder on board. The fire-control officer turns it on and selects which of the three sensors is giving us the best picture. The videotape goes to a new trailer they've set up strictly for making transfers to 16-mm sync-sound film. The contractors are still tweaking things like crazy, but the Pentagon wants all our turkeys converted to Cadillacs by the end of '72."

"Pretty impressive," I replied.

"Looks like you'll be seeing a lot of us over here," said Strbik. As they sauntered out, Horney added, "Don't worry, Leary. We've put in a special request for you to keep flying with us until we finish all the testing."

"Gee, thanks," I whimpered, but Strbik and Horney had already left and Wheeler and Baker were stepping in. I noticed Wheeler was carrying a small hardboard 16mm shipping case and wondered what the hell a clerk-typist and an Air Commando were doing together during work hours.

Zelinsky checked that the trailer door was locked and the red light to Wu's darkroom was still on before Wheeler handed him the shipping container and he began threading up the contents. "And *now*," he said, "one last project to look at."

"What's that?" asked Woody.

"Something that came in from the lab at Tan Son Nhut labeled 'TOP SECRET, NEED TO KNOW BASIS ONLY, attention Sergeant Link.' Airman Wheeler brought it to *my* attention and volunteered to look into it."

Wheeler stepped forward. "After checking a few leads, as you'll see, it made sense to bring in Sergeant Baker to assist me."

"*The Missing Link*?" I asked. "What kind of classified film would they be sending to our *administrative* NCO?"

"In the name of National Security we decided we'd better investigate," said Zelinsky as he finished threading up the projector, "but we suspect it might be a *blue movie*, gentlemen, produced at *taxpayers' expense*!" He started running the film, focusing as best he could. It was a grainy, bluish, black-and-white film that reminded me a little of the new gunship footage, except even on a poor-quality "dirty dupe" the undulating bodies in the blue movie transfixed us all. We were mesmerized even though the quality was so bad it was hard to distinguish who was the boy and who was the girl and if they were fully clothed, partly clothed or stark raving naked. The plot was a little iffy but might have been something about a magician's wife who got it on with a stagehand every time she got *poofed* on stage and disappeared into the wings. It was all over in ten minutes. The lights came up and Zelinsky quickly rewound the film.

"What a piece of crap," said Perez, who had heard the words "blue movie" and drifted over from the motion picture developing tank at the other end of the trailer.

"Does leave a lot to the imagination," I laughed.

"Or to wishful thinking," said Tom.

"*We* could turn out something better than that," said Shahbazian.

"You've got a motion picture lab right here that I can put at your disposal," said Perez.

"Hell, yeah," Zelinsky said as he boxed up the film and handed it back to Wheeler. "And with all these cameras and lights lying around, we could make a *Hollywood*-quality blue movie."

"Only what's the point?" I asked. "Who'd pay to see it?"

"Sergeant Baker and I can answer that one," said Wheeler. "I've been putting through a lot of calls for Link lately to Indian Joe downtown."

"The dude who owns the restaurant and the tailor shops," added Baker.

"What would he be doing with porn films?" I asked.

"Same thing he's doing with the black-market stereo equipment I've been selling him," Baker replied, "He's turning one of his warehouses into a private gentlemen's club."

"Do you think he'd buy some *classy* soft-core porn from us?" I asked. I was agreeable to another pleasant diversion from the war, but I had standards.

"I can ask tonight when I bring him a Sansui stereo and some Acoustic Research speakers."

"If it's *artistic*, I wouldn't mind getting some practice doing location lighting before I go off to film school," I volunteered.

"Hell, if it's artistic, I'll *act* in it," said Shahbazian.

"And Kristin won't mind?" Zelinsky asked.

"By the time it's been duped a hundred times like the one we just saw, my own mother wouldn't recognize me."

"I could probably get Tiger, the girl who does the Spectre floor shows, to co-star," added Harley. "She *tii-rahked* Pigpen Sachs awhile before she went free-lance."

Shahbazian spoke up hopefully, "Wouldn't we want more of a girl-next-door look?"

"For lifers?" asked Baker. "Why don't I ask Indian Joe about that too."

"*Mali* looks wholesome," said Zelinsky.

"And she's gonna stay that way. What about *Pueng*?"

"And bring her back to Dearborn to meet my family?"

"*Guys*," I piped in, "this is going to be for the private enjoyment of the patrons of Indian Joe's gentlemen's club."

"I get the feeling Indian Joe would like to go international," said Baker. "If he could utilize a couple of our C-130's to cut down on tariffs, shipping and handling—and censorship—he could get it at least as far as Hong Kong, Singapore, Manila and Sydney. That just happens to be the route Strbik and

Horney take on their 'training missions' when they do a little work on the side for the Airborne Opal Cartel."

So much for moral fiber, I thought. "We might be talking serious money," I piped in. "We could all use a little of that. I'm still making monthly payments to my lawyer. Larry's got a wedding coming up and a house to buy back in Michigan. Woody's got gambling debts and whatever he owes Kristin to pay off before he gets his Palm Springs wedding. Even Harley, with all that flight pay and combat pay, aren't you still paying alimony to your first two wives?"

"Did you have to bring *that* up?" he winced.

"And I could pay off the tab I've run up at Niko's," Perez confessed.

Zelinsky started thinking out loud. "If Joe's got overseas buyers lined up, we could charge him five thousand for a twenty-minute film and it would be a bargain. Bare-bones production costs for a 16mm flick back in the States run a thousand bucks a minute. Do you think we could get the equipment off base for a weekend?" he asked me.

"I take my drums out in a taxi whenever the band plays downtown. We could mix the film equipment in with band equipment."

"Piece of cake," said Harley.

"What time do you meet Indian Joe?" asked Zelinsky.

"Midnight, down at his warehouse. Why don't you come along?"

"If we can continue this meeting down at Ruam Chon Sawng beforehand." He gestured towards Jack Wu's darkroom door. "We've still got some serious brainstorming to do—in private. How does 8:00 PM sound?"

"Bitchin' Guys Productions rides again!" cheered Woody.

"What about the bicycle race?" I asked.

"We'll keep *Wu* busy with the bicycle race," said Zelinsky, "while Perez does the lab work on the blue movie." He paused briefly, glancing at each of the men in the room and checking the darkroom door. "While we're on the subject of Jack Wu, I have a funny feeling he *is* an OSI investigator, but that he likes us, that he showed us that out-of-focus picture of Wheeler and his friend Tukada as a warning shot across the bow. Watch your back, Tom. Who knows what he didn't show us."

"Does the OSI have jurisdiction off the base?" asked Perez.

"Who knows?" said Zelinsky. "We're in Thailand."

The trailer door started rattling and we could hear Link outside cursing,

"What the fuck is this door doing locked!"

Shahbazian motioned for Wheeler to follow him into the repair shop. Tom tucked the shipping box under his arm and skedaddled out the back door. Woody quickly pulled it shut behind him. Zelinsky unlocked the front door and was almost knocked over by Link. "Sorry," said Zelinsky, "we were just running some highly sensitive *Top* Top Secret test footage for a couple of Spectre officers."

Link was steaming. "Well I'm looking for some Top Secret footage myself that left Tan Son Nhut yesterday and hasn't shown up."

"It shipped out on a Sunday?" Zelinsky asked.

"It's *very* high priority."

"What's it about?" asked Shahbazian.

"None of your fuckin' business," Link snarled. "'Need-to-know' and all that."

Wheeler burst in the door carrying the container of film. "Sergeant Link! I've been looking all over for you. This came directly from the flight line this morning. Seemed pretty urgent."

Link snatched it away. "You guys better not be fuckin' with me. Remember I sign off on performance reports for every stinking one of you."

The red light went out and the darkroom door whooshed open. "Did I hear something about missing Top Secret footage?" asked Wu.

It was the first time I had ever seen Link look scared.

"No problem, sergeant. We just got everything straightened out. Sergeant Shahbazian," said Link with a pained smile, "could you please bring that projector over to my office when you have a moment?"

Clutching his film, Link stomped out the door, slamming it so hard it popped back open. Wu chuckled. "I'll be over at the chow hall," he announced as he coolly strolled out.

Shahbazian started packing up the projector. "Aren't we going to be stepping on Link's toes if we start making movies?"

"Link'll bail out voluntarily when he sees how bad his clip is," I replied. "If he doesn't, *Joe* will kill the deal."

"Unless Indian Joe decides he needs lots of films," said Baker.

"In which case the law of supply and demand would kick in," volunteered Shahbazian.

"And our price could go up," added Perez.

Zelinsky smiled. "The free enterprise system at its finest! See you guys at Ruam Chon Sawng."

We polished off a round of Singha beers out on the front porch at Bungalow #4 while the group trickled in. I had no trouble bringing Jamal Washington on board to help me light and operate a second camera. Perez assured us we could count on him to process the priceless footage while we distracted Jack Wu with a scouting trip to Big Buddha. We gambled that even if Jack *was* an undercover OSI investigator, he'd be too preoccupied snooping around for drug deals and black marketeering and serious crimes and misdemeanors, like the jeep that had gone missing a month earlier, to notice a little porn footage running through his lab. Zelinsky wanted to direct, arguing that his experience as an editor made him the logical choice, "the same way David Lean was an editor before he directed *Laurence of Arabia*." We stopped laughing when he offered to put up any front money that was needed.

The vibes for the Blue Movie Syndicate going into production were so good that Wheeler invited us back to his room for a celebratory smoke. We found places to flop down on his bed and on the floor, and as we passed the peace pipe, Baker and Zelinsky were in especially good spirits looking forward to their meeting with Indian Joe. "I can picture it now," said Zelinsky. "Indian Joe rolling out the red carpet. Asking if we can start tomorrow."

As we continued talking, Lek began showing an interest, and Shahbazian even volunteered to help Washington and me with the lighting as long as he was still allowed to play the lead.

"This isn't going to be a dirty dupe," Wheeler said. "If Leary does a decent job lighting, aren't you worried about being recognized by Link or someone higher up?"

Shahbazian whispered something to Lek. She tossed him a wig and a pair of sunglasses. "How about a British Invasion look?"

Zelinsky laughed, "Maybe a girl-next-door type can be bringing a rock star 'room service.'"

"I don't know what is this 'girl next door'—but I can be the girl in your movie." Lek was turning out to be a trouper. "I know *lots* about room service."

"In that case, maybe we should make her more a *spitfire* next door," said Shahbazian. "Is that going to be a problem for you, Tom?"

"I might need to be your stunt double on the close-ups. Will that be a problem for *you*?"

There was a moment of awkward silence. As the director of photography, I *was* concerned about what I was going to be asked to photograph. "If this is going to be classy, don't we need a *script*?"

"You helped Stevens edit the *sNorton Bird* back in San Bernardino, didn't you?" replied Zelinsky.

"What does that have to do with writing a porno script?"

"It means you're the only one here who has written anything since a ninth-grade book report—you're our writer, Mr. USC."

"What about Leo Guttchock? He actually graduated from film school."

"From what I hear, Leo can't stay sober long enough to tie his shoelaces."

"I'll think about it."

Zelinsky began to strut around the room like Eric Von Stroheim in imaginary jodhpurs and riding boots. "Now that you're the writer," he said, "Can you do something with the room-service idea?"

"*If* I decide to be the writer, how about something like in *Tom Jones* where they make eating fruit pornographic?"

"Only there won't be a fade out," said Zelinsky, wearing his Cheshire-cat grin.

"Lek," I asked, "can you make eating fruit sexy?"

Without losing a beat, she sliced up a mango, sumptuously licked the large pit, and then tossed it. "Whoo-ee!" shouted the Blue Movie Syndicate. She ripped off Tom's T-shirt and rubbed a piece of the sweet fruit all over his chest. "All right, Lek!" shouted the syndicate in a second burst of enthusiasm when she ran her tongue across Tom's chest before feeding him the mango slice. She slid another piece between her lips, but instead of taking a bite, she walked on her hands and knees over to Shahbazian and started rubbing it over his cheeks and neck and then, taking it in her hand, rubbing it under her blouse, closing her eyes dreamily. "Wheee-yu!" cried the syndicate as she fed that slice to Woody.

Secure now in the knowledge that all our bases were covered, we drank another round of Singhas, passed around Tom Wheeler's peace pipe and settled back, a big collective smile on our faces.

"I want thousan' dollah—up front," said Lek, breaking the momentary silence. "My father's water buffalo get hit by lightning. Very bad. Him also need gallstone operation—"

"Your father or the water buffalo?" Shahbazian asked.

"My *father*. Are you crazy? Water buffalo dead already. *Mahk mahk* bad luck."

"No problem!" replied Zelinsky, now playing a Darryl F. Zanuck executive producer. "Assuming Joe agrees to five thousand, I'll pay Lek out of my own pocket. In exchange for taking the financial risk and putting in a *lot* of time producing, directing and editing, I'll take half of the remaining proceeds. The rest of you split what's left."

"How many ways are we splitting this?" asked Perez a little skeptically.

Zelinsky's mental wheels were already spinning. "If there are six of you, with a double share for Leary as writer and DP, that makes seven shares for the crew. If Lek gets a thou and I cut my rate to nineteen hundred for seeing this through to completion, that would leave twenty-one hundred. Divided into seven shares, that comes to three hundred a share. More than most of you make in a month—for a day's work. *And* you'll get a percentage any time Joe orders additional prints."

The syndicate was buzzing happily when the door opened and Pueng barged in, dragging Zelinsky, our producer-director, out by his ear. "Ouch!" he yelled.

"You big baby!" she screamed. "Talking like *big man*. You know these walls are thin like paper. What's this about you be producer of porn movie? What about my teak furniture from Chiang Mai? You promise!"

"But this is an investment—I can make a 200% profit. I pay Lek a thousand and Indian Joe pays me *five* thousand. I'm splitting *four* thousand between me and the crew."

"You don' know Indian Joe. *He* make 200% profit, not you. Nobody but Indian Joe." She dragged him back to their room for the rest of her muffled harangue.

Zelinsky returned a few minutes later with his head drooping. "Looks like I'm going to Chiang Mai next week to buy wedding furniture. Say bye-bye to the front money."

Shahbazian remained optimistic. "Why don't you see what you and Baker can work out with Indian Joe?"

"See what he offers," I suggested. "Shoot for eight or ten thousand."

Zelinsky turned to me. "Maybe you should go. Pueng thinks I'm a pushover. Start at seven or eight. Don't go below five—and let *him* put up Lek's front money."

"The Bitchin' Guys won't get screwed by Indian Joe," promised Harley.

"Long live the Bitchin' Guys," yelled the crew as Harley and I headed out.

We arrived at Indian Joe's warehouse at the stroke of midnight and told the cab driver to pull around back where we could unload the stereo equipment in darkness. Just before we opened the trunk a dim porch light came on. Joe stepped out a door that led directly into his office, took a puff of his cigar and smiled, barely visible in the weak backlight. "What do you have for me tonight, Sergeant Baker?"

Harley carried in the Sansui receiver, still boxed, and set it in a corner of the office where a pile of other stereo equipment was stacked. I followed with the speakers. The room was barely brighter than the alley outside, lit only by a single bulb in a green metal shade that hung over the library table in the middle of the room that served for a desk. There seemed to be a lot more equipment sitting around than he would need for a gentlemen's club, but who was I to know? Joe himself was imposing, a blue-eyed Sikh who would have towered over me and Harley even without his turban. "Sit down, gentlemen."

A large wood-frame window looked out into his main warehouse, which was filled with bolts of material that supplied his custom tailor shops. Several young girls and old women toiled under flickering fluorescents at their Singer sewing machines, turning out rush-order sportswear for their GI clientele. Joe pulled out a thick roll of 500-baht notes and started counting them off for Harley. "Who is your friend?" he asked.

"This is Airman Leary, a cameraman with the 601st Photo Squadron. Reliable sources tell us you received a very poor-quality blue movie today, something not up to the high standards of your new club."

"And?"

"We can produce quality films to your specifications here in Ubon," I replied.

"And what will these films cost me?"

"We're prepared to offer you a twenty-minute film for eight thousand dollars. That's a substantial discount over production costs back in the States."

He poured us each a shot of Jack Daniels, which glowed warmly from the faint light overhead. "Drink up, gentlemen."

"Would you like to hear our story idea?" I asked before I tossed back the whiskey.

"I will definitely keep your proposal in mind. But I can only offer a thousand dollars."

Harley and I choked. "How can we pay our crew?"

"Maybe find some Thais whom you can pay Thai instead of American wages."

"But what will you do for entertainment at your smokers?" Harley asked.

Link stepped out of the shadows. "I'm afraid your 'reliable sources' only got part of the story. What kind of fool do you take me for? One look at the film from Tan Son Nhut and I went to Plan B. A quick overseas call and voila!—my reliable source for Danish porno films. The first one's shipping out tomorrow from the photo outfit at Rhein-Main, Germany. Lots of blondes to make Khun Joe's American *and* local customers happy. See you tomorrow, Leary. And Baker—I *don't* want to see you loitering around my photo squadron. Don't forget there's a goddamn war going on." He lit up a cigar and took a seat, leaning back comfortably.

Harley and I started to get up, but Indian Joe motioned for us to wait. He took a pull on his cigar and casually tapped the ash into his ashtray. Letting out a long stream of smoke, he refilled our glasses. "Drink up, my friends. Don't be discouraged. Your BX stereo equipment will always be welcome here."

Plan B, OR: Back to the Drawing Board

Heeding Link's warning, Baker left it to me to break the news to our little syndicate. I had just finished when Wu stepped into the editorial trailer. "How'd your meeting go last night?" he asked.

"What meeting?" I answered.

"Your meeting about the blue movie from Tan Son Nhut."

Perez, Shahbazian, Washington and Zelinsky glanced at each other uncomfortably. "You mean the Top Secret stuff addressed to Link?" asked Wheeler.

Wu smiled. "Just a little word to the wise—I wouldn't mess with Link if I were you. He's been planning his movie deal with Indian Joe for weeks. A month back, he asked me to partner up with him—making prints here at the lab. He doesn't want any competition."

Wheeler decided to come clean. "We might have been thinking about it, but there's no way we can match his price."

Wu's face lit up. "That's *great*, believe it or not. Because I heard some interesting news this morning. If true, this could turn out to be a very propitious time to be putting on a *bicycle race*."

We were all tired, hung over and skeptical. "How's that?" asked Zelinsky.

"Because this war has got to be about over. It's all very hush-hush, but I got word at breakfast that Nixon and Kissinger are supposed to be going to Peking in January or February."

I caught Jack's drift immediately. "And while they're wining and dining at the diplomatic level, we can be doing do our part at the *community-relations* level—putting on a bicycle race! Give our bosses here one last chance to put a feather in their caps before they have to go back to the States and sit around waiting for another war."

"The weekend before the President arrives in China!" smiled Wu.

"Our little inter-squadron wager is interesting," said Zelinsky, "but isn't there a way to make this bigger?"

Washington was loafing over in the corner. "Did I hear wager?"

"On a bicycle race out to Big Buddha," Zelinsky answered.

"An inter-squadron race between us and Spectre," Wu added. "We're taking a Special Services excursion out there in a couple weeks so we can scope out the route."

"'Cept if you open this up to the whole base and maybe charge a ten-dollar entrance fee," said Washington, "with six thousand guys on this base, plus whatever Thais from the host country want to join in—*now* you're talkin' *serious* money."

"Which is why I think you've just made yourself a full member of the Big Buddha Syndicate," I said.

"He can have my spot," said Perez as he headed back to the lab. "This is looking like a lot more than a day's work."

The door opened. "How do our dailies look today, Sergeant Zelinsky?" asked Colonel Strbik as he and Major Horney stepped inside the trailer.

"Haven't gotten them out of the lab yet, sir. But we do have something to discuss with you while we're waiting. Any interest in the little wager we talked about yesterday?"

"I was surprised," Strbik said, "but there just might be. There's buzz around Spectre that the war could start winding down in the next few months. Rumor has it that Nixon and Kissinger are going to go over Ho Chi Minh's head and start negotiating directly with Mao and Zhao Enlai. Our boys might need a little diversion to keep up unit morale if Seventh Air Force starts cutting back on our flying time."

"And they might need *a big* diversion," added Horney, "if this fucked-up war turns into a never-ending stalemate like Korea."

Personally, it was just the kind of diversion I needed—a chance to have some fun I could actually write home about while at the same time making some fast, easy money. "Sergeant Washington suggested opening it up to every unit at Ubon. Our little group can put out some feelers to get things going," I said, "but eventually we'd need to get the whole base involved. We'd need everything from porta-potties and first aid to a place for the pit crews to hang—"

"Not to mention security," Wu added helpfully.

"Sooner or later," I said, "we'd need to get the base commander on board." Strbik and Horney agreed.

"Now if the war's really winding down, that pretty much pulls the rug out from under any chance he has of making a mark for himself in combat operations, right?"

Strbik and Horney agreed again.

"Well, here's another way for Colonel Grimsley to get a spread in *Life* magazine or at least the *Pacific Stars and Stripes*—a feature about the colonel's 'New Innovation in Community Action.' Describing how lovable Americans are riding their bicycles through the Thai countryside to win Thai hearts and minds."

"We'll feel him out next time we bump into him over at the O Club," said Horney. "What do you think, Russ?"

"I think this might be doable," Strbik replied. Even in person his deep, whiskey-scarred voice sounded like it was coming over an intercom. "Maybe it's all turned out for the best, Bill, being grounded for the next two weeks."

His partner writhed. Perez brought in the transfers and handed them to Zelinsky.

"You'll be able to work full-time with Wu and Leary here cutting through any red tape that comes up."

"Did you get hurt on a mission?" asked Wu in his usual friendly manner.

"Depends on what kind of a mission you're talking about." Strbik replied cryptically.

"I'm taking medication for the goddamn *flu*," Horney insisted.

"Which is why my sidekick isn't allowed to drink or go downtown while he's rehabilitating," Strbik added drolly.

"I didn't know they had medication for the flu," said Zelinsky as he threaded up the film.

"Can we run the goddamn dailies?" grumbled Horney.

26 October 1971 (night)
Navy Exchange

The last half of October turned out to be the beginning of Spectre's serious hunting season, the monsoon rains dissolving into what the Thais called "cool season" and what a Georgian back home would have called summer. My hands quit shaking but the hairs kept standing on the back of my neck whenever we made contact. We destroyed convoy after convoy, but the North Vietnamese 559th Transportation Group wasn't cooperating with the planners at Seventh Air Force in Saigon. They kept fighting back, seeming to throw a little more triple-A at us with each succeeding week. It was the triple-A that kept my stomach tied in knots, and the knots were taking longer to come untied when we got home. Baker called the feeling in his stomach "gnarly" and claimed to like it. I wasn't sure he was telling me the truth, and I was damned certain *I* didn't enjoy feeling like my testicles were stuck in my throat every time we hit a downdraft while engaged with the NVA.

I settled into a routine, sleeping during the day and flying Spectre missions a couple nights a week under Harley's watchful eye as part of Colonel Strbik's hard crew. My off nights were spent rehearsing with the band at the chapel annex or playing downtown at the Soul Sister or on base at the NCO or Airmen's clubs. Playing soul music was needed balm for my jittery nerves and took a little of the sting out of sending monthly payments back to my L.A. lawyer for services he may or may not have rendered. Stateside, I might have sued Edward Poser, Esquire, for non-support, but this wasn't stateside. I would have rather *not* been earning flight pay and hazardous-duty pay, but at least it took care of my share of the rent at Ruam Chon Sawng and let me put a tiny bit away for film school and maybe a zoom lens and tripod for my spring-wound Bolex. Bungalow #4 had become as necessary as my music to escape the war for a few hours every day.

Even though she was back at school working under a lot of tight deadlines, Danielle was still writing a couple of times a week, still worried sick about my doing aerial photography in a combat zone. She was apologetic how the anti-war movement was petering out now that *American* ground troops were coming home and American casualties were down, which were all that Americans seemed to care about. And as much as she liked the University of Redlands, she was disgusted how college campuses, Redlands included, quickly grew apathetic once a lottery replaced the draft. I was sorry to have missed the lottery, but there was an unfathomable, cantankerous part of my psyche that would have been sorry to miss the war. I still wasn't able to tell her much in my letters other than that I wasn't able to tell her much, especially the part about thumbing our noses at the Geneva Accords by being in combat in Laos. The war over Laos hadn't cooled down one bit, but I had to keep talking in riddles about possibly doing sensitive work in places where we were or weren't that might or might not be dangerous. I think I managed to get across to her that even though our grunts were being replaced by South Vietnamese ground pounders, the US Air Force had been left out of the exchange program, flying more sorties than ever.

"I love you," she wrote. "I wish you could be here with me right now camping up in the mountains or out in the desert or taking a drive up the Pacific Coast Highway to see the redwood forests. Please don't get hurt over there."

But flying combat was taking its toll. Even if I could have written freely about what was going on over here, I would have had a hard time reciprocating her deep feelings. Instead, I often felt like I was writing to a blank piece of paper or to thin air. About the best I could usually do was to end my letters by telling her that I missed her.

That afternoon, however, thinking about how dreary my letters had gotten, I was glad to have some good news to send along for a change. "I can't go into details about it, but some reliable inside sources tell us that air operations over here might be winding down in the next six months. We're going to celebrate by putting on a fifty-mile bicycle race and *I'm* going to be one of the organizers! Hope that helps you sleep a little sounder."

That night we had a Navy exchange pilot come over from a carrier in the South China Sea to check out what it was like to use a runway that was actually attached to the ground and to see what a propeller-driven modified trash-hauler could do that they couldn't do flying a state-of-the-art, jet-powered fighter-bomber off a boat. Operation Pave Pronto, Spectre's nocturnal effort to *un*pave the Ho Chi Minh Trail, was apparently getting a lot of buzz down at Seventh Air Force and out on the carriers in the South

China Sea. Before we took off, Harley got a chance to elaborate on his theory that four engines are better than one or two when people are shooting at you, which seemed pretty convincing to our guest. The bags of popcorn Captain Rush brought along for the officers in the control booth were a little harder to explain to a fighter pilot.

About three hours into the mission we were orbiting in a thirty-degree bank, pulling G's and flying through clouds that were bouncing us around even worse than the usual mountain thermals. I was off headphones when I made my way forward to film with the NOD-cam. Nearby, I could make out Harley crouched over in the aisle, holding a penlight in his teeth, working pretty much blind while he laid out lengths of 20-mm Vulcan ammo. Connecting them together by stomping on the rounds and yanking up the links, he carefully counted out the rounds as he laid them back and forth into the ammo cans, knowing that if the can wasn't laid out properly, the gun jammed. I plugged back in to the intercom just in time to hear Strbik calling Harley over his headphone—the Vulcan had decided to jam anyway and he needed Baker to clear it. Strbik had decided to pass up a second M-61 Vulcan in order to keep my NOD-cam on board, so I stayed back, feeling responsible, not wanting to get in Harley's way while he worked on the only Vulcan we had. "Jam cleared!" he called over the intercom. He took off his headphones and hurriedly turned back to finish up with the ammo. We often worked off-headphone and rarely wore our parachute harnesses, which freed us up to get our work done quickly. It hadn't taken me many sorties to figure out that off headphones and out of our harnesses it was easier to work—but we had considerably lessened our chances of making it home if we took serious battle damage.

Voom! Voom! Triple-A caught us off guard, exploding right outside the open ports where we were working. A moment later the Navy pilot came running by, his chute in his hand, his eyes as big as saucers. Harley and I gave each other a serious look, thinking, *Shit, this is it!* In the faint glow of a red recessed work light, Baker grabbed his harness and slipped it on and started clipping on his parachute. I stashed my camera and tried to do the same, except I couldn't find the damned harness. When I finally found it and got it on, I had trouble locating my chest-pack parachute. In a flash, Harley had cinched up his harness and was following our Navy friend toward the open tail ramp. I followed behind, hoping I had the chest pack snapped on correctly, crashing hard into Harley when Pigpen Sachs swung up his tattooed biker arms and stopped us dead in our tracks. I couldn't hear a thing over the whine of the turboprops, but I could lip-read Sachs asking, "What the *hell* are you doing?"

"That Navy dude just bailed out and we're going with him," shouted Harley.

"No, you're not," Pigpen answered, turning toward the ramp. He flicked on his little penlight, and there was the Navy lieutenant JG with his trousers down to his ankles and his rear end hanging over the ramp, suffering from a serious case of diarrhea.

Back at operations, Harley and Pigpen invited me to change into civvies and do our unofficial debriefing as their guest at the NCO Club. We found a dark corner booth and had just settled in when I noticed that now my *knees* were shaking. I hoped it was from the rough ride that night and was relieved when a pretty Thai waitress brought us our three bottles of Singha. "That will be the *last* time I ever get caught without my parachute harness on," I said, forcing out something like a laugh.

"You got that right," Harley said.

"Why didn't somebody brief that Navy clown," pronounced Pigpen authoritatively, "that if you can't fly with a hangover—or a little touch of dysentery—you got no fuckin' business flying with Spectre?"

A second round showed up and Harley began pontificating. "Goddamn! We almost took a flying leap into Steel Tiger East, one of the nastiest NVA outposts in the entire theater! All because some joker who thinks you should land airplanes on floating postage stamps drank the tap water at his girlfriend's bungalow the last time he was on shore leave."

By the time I bought the third round I noticed that my knees had stopped rattling and my legs had reverted to their normal post-flight rubbery condition. I was still wired, though, so I invited Harley and Pigpen to stop by Ruam Chon Sawng for a nightcap.

Tom was sitting out on the porch in one of the throne chairs having a late-night toke when we arrived. Harley took the other throne chair and Pigpen made himself at home while I dug some cold beer out of the music room fridge. We popped open our Singhas and took a couple of sips before Harley broke the silence. "Now that's what I call a fucked-up night."

"What happened?" Tom asked.

"A friggin' Navy pilot asked to come along," replied Sachs.

"And in the middle of taking some incoming fire the fucker comes charging down from the cockpit and heads for the tail ramp—because he has the runs! Brendan and I thought we'd been hit and just about jumped out of the plane—directly into a *very* evil NVA stronghold."

"Damn!" said Tom.

"You got that right," said Harley.

"Fuckin' Navy," Sachs added.

We sat there a moment in silence. "You won't believe this," I said finally, "but I had a dream last night that was scarier than the mission."

"Bullshit," Harley responded.

"Must've been one hell of a dream," said Tom.

"The funny thing is I've had dreams about plane crashes my whole life. In the ones that started when I was a kid, they always seem to be in slow motion and I always seem to know I'll survive them. I dream I'm a passenger in the back of an old olive-drab C-47, which is strange because the interior is always a commercial passenger plane, an airliner. None of that matters, though. I know I'll be okay, because my dad's flying, and Dad has always been the perfect pilot, every landing as smooth as butter. So even though we're in a nosedive, I figure the old man will grease it in somehow. I sit there, scared shitless but staying cool.

"The dreams that really frighten me started when I was in college. Now *I'm* flying. At first it was a 707. Lately it's been a C-130, but it's always when I'm trying to land. We're supposed to be lined up on final except I'm on the wrong heading and don't see the airport. Suddenly we have some son-of-a-bitchin' loss of power and drop like a rock, and the next thing I know I'm roaring down a New York street, fifty feet off the ground, dodging high-tension wires and telephone poles and barely fitting between the high-rise buildings at a hundred and fifty miles an hour, passing over the wreckage of another recent air disaster. Other times we're out in the country somewhere, but it ends up the same—I'm stuck fifty feet above the interstate and all of a sudden we're heading straight for a bunch of mountains and I've got to fly the crazy plane through a tunnel. It's like one of those racing-car games in a penny arcade, except I'd swear it's life and death—I mean this is *real* and we're gonna eat it and somehow I keep faking my way through."

"You sure this isn't some Oedipus thing?" asked Tom. "Maybe you *want* your dad to crash. Maybe flying through those tunnels symbolizes—"

"You two are saving us a bundle," Harley said, pouring the rest of his Singha down his throat in a grandiose gesture. "We won't need any more booze *or* grass to put us to sleep tonight." He stretched out his legs and let his head rest against the high back of his throne chair.

"Wait a minute!" I continued. "I still haven't told you about the dream I had last night."

"I've *been* in a plane crash, asshole. If I wasted my time dreaming about them or even thinking about them, I'd be shitting in my pants before I ever got out of bed in the morning."

"Well, this one was *weird*, because it was scarier than when we're really shot at. I mean I just knew I was going to die. And this was a nice quick real-time dream, not dragged out in slow motion. Not a clue of it being just a dream. I knew we were going to die because when the plane blew, it pancaked through the air like a hockey puck. Now whether or not God wanted man to fly is debatable, but God sure as shit didn't want airplanes swirling through the sky like Frisbees. We ended up blown around backwards, and that scared me. I mean I literally put my head between my knees and started praying. And then I woke up."

"And *now* it's time to go back to sleep," Harley said as he stood to go. "Don't forget to say your prayers."

Triumph of the Will

Sergeant "Missing Link" Link announced to Lieutenant Billy Hill that Wu, Zelinsky and I were outside. We could hear him hesitate and then confide sarcastically that it was something about a bicycle race. Now I may not have been much of a military man, but I knew the Big Buddha Bicycle Race was never going to reach its fullest potential in spreading international goodwill and understanding and in making big bucks for the syndicate without going through the Chain of Command. The syndicate was going to have to get a lieutenant or two on board who could sell a few squadron commanders on it before we ever worked our way up to pitching a bicycle race to Colonel Elmer Grimsley, the base commander. A good place to start, I figured, was Lieutenant Hill, our ambitious director of combat documentation, who wouldn't be able to pass up the idea of making a live-action documentary. Wu and Zelinsky concurred, hoping that Hill would sell it for us to Captain English, our detachment commander, and we could take it from there.

Hill sounded suspicious but intrigued and told the sergeant to show us in. Zelinsky and I mustered up military bearing far beyond our ability level by self-consciously copying Wu, the career soldier, snapping off a couple of smart-looking imitation salutes as we reported in, which seemed to get Hill even a little more suspicious.

By the time we left, though, Lieutenant Hill was convinced that coverage of the race by the Rat Pack could be so thorough and inspired that he'd be a shoo-in to win the coveted Aerospace Audio-Visual Service Newsclip-of-the-Year Award and any other government kudos he would go after. He called excitedly for Lieutenant Liscomb, who looked tired and depressed when he came in, but as Hill brought him up to speed, a switch clicked and Liscomb's mood suddenly brightened. "How about getting the machine shop to build some custom camera rigs?" Liscomb asked.

Hill's eyes lit up. "We'll use helmet cameras! I could never find a fighter jock willing to wear one."

"Hell, I'll wear one, Lieutenant," my mouth blurted out before my brain had a chance to put in its fifty cents worth. "That's the least I can do for you while I'm racing."

Liscomb, the experimental filmmaker, was getting his old enthusiasm back. "If Leary's gonna wear a helmet cam, get one for me too."

"We'll make Hollywood jealous," beamed Hill. "We'll do truck mounts and bicycle mounts. Damn! I can see it now! We'll open with a helicopter shot of the start and we'll get that lunatic cameraman Sliviak over here from Danang to do some of that crazy-assed flying around upside down he loves to do!"

"Sliviak's the best," enthused Liscomb.

"Didn't his soundman do some work for you on your *Air Force Now* series?" Hill asked.

"Frank Lutz? Yeah, I used him over in Nam and I've used him back at Norton."

"Tell him I'll bring him over with Sliviak if he can smuggle in a few cases of San Miguel with his sound equipment," said Hill. "This stuff the Thai beer monopoly puts out is starting to taste like elephant piss."

"I'll get right on it," said Liscomb. "I owe him one now that the 'Surfing Southeast Asia' segment's cancelled."

"How about if we use the gun cameras on a couple of F-4s for some extra coverage?" Wu suggested.

"Except some fool might forget to unload the machine guns," warned Zelinsky, hating to break into the euphoria.

"Forget the gun cameras," whooped Hill. "We won't need 'em. Sliviak will get us plenty of aerials. We're gonna shoot the works— ten, fifteen, *twenty* cameras! It's gonna be great!"

"Can we dig a few ditches and do some of those cowboy-movie stampede shots?" Wu asked hopefully.

"You got it!" replied Hill.

"I want to *parachute* in with my new helmet cam!" shouted Liscomb.

"Moonbeam, you might have just saved your career. We'll be cutting back on your reconnaissance missions, because from now on you're our official Bicycle Race Liaison Officer. Okay men, let's get started!" yelled Hill like a quarterback going for the win against Alabama.

The three of us marched smartly back to the ComDoc editorial trailer, joined now by Lieutenant Liscomb. "Hot damn!" I said, stepping inside and clinking the door shut behind us. "With Hill, Strbik and Horney in our corner, this is going to be an easier sell to Colonel Grimsley than I ever imagined!"

Zelinsky gave us a conspiratorial half-smile. "And the nice thing is we didn't even have to confuse Billy with the tie-in to Nixon in China."

"Which is?" Liscomb asked.

"Reliable rumors have it that Nixon and Kissinger will be visiting Chairman Mao and Zhao Enlai early next year," Wu replied.

"Which has gotta mean this stinking war is finally winding down," said Liscomb. "Far out!"

"We figure if we can get some upbeat coverage of the bicycle race it'll give the brass here one last chance to get their names in the paper," I explained.

"And maybe *this* is one for Walter Cronkite!" said the good lieutenant, smiling broadly as he left. "I'll be over in my office ordering some helmet cams. Call if you need me."

"Let's get over to the Little Pentagon right now and set up a meeting with Colonel Grimsley," said Wu.

"How about a drink at the NCO Club first?" asked Zelinsky.

"Because that would leave out our partner, Airman Leary, until he earns another stripe," Wu replied.

"I guess I could take you gentlemen to the Airmen's Club. We *do* have bars in our overseas branches." I had no sooner finished speaking than I started to hear a familiar tapping sound on the trailer roof. Looking out the door, I saw that it was pouring.

"Except not today," said Zelinsky. "I joined the Air Force so I *wouldn't* have to walk around in the mud."

For the next two days we hung out at the editorial trailer, playing poker and waiting for the last of the monsoon rains to go away. With little combat footage to cut, Zelinsky and Wu went through the film cans on the storage rack and in the classified file drawers, hoping to find some more of Link's blue movies. What he found instead was a mish-mash of documentaries. Later that afternoon Lieutenant Liscomb happened to dropped back while we were running Leni Riefenstahl's *Triumph of the Will*, her little valentine to Hitler. "Damn," said Moonbeam, "that stuff makes *me* want to join the Nazi Party."

The second day we watched *Anderson Platoon*, a French-produced cinema vérité documentary that opened with a church service conducted in the field by a chaplain at a forward artillery base, explosions audible in the distance. The narrator, in a thick French accent, told us the Buddhas in the pagodas were draped in saffron for a Vietnamese holiday trying to appease the souls of the unburied dead—"wandering souls: beggars, prostitutes and soldiers."

"Sounds like us," said Wheeler, who had been bored to death in the orderly room and decided to drop by. Baker and Horney had been equally bored over at the 16th SOS and dropped in a few minutes later. For the rest of the film the French crew crawled through the jungle and sloshed through the leech-infested mud right alongside the grunts they filmed with about as much respect and admiration as Frenchmen could ever be expected to give barbarian Americans.

"Wouldn't want to be them," I said. "The film crew *or* the platoon."

"Makes you appreciate having an ugly aluminum trailer to go to on a rainy day," Zelinsky commented.

"Have to admit," said Washington, "I prefer an airplane to a foxhole, even if it does mean filming over the Ho Chi Minh Trail. Anybody happen to know how leeches do at ten thousand feet?"

Baker and Horney were our guests of honor that day. "They jump," Harley said in his raspy voice.

"And then they pull the rip cord on their little parachutes," added Horney, and we laughed our GI laughs.

Later that day Zelinsky found several captured North Vietnamese propaganda films. In one of them, singing, smiling peasant children rode their bikes to school in a formation that looked like something out of a Busby Berkeley musical. The mood was broken by the sight of B-52 contrails high above them and shots of what looked like a bombed-out Hanoi school or hospital. In another, singing, smiling peasant adults broke their backs together churning happy, bubbling klong water out of a sparkling, back-lit irrigation ditch into a nearby rice paddy where other eagerly awaiting peasants were singing and smiling as if transplanting rice shoots in 110° tropical sun were a form of going to heaven.

"Sure glad I'm not *them*," I said.

"Gives my people some bad déjà vu," said Washington.

"But maybe we *should* be singing more patriotic songs around here," taunted Zelinsky.

"They don't pay me enough to listen to you sing," Wheeler replied.

Sergeant Link stepped in, immediately putting us on our best behavior.

His permanent five o'clock shadow gave him a Ten Most Wanted look that was creepy enough, but today he was flashing me a smile that would have given Machine Gun Kelly the shivers. "Leary—Captain English and Lieutenant Hill want to see you over in the orderly room."

I followed him out into the rain and mud, dreading what new misadventure might be in store for me. A new high-tech camera that could film through rainclouds didn't seem possible. Maybe they were sending me off to the one spot in all of Southeast Asia where the sun was shining. Link knocked on Captain English's door and swung it open when we heard, "Come in."

"Airman Leary reports as ordered, sir." Hill and Liscomb were standing behind English, who was seated at his desk wearing his usual sphinxlike expression. I gave them a little salute that was sadly lacking in enthusiasm.

"We've got some good news for you, Leary," said the captain, his granite face giving off the slightest trace of a smile on his tight lips and a glimmer of light in his dull, dark eyes. I gulped. Good news wasn't possible. He handed the telex message back to Liscomb, who studied it a second and then broke out laughing. "Hot damn, Leary! You're promotion to sergeant just came in!"

I was mildly stunned and relieved. "Thank you, sirs."

"You've earned it," said English. "Better late than never."

And damn if that long-overdue promotion didn't get me a little choked up, although I never would have admitted it. Hill had on a shit-eater so big I could see every tooth in his mouth. "Didn't we tell you flying was going to be a great opportunity? Besides, it won't hurt to have a little extra rank now that you and Liscomb are organizing that bicycle race."

Tora! Tora! Tora!
(OR: The Element of Surprise...)

Having an extra stripe didn't help me feel any better flying over the Ho Chi Minh Trail. The NVA didn't seem to be impressed. The trucks kept coming. We kept killing them by the hundreds. The NVA kept shooting back. On a clear night we could still see blurry shadows of drivers climbing out and trying to escape the carnage. Pigpen Sachs started wearing a T-shirt that read: "You can run, but you can't hide." Danielle's letters started piling up. I was having trouble writing back when I wasn't allowed to say a word about Spectre or Operation Pave Pronto. Compared to nighttime combat seventy-five hundred feet over Steel Tiger East, the usual chatter about sports and weather, college protests and college apathy, drugs and booze, getting strung out and going into rehab, getting a one-stripe promotion and even a fifty-mile bicycle race all seemed trivial.

And the trucks kept coming. Triple-A gun emplacements kept inching south, not stopping at Sepone but ever deeper into Laotian territory and ever closer to the end points of the Trail in South Vietnam and Cambodia. They weren't immobile German-style pillboxes or nuclear-age American missile silos. They were *maddeningly* mobile and always seemed to be hiding in caves or some unknown spot under the triple-canopy jungle just enough farther down the Trail that flights of F-4s could never seem to find them in the daytime when they went back to take them out for us. SAM missiles, Russia's finest, which weren't supposed to exist outside Hanoi, started turning up, following in an eerie progression after the 57-mm radar-guided guns that followed the thirty-sevens that followed the twenty-threes that slowly but surely followed the dual-mounted 12.7s down the Trail. The days of potshots from small arms fire were long over. In-tell tried to convince us otherwise, but we knew a flying telephone pole when we saw one, especially when they had pointy noses and little shark fins for tails. Apparently Command Post decided flight crews didn't have a "need-to-know" regarding what was being shot at them. The flight crews deeply appreciated the way Command Post looked after their morale.

Cooper was still stateside, Harwell and Spitzer were on TDY over at

Danang, and Spinelli and Nevers were still dead, which meant Jamal Washington and I had to fly five nights straight. I used my day off to bring every decent album I could find at the BX down to Woodstock Music for a little of what I called *spiritual* black marketeering—spreading international peace and goodwill like Satchmo Armstrong did when he toured for the State Department. While I was there, Sommit showed me an article in a Chinese-language newspaper from Bangkok. "It say the national police raid a warehouse in Mukdahan. Find much Communi't propaganda. Some show pictures of Thai bar girls dancing with American GIs, ask 'Does this bring democracy?' Others say 'No American bases in Thailand! Americans go home!' Except Thai people *like* American, say they *sanuk*, have good heart—*jai dii*—which mean they fun and spend money. Thai government blame opposition party. But much opposition is *anti*-communi't. Says government blame them anyway so they can stay in power."

"That's pretty confusing for an American," I told him.

He laughed and said, "It confusing for a Thai!"

Back at the Ghetto, I was walking my bike through the front gate when Sergeant Prasert stepped out of Mama-sahn's restaurant. "Khun Bren-dan," he called, "my sis-ter will go with you tonight, if you still want to go to movie. Get dressed and I will show you where she live."

"What about Dave?"

"He stay in detox at least two more week. I think she need to go out, stop being sad."

Expecting a bungalow in a crowded alley like Ruam Chon Sawng, I was jarred when our *sahmlaw* pulled to a stop at the gate to Tukada's residence. Even though it was on a dirt lane well off the section of Route 66 that was in reality called Chayangkul Road, the place was impressive by Thai *or* American standards, with a gently sloping roof whose wide, flared eaves shaded a long veranda. I wondered if the affluence might have originally had something to do with being located near the provincial hospital. As we pushed open the gate, I saw that the yard was overgrown with weeds but that the garden itself had once been beautifully landscaped, especially the lily pond towards the back that had a small wooden bridge running across it. When we knocked at the door a girl of about thirteen answered, asking us to come in.

After seeing the insides of nothing but overcrowded hootches and cramped bungalows for the past six months, I was amazed by the roominess and comfort at Dah's abode. The floor was tile instead of worn plank. A spacious kitchen could be seen in back of the large living room, and stairs ran down to what seemed to be a basement, the first I had seen in a country where most homes were elevated on stilts. In addition to floor pillows, there was a new rattan sofa by the door and two new rattan chairs by the window. The housegirl motioned to the chairs and asked us to have a seat. "Please," she said, disappearing for a moment to announce us to Dah. When she returned, she sat down on the floor next to a four-year-old child, who was hypnotized by the picture from a jukebox-sized, Chinese-made television that seemed to take its styling from a two-tone '57 Plymouth. "Who is the kid?" I asked.

"Tukada was married once before, to American captain who send her money."

"I remember you saying something about him out at the falls." I looked around the room again. The little girl glanced up at me, gave me an intense look of hatred, and ran off, disappearing down the stairs.

"She does not like *farang*," Prasert apologized.

"And she's half-American?"

"None of us can understand," he replied elusively.

"Is that a basement she ran off to?"

Prasert did not know the word. "A room under this room," I explained, looking towards the stairs.

"Oh, yes," said Prasert, following my gaze. "The doctor who built house made his shower room in the ground under the house instead of outside. He say it will make house cooler in hot season and—"

The little girl reappeared at the top of the stairs, spotted me, and ran back into the darkness.

"*Sawatdii, kha.*"

I turned to see Tukada greeting me with a gracious *wai* as she stepped into the room. She wore a long, traditional Thai silk skirt and white blouse, and I couldn't help wondering if it was something she wore to the Officers' Club in her days with the captain. "*Sawatdii*, Khun Dah," I answered, giving her a polite *wai* in return. "You look lovely." She gave me a half smile. "I hope Dave is feeling better."

"Me too. I worry about him too much."

"It must be tough for both of you." I didn't know what more to say. "Shall we go?" I asked.

She nodded yes.

"Khun Prasert," I asked awkwardly, "would you like to come with us?"

"Not today, Khun Brendan. I think maybe I stay here, watch television."

The Chalerm Seen Theatre was aging but still imposing, reminding me of old-time movie palaces like Grauman's Chinese back on Hollywood Boulevard. About the only difference was that, before the film began, a giant image of the King appeared on screen and the audience stood at attention for the playing of the Thai national anthem, a ritual I expected back in the States before a sporting event, not for a movie. Instead of a Thai tearjerker or a Hong Kong gravity-defying martial arts film, I was pleasantly surprised to discover that *Tora! Tora! Tora!* was playing. The buzz among the film buffs back at the base was that it was Hollywood at its best, and the film lived up to its hype. I was especially impressed how details I had seen in period documentary footage were carefully incorporated as the film cut back and forth from the Japanese to the American perspective. What I did not expect in the darkened theater was the boisterous cheer from the mostly Thai audience when the Japanese finally attacked and American ships started sinking. *What's going on here?* I wondered. *How hard did our Thai friends really resist the Japanese occupation during World War II? Did they resist it at all?*

I think Tukada sensed my discomfort at the anti-American vibes and put her hand on mine. I didn't notice at first, too deep in thought about how the subject of the Japanese occupation during World War II never seemed to have come up in the months I had been here. I wondered if the Japanese had actually occupied Thailand or merely been allowed to think they were running the show. Dah squeezed my forearm and I snapped out of my reverie. In the dim light reflecting from the screen I could see her glancing up at me with a sympathetic smile. I surprised myself by kissing her lightly and was about to kiss her again when the lights started coming up as the picture came to an end. Inching our way toward the exit, I couldn't help glancing around, wondering who among these lovely, smiling people had been rooting for the Japanese pilots as they dropped their bombs and torpedoes and strafed American aircraft trapped on the ground, unable to even reach a taxiway. Outside we were pushed along with the crowd a little further until we reached the beginning of a line of *sahmlaws*. "Can you stop by for a drink or do you need to get home?"

"I can stay out another hour."

"*Bai 'Ruam Chon Sawng' tawrai, khrab*?" I asked the first driver we came to.

He overcharged me an outrageous *farang* price, but I didn't feel like haggling. I didn't feel like hanging around a bunch of Hirohito-lovers, and I wanted to spend some time alone with Tukada, just talking. Prasert had said that I was the one GI who could straighten her out. I didn't want to get my hopes up, but everything I had seen that evening was telling me she was a divorced mom who had once married well. I had been with Tukada over three hours and saw no sign of a drug habit. If she was willing to try, to meet me halfway, maybe Prasert was right. Maybe I could save her from falling into the abyss.

The night was cool and clear. I put my arm on hers in a polite attempt to keep her warm and she slid close. I felt bad for Dave, but not bad enough to push her away. "You have a beautiful house—and a beautiful daughter. Dave never mentioned that you were married."

Dah's face grew glum. "I don' like to talk about it. Husband was good to me. But after he take me to S-tates to live with moz-zer in San Fran-cis-co, he get sent to Korea."

"San Francisco's a great town."

"I don' know—she always make me stay at house after I get big from baby. I think she ashame…."

We rode on in silence. Finally, Dah continued. "Husband still good to me, though. When I tell him I want to come back to Thailand with baby, he give me money. He still send me money every month to take care of Pranee."

Just before we reached the Ghetto, she slid back to a proper distance in the seat. I paid the driver and we started up the alley. "Do you want to marry me too?" she asked coolly.

I was caught flat-footed. "If you weren't already married—and already engaged—and if *I* didn't have a fiancée at home, it might be interesting to consider."

By the time we reached the stairs to Bungalow #4, I was beginning to have second thoughts—about whether she should be coming up with me, about what we might be getting into. I wanted to say something and at the same time I was afraid to say a word, half wanting to let the evening unfold in mystery. When I looked down, I was jolted to see that her expression had become sullen, her eyes had become dull and pitiful, the flesh on her face had turned wan. "I have to go," she pleaded. "Jus' for ten minute. I promise."

I turned and climbed the long, steep stairway, glancing back several times as Tukada walked down the deserted alley, spoke to our loitering *sahmlaw* driver, and rode off. Dreading the thought of staring at the walls of my empty room, I crossed the porch and knocked on Tom's door when I heard familiar laughter.

"Come on in," he said. He and Lek were sitting on the bed smoking his bong. I found a floor cushion and made myself comfortable, but when they passed around the water pipe, it gave me no pleasure.

"You sure she coming back?" Lek asked.

"Not anymore." I glanced at Tom's Baby Ben: it read midnight. My eyes were burning and my body felt tired. "I've gotta rack out. Wu set up a meeting with Sagittarius Smith over at the NCO Club first thing in the morning to sell him on the bicycle race. If we can get *him* on board, and maybe the community-action officer, it's going to make it a hell of a lot easier when we approach Colonel Grimsley. Believe it or not, this might even help get Liscomb released from house arrest."

"So I was gathering from Link and Hill's powwows with English. They really put it to you guys for one stinking peace march."

"Except we're not doing anything other dudes aren't volunteering for."

"You're doing stuff *lifers* volunteer for. Let me know if you want me to type up a formal proposal for Grimsley. It's the least I can do for you."

"Thanks, Tom. We might just take you up on that."

I closed the door behind me and walked over to the balcony to look one more time for Tukada before turning in. A couple of mutts were sniffing hungrily at bags of garbage strewn around the alley. Another was gnawing on a bone. I could still hear Lek's earthy voice bleeding through the thin walls. "You dudes are crazy," she teased. "What you wanna ride bicycle to Big Buddha for, huh?"

The Age of Sagittarius

Saturday morning, Larry Zelinsky, Jack Wu and I strode confidently into the office of Senior Master Sergeant Sagittarius Smith, the imposing, Roosevelt Greer-sized Non-Commissioned Officer in Charge at the NCO and Airmen's clubs. I started it off. "Looks like things have slowed down around here since they took out your slot machines, eh, Sarge? It's a shame a scandal all the way back in Washington can put a crimp on your operation here."

Sagittarius was not a man who enjoyed small talk. His dark, jaded eyes were already looking us over hard, trying to scrutinize exactly what our angle was.

"And we think it's a disgrace," I continued, "how those twerps over at the Airmen's Club got up that petition to make you get rid of the Chirping Sparrows."

"What's the Air Force come to when one- and two-stripe airmen can go over the head of a senior non-commissioned officer of your stature?" added Tech Sergeant Wu sympathetically.

Zelinsky picked up the ball. "Must be kind of lonesome down at your bungalow without an all-girl Korean rock band rooming there. How long were they there? A couple months?"

The giant sat up in his seat and lit a cigar, exhaling a long cloud of smoke. "Let's cut the shit," he boomed. "What do you want to lay on me?"

"To put it bluntly," replied Wu, "we want to lay a bicycle race on you."

"The Big Buddha Bicycle Race," I said with a smile. "In honor of Nixon's upcoming visit to China. In celebration of the war winding down."

"A final chance to put a feather in your cap before the Air Force shuts all this down and sends you to Minot, North Dakota, to entertain the missile silos," Zelinsky added with his usual Cheshire-cat grin.

We spelled out the carefully rehearsed details, with Wu leading off. "*You* handle the business end—processing entrance fees, banking money coming in from sponsors, maybe helping us pull a string here or there, and paying off the winners."

I jumped in. "We'll do the down-and-dirty leg work, going out to every unit on base to promote this and sign people up, and we'll go door to door to any business we can think of that caters to GIs. On race day we split the entrance fees and wagers—30% for you, 30% for our little syndicate. We're budgeting 10% to cover expenses like 'gifts' for Thai officials and mid-level people on base like the hospital and Air Police commanders. That still leaves 30% for win, place and show money for the bikers."

"What would make these guys want to do their wagering through us?"

I let Zelinsky handle this one. He and Washington had been doing some deep thinking about the gambling angles. "Obviously, there will be some side-betting we can't control. But we can up the ante by making it unit against unit in addition to individual prizes." He gazed outside at the large, empty lobby and smiled sagely. "You've got plenty of space to set up ticket windows now that the one-armed bandits are gone."

Sagittarius knotted his massive forehead and narrowed his weary eyes. He'd had his share of setbacks lately. The NCO Club scandals being investigated back in Washington involved some old friends from his tech-school days who had done very well in the Air Force. "You say the brass will be on board as far as tying this in to Nixon's visit to China?"

"We're getting a meeting with the base commander set up as we speak," said Wu.

Sagittarius took a long drag on his cigar and thoughtfully scratched his chin. My Rat Pack crewmates exchanged glances. "And I'm in charge of the 10% that covers 'expenses?'"

We nodded, happy to have a pro handling that part of the operation.

He stood up slowly, his big body towering above us. Breaking into a smile, he grabbed my hand in a bone-crushing handshake. "It's a deal."

A Turn for the Worse

Having Sagittarius join the Big Buddha Syndicate was a little like making sergeant—it felt great all day Saturday until the sun went down and I was once again crossing the Mekong with Spectre in a flying coffin. I was relieved at first that it was a slow night, but soon I was regretting having too much time to think. I thought about how on a Saturday night back in the States, I would have been taking Danielle out for dinner and a show. I thought about how on a Saturday night with Spectre, we *were* the show. I thought about how the show was awfully boring tonight, giving me way too much time to think about Miss Tukada Maneewatana and wonder what happened to her since I saw her last. We cruised for hours looking at miles of empty trail. About the time I finally stopped fretting about Tukada, it dawned on me that *nobody* was firing at us and I started worrying that it was some kind of a setup. When we finally found a truck and went into orbit to make the kill, I was certain it was a flak trap—a barrage of anti-aircraft waiting patiently in ambush. My stomach tied itself in knots. Nothing. Not a shot was fired at us, and I wondered if we had actually been on the Trail or had gotten lost. I did some arithmetic on the way home and figured it had cost the U.S. government over $50,000 to take out a single Russian-built truck.

I slept deeply Sunday morning at Ruam Chon Sawng, oblivious to the thin mattress on my hard bed, not waking up till noon to the sound of a mosquito whirring in my ear. Mid-afternoon, Tom Wheeler and I took a leisurely ride out to the Base Exchange and killed a few hours lusting after the latest state-of-the-art stereo gear. It was dusk when Tom and I rode our bikes up the alley to Bungalow #4. Larry Zelinsky was waiting for us at the top of the steps. "Dah's here. She's pretty bad."

When Tom and I reached the top of the stairs, we saw Prasert sitting in one of the wicker chairs, asleep, his uniform rumpled and his face gaunt. "Lek and Pueng are with her," Larry told us, leading us into Tom's room.

Dah was hanging out of the bed, going through the last throes of dry heaves when we entered. Tom and I knelt down beside her. Lek brought over a washcloth and a bowl of water. I held the bowl while Tom washed off her face, which was pale and clammy.

"I feel sick all the time, Tom," she said quietly, in a state of delirium. "If I do rock I get sick. If I don' do rock, I feel terrible."

"She don' eat for two, three day," added Pueng.

"How about drinking some tea?" I asked.

"No, I can't…." She was withdrawing into herself, defeated.

Tom lit a joint. "Try this," he told her, "It might give you an appetite, and maybe you can at least get some sleep."

She took a hit and seemed to relax a little. I gave Lek the bowl of water and pulled up the blanket, covering Dah's shoulders. Larry, Lek, Pueng and I each took a short, nervous drag on the hand-rolled cigarette. Tom took a puff and passed it back to Dah. She began to inhale, but pushed it away. "It making me sick," she whispered sadly. "Everything making me sick."

Lek handed the bowl and washcloth back to me. "Can you go get some more water?"

Tom followed me across the hall to the *hong nam* and relieved himself while I filled the bowl, dipping it into the large earthen *klong* jar. Rinsing out the washcloth, I wondered how she had gotten so bad so fast and wondered if Tom understood how quickly she had taken this nosedive. "There was *something* wrong Friday night," I said, "but Christ, I had no idea she was in this kind of shape."

"You remember when we went off together at the falls?"

"Yeah. I filmed it. Got a beautiful shot of the two of you. I'm embarrassed to admit it, but you made me a little jealous. And here I thought you said it was *Lek* who was going to do a head trip on us."

"Let me finish—that's small potatoes now. We went off down to the stream because she was sick *then*. She couldn't hold down her lunch."

"*That's* what I was jealous of? Good God. It looked romantic through a telephoto lens."

Larry quietly poked his head in. "She can sleep in my room tonight. I'm taking Pueng to a movie and I'll stay at her place."

"You're not going to see *Tora! Tora! Tora!* are you?" I asked.

"Why not? I hear it's good."

"When Dah and I saw it, at least half the audience was rooting for the Bad Guys. And the other half didn't seem to be taking sides."

"Whew! Our friends, the freedom-loving Thais?" Larry took the bowl and washcloth from me and crossed back to the bedroom.

Tom and I waited out in the hall. "Remember," Tom said, "these are backwards, rebellious *Issan* Thais. Bangkok Thais might behave a little better."

Larry stayed with Lek and Pueng while Tom and I went out to the porch. Pacing slowly, our thoughts back again on Tukada, both of us were deeply troubled. "You know," I said softly to Tom, "Dah and Prasert both told me she used to be married to an American captain. If that's on the up and up, maybe she's still a dependent. They might be able to put her through detoxification at the base hospital the same as they're doing with Dave."

"Let's go see Dave tomorrow."

Lek came out from the bedroom to talk to us. "You know what she say when she come today? She say she shoot with needle five time yesterday."

"*Jesus*," I said to no one in particular.

Tom sat down at the top of the wooden stairway and lowered his head, shaking it slowly from side to side. "You know I've been dealing grass since tenth grade. But I always swore it would be grass and only grass. I really don't know how to handle this seriously strung-out business."

"I'm a *total* baby at this," I replied, hitching myself up on the railing. "I was at a drinking school. Never got beyond curing a hangover and mopping up after guys who mixed their drinks. Pot smoking was just a rumor."

Lek sat down next to Tom and put her head on his shoulder. I was scared for a moment—and then lost—at the realization I could no longer remember what Danielle's head felt like on *my* shoulder. I smiled at how close Tom and Lek had become, until I picked up the drift of their conversation, which was growing louder. "Why she talk to you all the time, huh? Why she don' talk to Bren-dan? Why she ask for you when she come today? Why she not ask for Bren-dan—or Dave? Are you using needle like her?"

The conversation woke up Prasert, who came over and leaned wearily against the support post nearby. "Do you think you can help my sister?" he asked quietly.

The nurse pushed open the swinging doors and pointed out the direction for Tom Wheeler, Larry Zelinsky and me. "Next corridor on the left."

Dave Murray had dozed off reading a copy of *Playboy*. I did an awful imitation of a bugle playing reveille while Larry grabbed the magazine out of Dave's hand and inspected the patient's palm. "I think you got some hair growing there, buddy. No wonder you're so exhausted."

Murray sat up, drowsily rubbing his eyes. Finally recognizing his visitors, he broke into his hangdog smile. "Hey, guys. Thanks for dropping by. I never realized it, but they got some pretty good articles in that magazine. I just learned you're not supposed to wear white socks with a black suit."

"You brought a black suit to Thailand?" Zelinsky asked.

"Forget about him," said Tom. "How they been treating you, Dave?"

"Oh, not bad. I feel a lot better. Got to the point I didn't know if I was gonna make it before they brought me in…. How's Dah?"

Tom and Larry hesitated. "That's one of the things we came to talk to you about," I admitted.

"She's started on the needle," Tom continued.

The sedation slowed Dave's reaction. "What's she doin' that for. She promised—"

"Sometimes it's hard for people to keep their promises," I said, looking off a moment before asking, "Is Tukada still married to that American captain?"

"Yeah," Dave responded slowly. "She only wrote him last week to ask for a divorce."

"Then she can still come in here for treatment," Tom said.

"I guess so," Dave agreed. "But before you bring her in, be sure to see Chaplain Kirkgartner. He'll make sure they take care of her the way he did for me. Otherwise, a bunch of these doctors just hand you a bottle of Darvon and say, 'You got on it yourself, you can get off it yourself.'"

"A *chaplain*?" asked Zelinsky skeptically.

"Kirkgartner," I replied, "is the cool *young* chaplain who runs the rap sessions at the Coffee House of Free Expression. And he's the one who came up with a place for my band to rehearse when they were starting up. We still use it."

"That's the man she wants," said Dave. "Dr. Harvey's been okay now that I'm in, but she needs to see Kirkgartner first."

As we started to leave, Dave called after us. "Can I ask one of you for a little favor?" He pulled out a plastic bag filled with virgin stalks of grass from under his mattress. "It was really nice of Mole to bring this in for me, but he forgot to cut it."

"I'll take care of it for you," Tom promised, stuffing the bag into the cargo pocket on his jungle fatigues. "See ya tomorrow."

Dealing with Dah and Dave the past couple of days had been draining, but Tom and I were feeling optimistic that afternoon when we rode home from the base. We had gone with Zelinsky directly from Dave's bedside to Chaplain Kirkgartner's office. The chaplain agreed to help us cut through the red tape and do a quick intervention to get Dah into detox. Zelinsky had swung by Pueng's and was on his way over to join us. When Tom and I climbed the wooden stairs, it was reassuring to see Prasert, in a clean change of clothes, sitting in the same high-back wicker chair he had been sitting in the night before. We asked how Dah was doing. "She want to go home," he said haltingly. "She worry about baby.... I don't think she and Lek get along too good, either."

Tom could see our well-laid plans going up in smoke. "You mean she *wants* to go home or she's gone already?" he asked.

"Not yet."

"Could you go talk to her?" I asked. "The chaplain who helped Dave is coming at 6:30. Dr. Harvey, Dave's doctor, won't come, but Chaplain Kirkgartner *will*. Dave told us he's a great guy and he is. But if he's going to help her, she has to be here so he can talk to her." Prasert seemed reluctant to budge. I guessed that he didn't think she would want to get involved with a Christian minister who also happened to be an Air Force officer and might end up reporting her to the authorities. Prasert knew better than any of us how stubborn Dah could be, especially if she were fearful and it involved her daughter. "Do you think she's afraid her husband will find out?"

"I think so, Khun Bren-dan," he responded, deep in his own thoughts.

"Just tell her that Leary and I saw Dave today and we have a lot to tell her," Tom urged.

"I understand," said Prasert, getting up slowly. But before he could take a step, the door to Zelinsky's room opened and Tukada crept out gingerly, dressed to go home but still looking haggard.

"Tukada," I pleaded, "please stay. Someone is coming who can help you." She inched past me, averting her eyes, and started making her way down the steps. "It's someone *Dave* wants you to meet with."

"Sorry," she called back to us, smiling weakly, "tomorrow is Loy Kratong. I must to go see my mother in Pimai."

Tom and I glanced back at Prasert, but he just stood there. We turned and followed her down the stairs, but by the time we reached her she had already climbed into the *sahmlaw* parked in the shade of Leclerc's bungalow next door. The *sahmlaw* brushed past us, pushing us aside. We followed, calling after her one more time, but she ignored us and soon her *sahmlaw* was disappearing though the gate and out onto the street. We stood there a moment catching our breath and then returned to Prasert.

"What is Loy Kratong?" I asked.

"Holiday for the River Goddess, the goddess of life. We pay respect and ask forgiveness," he replied wistfully. "Very beautiful—everywhere in Thailand and Laos, people make little boat out of banana leaf and put a candle inside. At sunset we put the boat in the water and light the candle. You can make a wish. And you can also pray for your sin to be washed away."

"Why can't she light her candle here in Ubon?"

"I think today Tukada is sad that her father is in Wietnam wis Thai Navy. I think she is missing her mother, even though they do not get along. Also, I think she afraid she has much sin to wash away. I better go," he said, starting down the stairs. "Maybe I can get her to come back for meeting your friend."

"Where's Lek?" Tom called after him.

"She is in your room taking nap," answered Prasert before he hurried off to hail a *sahmlaw*.

"I better go tell her what we've got up our sleeve," Tom said to me warily.

Last Supper, Maybe

Dinner was tense. Zelinsky had come home with Pueng, but there was no wisecracking from him nor playful sweet talk from her. As we sat around the porch eating, Tom asked Lek why she didn't make Dah stay. Lek slammed down her plate and stormed back to Tom's room. "She say she feel *better*, goddamn! She wear me out."

We continued eating in silence, nobody very hungry even though the food was delicious. Prasert got back from Tukada's just as we were finishing and Tom, in a melancholy mood, was rolling an after-dinner joint. "Dah will come at 6:30," said Prasert, "but only if Lek is not here."

Larry and Pueng got up silently and retreated to his bedroom. Tom took a long, slow hit on his doobie. Finally, in super-slow motion, he gathered himself up and went back to talk to Lek. "She want me to do *what?*" we could hear through the thin walls. "She want me to leave my home? After I help her for two day! No way, Tom."

They came out a moment later and Lek sidled up to me. "You want me to go too, huh?"

My throat felt dry. "Just for a few minutes while we talk to Dah. You understand better than any of us how sick she is."

"Sure. I understan'—I peel your fruit, roll you joints, make dinner and sweep floor, and then you ask me to go—JUS' LIKE DAT. Sure—I go."

"She'll be here in ten minutes. No hassle, okay?" I took Lek's elbow and led her around the corner towards the *hong nam*. "You've seen how strung out she is."

"I know. But why I can't wait here?" She stood defiantly in front of Tom's bedroom door. "This is my house. I *live* here with Tom, goddamn."

I stepped out on the porch to pull myself together. I looked at Tom for help, but my friend tuned me out, talking quietly to Prasert and lighting up his umpteenth joint of the day. When I saw Tukada getting out of a *sahmlaw* down at the gate, I went back to Lek in desperation, catching her halfway back to the porch. "Please," I begged. "No hassle. Just walk out of here and don't say another word. Go see *Tora! Tora! Tora!* for chrissakes. Here's a hundred baht."

She pushed my hand away. "I do everything for you guys and I get nothing! You know when I eat? When I cook dinner for Tom, that's all. No way I'm gonna go now, just for some Suzy Wong, some whore—"

I stared into Lek's eyes. They were dull and hard, shutting me out. I took a step toward the porch. "Tom," I whispered, "could you...." He wasn't listening. Dah was climbing the stairs. I turned back to Lek, quickly running out of patience. "Lek," I pleaded, "I know this isn't fair to you. Life isn't fair to a lot of us. There wouldn't be a war going on if life was fair. But then if it weren't for the damn war, we wouldn't have gotten together, we wouldn't be here right now having this little love-in. You've got to listen to me! We're more than friends, we're practically family. And our real families can't help us here. We've all got problems, and all we've got is each other to get us through them. We've all got problems, Lek, but Dah's gonna *kick off* with her problems, she's gonna leave her baby without a mother—"

She looked at me coldly. "So?"

I slapped her across the face. Immediately, I was disgusted with both of us, but she scarcely flinched. Years of hauling buckets of well water and planting and harvesting rice had made her sinewy and tough. Slowly she turned and stared off across the alley. Tears began to well up in her eyes, but it took an inhumanly long time and they stubbornly refused to fall.

Disoriented, I muttered, "Sorry," and joined the others out on the porch. Tom was lighting Tukada's cigarette. They leaned against the railing together at the top of the steps. Prasert, her mysterious "brother," sat across from them, saying nothing.

"*Sawatdii*, Khun Dah," I said awkwardly.

"You say Lek wouldn't be here." Her face was dull, sallow, pained like a person dying of cancer.

I choked, trying to laugh. "How can I be responsible for Tom's *tii-rahk*?"

She did not answer. Instead she ran her foot under Tom's bell-bottoms and up over his calf, pulling him close to her. She looked into his eyes. Tom looked back, too high to express anything.

I went back to Lek, who was now standing against Zelinsky's door, defiantly looking over the scene on the porch. "Lek, please?"

She turned away.

"Please look at me?" I put my hand on her shoulder. "Will you *look* at me, goddamn it?"

215

"Don't touch me!" she shrieked. "Get away from me!"

I cursed to myself in resignation and turned back to the others on the porch. Dah was already heading down the alley to her waiting *sahmlaw.* For the first time, I saw Prasert take a hit from one of Tom's marijuana cigarettes. He passed it to me, but I ignored him and took the stairs two at a time racing after Tukada.

I caught up with her just before she reached the gate. "Where are you *going?*"

"I have to meet Mole over at Dave's bungalow before I take night train to Pimai."

"So he can take you across the river to Papa-sahn's and shoot up?"

"I not shoot up. Just need some red rock to take wis me."

"But this is killing you!"

"I no shoot up. And no more do red rock. Just bring a little. Just in case."

"Dah," I cried, "you've got to stay here!"

But she had already slipped through the gate. After saying a few words to her driver, she climbed into the *sahmlaw.* He pushed a few steps and then jumped on and pedaled away.

I trudged back up the alley and rejoined Tom and Prasert. This time I took a hit when Tom passed me what little was left of his freshly rolled reefer. Slowly my scowl dissolved into a bitter laugh. "I give up. I mean, Christ, here I am back there screaming at Lek and begging, 'No hassle! No hassle!' and we've gotten ourselves into a *giant* hassle we've got no damned business being in." I calmed myself, then said to Prasert, "Tell Dah that if she ever wants help, just come and ask. But until then, forget it!"

I knocked over the empty chair on my way to my room. "Tom, tell Chaplain Kirkgartner I'm really sorry. Tell him to come over to the Cub Miami and I'll buy him a Thai ice tea for his trouble. Or a Long Island fuckin' ice tea. I'm not staying around here, though."

The Accidental Tii-rahk

The Club Miami was going full blast. Harley and I were trying to push our way through the mob to an empty table, but we couldn't budge because someone with long sideburns and sunglasses wearing a bangly white Elvis suit and surrounded by giggly bar girls was coming towards us from the dance floor. "What an asshole," said Harley.

"It's Shahbazian," I replied.

"Hey, dudes!" Woody shouted, lifting his shades and giving us a big grin. "Follow me!"

We groped our way through the smoky darkness toward an empty booth, one of several that had recently disappeared from the NCO Club. Woody piled in with two girls on his lap and another sitting next to him. Harley and I squeezed in on the other side. "Where the hell'd you find *that* outfit?" Harley asked.

"A tailor shop out on Uparisawn Road. Gotta helluva deal! *And* I intend to get a lot of use out of it." He hugged his companions, who laughed and started jabbering in Thai. "See? They love it!" Woody was already high, which reminded me of the time back in San Bernardino—the night before he was supposed to run time trials in his vintage Porsche—when we sat at a stop *sign* for fifteen minutes waiting for it to turn green. It was scary to think he had nearly become an Air Force missile technician before he turned up as an apprentice camera repairman and part-time bingo-caller back at Norton. Losing to him on Talent Night at the Ubon Hotel suddenly seemed like a full lifetime ago. "The only trouble is," said Woody, trying to study the faces of his little fan club, "it's so damn dark in here that I can't tell who's actually beautiful and who's just a great makeup artist."

"In the kind of shape you're in," Harley said, "just make sure she's really a *she*. The lady-boys can be even better makeup artists."

The girls ordered overpriced drinks and showered Woody with sweet talk, but when he turned down a short-time threesome—or foursome—they went off to work on other customers. They hadn't touched their drinks. We finished up a couple of Mekong and Cokes and crossed the street to the Soul Sister. None of the brothers I hung out with were there, but when the girls started fawning over Woody, one of the guys at the bar offered to buy the Elvis suit off him on the spot. We had one drink and moved on to the Corsair Club, where we had one more. From there we took a cab to the Sampan, which had become a lifer hangout and was so totally dead that nobody even noticed Shahbazian's get-up except one old-timer who asked if he was with the Bob Hope tour. In honor of being in Lifer Land, we each had a Jack Daniels straight up and then tried to jam ourselves into the back of a two-seat *sahmlaw* for the short ride to the New Playboy. The driver didn't need his livelihood destroyed by three drunks, however, and drove off without us. So we walked.

"A little fresh air'll do us good," Woody said.

"'Cept Air Commandos don't fuckin' walk—an' you'll get those white shoes all dusty," grumbled Harley.

"Pretend we've been shot down along the Ho Chi Minh Trail and this is the only way out."

"Fuck you, Leary, or I'll start making you wear snowshoes when we fly."

It was the first time in the course of the evening that we could talk without bar music blasting in our ears. Even the visibility was better under the dim orange streetlights. "Word back at the base is that you've got a stone-fox Thai *tii-rahk*," said Woody. "What the hell are you doing out bar-hopping?"

"It's her bowling night," growled Harley.

"Sometimes stone-fox Thai girlfriends get pissed off at their American boyfriends," I said to Woody, sotto voce.

"Air Commandos never let a bar go unhopped," Harley roared as we burst through the door of the New Playboy. Even though it was the most popular club in town at the moment, it looked much the same as the others. The place was usually too dark and the music too noisy, but with the crowd beginning to thin early and the house lights coming up, its bleakness was hard to miss. All the clubs had been thrown up quick and dirty, almost the way the nomadic slash-and-burn hill tribes threw together their huts, except on a scale to handle six thousand GIs instead of a hundred villag-ers. Like all the clubs, the floor was an unplanned mixture of concrete and linoleum. The walls were a make-do pastiche of cinder block, low-grade packing-crate plywood and rattan mat. The cinder block was painted in hideous bad taste, a poor attempt at psychedelic. The roofs were a mix of corrugated steel and thatch, held up by a maze of tubular beams that hinted of belonging somewhere on an Air Force base. The front door looked like it was copied from a Playboy Club stateside, but the emergency exits and windows were chained shut. I shuddered at the thought of a fire on a busy night.

We sat down at a couple of folding chairs that looked and felt like they had been part of a saloon fight in an old John Wayne Western. The table's cover had been torn off opening night, leaving particleboard that was now full of liquor stains and cigarette burns. It was so impermanent that nobody was even wasting time with graffiti. Harley's chair rocked precariously, nearly dumping him on the filthy floor. "We had our last Spectre party here. They may never get these chairs straightened out."

We waited too long to order drinks, ordered them anyway, chugged them down and left. We asked a cab driver to take us back to the Corsair, but smoking a loaded Blue Moon along the way, we came down with a serious case of the munchies and stopped instead at Tippy's for pizza. Larry Zelinsky and Pueng were on their way out, back in wisecracking kissy-face mode. We ordered a large thin-crust cheese pizza—the only kind they had—and then waited *forever*, so desperately hungry that we began shaking the Parmesan and salt into our hands and licking it up. When the pizza finally came we inhaled it in less than a minute and hurried out to catch last call at the Corsair.

It was just before closing time when we fell into our flimsy plastic chairs. All three of us were suffering from the combined effects of too much booze and grass. "It's ridiculous," I griped, "getting myself involved in a cat-fight between a semi-retired bar girl and a strung-out masseuse."

"Didn't you say they're romantically involved with friends of yours?" Woody asked. "That might be a red flag right there."

"You're right," I conceded. "What a mess. Dave Murray has to be spoon-fed by a nurse right now, and he's gonna take Dah and a half-American daughter who hates Americans back to America."

"Yeah," said Harley cynically, "but they're gonna ride their love bus off to a commune in New Mexico where they won't need food or money. They'll live on Love."

"For about a week," I said. "At least Tom hasn't lost his mind yet, making promises to Lek he can't keep."

Woody was amused. "Ubon is something else with all this getting married and having live-in girlfriends. Over at Danang, the brass seemed to like it better if we kept our love affairs to thirty minutes or less."

"Too much time on our hands," I blurted. "You had a genuine guerilla war going on. These rear-echelon cooks and file clerks here at Ubon think they're on protracted spring break. Meanwhile, the war's winding down and these Thai chicks see that the gravy train is rolling to a halt. Get their hands on a bunch o' mama's boys who never had a shot o' leg before. Give 'em one roll in the hay and the hayseeds think they're in love...."

I had no idea how much Mekong whiskey I had consumed. It went down way too smoothly with cola or soda—or on the rocks. It had been a family disgrace that I couldn't stand Irish, Scotch, or Canadian whiskey, but now I understood why my Irish brethren would never rule the world. The Mekong lifted me out of my seat in the middle of my diatribe and carried me out to the dance floor where a girl was standing alone, attempting to make eye contact with the disc jockey up on the stage. She tolerated me while I tried to dance, unable to shift out of ultra-slow-motion. At the end of the song, she gave me a haughty look and excused herself.

Back at the table I tried to pick up where I left off. "All they really want is a shot o' leg, but they go an' get themselves tied down for life with some Thai whore. Love!"

Woody jumped in. "What about Harley and his stone fox? Harley's no cherry."

"They're the exception," I replied. "Mali went to Ubon Teachers College."

"Before she and a girlfriend did the arithmetic," laughed Harley, "and figured they could make more a night working the bars than a country schoolteacher makes in a month."

"It's all nuts," I said and started to put my head down for a nap.

Shahbazian and Baker pulled me back up. "Come on, Brendan, me lad," Woody said, "we can pick this up tomorrow night—"

"Jus' one more dance," I mumbled, feeling now like I was in the middle of my old dream, searching for a forgotten someone I had lost back in Boston, feeling strangely chilly in the tropical night. It seemed like I had to swim in order to fight my way out of my chair and over to a nearby table. An attractive young girl wearing no makeup sat there by herself.

She and I danced a couple of numbers, trying to talk, but her voice was softer than a whisper and the music still blared. I made out in the din that her name was Sii-da and that she came from Laos but that she had lived in

Nakhon Phanom before coming to Ubon Ratchathani. Yes, she seemed to say, she can come home with me. She picked up a satchel not much bigger than a purse that I suspected contained all her worldly possessions. And suddenly we snapped into real time and her voice became completely, totally audible. "Can do for *roi baht*."

The currency conversion part of my damaged brain wasn't positive, but it seemed like I was getting a 50% discount off the customary rate. When I got back to the table, it was Woody and Harley who had nodded off into a sound sleep. We stumbled outside and found a cab driver willing to drop Woody off at the main entrance to the base and swing by the compound that Harley and Mali shared with Pigpen Sachs, the crazy door-gunner, and a Peace Corps volunteer named Jim Scott, who lived in a converted rice barn in back with his Thai girlfriend, Pye. Sii-da and I were the last stop. Between my drunkenness and Sii-da's soft-spokenness, I could scarcely make out anything she said to me on the way home, until I thought I heard, "You be *tii-rahk* me?"

"Whoa!" I blurted out, gasping for air. "You stay with me tonight and then go home tomorrow. That's it. *Khaojai mai?*"

She looked up at me with an inscrutable, albeit lovely, smile that was either complete naiveté or complete stupidity—or a great imitation of both.

When I came to in the morning, just before I opened my eyes, I could hear the soothing sound of two female voices and thought for a moment I might be in heaven until I realized that instead of speaking in French or Italian—the language of angels—they were talking rapidly in Issan Thai. The body lying next to mine was naked and in my grogginess felt warm and comforting at first, as though it naturally belonged there and should be there every night. And then, in horror, I remembered the night before and how it all careened out of control. I started to remember the soft-spoken girl I had danced with at the Corsair. And I was hit with a wave of self-loathing, slowly remembering how I had gotten into a cab with her and brought her home after we dropped off Shahbazian and Baker.

I gingerly opened my eyes. The girl lying next to me had let the sheet slide down to her hips and with her breasts uncovered looked like Aphrodite in the morning light. And I was convulsed with a wave of nausea, remembering that I had made love to her. I felt disgusted and lost, never to be able to undo last night's misadventure and realizing now that she spoke softly because she could barely speak English. I realized I had forever broken the sacred vow I made to Danielle—and I couldn't remember the girl's name. "Lek, I made a terrible mistake."

"She say you make love to her very good." Lek had made herself at home on the edge of the bed and happily interpreted for her new friend. "I think she want to be your *tii-rahk*. You *should*, Bren-dan. See? She young, healthy, she have good body—beautiful breasts, flat stomach, nice legs, strong arms. Look at her face—so sweet. Listen how quiet she is—not like me. An' she say, don' worry, she cannot get pregnant."

I crawled between them out of the bed and wrapped a bath towel around my waist. "Lek, I've got a very important meeting in an hour. I'm hung over. I need a shower to snap out of it. You've gotta go. And please take your friend with you."

Lek followed me to the porch, "Sii-da mean it. She Lao—very poor. Two year ago, her village burned by Communi't. Last year they bombed by Lao Air Force. This year Communi't come again. An' this time U.S. Air Force drop many bomb. Communi't go, but no more village. Come on, Bren-dan. You nice guy, you have nice room with big bed. She don' have any place to stay."

I was unable to think clearly, proving it by forgetting my shaving kit. I ducked back into the room, picked up my shaving gear and took a good look at the lovely young Laotian war refugee sitting up in bed smiling sweetly. "Look, I don't want to throw her out on the street, but I don't have time to figure this out right now." My head was throbbing with every word I spoke. The girl just sat there, continuing to smile sweetly. "I'll tell you what—tell her she can stay here while she looks for a place of her own. But she's gotta be out by Friday."

Lek said something to my houseguest that must have seemed all right. Sii-da gave me a little *wai* and another smile. "She tell me to thank you very much."

I gathered up the shaving kit and a clean uniform and turned to leave. "Please tell her that I left an extra hundred baht for her on the table."

I was barely able to keep up with Larry Zelinsky, Lieutenant Liscomb and Major Horney as they walked briskly along the inner promenade of the Little Pentagon on our way to the base commander's office. When we entered, we were stunned by the wall-to-wall carpeting, teak veneer paneling, teeth-chattering cold air conditioning, Corinthian-leather upholstery or a damned fine imitation, and numerous pieces of Thai art and crafts. We were even more stunned by the commander's preening receptionist and his tall, elegant secretary, who both looked like they had received their training at a Bangkok modeling academy.

The carpeting in Colonel Elmer Grimsley's inner office was a full inch thicker yet than the already-plush reception area. The walls were hung with a display of Colonel Grimsley's photographs and commendations collected in three wars. One of the most prominent photographs was of the colonel, dressed for battle, climbing into the cockpit of an F-105. On his desk sat an impressive model of an F-4 Phantom. Larry and I did our best to mimic Liscomb and Horney, marching in and saluting smartly. Glancing down, I realized my boots hadn't been shined in three months. I squirmed around briefly while standing at attention, trying to figure out some way to hide my feet in the plush carpeting.

"A bicycle race, eh?"

"Yessir," I blurted. "The Big Buddha Bicycle Race. With the President's visit to China coming up, we figure the war's got to be winding down soon, and a lot of the support troops are going to be sitting around with too much time on their hands. The guys that do fly won't have their heart in it because they'll start figuring, 'Why should I be putting my butt on the line when the war's practically over?'"

Lieutenant Liscomb took over. "It will give us a chance to refocus on our primary mission, Colonel—winning hearts and minds. It'll be a *volunteer* community-action project, so the guys involved will be genuinely committed to it. And the Thais will see us doing something besides carousing with their women and flying our fighter-bombers."

Zelinsky stepped in. "We know how the Thais love making everything *sanuk*—they can have so much fun singing and dancing and joking around that even a rice harvest can be festive. What could be more *sanuk* than a few hundred GIs zooming through the countryside in a road race?"

I jumped back in. "Imagine the American ingenuity they're going to see with the way these guys customize their wheels! No one outside the base ever gets to see that—"

"Until now," said Major Horney, wanting to wrap things up.

"It might be even more *sanuk* to invite the Thai Air Force units to race too," added Liscomb. "Either way, Lieutenant Hill, the operations officer over at ComDoc, has promised one hell of an *Air Force Now!* segment with plenty of coverage—helmet cameras, jeep mounts, maybe even a para-chute-cam!"

"And," I added boldly, "Captain English, our executive officer, is from Connecticut. His family has connections with some of Walter Cronkite's people. This could easily end up getting some play on CBS World News."

"Walter Cronkite, eh?" Colonel Grimsley thought about it a moment. "And Colonel Della Rippa over at Spectre thinks a little inter-squadron rivalry will be good for morale, eh?"

"He's quite sure, sir," replied Major Horney. "These men thought, and the colonel concurs, that a celebration of international goodwill like this could be a perfect lead-in to President Nixon's visit to China."

I was elated. Grimsley seemed to be buying in. It was time for the coup de grâce. "With a little luck," I said, "Air Force One might even be persuaded to drop by for a visit on the way to Peking."

"Kissinger and Nixon in Ubon! Now *that* would be good for morale! A little far-fetched, but hell, it wouldn't hurt to extend an invitation." It took him only a moment to make up his mind. "Well then, you've got my bless-ing. Anything you need—Air Police, Dispensary, Chow Hall—tell 'em I okayed it. And I'll personally put in a call to General Gong over at Seventh Air Force to see if we can't re-route Air Force One."

"*Thank* you, sir," we answered, saluting and marching out as quickly as possible before he could change his mind.

Zelinsky and I reported back to the guys at ComDoc. Jack Wu was especially happy to hear about including the Thais. "This is getting big," he said. "And the bigger it is, the more *sanuk* it'll be. And the more *sanuk* it is, the more the fun-loving Thais we get along the sidelines and into the race, which will make it even more *sanuk*."

"Which reminds me of one of Pueng's old folk expressions," Zelinsky commented drolly. "Whenever two Thais gather together, there will be *gambling!*"

"This might get too big for Sagittarius to handle, betting-wise," said Washington.

"If it gets that big, let the side bets roll," answered Wu. "Our little syndicate will clean up on entrance fees alone—and don't forget, we'll be collecting money from our sponsors for programs and posters and maybe even some banners and billboards."

"A chance to clean up on some of the bastards who have been cleaning up on us," Zelinsky laughed.

"And if we get the *sponsors* to foot the bill for T-shirts," I added, "we can sell them for a couple bucks each of pure profit!"

When Wheeler and Zelinsky and I got home that afternoon, the Loy Kratong song was playing on several radios along the alleyway. Nearing Bungalow #4, we could hear Lek and Pueng singing along sweetly:

> Wan pen deuan sipsong,
> nam gor nong
> tem ta-king
> Rao tang lai, chai ying
> sanuk gan jing wan loy krathong!

I couldn't translate exactly but knew enough of the words to figure out that Loy Kratong fell in the twelfth month of what must have been their old lunar calendar. And like most things Thai, it was going to be *sanuk*, which for us began the moment we reached the porch. Lek and Pueng had been to the market and bought us little Loy Kratong boats made out of folded banana leaves, a tradition that went back centuries. They poured us all a Mekong and Coke and explained that we'd be going down to the River Mun after dark and launching the boats, each carrying a single candle. "It so beautiful!" they cried effusively.

"Where's Sii-da?" I asked.

"She was sleeping when we go to market," answered Pueng. "Tell us *mai sabai*—she not feel good."

I whispered to Lek, "She understands she needs to be out by Friday, right?"

"She know," Lek replied.

I opened the door to my room, expecting to see Sii-da lying there asleep, but the bed was empty. "Blen-dan!" I heard her call through my side window. I opened the shutter and looked outside, where I spotted her walking woozily down the stairs from B.J. and Leclerc's front porch and stumbling back to Bungalow #4. "B.J. and Leclerc very nice," she said. "Let me smoke ganja with them today."

When she noticed Pueng and Lek holding the banana-leaf boats, her face lit up. "We have same thing in Lao. We call Bun Awk Pansa. Do we go together to the river?"

I didn't have the heart on a day having something to do with atonement to disappoint her. "Yes, we're all going together. Let me get my camera so I can take some pictures."

While we were waiting for nightfall I took some playful snapshots of Tom and Lek and then Larry and Pueng. Sii-da sat pensively in a corner, perhaps thinking of Bun Awk Pansa back home, remembering her childhood before the war when her mountain village was still standing at the side of a winding stream. The magic-hour light was soft and she was mostly in shadow when I snapped the shutter, creating a delicate portrait of a village girl too shy to look into the lens of a camera.

When night arrived we took a taxi down Robmuang Road to the Mother River Mun for dinner at Hat Khu Duar, an outdoor restaurant made up of thirty thatch-roofed decks built on pilings out on the river. Connected to each other by narrow wooden gangways, they seemed to float tranquilly on the water like rafts. We ate together in the private dining hut furthest from shore and made our own drinks, a little too strong, from a bucket of ice and a bottle of Mekong and some smaller bottles of Coke and soda. When the time came, we floated our leaf boats peacefully down the swollen river, hundreds of candles lighting the way to Pakse and Champasak, the southernmost of the three ancient kingdoms that made up Laos. Sii-da didn't speak much, and when she did, it was mostly to Lek, but she seemed to be having a pleasant time.

As for myself, I slipped off into a dreamy mood, a little intoxicated from the Mekong whiskey, enjoying the delicate fragrance of incense in the air, barely noticing Sii-da sitting nearby while I took a few pictures that were hard to focus in the faint candlelight and that I could only hope would come out. Watching the candles floating by, I remembered the candles my fellow GIs and other peace marchers placed on the iron fence in front of the White House on a brisk November night two years earlier—the night I met Danielle. I thought of Danielle, reflecting on how she too was becoming a flickering light drifting quietly away from me. And I wondered if Tukada was with her mother and if her sins were being cleansed.

I flew the night after Loy Kratong. Lek assured me before I left that Sii-da would be out looking for a permanent *tii-rahk*. On our way to the pre-flight briefing, Harley offered me some amphetamines to "pep me up" during the operation, but I passed. Fear and adrenaline were all I needed to stay on my toes when we were airborne. Coming home drained had been enough to put me into a blissful coma, barely aware of Sii-da curled up on the other side of the bed. Waking up as usual when the afternoon sun turned the air hot and stale in my room, I was relieved to discover that Sii-da had gone out and her satchel was packed up and sitting by the door. I rode my bike down to the Noy Market for a late lunch and stopped by Woodstock Music to hang out for a while with Sommit and his younger brother, Chai. Walking my bike through the gate to Ruam Chon Sawng, I ran into Prasert. "Tukada come here to see you," he said as we walked up the alley together.

Now she comes! I lamented to myself.

Prasert lingered behind when I started climbing the wooden stairs. Tukada was sitting majestically in one of the high-back wicker throne chairs. I sat down next to her in one of the smaller rattan-framed models and asked, "How was Loy Kratong? Was your mother happy to see you?"

"Yes, it was big surprise for her. And you?"

"We went to a restaurant down by the river. It was as beautiful as Prasert said it would be."

"I sink Loy Kratong my favorite holiday. But zis year I get sick. Try to no do heroin, but I cannot help. I must do or I throw up, and my moz-zer find me—sniffing red rock wis my key—an' tell me go back to Ubon. She don' understand. I'm getting better. I don' use needle. That's getting better, but she don' know."

"I'm sorry she doesn't understand. It must be difficult for her."

Dah continued without looking into my eyes. "When I come back to Ubon yesterday afternoon, I go see Mole for more rock. And while I'm there, we have a different big surprise—Dave come home early from hos-pi-tal. I'm so hap-py, but when he see me with *Mole*, he get *mahk-mahk moho*, call me whore, tell me go home to my house, never come back, he never want to see me again. I don' understand Dave. He never jealous like this before. Mole! He is nos-sing to me. We jus' do red rock because he and Dave are roommate. That's all. But Dave is just like my mother. He don' understand either. And now he say we no get mar-ried."

"Dah, this is crazy. You've got to stop. Completely. Prasert told me about Takhli—how you almost died. Lek told me you were shooting up again last week. Why is Mole still doing red rock with you? He knows how sick you've been. You've got to stay away from him. And Dave too. I mean, I love Dave like a little brother, but if you two stay together, you'll end up strung out on drugs for the rest of your lives. Aren't you worried about your baby? What does Prasert think?"

She turned to me, looking squarely into my eyes. "Prasert say you want to help me. Prasert say you a good man. I believe him. I want you to help me too. I want that very much. I think I want you to be my best frien'. I think maybe I want you to be wis me every day, take care of me."

"Jesus, Mary—are you asking to be my *tii-rahk*?"

"Except Lek say you have *tii-rahk* already."

"Lek's wrong."

"Lek tell me you find *tii-rahk* the night I go home to Pimai."

"She's not my *tii-rahk*, she's a hill-tribe girl from Laos. She came to Thailand because her village was destroyed in the war. She has nothing now, and Lek talked me into letting her stay until she can find a place of her own."

"Maybe I should go."

"*Whoa.* Hold up. Dah, this is very confusing. You know I've got a girlfriend in the States—but I care about *you*. A lot. I want to help you get off drugs so you can take care of your baby."

"*Prohd pud chah-chah noy*—you speak too fast."

I looked at her imploringly and took her hands in mine. "Wait here while I wash up and put on a clean shirt. We'll get away from here. Away from *Lek*."

Tukada rode behind me on the back of my bicycle, her arms around my chest and her head resting on the back of my shoulder. Dusk turned into a clear, balmy night, softly lit by the crescent moon. We flowed together as we leaned into the turns. The evening breeze refreshed us as we rode through the gravelly streets to the outskirts of town.

We came to a small monastery where the monks were doing their evening chanting. "Can we stop?" Tukada asked.

She led me quietly to the back of the meditation hall and we sat cross-legged for half an hour while the monks and a few villagers completed their evening ritual. At first I was confused, wondering why I could sometimes make out Thai and other times I couldn't. "What language is that?" I whispered.

"Pa-li," she replied. "Very old. Language of ze Buddha from two zousand five hundred year ago."

Even though I couldn't understand it, I found the rhythm to be hypnotic. It wasn't quite as musical as the Gregorian chants of my youth, but the tones seemed to have been chosen carefully to produce a soothing vibration. As the liturgy came to an end, the monks and villagers kneeled and made a series of prostrations toward the golden Buddha at the front of the hall. The villagers made three more prostrations towards the senior monk. I mimicked Dah as best I could and lingered behind with her when everyone else had left. She led me to the front of the temple and made three prostrations to the Buddha. "I feel so peaceful when I hear the monk praying," she said softly. "Life here at *wat* look simple, but monk must give up so much. Prasert came to stay for one rainy season retreat, but he could not do it. So simple but so difficult."

She stooped humbly and made her way to an offering box next to a large vase filled with sand and the stubs of burned-out sticks of incense. She put some coins into the box and picked up three sticks of incense, lit them, and then blew out the flame. They were emitting a steady fragrant plume when she stuck them gently into the sand. Sitting next to me again, cross-legged, she whispered, "I want to pray just for a minute for my moz-zer and faz-zer and Prasert. Is that okay?"

"Of course," I said and sat there next to her, also cross-legged. It looked completely natural for her to sit there in silence, but my knees were already beginning to ache and my mind race and I had a taste of why Prasert found it so difficult to do this for days on end.

After a few minutes she opened her eyes. When she did three more prostrations, I copied her as best I could, backed up several steps as she did on our hands and knees and then walked humbly out, stooping respectfully in the presence of the serenely seated Buddha.

On the way back to town Dah asked if we could stop at the Ubon Hotel for cigarettes. It was only eight o'clock and the downstairs bar was nearly empty. While she visited the *hong nam*, I bought her cigarettes and ordered us a couple of Cokes, without Mekong for a change. We sat down at a quiet corner table and she took my hand in hers. "Bren-dan," she said, "I don' want to do rock anymore."

"I can't tell you how glad I am to hear that," I said, squeezing her hands and smiling, thinking how pretty she looked. I touched my glass to hers and took a sip. "Maybe we don't need booze either."

"No defilement is very good," she smiled with a trace of sadness in her eyes.

Setting down my glass, I couldn't help glancing around the room.

"You *sure* you don' have *tii-rahk* ?" Dah chided.

"Sorry. I've been jumpy ever since I started flying."

"Let's go over to Soul Sister. I want to hear you play drum."

"Is that okay after going to the monastery?"

"It's okay. I like watching you play."

"No guarantees I'll be able to sit in," I told her, "but let's see what we can do." I liked the idea of getting lost in a crowd, hidden in lots of shadow and smoke.

We could tell from the size of the group waiting outside that the Soul Sister was jumping. We glided up on my trusty bicycle, feeling like we were making an entrance at a Hollywood premier, except I wouldn't have been chaining up my limousine at a Hollywood premier. With the exception of a handful of Thai waitresses and bartenders and a couple of hipster white dudes, the place was pure soul. Jay and the Ugly Americans, the Band of Brothers' favorite competitor, was playing—in fine form as usual—the reincarnation of Sly and the Family Stone even if they came mostly from the Philippines. Dah and I fought our way through the crowd until I spotted Washington and the Giggler at a table by themselves. "How's it goin', Jamal?"

"'Zappening, Leary?" My former bunkmate said something else that I pretended I could make out in the din before he and I exchanged ritual soul handshakes and I accepted his invitation for Dah and me to sit down and join them. The Giggler giggled and went back to watching the band. I managed to get a waitress and ordered a couple of Mekong and sodas.

"I'll be right back," I told Tukada and headed over to the bandstand. After talking a moment to Marcos, the band's leader, their drummer moved over to the congas and I climbed up on the drums. We launched into a lively version of "Everyday People," a great tune to warm up on. And then, just as we had pre-arranged it, the bass player and I started up a syncopated opening riff to "Gimme Some Lovin.'" We kept the riff of bass and tom-toms going even after the rest of the band joined in until we built up to the big refrain: "Gimme gimme some lovin'..." After a few more verses, I did a kick-ass solo, Marcos sang the last verse, and we took it out with some more heavy-duty bass and drums before the whole band came crashing in for the finale. When I climbed down I was drenched with sweat, but I had been checking out Tukada throughout the performance—and she had been digging it.

She gave me a quick kiss on the cheek as I sat down. "Now *this* is a little more like it!" I laughed.

Washington high-fived me and the club was still echoing with "*Right on! Right on!*" when, from out of nowhere, I thought I heard my name being called faintly in a weak, insipid voice that sounded dimly familiar. Sii-da appeared as the smoke parted behind Washington. "Blen-dan—I look everywhere for you. Lek say you like to come here. Where you been, huh?"

I looked over to Dah, but her chair was already empty.

"Sir—like more drinks?" asked our beleaguered waitress.

"I'll just pay for these," I replied, quickly giving her a couple dollars in *baht* and glancing dishearteningly through the mob for Tukada. By the time I spotted her, she was heading out the door, an impassable mass of people separating us. I chased after her anyway, trying to squeeze through the crowd without knocking over any of the revelers or their drinks. When I finally got outside, I looked in both directions and then around the corner where I had left my bike. The streets were hauntingly deserted, as though a wizard's incantation had made Dah disappear. I was numb and, without thinking, let the music draw me back inside.

"This for me, Blen-dan?" Sii-da asked blankly, looking up from the cocktail I hadn't had time to touch.

I stared at her, wishing it was a bad dream, and pushed the glass into her hand. Sitting down in the seat Dah had abandoned, I fingered her half-empty Mekong and soda and then gulped it down. It tasted as watery as it looked. The band finished its last song of the set and Marcos announced a short break. The crowd noise turned to a soothing buzz as the musicians started to leave the stage.

Washington called me from his end of the table. "You hear what I said before about the inspection for General Gong tomorrow?"

"No," I confessed, "I was faking it."

"He wants to make sure the base is ready in case Nixon and Kissinger decide to swing by on their way to China."

I rolled my eyes. "But that's not for another couple of months! And how the hell can you have an inspection in a combat zone, for chrissakes?"

"Ours is not to reason why, my brother. Maybe we're winding down to something like those NATO bases over in Europe. Might be more of a practice inspection."

I needed a drink and almost took Sii-da's out of her hand, but I didn't quite have the heart. Instead, I ordered another round—on the rocks, without the soda—drank it down in one swallow, waited for the burning in my esophagus to turn into a soothing numbness in my brain and then looked sadly into Sii-da's tragic countenance. "What are you doing here?"

"Lek say you like to come Soul Sister. She an' I talk tonight *mahk mahk*. She still think you should let me stay with you, be your *tii-rahk*."

"I'm sorry, Sii-da, but Lek's wrong. I need you to move out tomorrow. Tonight's a good night to find a new *tii-rahk*. Many lonesome GIs at Soul Sister. *Khaojai mai*?"

She shook her head meekly, not giving me a clue whether she truly understood or was just being agreeable. My heart ached for her, but there was nothing more I could do. I got up before I felt any lousier and left. It was dark when I got to Tukada's, but I knocked anyway. Her housegirl looked exhausted when she cracked the door open. "Dah *mai yu*. She never come back tonight. Sor-ry."

I felt like crap when I got home. Unable to sleep, I wrote Danielle a letter.

The next morning every low-ranking enlisted man in the 601st was outside raking or sweeping or scrubbing or painting. Homer Harwell, NCO-in-charge of combat documentation, had gotten back from TDY at Than Son Nhut in time to supervise the operation, assigning Tom Wheeler, Larry Zelinsky and me to paint the white ComDoc admin trailer white. We did such a great job that we were rewarded with the opportunity to do the same thing with the latrine trailer, which was only the slightest bit smaller. "What the hell does General Gong care about the paint job on a trailer?" asked Wheeler, removing his field cap a moment to brush long strands of his surfer blond hair out of his eyes.

"Maybe because he doesn't have a clue what goes on *inside* a photo lab," Zelinsky answered, "but he knows his white paint." Zelinsky's uniform looked especially shabby with the harsh sun beaming down on his frayed pockets and paint-splattered boots.

"Link says we'll be painting this all over again if and when Nixon and Kissinger actually come through," Wheeler said with a sigh.

"But that's only a couple months from now!" I groaned.

"You greenhorns are starting to catch on," said Jack Wu, coming from the direction of the admin trailer, his beloved Nikon hanging comfortably around his neck. "Harwell wanted me to look in on you before I head over to the lab to see how Price and Perez are doing polishing up the developing tank. Before I forget, though—are we still taking that group trip to the elephant roundup in Surin? It's only a few weeks off."

We told him to count us in. "And don't forget Lek and Pueng," said Tom.

"Leary, what about your new girlfriend?" Zelinsky asked.

"Unless *you're* taking her—no way."

"Sorry I asked."

"I'm pretty excited," said Wu, checking over his camera and lens, "I heard that last year two of the old bulls went on a rampage and knocked down a couple of the refreshment stands. Sure would have liked to have gotten some shots of that! I'm hoping that 1000mm telephoto and the monopod I ordered from Hong Kong get here in time."

He gave our handiwork a once-over. "The trailers look good, gentlemen. And so does the bicycle race, from what Lieutenant Liscomb's been telling me."

"Our meeting with Colonel Grimsley couldn't have gone better," I said.

"He's completely on board," added Zelinsky. "Anything we want, just ask."

"As soon as we get General Gong out of here, I'll stop by the NCO Club and brief Sagittarius Smith," Wu responded happily. As he headed off, he called back to us, "The Saturday before Nixon meets Chairman Mao should be a perfect day for a bicycle race!"

Once he was around the corner, Zelinsky started laughing. "That guy should be a cruise-ship activity director."

"When he isn't spying for the OSI with that new telephoto lens," I added.

"Brendan," Wheeler asked, "what was all that jabbering about this morning between you and Sii-da?

"I was reminding her that she needs to move her butt out *today*," I answered, slapping my brush a little harder than necessary onto the side of the trailer.

"Now what?"

"Why did I allow Lek to push me so hard to let her stick around?"

"Maybe Lek's using Sii-da to keep Tukada away so she can have you all to herself when I go back to the World," said Tom, squinting his eyes in thought.

"Lek may be clever, but she's wasting her time," I replied. "Get *this*—when I was leaving for work this morning B.J. next door asks me if I knew Sii-da's been turning tricks in my bed while I've been out flying over the Ho Chi Minh Trail."

"What's wrong with that?" Zelinsky said. "At least you weren't sleeping in it."

"If I am, Larry, can I send her over to your room?"

Wheeler sounded the alarm. "Pretend you're working."

"Over here, sir," said Harwell, leading the perpetually sunburned Billy Hill around the corner of our trailer. We started slapping on paint in silence. Harwell and Lieutenant Hill gave it a quick once-over and couldn't find anything to complain about.

"Boys," the lieutenant announced proudly, "you've done so well here on the exterior of the latrine that we've got another job for you on the inside.

There's been entirely too much graffiti-writin' goin' on. So we're—I mean *you're*—gonna take down the walls on the latrine stalls."

Wheeler looked worried about losing the privacy he needed for his daytime rock tooting and pot smoking. "Lieutenant, don't you think that's a little drastic? Isn't this really just a practice inspection in case Kissinger and Nixon come in February?"

"You've got something better in mind?" asked Harwell.

"Yes, I do," Wheeler replied.

He whispered something in Hill's ear, who thought about it a moment and then replied loudly, "Okay, but if I don't like it, those walls come down."

An hour and a half later General Gong's staff car was sitting conspicuously in the middle of the Rat Pack driveway, a blue pennant with three white stars mounted on the front fender. The driver and an air policeman in dress blues were standing alongside it, and two other staff cars were parked behind it. General Gong, Captain English, First Lieutenant Hill and Second Lieutenant Liscomb came out the lab trailer, followed by an entourage of rear-echelon staff officers and ComDoc NCOs. "Very impressive, gentlemen, all that bomb damage assessment footage being processed and edited right here. Sergeant Wu, that is one of the shiniest motion picture processing tanks I've ever seen."

"Thank you, sir," said Wu, beaming a smile so ruggedly handsome and nonchalant that he looked like a Taiwanese Errol Flynn.

"And Sergeant Harwell and Sergeant Link, that silver recovery unit on the film processing tanks is ingenious."

Harwell and Link gave the general a couple of their craggy, crooked good-ole-boy smiles and said thanks.

"And they didn't even tell the general the *most* ingenious part about selling the recovered silver downtown to Indian Joe," whispered Zelinsky.

"Before I leave, could someone point me to the latrine?" asked General Gong.

"I'd be happy to, sir," said Lieutenant Hill. "The Rat Pack has even done some innovating *there* that might come in handy if the President decides to pay us a visit."

"Is that so?" Gong replied. "Colonel Watley—come with me and take notes. The rest of you men—at ease!"

Most of the general's entourage waited outside. Wheeler, Zelinsky and I managed to get a view peering in a small side window from the back of the Rat Pack pickup truck. Billy Hill proudly opened the door to the first stall. The walls were covered with Plexiglas; red china markers and clean white rags hung in front of each panel. General Gong was mildly amused until he squinted, stepped closer and saw "General Gong is a horse's ass" scrawled boldly next to the toilet bowl. "Graffiti like that *used* to be a problem, sir," explained Hill, recovering quickly. With a flourish he took the rag and wiped the wall clean.

After a moment of scrutiny, Gong smiled. "Well done, Hill. Colonel Watley, see to it that these are put in anywhere that President Nixon and Secretary Kissinger might be visiting on their way to China."

Watley duly noted the command on his clipboard. "I was tempted to steal the cleaning rags," laughed Zelinsky as we climbed down from the truck. The caravan drove away, and most of the Rat Pack went back to work. Zelinsky, Wheeler and I went into the shiny white latrine trailer to clean ourselves up. Zelinsky was drying his hands when his eyes caught Wheeler's back reflected in the mirror. Wheeler stepped away, revealing "Zelinsky did it!" on the Plexiglas door. Larry walked over to wipe off his name when he noticed someone had stolen his idea and taken the rags. "Cute," he said as we headed back to work.

I stopped by the ready room and checked the board. I wasn't scheduled to fly and headed over to editorial to hang out some more with Zelinsky while he finished up the latest *Hits of the Week*. During one long sequence, the F-4s flew through exploding cloud after cloud of smoke and flame, so close to the treetops that it seemed like they should be blowing *themselves* up with their own ordnance. The good news for cameramen was that whenever gun cameras were mounted on Wolf Pack fighter-bombers, there was no need to send a photographer along in the back seat.

I fixed myself a cup of coffee and was settling in for a pleasant discussion of our plans for the weekend when Harwell barged in, followed by Wheeler. Harwell looked serious. "Gather 'round, men."

It amazed me how many of us were tucked away in the sundry cubbyholes of a single trailer. Shahbazian came in and joined Zelinsky, along with Price, Perez, the rest of the lab guys and a couple of passers-by like me and Washington. Watching Wu coming through the revolving door of the darkroom, I speculated on what the heck he was really up to in there—prepping bomb damage assessment footage for the developing tank, processing film for the undercover OSI work that we half-believed he actually did, or putting his heart and soul into sorting slides of his latest travels?

Wheeler posted the announcement on our bulletin board while Harwell read his copy. "Boys, we're going on Red Alert. Might just be for the night, but for all you slimeballs living downtown, get yourself mentally prepared to be without your *tii-rahks* for a couple of weeks. We're all staying on base, and there *will* be bed checks. I'll have some teddy bears over at my office for any of you guys that have trouble sleeping alone."

It had been a quiet year in Ubon Province. We hadn't been on anything but an hour or two of Yellow Alerts, and they had always been called off in time for us to get downtown by nightfall, which for many of my mates on the Thai-Lao frontier was their reason for living. "It'll be nice to tip a few beers with Woody over at the patio," I said philosophically to Zelinsky. "I just wish I could be sure Sii-da has moved her butt out."

Zelinsky wasn't so philosophical. He had wedding plans to make and had finally gotten a hop on a C-47 set up to take him and Pueng over to Chiang Mai to order their teak furniture. "Excuse me, Sarge, but I thought the inspection today and the bicycle race and the President going to shake hands with his old friend Mao Tse-tung was all because the friggin' war was supposed to be winding down."

"Apparently somebody forgot to tell our local Communist insurgents," Harwell snarled.

Captain English stepped into the trailer wearing freshly starched fatigues, followed by Senior Master Sergeant Link, who scared the hell out of us with a Strategic Air Command "Ten *hut!*"

No sooner had English put us at ease than Wu raised his hand. "A buddy of mine over at In-tell told me a hard-core NVA battalion has been spotted moving west out of Attapeu. Is there any connection?"

"Sergeant Wu," replied English, "an experienced NCO like you should know better than to speculate. You know as well as I do that the only Bad Guys who have ever turned up in Ubon were rag-tag *Thai* insurgents fighting their own private war."

Zelinsky's chubby hand shot up. "Sir, these Thai insurgents you just mentioned. Any connection to the train robbers over in Surin Province?"

English smiled condescendingly. "I think you can answer that for yourself, Sergeant Zelinsky. In Surin you had a couple of criminals try to stick up the Bangkok train. Out here and up at Udorn and NKP we've had an occasional platoon of local malcontents, probably stirred up by some Pathet Lao propaganda, go on a suicide mission and get their butts kicked. How in the world could there be a connection?"

"Drat!" cried Wu. "You've just reminded me—a big elephant festival is coming up in two weeks over in Surin. A bunch of us were planning to go."

"I can't imagine we'll still be stuck here in two weeks," English replied.

"Thanks!" smiled Wu. "I've got a new lens and a monopod coming in from Hong Kong that I ordered especially for the festival."

"Mark my words," said English boldly, "the 1971 Surin Elephant Festival will go on, and you'll be there to see it!"

My Rat Pack brethren were inspired, applauding wildly before Captain English, Sergeant Harwell and First Sergeant Link turned to leave. "Carry on," growled Link.

16 November 1971
Red Alert

We were locked down on base and I didn't like it. Lying in my bunk, every sound, roaring loud or pin-drop soft seemed to keep me awake. I would no sooner get used to the rumbling of jet engines taking off or landing or, loudest of all, being tested down on the flight line than the compressors on the air conditioner and the refrigerator would start humming discordantly. And no sooner would they switch off than I would spring awake to the buzz-sawing of cicadas, the *weeeing* of a mosquito, the clucking of a little household lizard called a *jingjok*, or the clinking of an empty beer can kicked by a combat boot just outside the door. In an uncanny way I preferred the high-intensity terror I felt in the air over the jagged mountains that divided Laos from Vietnam. *That* terror I knew would end in a few hours with our AC-130 Hercules parked safely on the tarmac at Ubon Royal Thai Air Force Base and with Brendan Leary tucked snugly in his bed at Bungalow Ruam Chon Sawng. Either that or it would end in quick, sweet death. A Red Alert, though, meant being stuck here on the ground, never knowing when you might be the target of a random mortar round or an anonymous sniper's bullet. Never knowing when the local Bad Guys might launch a shoulder-mounted rocket like the one that killed Shahbazian's buddies over at Danang.

An added complication on the ground was that Tom Wheeler and I had made a pact around the time of my discharge hearing not to use a gun if we could possibly avoid it, even in self-defense—our pale, private gestures at atoning for the sins of Lieutenant Calley and his men at My Lai. The first morning after going on alert, Tom and I talked it over during breakfast and decided the time had come to take action. We quietly stopped by Captain English's office and told him we wanted to turn in our gun cards, which meant the armory would not be able to issue us an M-16 if the base were attacked. He took it coolly, almost like he had been expecting something like this. "I read your request for discharge, Leary, and your supporting letter, Wheeler. We know this isn't something spur of the moment. Your request is granted. Just stay close and report to Command Post if we're attacked. Hill and I will keep you plenty busy."

Stepping out of English's office we breathed a sigh of relief, knowing that if we had been in the Army over in Nam we'd probably be headed for Long Binh Jail. We were left with a moral conundrum we tried not to think about, however, in that *other* GIs would still be putting their lives on the line to protect *us*. I worried about the Air Policemen who were guarding the perimeter, on alert for a hard-core sapper team on a hell-be-damned suicide mission. When I thought of the cooks and clerk-typists being held in reserve who had not touched an M-16 since the day they shipped out, my head reeled. I shivered at the thought of them being sent out on night patrol, out beyond the guard towers, cloaked in darkness, probed by their own slithering shadows. I shook my head sadly, unable to imagine these ragtag amateurs inflicting more damage on their enemy, real or imagined, than they would inflict on themselves or other innocent bystanders.

"Leary, go get some chow." I snapped out of my reverie and bolted up from the ready-room bus seat into something like attention. First Lieutenant Billy Hill, the night duty officer, had a voice that sounded like the cracked reed of a beginning clarinet player. He was the product of the Reserve Officer Training Program at a small college tucked away in the back woods of western Georgia. Hill once had a silken, mellifluous voice, he claimed, until he threw it out barking commands on the drill field during his tenure as cadet commander, one of the unpublicized perils of ROTC, Zelinsky had surmised. "If you get a mind to drink dessert at the NCO Club, it's okay by me. Just make sure you don't fall off your barstool. I'll need every man I've got back here at ComDoc if there's any real action. Even with your limited soldiering abilities, Leary, I'm countin' on you to get us some pretty pictures."

Leo Guttchock, apparently cured of jaundice, was off in the corner looking surprisingly efficient pointing a tripod-mounted Arriflex at a technical-looking grid chart taped to the wall. He paused a moment from running his focus tests and looked up. "I got you covered, Brendan."

I might have been a little too eager grabbing my cap and bolting for the door. "Make sure you get your ass back here pronto if they sound the alarm," called Hill.

The words felt like melted ice dripping down my back. "I've been thinking, Lieutenant—what happens if these sappers turn out to be from that large unit of hard-core North Vietnamese regulars that Sergeant Wu was talking about and they break through and start really tearing this place up? Even if some of our planes got off the ground, wouldn't they be useless if the base were overrun, with GIs and VC going hand to hand, fighting door-to-door?"

"That's why cameramen take pictures, Leary, and officers do the thinking. We've already got a flight of F-4s out cruisin' the boonies, and those Phantom jocks ain't gonna let any VC or terrorists or anybody else get within fifty miles o' here. And even if the Commies were lucky enough to reach the perimeter, that's where they'd be shit out of luck, because we got a couple o' them ole Spectre birds up circling the base as we speak. You of all people oughta know how gunships can pick fly turds out of pepper when they fly close air support. Our boys in the 16th SOS are so ticked off at being cooped up on this rat-hole base for six straight days, deprived o' their *tii-rahks* and massage parlors and conscience-alterin' substances and rock 'n' roll and pizza at Tippy's that I'm afraid they would severely kick the butt of any Communist troublemaker who was foolish enough to show up."

I couldn't help admiring how well Hill had mastered his LBJ imitation, which got me wondering if the brash lieutenant might give up his movie-directing ambitions and run instead for a seat in congress. "The guys *do* seemed to be ticked, sir," I said, stepping outside.

I had no sooner turned the corner of the ComDoc camera trailer than First Sergeant Link stepped out of the shadows. "What's this I hear about you and Wheeler turning in your Gun Cards?" he growled.

"You heard correctly," I answered, suddenly wanting a Mekong and soda to wet my scratchy throat.

"You put him up to this, Leary?"

"I'm afraid we put each other up to it, Sarge."

"Well, get this, Leary—if this base is attacked and I tell you to pick up an M-16 and get out to the perimeter to shoot some gooks, you'll either do it or I'll personally put a bullet through your head."

I was having trouble thinking of a funny retort when Lieutenant Liscomb appeared from I don't know where. "You put a bullet through Leary's head and I'll personally return the favor, if you've got any brains inside that thick skull of yours to blow out."

I suddenly wanted a *bottle* of Mekong, neat. Link tried to glare at Liscomb, but Liscomb wasn't wasting any effort glaring back. He was the epitome of cool, looking at Link with his eyes wide open and clear. In fact, he gave Link a little smile and a little tip of his head. There might have been a pause.

"We'll see about that," said Link with a final glare at Liscomb and then me before he gave the lieutenant a half-hearted salute, made a slow about-face, and skulked off.

The enlisted men's dining hall, offering free grub twenty-four hours a day, was located at the bottom of a knoll along the west side of the main taxiway near the gym and the engine test area. I headed in the opposite direction, towards the NCO Club. It had taken me a full year longer than anyone else I knew to make sergeant. For two and a half agonizing years I had been confined to cheaply paneled airmen's beer bars and Sunday-school-wholesome USO clubs to while away my off-duty hours. I felt instantly at home in the Non-Commissioned Officers' Club, the same sort of womblike security I used to find in my old East Coast fraternity house and in New England bars that served underage college guys. Except New England bars and East Coast fraternity houses didn't have strange characters in khakis hiding outside in the shadows of palm trees. I stopped dead in my tracks, certain for a moment it was Link. Once I realized it was the deputy base commander checking haircuts, I made a hard right and ducked in the side entrance Harley Baker and Larry Zelinsky used to use to smuggle me in.

Safely inside, I headed for the bar and wasn't surprised to see that Harley Baker had gotten there ahead of me. I wasn't thrilled about sitting with him, especially if he got off on one of his drunken tirades about Fuckin' New Guys, which for him was anybody still on their first tour, or any of his other pet peeves, but since I didn't see anyone else I recognized I figured I'd better not snub the closest thing I had to a guardian angel. His elbows had settled deeply and comfortably into the burgundy imitation-leather armrests that ran down the edge of a long, polished, Philippine mahogany bar that seemed to follow the curvature of the earth before disappearing into a thick cloud of cigarette smoke. The hard-drinking, mescaline-eating Spectre gunner barely noticed when I sat down at the stool next to him. "What in the name of Sweet Jesus are you going to do when they throw your ass out of the Air Force and make you get a real job where you've got to go eight straight hours without a drink?" I asked.

"Never gonna happen, draft dodger." Harley did not bother to look up. He studied his swizzle stick as though he were looking through a gun sight at an enemy convoy—ambiguous shadows hidden in limestone caves and woven into dark tendrils of the jungle canopy. He squinted at the tiny trucks and squeezed his imaginary trigger. "There aren't enough dumb shits around willing to go the places I go, do the things I do, fly the places I fly. An' live to tell about it. Or, more precisely, tell about it if we were *allowed* to tell about it. That's what I like about your Top Secret fuckin' security clearance—if I decide you have a 'need-to-know,' I can talk to you about stuff I can't tell my own mother. I go anywhere they send me an' I get back. How can they ask for more'n that?"

"How about not disgracing the regiment when you're off duty?"

Harley leaned over and gave me one of the three-inch-away glares that I might have hated most of his many quirks. "Where the hell do you come off with your holier-than-thou crap, you scrawny pacifist pinko? Mr. Crystallization of His Deeply Held Beliefs. You're the kind of disgusting puke who'll screw our women and smoke our dope and then turn right around and write to your congressman and the *New York Times* complaining about how this has corrupted your pure virgin soul."

"You may or not be full of shit, but one night with Sii-da that I was too stoned to remember isn't exactly 'screwing your women.' It just so happens that while we've been stuck here sitting around wasting our time the last few days, I've had nothing better to do than start worrying about what's going to happen to you when you reach forty."

"Never gonna happen. You of all people know I'll never make it to forty."

"But just in case God decides to play a cruel joke on the world and let you live—what then?"

"I'll get another band together and take it on the road. I'll have my pension to tide me over while we get started—"

"How many balding, pot-bellied forty-year-olds tour with rock bands? What are you going to do, switch to country and western?"

"*Hell, no.* Maybe I'll get into construction with my brother. Maybe Mali and I'll have a couple of kids—"

"Now I know you're jiving me. Your cock'll fall off before you ever get around to having kids."

"You got that right, dude." Harley took a sip of his drink and stared at the swirling ice cubes. He suddenly turned serious. "Maybe I'll clean up my act. Maybe I'll start right now, while we're stuck on this goddamned base. Mali's the best thing that's ever happened to me, y'know. She ain't nothin' like those first two wives. Gotta treat her right. She's gonna make a helluva great mom."

"I'll drink to that." I clinked my glass against Baker's. "To Harley and motherhood!"

"Fuck you, you over-educated, elitist son-of-a-bitch. Fuck you and your draft-dodging fellow travelers. You depend on us real soldiers to protect your ass, and then you turn right around and preach all this Peace, Love, Dove, Higher-Consciousness-than-Thou crap. Wait till you're out on the perimeter and some asshole is shooting at you just because you've got round eyes. You'll shoot back and you'll kill the mother and you won't exactly feel good about it, but you'll have had your first taste of blood and you'll turn into a hungry shark, just like the rest of us, surviving on instinct. You've been trained to kill since you saw your first John Wayne movie, and when you finally do, when you reach down inside yourself and see what you're really made of, you'll have finally joined the Wolf Pack. Maybe you'll finally know what it's like to be a man. Think about it."

I cleared my scratchy throat. "Wheeler and I turned in our gun cards."

Harley was leaning so far over that he and I could barely keep from sliding off our well-worn Naugahyde bar stools. Firmly but gently straightening myself up, I forced him to back off. "You are about the dumbest son-of-bitch to ever come down the pike," he said, still managing to get a little spit on my face. "On base alert and you're gonna let your M-16 stay locked up in the armory? You and Wheeler gotta be kidding me."

"I haven't touched a firearm since I applied for discharge as a conscientious objector. That wasn't an act. Just because the brass shot me down doesn't mean my beliefs have changed."

Harley's eyes were starting to bulge. "What the hell do you call that .38 in your survival vest?"

"I leave it in my locker. I'm not planning on getting shot down."

"None of us are, genius. But if you *are* shot down or if I decide to throw your ass out of the airplane some night and those little brown bastards in black pajamas march you up to the Hanoi Hilton, try preaching to *them* about Peace and Love!" Harley waved for the Filipino bartender who came with the mahogany. I tried to quietly slip away, but Baker caught me by

245

surprise, throwing out his arm like a big fishnet and hauling me in. I fully expected to be put into a chokehold. Instead, he turned to the barman and commanded, "Bring us a bottle of Mekong. We're gonna get ripped."

By the time we finished our first shot of fermented formaldehyde, the house band had started playing. In what seemed to me like one hot gulp, the band was on its second set and Harley had ordered our second bottle. Tiger, one of Sagittarius Smith's secret weapons in the worldwide struggle to defeat Communism, appeared on the smoke-shrouded stage a few minutes later amid a surprised burst of applause and began dancing a woozy, sleazy striptease. The crowd went crazy, impressed as much by Smith's ingenuity at smuggling her on base as by Tiger's stab at dancing. There had never been a barbed-wire barricade that could deter Sagittarius from his life's calling—bringing debauchery to his boys. Harley and Tiger, of course, were old friends from her days living with Pigpen Sachs. She joined us for a drink when she finished her floorshow, not bothering to put on more clothes than were necessary for medicinal purposes. She gulped down a whiskey and soda and dragged us back to her dressing cubicle, a dismal storeroom long abandoned by the janitors. Careful where I placed my feet, I worked my way across the remains of a linoleum floor. The air was stagnant, the heavy scent of disinfectant unable to camouflage a faint but persistent stench reminiscent of a back alley on skid row at high noon.

I collapsed into the twisted wreckage of a love seat upholstered in cracked, faded plastic splattered with stains that curdled my imagination. Harley sat in a hard wooden chair that belonged to a long-lost school desk. After throwing herself into Harley's big, strong lap and covering his cheek with slobbery blisses, Tiger poured each of us another shooter of Thai embalming fluid, but I was unable to pay much attention to Harley and Tiger. I had gone involuntarily into a state of full combat readiness, my eyes dancing across the charred landscape, bracing for an invasion of rat-sized cockroaches. After a second shooter, my brain summarily CUT TO BLACK.

As Harley explained to me later, he had protested too little after I passed out and allowed Tiger to show him the desk drawer in the club office where Senior Master Sergeant Sagittarius Smith kept the keys to his jeep. They drove unmolested past several guard towers before ending up at the base garbage dump, where Tiger led Harley to a hole in the fence utilized regularly by the town's *nouveau riche* rag pickers. According to reliable reports from the house band, Smith's stomach tied itself into a sheepshank when he discovered Tiger's dressing room was empty. He went to his office, opened the drawer where he kept his Maalox and discovered his keys were missing. The rest of the evening he stewed over the libidinal drought that began when the club membership mutinied more than a month earlier, forcing him to ship the Chirping Sparrows—the most voluptuous, tone-deaf, all-female rock band in all of Asia—back to Korea, at least until they could find a new lead singer. As usual, Harley had not concerned himself with the nuances of the big sergeant's emotions any more than he gave a hoot about any support troop's thoughts or feelings.

I had only needed a quick glance at Sagittarius Smith's king-sized gut to figure that Tiger would try to sweet-talk Harley into being her chaperone. What I could not figure was why my deranged cohort would let himself get sucked in, risking every possible flavor of tropical scourge with a wicked vixen in leopard-skin toreador pants when he had the picture of modest grace, intelligence and beauty languishing in his half-empty bed at home. Mali was Mom material. All Tiger could promise was trouble.

Soggy thoughts of pot-bellied Smiths, languishing Malis, rampaging Harleys and syphilitic vixens were floating through my brain when I regained consciousness. My private movie must have jumped ahead a couple of scenes, however, because I was already outside and had no idea how I got there. Suddenly I desperately wanted to find my way back to the 601st. I needed to be standing by vigilantly at the ComDoc camera trailer. I felt a powerful need to pick up a camera and film heroically if I wasn't going to be picking up a gun. I suddenly felt homesick for our squadron mascot, the Rat Pack rat. *"We Kill 'Em with Fillum,"* I thought. *Now there's a motto I can live with.*

It should have only been a short four-block walk back to the ComDoc ready room, but I was hopelessly lost. I found myself near the Base Exchange and then up near the laundry emporium. I tried to carefully retrace my steps but instead of ending up at the club found myself at the base arts and crafts center. I heard gunshots coming from the northeast end of the main runway—the end pointed towards Laos and the Demilitarized Zone of Vietnam—and hoped it wasn't Harley and Tiger getting pinned down. The night sky began to light up with mortar rounds and searchlights and tracers. I panicked and began running, feeling like the doomed, dumb-but-lovable character from Brooklyn in one of the old war movies I had watched with my grandfather as a kid. Back then I assumed I'd be playing the Errol Flynn part.

Persevering, I sprinted half the length of a football field—until a wave of dizziness spun me around in my tracks. I bent over double and tried to throw up but all I could produce were dry heaves. Dying would have been more fun. The mortar rounds seemed nearer, pounding at my guts as if I were a street urchin's punching bag. When I looked up, I noticed I was amid the hootches occupied by the Rat Pack's non-flying enlisted men. I felt a flash of relief—until I looked inside. The hootches were empty, and I could only vaguely remember that the revetment where they tested F-4 engines was only a stone's throw away and that ComDoc was only another hop, step and jump from there.

"Why if it isn't Brendan Leary, himself! What the hell are you doing over here? I thought you were on duty tonight."

Zelinsky was sweaty and covered with mud. Chewing nervously on a wad of bubble gum, he looked like a dogface out of one of Ernie Pyle's World War II-vintage cartoons, his helmet cocked jauntily to the side, the strap undone.

"They must have slipped me a Mickey at the club. Should've known it wasn't a Shirley Temple when the straw melted. Hah hah."

"You doin' bad acid or what? Let me get you back to the ready room before Hill has your ass. Rumor had it that you'd headed downtown in a stolen jeep."

I could still smell sulfur and cordite in the warm night air. Soon I was hearing the familiar clanging of the erector-set stairs that led to our tin and aluminum camera trailer. Just before I opened the door, I asked, "Are we still fighting?"

Zelinsky stared quizzically. "You haven't started on opium, have you? The shooting stopped fifteen minutes ago. Kicked their ass. Ran them off before they made it onto the base. Word has it there were twelve of them, but for all their trouble, all they did was shoot out a few windows and put a couple of holes in the runway. Washington says he got some great stuff. Luckily for you."

The door opened by itself and I took half a step inside. Washington gathered me up like a sack of potatoes and waltzed me right back out. "Got you covered, man. Duty report says you were diverted to perimeter defense. You might even get put in for a medal if they pull any bodies off the wire in the morning."

"I think they might have a little trouble giving a medal to a guy who was never issued a weapon."

"Don't sweat the small stuff," Washington replied. He was about the same size as my maternal grandmother. She'd developed her physique eating meat and potatoes on a small farm in Western Pennsylvania. Washington's mama had fattened him up on the same southern soul food she'd been raised on before her family gave up sharecropping and moved north.

I was still on my feet, but my partner was shouldering two thirds of my weight. "'Sreally nice o'you t'smooth things out with Hill," I told him. "Guess I'll jush head on back wi' Zhelinsky."

"'Ceptin' you haven't been assigned to Larry's hootch for over a month—you're a cameraman now, remember? Say good night to Sergeant Zelinsky."

"Night, Lare."

"Get some sleep," Zelinsky replied before he disappeared into the smoke and fog. No sooner had he vanished than two shadowy forms called down to us from the roof of the admin trailer. "Leary, Washington—wait up."

The silhouette who sounded like Tom Wheeler climbed down first. "Hey, man," he said, "you look bad. I mean *bad* bad. You haven't started drinking that *Laotian* rot-gut, have you?"

"I've got some *real* Laotian shit," said the laconic, towheaded second figure who followed close behind. Dave Murray had been kicked out of detox and sent back to the ComDoc orderly room a couple days before we went on alert, not because he was cured, I suspected, but because they needed every breathing human being on the base at their disposal.

"What were you doing on the roof?" I asked.

"It was Shahbazian's idea," said Dave. "He got telling us about all the pleasant evenings they spent back at Danang getting thoroughly wrecked and watching firefights off in the distance from their barracks rooftop, so we thought we'd give it a try."

"Luckily, tonight was a dud," Tom added. "It wasn't until we got up on the roof that Woody remembered how the VC turned out to be lousy sports and started firing rockets at *them*."

"Where's Shahbazian?" asked Washington.

"He said he's not coming out of the latrine till this friggin' alert is over," answered Dave.

"Last time I checked he was sound asleep," said Tom.

Wheeler and Murray might not have been considered virtuous in the conventional sense of the word, but when it came to generosity, the boys were virtuous to a fault. They insisted that Washington and I join them over at their hootch in the semi-privacy of the lockers and double bunk beds at the back of their quarters.

Dave was as high as I had ever seen him. "We get some good shit around here, but this is the best of the best—the stuff Papa-sahn usually keeps for himself," he warned us. "Mole gave it to me for my getting-out-of-detox present." Putting a hand-tooled metal pipe to his lips, he lit up and took a deep drag before handing it to Tom.

"He's not kidding," Tom said, gasping a little and passing along the pipe. We all did a couple of tokes while our two connoisseurs of weed searched their lockers for some clean clothes.

"Did you hear about the Chirping Sparrows?" Dave asked, savoring the inside information he was picking up from the orderly room radio and switchboard. "They were circling the base in a Klong Airways C-130 during the mortar attack."

"Whoo-*ee!*" grinned Washington. "I can picture them on final now, primping their bouffants, freshening up their lip gloss for their triumphant return to Ubon."

I needed to throw a cold water bucket of reality into the conversation. "We've got a goddamn war going on," I said. "What the hell are the Sparrows doing using up airspace that belongs to gunships and fighter-bombers?"

"It's the *New* Chirping Sparrows," said Dave. "They got a lead singer who can carry a tune now."

"If those warbling lovebirds really do show up in the middle of a Red Alert lockdown, aren't you afraid Lek will get wind of it and have your tushie?" I asked Tom.

"I'm kinda hoping she's forgotten about the night I got kidnapped by the Sparrows," he answered. "Besides, she was still living with Mole back then." He had peeled off his dusty fatigues and jungle boots and was exchanging them for a tie-dyed T-shirt and jeans. "She did have another one of her snits, by the way, and took off for Korat the night before we were put on alert."

"I didn't see her around when Dah stopped over, but I assumed Lek was avoiding her. She must have been in one pissy mood, though, because she filled Sii-da's head with the crazy idea I wanted to *tii-rahk* her after all. And then Lek sent her out looking for me."

"What was Dah doing at Ruam Chon Sawng?" Dave asked.

"She wanted to talk to Lek about *you* throwing her ass out," I lied.

"This is really fucking up my head," said Dave. "I don't know whether to believe it or not that she and Mole were just snorting rock when I walked in on them. It's so weird—Mole gives me a bag of Laotian weed, tells me it'll mellow me out, and now we're cool. Meanwhile, I'm in *love* with Tukada, but I can't get hold of her while we're stuck here on base. I *love* her, but I don't *trust* her. I'm afraid I don't trust anybody—just look at the way Lek dumped Mole to move in with you, Tom."

"Mole was screwing up in the end," said Tom said. "He was going broke from his drug habit and wanted her to start working the bars again."

I let out a long stream of ganja fumes. "Mole must be doing all right now if he can be giving away shit like this."

"I don't know whether to make up with her or trust my gut feelings," Dave said. "My heart says one thing and my gut says something else. It's making me crazy." Tom and I shot each other a look but kept our mouths shut.

Washington collapsed into Tom's unmade lower bunk. "What *is* it about these Thai bitches?" he asked. "When you watch them from a distance they look so cool and graceful and serene. And when they first shack up with you, all they need is a coupla hundred baht a month and, like magic, the laundry's done and the floor's swept and fresh fruit seems like it's falling from trees."

"It *is* falling from trees," said Dave.

Oblivious, Jamal kept talking. "And when they peel it for you, they don't just peel it, they carve it into little flowers and birds. You get thinking, *Man, this is a helluva deal!* Once you get used to it over here, you figure, *Shee-it, man, who needs America with all its cars and electric appliances and the monthly payments that go with them? This is better—the best grass and tastiest food and the most beautiful women in the world and it's just pennies a day, man, like the encyclopedia salesman says, except this isn't looking at the pictures—this is the real thing."*

I had melted into the corner. To be more precise, the killer stuff from

Laos had melted me. Dave's battered footlocker felt like a stack of Persian pillows. "This scene is great for the short run all right," I muttered. "But what happens twenty years down the road when she's fat and her teeth have turned black from betel nut and you decide you'd like to have a conversation with her in real English—not bar English?"

Washington let out one of his room-shattering laughs. "Ain't worried about no *conversation*, man, and I ain't worried about no twenty years from now. Ain't none of us gonna live that long, anyhow, the way we been carryin' on. I'm more worried about three *months* from now. When they start hitting you up for TV sets from the Base Exchange for their tired ol' dyin' daddies. I'm deeply concerned about how the *minute* you don't deliver the goodies, there's no more nooky. Just when you've gotten used to that four-foot eleven-inch body curled up next to you every night. So you give in and the next thing you know your year's up and it never fails—I've seen in a hundred times now—you've gotten so used to that ninety pounds of Indochinese womanflesh that you want to wrap her up and take her home with you. Exceptin' she's got this kid back in Phitsanulok, see, and her papa-sahn's got TB and she can't go. Or it goes the other way—she's just dying to go that great BX across the Big Pond. Got her bags all packed. Only you're the one guy in a hundred who *didn't* get a Dear John. So you've still got your fiancée back home and you figure you better go back and check *that* out—you get thinking how she already speaks pretty good English and if your memory serves you right she was a pretty good kisser to boot. You kinda cross your fingers and in the recesses of your dim little mind you figure if things don't work out back in the World, you can always get back to Thailand and fetch your *tii-rahk,* your truest of true loves, who has *no doubt* been waiting faithfully on the back burner while you sort all this shit out."

"And then there's the Dave Murray Syndrome," blurted Harley as he slammed through the screen door, caught his toe on the steel leg of one of the bunks and careened with a roar of thunder into Dave's wall locker. "Dave here finds Miss Tukada Maneewatana, the perfect Asian hipster-lady, chomping at the bit to pile into a VW van covered with day-glow rainbows, ready to live Jack Kerouac's dream and strike out across America, living on love and the twenty-three dollars they've managed to save."

"Who's Jack Kerouac?" asked Dave.

"He's the beatnik writer dude who gave Dennis Hopper the idea for *Easy*

Rider," Tom explained.

"And if things get tight," Harley said, "no sweat! They can always do a little panhandling or just a teeny-weeny bit of dope dealing. No hooking, of course. In Hippy-Dippy America, love is 'free.' But now comes the interesting part, because sooner or later he's gonna have to show up in that little home town of his in Iowa for a shower and a home-cooked meal. Maybe sign up for unemployment. And the last person there who didn't have skin as white as the driven snow his great-grandfather personally rounded up and shipped to a reservation in Oklahoma." He turned to Dave. "Have you ever wondered how your little Thai wench is gonna do at the local Safeway trying to bargain with the head butcher over the price of dried squid?"

"My family's from Nebraska," said Dave after his usual fifteen-second audio delay.

"I thought you went AWOL," I said to Baker. "Thought you were spending the night at Tiger's dump over in Hanoi-West."

Harley shot us a pained grin. "I got thinking how I'd rather spend the night shooting at SAM missile sites over Dien Bien Phu than put any part of my body near someone touched by Pigpen Sachs."

Harley was up to his usual no good and enjoying every minute of it. "I swear I could hear your bullshit clear out by the main gate. You realize of course that Washington here, for all his bitching and moaning, has actually got it made. Bringing a Thai chick back to Newark is gonna be like bringing home a blonde as far as impressing the brothers."

"I ought to take *you* back to Newark. Have my momma fatten you up, pencil prick. Then maybe we could get you into the albino branch of the Panthers."

"And so what *is* the question here?" Dave asked, staring deep into his gurgling water pipe. "Who amongst us can decipher whether Ubon is heaven or a common whorehouse?"

Tom smiled with innocence and experience. "Maybe heaven *is* a common whorehouse. What else is worth doing for eternity?"

Harley cracked a shark-toothed grin. "We *are* down to basics now, *aren't* we? Fucking and dope-smoking and killing and dying."

"Is life really that simple and crude?" I asked, curling up on the floor.

Wheeler was smiling sweetly at a private joke. "Lek took me home with her last month to Ban Nang Sarawng over near Korat to visit her dad and her little boy. And it was amazing watching Lek with her dad. Dig it—there was none of the brash bullshit like when she's hanging out with us. She's just like the girls in the travel posters—sweet and respectful, you know? Shoes left at the door, the way she was brought up. She glides around her father's bungalow in delicate, pattering footsteps, and her voice is gentle while she carves up vegetables and fruit and does the cooking. And the love and respect she showed her dad—it was real. She bowed down when she was near him as much as she seems to bloat up around Americans. I think she genuinely respects him for breaking his back in the rice fields from sunup to sundown."

Tom gathered his thoughts a moment and then went on. "Shacking up may be popular back in the States, but it's done pretty much on equal terms. Here it's a life-and-death gamble. Imagine a worst-case scenario and the North Vietnamese Army ends up occupying Northeast Thailand? What would they do to a bar girl who had been sleeping with the enemy?" Nobody answered. "Even with a *best*-case scenario, what's going to happen to her body and soul from ten years of sleeping with strange men? What she's doing has got to be degrading, but can she worry about self-respect when this might be the only chance her family will ever have to own a TV set and buy some new land and rebuild their cottage on good teak stilts and maybe buy a new plow and harness and a couple of strong, young water buffalo? All thanks to the money she's sending home."

"Amen, Brother Tom!" cried Washington.

By three in the morning Harley had returned to his air-conditioned trailer over at the 16th Special Operations Squadron. My ears seemed to be working okay, but my eyes didn't want to stay open. More perplexing, my body, which had been floating pleasantly, was now starting to shrink. Some New Guy nobody had ever seen before stopped by Tom's hootch on his way back from the base bowling alley and swore that not only had the New Chirping Sparrows safely returned from Korea, they were setting up for a late-night performance over at the club.

Washington, still stretched out on Tom's bunk, seemed excited by the report, weakly shouting, "Praise God! And praise Sagittarius Smith!" He promptly fell into a deep slumber that made him look like an overstuffed teddy bear. Tom and Dave got it into their heads to go check it out over at the club. I had stopped shrinking, but now I was staring back at them from the dead, unable to move my lips.

I was certain I had become a Self-Contained Unit. An SCU. An indestructible steel box that could be dropped from a C-123 at any altitude over the nastiest mountain ranges of Laos, blow-torched, hand-grenaded or nuked. Nothing would make me squeal. Enough food, water and medicine to hold out indefinitely. My field radio-transceiver was powered by a high-efficiency generator with plenty of back-up batteries. The SCU was steel, all right. I felt cold and hard and indestructible and absolutely numb. Self-Contained Unit. Ball of steel wool. Fetal, pre-conscious. Almost invisible.

So this is what Dave Murray's Laotian shit does to you after the orgasms in your lungs die down. Laotian Leh. What the hell does "Leh" mean? I tried blinking my eyes in Morse code like I had seen in an old Lone Ranger movie when one of the Good Guys was about to be buried alive. Nothing happened. I didn't want to be buried alive. I didn't like being invisible. I blinked again, trying for a simple SOS like we had learned at Boy Scout camp. Again nothing happened. I felt a tiny knot of fear beginning to grow in my belly, a little shrapnel wound of anxiety that they might really, truly, inexplicably bury me alive after a day or two of non-blinking.

Tom and Dave nudged me and tried to stand me up. "Come on, man," Dave implored, "we gotta get going if we're gonna check out the Chirping Sparrows."

Their voices echoed from across the North Rim of the Grand Canyon, powerful and loud like the voice of God. I yelled back with all my strength, but my little cricket lips could only produce the faint sound of a midget after inhaling helium.

"What's he saying about a self-controlled eunuch?" Dave asked.

Tom threw a blanket over me and tucked it under my chin. "See you over at the club if you feel better."

"Later, man," said Dave.

I could hear my voice, deep inside my SCU, say that I could not move, could they please bring a forklift. My voice was growing smaller and seemed trapped inside my corrugated stainless-steel walls. Footsteps. Creaking hinge. The slam of the rickety screen door, an after-slam, and then silence.

My chest started to burst with fear that I *was* actually paralyzed permanently, that even though my mind had turned itself inside out, it had made a correct assessment of the situation after all. I felt desperately alone until, finally, the spasm in my chest loosened its grip and I sank into a deep, dark sleep.

The Best Night in the Sweet, Short Life of Tukada Maneewatana

It was already growing dark Wednesday when I began to regain consciousness. I was not certain at first if my bunk was in Thailand, China, San Berdoo or Boston, nor if this was the morning or evening of the previous or following day.

"Wake up, Leary, it's time to go home," called Tom. Somehow I had gotten back to my old bunk above Washington's. Tom and Dave helped me down and pointed me towards my locker, where it took me a few tries but I finally got the combination to open. I swapped out my musty jungle fatigues for a pair of jeans and a T-shirt and let Tom and Dave lead me to the bus stop across from the chapel where three pint-sized *baht*-buses were waiting to take GIs out to the gate and on into town. It was going to be one of those evenings in early cool season when the air stayed pungent and clammy long after the sun went down. The first bus was nearly full but we climbed on anyway. By the time we squeezed into the tiny back seat our skin was covered with a thin film of perspiration. Even with the windows open it didn't get any cooler when the bus pulled out

"You missed a great show last night," Dave told me as we headed for the gate.

"It was amazing—they fired their old lead singer and now they actually sound decent," said Tom. "Sagittarius has come out of this base alert thing smelling like a rose."

Dave's mood darkened suddenly and he just sat there quietly staring at his hands as the bus rumbled along. "I've been giving it a lot of thought about Tukada," he said. "And I think we can work things out."

Tom and I glanced at each other, afraid to open our mouths. We knew that Tukada hadn't found a new *tii-rahk*, but we wouldn't have been surprised to hear she was shopping around. The Thai women we knew didn't spend a lot of time looking back with remorse. We were afraid Dave *might* be the type to start having second thoughts, though, which he had confirmed the night before. I felt like a jerk for letting it slip out that Tukada had been hanging around Ruam Chon Sawng after Tom and I had gone to such great lengths to avoid bringing up her name.

The bus squealed to a halt at the main gate, where the guardhouse was still being reinforced with extra Thai and American MPs. "Later, dudes," grunted Dave, climbing down and heading off to a line of waiting cabs and *sahmlaws*.

"*Chok dii*," I called to him. "Good luck out there."

"And good luck with Dah," added Tom.

Dave looked like a sleepy-eyed hound dog as he walked away, bewildered by the clash of bright neon lights and the cacophony of street-hawkers and drivers vying for his attention. I was glad to be staying on board, because the scene on the street looked pretty bewildering to me too. And then he surprised us by climbing unsteadily onto the back of a motorbike, giving the driver some instructions, and racing off. "Looks like a man in a hurry," I said, pitying our wayward compadre.

"I wonder who he's looking for—Papa-sahn or Tukada?" asked Tom.

"Maybe it's a package deal," I sighed.

The bus was still crowded when it pulled out into the steamy night and soon our T-shirts and bellbottoms felt like warm, wet dishrags. When we saw that the New Playboy Club was jumping, we thought it might be a good idea to cool off there with a Mekong and Coke and a blast of air conditioning. It would have been a great idea, except the patrons were lined up four deep at the bar, so we didn't end up any cooler than if we had stayed on the bus. Somehow we didn't mind, though, thanks to the feeling of Mardis Gras that was in the air. Smiling couples were dancing on the dance floor and overflowing into the parking lot and out onto the street. Bus after bus was passing by filled with laughing GIs and their fat wallets. We knew that club owners and merchants like Indian Joe would be overjoyed to see currency once again in circulation, and the girlfriends of the GIs seemed even happier to see their unofficial BX privileges restored. Tom and I got caught up in the festive mood and had started on our second Mekong and Coke when Washington snuck up on us from behind. "Did you hear the rumor that they're gonna put us back on alert tomorrow?" he asked.

"Why the hell would they do that?" asked Tom.

"Because Colonel Grimsley is pissed," answered Washington. "When the Air Police searched the perimeter this morning they didn't find a damned thing. Either the Bad Guys dragged away their wounded without leaving a speck of blood or the firefight in reality was our own guys having a panic attack."

"Sergeant Prasert has already told us that there aren't any Viet Cong, North Vietnamese regulars, Pathet Lao, Pathet Thai train robbers or any other crazy Commie SOBs within a hundred miles o' here. Captain English said the same thing. I've got a strong suspicion it was a panic attack," I groaned.

"Then who the hell was rocketing the base yesterday?" Tom asked.

"Those weren't rockets, they were just mortars," I winced.

"We were probably mortaring ourselves, shooting at palm tree shadows like the New Guys do over in Nam," laughed Washington.

I sighed philosophically. "Makes me yearn for Boy Scout camp. They always made us put our guns away at night."

"I'm with you on that one, bro," said Tom. "Nothing in the world scares me more than a bunch of bottle-washers and titless WAFs running around with clips of real bullets shoved up their collective M-16s."

I sighed again. "You *are* a titless WAF."

"I rest my case," said Tom.

"Kinda sends a chill down your spine, don't it," Washington said, scrunching up his forehead and half raising his eyebrows. "Somebody's gonna get their ass shot, sure as shit."

"We're doomed," I said, glancing helplessly at my companions.

"Here's to our impending demise," said Washington with a laugh, clinking our glasses with his beer bottle. He was still laughing when he disappeared into the crowd. I tried to get our check, but the bartender misunderstood and brought us another round, which seemed like a shame to waste. It also seemed like a shame to waste the doobies I discovered crumpled in my T-shirt pocket, so we ducked into the alley around back to smoke one on our way out to catch the next bus.

We were so generally anaesthetized by the time we crawled onto another crowded pink and blue *roht meh* that we didn't mind at all having to squeeze our six-foot bodies into seats built in Japan for five-foot Asian passengers. As we bounced along, heading at last for home, I remembered how shocked I had been a week earlier—just before we went on alert—to see our first lifer moving into Ruam Chon Sawng, which in turn got me thinking about my latest, most serious run-in with Link. It didn't take me long to notice that thinking about Link and lifers and death threats was ruining my good mood, which soon got me thinking how it might be a good time to take a little nap.

It was not until we climbed off the tinny bus on the opposite side of the street from the Ruam Chon Sawng bungalows that we fully realized how much fresh damage we had done to our bodies and souls. Drunk, stoned and still hung over, Tom and I hobbled blindly across Thanon See Narawng, nearly getting hit by a *roht tax-ii* and two motor scooters in the process. "Where else in the worl' can you get chauffeured around in style like that for only a nickel?" asked Tom, unperturbed.

"There's another one for Washington's list, right up there with sliced mango," I said as we passed under the archway that connected Mama-sahn's house to her little restaurant. Several of the bar girls who lived upstairs above the *rahn-ahahn* were helping themselves to sticky rice and soup that suspiciously resembled battery acid and river eel. Mama-sahn opened the noodle shop whenever she was in the mood. By some inscrutable Asian coincidence, for almost six months she had never once been open when Tom or I were hungry or dying of thirst except on a day like today, of course, when the old witch saw in her crystal ball that we had already stuffed ourselves with booze and pretzels at the New Playboy.

I bashed into the wrought-iron gate, bounced off without feeling a thing, and continued hobbling along. Entering the valley of the shadow of death, I called to Tom, "Honey, we're home!"

"*Sawatdii*, Mama-sahn," said Tom, bowing a little as he passed the old medicine woman. As usual, she sat contentedly on her porch counting a thick wad of Yankee dollars, mildly zonked from the cud of betel nut that turned her teeth ever-deepening shades of magenta. Her uncovered breasts were almost as lovely as her stained teeth, hanging as they did down to her navel.

"*Sawatdii, kha*," she cooed, beaming her biggest, blackest, most flirtatious schoolgirl grin that she saved just for Tom.

The Homecoming-Mardi Gras was in full swing as Tom and I staggered up the debris-strewn cul-de-sac. We tripped over the feet of a couple of guys who said they were "resting" in the soggy gutter. Simultaneously we reeled to a bizarre mixture of soul and acid rock that was bouncing every which way out of and off of the bungalows, a mixture of musical nitro and glycerin that was threatening to blow up the lab: "In A Gada da Vida,"

Buddy Miles going through his changes, "American Woman," James Brown with his brand new bag, and Jefferson Airplane singing "White Rabbit" out of one bungalow and "Somebody to Love" out of another. Down near the spirit house, "My Generation" clashed with "Eight Miles High" and the Ghetto theme song, "Who's Making Love to Your Old Lady?" Several brothers, already high, were hanging out, sitting around comfortably on the patio wall of one of the chicken coops, openly sharing a factory-rolled marijuana cigarette. Upstairs to the left, what sounded like a madman driving nails through his bedroom floor cut through all the ear-splitting music, pounding that was actually the sound of more red-rock heroin being ground to perfection with an empty Coke bottle.

"Phom Daeng!" called Bun-lii from a dark corner five feet or a mile away, we weren't sure which, a corner we had passed every day for months and never knew existed. She had aged in the six months since I had seen her with Shahbazian at the Ubon Hotel. Now she glided past and around Wheeler as if he were the last survivor of a burning destroyer turned belly-up in the Coral Sea and she were a frenzied shark. She and every other bargirl in Thailand loved Tom for his yellow mane the way counter-culture groupies back in the States had loved him for his cool in the midst of complicated and potentially deadly dope deals. I once asked Tom how he maintained his Buddha-like serenity. "It's easy," he had said. "Light up a joint before you get out of bed in the morning, and smile knowingly the rest of the day, especially if you're spaced out or seriously wasted."

"Phom Daeng!" Bun-lii called again. Soon she would be selling mangoes at the market. She was past thirty, washed up as a whore. Even the lifers were no longer buying drinks for her at the Sampan.

"Want red?" asked a brown-skinned flower-chick, floating among the stilts beneath the bungalows. Her feet were barely touching the ground, but her slobbery lips had become so heavy she could barely speak. Her eyelids were drooping nearly shut and her hair and clothing looked matted and rumpled like she had been sleeping in a haystack. She opened a chubby hand full of red capsules and thrust them toward Wheeler and me.

Her girlfriend, an emaciated skeleton, asked, "Want white?"

Ordinarily I *liked* being surrounded by my fellow freaks and soul brothers at Bungalow Ruam Chon Sawng, suspecting we had something going closer to Haight Ashbury than Haight Ashbury did. Now, though, my chest was heaving, brought on by shortness of breath and paroxysms of anxiety. I tugged at Tom's shirt, pleading, "Let's fuggin' get outa here, man."

Instead, Tom and I collapsed on the ramshackle bamboo bed that someone had abandoned underneath our stairway and where the *sahmlaw* drivers often sat around gambling on quieter nights. "I'm," mumbled Tom, pushing back a mass of his straight blond hair. "I'm…." His eyes shone dully through clumps of golden locks that Thai black-brown-bronze-skinned women who hated looking at themselves loved to look at. "I'm—what can I tell you—I'm back on red rock."

A switch clicked and I started dreaming with my eyes wide open, remembering Tom and Tukada tooting red-rock heroin in his room late at night and out at Kaeng Sapue Rapids and Tadtohn Falls in broad daylight.

"Who want pussy?" came a muffled voice from inside the stilt-shack eight feet above us next door. B.J. and Leclerc were sitting outside on the porch railing rapping with another group of brothers while a couple of their buddies danced solitaire to the familiar refrain of *"Who's making love to your old lady—while you were out making love?"*

Sii-da, the once-shy Laotian farm girl, appeared in B.J.'s doorway wearing a wrinkled T-shirt and sarong. She sleepwalked tipsily out among the brothers on the porch, but they kept rapping or dancing without paying her any attention.

"What happened with Lek?" I asked.

"When I told her I couldn't give her any money till payday she had a fit."

Sii-da caught me in her sights and came to a wobbly halt.

"She knew I was a poorly paid airman first class when she moved in," Tom lamented.

"Jus' like a woman to think she can change your pay grade."

Sii-da began calling with her wispy voice, "Blen-dan! Blen-dan! You wan' pussy?"

She opened the sarong, revealing her perfectly shaped legs and pink satin panties. Tom and I lit up a new doobie, trying to ignore her as she showered us with her sarong, her tee-shirt, and her bra. When B.J. noticed that Tom and I were on the receiving end of Sii-da's little barrage, he decided to come downstairs for a visit, soon followed by Leclerc and the other brothers. Gathering around me and Tom on the bamboo bed, they left Sii-da to finish her nightmare alone. "Your girlfriend's got the clap," said Brother B.J.

"She's not my girlfriend," I responded. "And besides, I'm clean. I'll bet it was one those midnight ramblers you told me about. How the hell's she gonna find a *tii-rahk* now?"

"We hired her to do some cooking and cleaning over at Bungalow #3," said B.J. "At least she ain't gonna starve, and she don't mind sleeping on a grass mat." Which was a good thing, because she wasn't going to be working at the Club Miami or the Soul Sister for the next two weeks, except maybe the afternoon tea dances when the police weren't around, provided she could find someone who didn't mind "wearing the glove while making love," as B.J. liked to say. Even for someone as resourceful as a Laotian bar girl working on the Thai frontier, the prospect of two weeks without food was an unsettling experience. From my perspective, it meant two more weeks before Sii-da could look for a *tii-rahk*.

With his deep, beer-barrel voice, Leclerc asked Tom, "You got any rock, man?"

Tom, the stoned Buddha, handed me the doobie and fumbled blissfully in his T-shirt pocket, pulling out a Vicks inhaler, a crumpled hundred-baht note, and a carefully folded page from a Thai movie magazine. He unwrapped the paper, rolled the Thai five-dollar bill—a rice farmer's weekly earnings—into a short straw and drew the red powder into each nostril. Closing his eyes, he paused a moment before he passed the paper on to Leclerc. Wheeler put the inhaler to his nose and breathed deeply, feeling his nasal passages tingle and sting before they finally cleared and he could sink back onto the weathered bamboo bed. He put his hands behind his head and closed his eyes again, looking so comfy he could have been lying on a blanket at Pattaya Beach. So comfy he could have been lying in a coffin, smiling from inside his own death mask. "Where else but Thailand," asked Tom sentimentally, "can you get the purest scag in the world for a quarter a bag?"

"Right on!" boomed Leclerc and a few echoes.

Tom continued smiling, looking his death mask calmly in the eye. "I can stop any time. That's the beautiful thing with this 99% pure stuff—you can quit any time you want, no problem."

"You're starting to sound like Dave." I said. "Remember when you used to tell me, 'No doubt about it—this shit's cocaine'?"

"Papa-sahn promised it was. Got to trust your local pusher, even if he *is* half-rodent and half-reptile and lives on the wrong side of the river."

I laughed bitterly. "Why can't we be happy with the best friggin' *grass* in the world?"

"Easy, man. Nobody's forcing nobody to do nothin'. This be the *all-volunteer* Air Force down here in the Ghetto." B.J. was the shortest, stringiest, fastest-talking of the visitors. He might have been the fastest-talking dude in the entire Seventh Air Force.

Tom was still smiling blissfully. I continued, saying, "All I remember, Mr. B.J. Jones, was how proud Dave was the day you sent him home with some o' your red-rock candy. First white guy on the block. A step ahead of the avant-garde."

"You cats should be very, very flattered. I don't hawk my wares to just anybody comes down the street," said B.J., flashing a broad smile.

I was less stoned than drunk and less drunk than hung over. I watched Tom hold up the empty packet and light it with his Ronson lighter. My grumpy switch clicked on. "Damn you, Tom. How'd you ever let some fool like Dave get you started? I mean, you're talking about a guy who let his hamsters overdose on LSD."

"Maybe Dave jus' *thought* he was the first white dude on the block. Maybe Brother Tom here picked his poison all by hisself, Preacher Man." B.J. was still smiling, amused at my naiveté.

"Who want pussy, goddamn!" cried Sii-da, wearing only her bikini panties.

B.J. didn't notice. His drugs had kicked in and he was having a vision as beautiful as anything he had ever experienced back home as a kid at the Garden of Eden Missionary Baptist Church. "Wow, man!" he enthused, his smile spreading into an infectious, toothy grin, "You know what we gonna do when we get back?"

"Tell us, brother."

"This is gonna be better than goin' to church—"

"How's that, bro?"

"We all gon' bring a *lotta* this shit back to the Worl'…an' then we can meet up—in Vermont, maybe, or Montreal, or California—an' get HII-IGH!"

"Far out, man."

"That's a groove."

"We gonna be in the mountains—beautiful mountains covered with fresh snow. An' we gon' ski like hell all over those mountains and think back to all the good times we had together here in Thailand."

"Right on!"

Sii-da threw down her panties, which glanced off my head and settled on my shoulder. I tried not to flinch. Something was going on inside my head that was more important. "Do you really think it's all over between Dah and Dave?" I asked Tom.

"She told you last week Dave threw her out, right?" Tom replied. "And yet Dave sounded tonight like they're going to patch it up."

"So who's been kidding whom?" I asked. "Was she just telling me what she *wishes* would happen? I'll be damned if I know—and yet I figured *I* can get her off scag. In the meantime, I can't even help *you* get off this shit—"

"Blen-dan!" Sii-da shrieked from the porch next door. She was getting hard to ignore. I ignored her anyway,

"I dunno," said Tom, "maybe she resents you *because* you want her off—"

"You wanna eat my pussy, Blen-dan? You wanna eat my beau-ti-ful, clean pussy?"

Sii-da's livelihood danced above us like a miniature fighting kite. No one cared. The brothers had all watched the same pageant played out before, performed better by a different actress. Sii-da was on call. They could view her body, clothed or naked, singly or in groups, twenty-four hours a day. This might be the only chance they'd get to watch Tom and B.J. overdose on red rock. Sii-da ran back inside, slamming the door shut and locking it behind her.

I was beginning to fade fast and was feeling a powerful urge to go upstairs to my room and crash when Tom startled me with a nudge. "Your ESP must be in high gear tonight—"

Miss Tukada Maneewatana was walking toward us up the alley. I froze a moment and would have stayed frozen if the reefer I had been holding hadn't burned itself to near-extinction, singeing my fingertips. "Ouch!" I winced.

I dug out an old alligator clip and used it to hold the roach while I relit it, taking a long, deep, intoxicating breath in the process. "What the hell is she doing here? This is too weird."

B.J. could never get too much entertainment from us middle-class white dudes. "*Easy*, man. She's a stone fox. You may think you're a preacher man, but not even a preacher man should mind havin' a stone fox stop by his church once in a while."

I wanted to explain my pure intentions to B.J. How I just wanted to help Prasert get Tukada off scag. I wanted to write a letter to Danielle and explain my pure intentions to her too. Except B.J. was already on to me. Danielle would read between the lines. Baker and Shahbazian would have told me to lie. I hated Baker and Shahbazian, especially when they might be right and my moral fiber was unraveling before my eyes.

"*Sawatdii, kha*," said Tukada, pressing her hands together and bowing her head in a graceful *wai*, lip service she still paid to her Thai heritage.

Tom and I *waied* back. B.J. and his gang sensed that ten was a crowd and began drifting away. "Later," boomed all six feet four inches of Leclerc as Tukada squeezed between me and Tom on the bench.

"How are you feeling?" Tom asked.

"I sleep all day last two days, no do rock. Before I sink I'm gonna die," she said solemnly, "but today I feel bet-ter."

I stared at the man-sized shirt she wore. *Stone foxes should be wearing sleek silk dresses and styling their hair like Diana Ross*, I thought. I recalled the first time I had seen her in that navy work shirt that was de rigueur for her. How incongruous it had seemed. What young, attractive Thai woman would want to drape her body with coarse blue denim when silk was cheap and plentiful even in the remotest *ampuhrs*? Perhaps it was a gesture—tired of being hit upon, maybe she was trying to camouflage her loveliness. And yet she would almost always add just a touch of a certain something—hoop earrings, hill-tribe bracelets, a batik bandanna…. It drew me to her like a demolished car to an electromagnet in a wrecking yard. She glided with such grace and elegance that a piece of clothing suitable for a prison road gang on Dah became Parisian haute couture.

And then another mind-flash. It was Dah's size. The man-sized hugeness of the shirt accentuated her tininess. I enjoyed the realization that she was full and soft and rounded in almost perfect proportion but that she was nearly doll-like in scale. Even a lanky long-distance runner like myself could lift Tukada up like a little cloud and hold her high over my shoulders.

Something else, equally superficial and far more destructive, drew me inexorably toward her. She had a wounded, Edith Piaf, Parisian-street-singer look. The soft and vulnerable look of someone who grew up too soon, who missed her childhood, and who was reaching out to hippiedom as a second and last chance at a carefree adolescence. Foolishly, I chose to overlook important details. Her skin was flawless everywhere except the tiny wrinkles beneath her eyes. There the flesh was just a little puffy and just half a shade too dark. The scars on each of her tiny wrists, I surmised, came from the slashing of a razor blade—that was not uncommon among the seemingly carefree Issan girls who had left their villages to do business with GIs. But I could never bring myself to ask about those wounds. I chose to ignore the pain so poorly hidden in the depths of her dark and watery eyes, pain that never failed to betray her and the people around her.

"You have a cigarette?" she asked, tugging gently at my arm.

"Sorry, I'm fresh out. Be a *dahling*, would you Tom?"

Wheeler pulled out a pack of Salems. She took one, and while I lit it she steadied my hand with her own, surprising me once again with its softness and warmth. She inhaled deeply, closing her eyes, and asked, "Where is Lek?"

"She split," answered Tom. "Moved out. Gone."

Gingerly lifting Sii-da's panties off my shoulder, she asked, "How abou' *your tii-rahk*, Bren-dan?"

I snatched the satin undergarment out of Dah's hand, balled it up, and threw it back where it came from in a flash of peevish intensity. The panties seemed to float forever in an updraft rising between the stilt shacks. "I've already told you—she was never my *tii-rahk*. It was all *Lek's* idea, remember? I was just letting her stay a few days."

"Lek can make you sleep wis a girl you don' like?"

"I was drunk—from you and Lek fighting, remember?"

"I sink I'm tired of hearing abou' Lek."

"You want a hit?" I asked, passing Tukada the small roach left on my clip. She took a long, deep drag and exhaled coolly. "Where she go?"

The bamboo bed was starting to make my butt ache. Tom shook his head and smirked. "Next door," I said in a whisper.

"*Arai na?*"

"Sii-da moved next door. Now she has *four* fuckin' *tii-rahks*."

Tukada studied me a moment before giving me one of her jaded smiles. "All zis talk abou' *tii-rahks* is wearing me out." She looked at Tom and then back at me, her voice softening. "Can you take me on your bicycle? Have too much noise here. Make my head hurt."

"Where's Dave?" I asked.

"We're finish. Done. Prasert right abou' him. He and Mole smoke opium now. I tell him he should marry Mole."

Tom and I unchained our twin five-speeds from the porch railing upstairs and brought them down. Without speaking, Tukada climbed on the back of my bike, put her hands lightly on my hips, and the three of us rode out of the cul-de-sac and onto the deserted side streets of Ubon. Tom lit up another joint and we passed it around as we rode. "I think we've got another chapter for *The Air Force Aerobics Manual*," I called. "High-Efficiency Dope-Smoking."

Tom laughed. "We could rip it off and turn it into a best seller. 'Fight inflation! *Bicycle* your way to optimum grass intake!'"

"What is zis *aerobics?*"

I loved the idea of teaching Dah about America. "Some crazy Air Force doctor wants us to believe that exercise is *good* for you."

"Here's to having it all—" Tom called as he raced by, "a healthy body and a wrecked mind!"

A mile out into the countryside the night was dark and silent. The rice farmers and their families would be getting up in a few hours to begin another grueling day. The snorting of water buffalo was enough to make Tom and me imagine we were surrounded by Viet Cong or Pathet Lao or whoever it was that were rumored to be putting bullet holes into the sides of airplanes coming in to Ubon. With nothing more than a Ronson Comet cigarette lighter and Tukada to protect us, the last thing in the world we needed was to run into a real group of terrorists.

We turned north when we reached the outskirts of town and circled the grounds of a tall Buddhist temple with majestic, sweeping tile roofs that reached to the heavens. "Why do the temple roofs curve up like that?" I asked.

"Thai people believe it keep away evil spirit," Dah replied.

Heading east on a street called Thanon Pah Loh, in the general direction of home, we came upon the Siam Hotel. It was smaller than the Ubon Hotel downtown, which bustled with nightclubs and restaurants and bars, and it was landscaped like a small country club.

"Did I hear they have a nice pool here?" I asked Dah.

"*Mii.* They have. You like swim-ming?"

We slowed down before we reached the main entrance. "How 'bout it, Tom?"

"Can we rent bathing suits?"

"*Mai pen rai*, don' worry," answered Dah. "It closed already—they turn off lights."

The gate to the pool was locked, but Tom found a spot in the hedge where we could squeeze through. As soon as we got inside, we lit up some more pot and began scouting around. We found an ashtray that we kept with us, some towels, which we stowed on a lounge chair, and three inner tubes that we tossed into the water. Flinging off our sandals and rolling up our pant legs, we sat down along the edge of the pool and began kicking, turning the glassy water into a bubbly froth. By the time we finished smoking the number even Dah was feeling giddy. We slipped off our clothes and jumped in, racing like little kids to see who would get the best tube. Mine was made by an American manufacturer, aviation quality—probably from an F-4, I figured. I felt more secure floating in the murky pool but wondered how safe my next landing would be coming back from the Mu Gia Pass.

The three of us spent a demented minute paddling furiously in circles before Tom ran out of steam and made his way back to the side of the pool. Hiking his chest up high from inside the tube, he reached over to his clothes lying nearby. It took some rummaging around, but he finally found his packet of red rock and pulled it out. Dah and I paddled over to him to see what we were missing. Tukada stared at the rock, tried to look away, and stared again. "You think it would hurt if I do jus' one last time?"

Tom rolled up his hundred-baht note and snorted. His eyes went glassy as he was blasted with a head rush. "It's up to you, Dah."

My eyes flashed darkly. I tried to remember ever being put out with Tom in the two years we had known each other. His mellowness had always been a blessing, a refuge from the sharks and barracudas who were taking the war seriously. Now, abruptly, his sweetness had become another wrap in the noose that was strangling Tukada. I put my hand on her arm. "Please, Dah. Your baby needs you to take care of her."

She looked melancholy as she turned away. I was startled at how quickly her face had turned ashen and drawn, as if something inside her was dying. Carefully, Tom folded up his powdered happiness and tucked it back where he'd found it in his pile of clothing. "Got any more *ganja*?" he asked, reaching for the shirt I'd left crumpled on the ground.

"There might be one more number rolled."

Tom found the cigarette and lit it and passed it over to Tukada. She took a long drag and held her breath for several seconds before exhaling the smoke in a thin, steady stream. "Sorry I get too sad," she said, a sensual smile returning to her face as she reached across the sides of our inner tubes and passed the reefer to me. "Actually, I very hap-py. This night is *so good.*"

I took a deep draw and gazed at Tukada. She returned my gaze and then closed her eyes, contented. After tapping off the ash and pressing the doobie into the notch on the side of the ashtray, I pushed off, floating back out into the middle of the pool. I started kicking myself around in a circle, and soon Tom and Dah came out and joined in, unable to keep from laughing like school kids. I spun around wildly, spinning myself back in time to a backyard tree swing and a rocket ride at a church carnival that promised to fling us into the heavens. I spun wildly across the plains of Kansas and I skimmed along the Yellow Brick Road to Oz. I spun myself into distant galaxies and could not remember if I were seeing the past or the future or if the whirling blue and magenta that filled my mind's eye was another dimension that had always existed but which I could only see in moments filled with overwhelming love and extrainteruniversal timelessness and spirituality brought on by incredibly fine dope and two debauched friends whom I cared about at that moment more than anyone else in the world. I spun madly and perfectly—until I caught a glimpse of Tukada at the side of the pool, reaching into the pocket of Tom's pants, tightly rolling up the Thai note she found and snorting from the packet of red-rock heroin.

I watched her through a magical slow-motion camera and then crawled inside my own movie, paddling in a hazy dream to the ashtray near the ledge of the pool where I had left the roach. I picked it up carefully with my fingernails and lit it, managing to take a few drags on it before my fingertips turned to fire and I had to flip the ashes into the dark landscape. Tom watched from the middle of the pool as I slipped out of my tube and swam over to Dah. "Are you sure you want to do that?" I asked her.

She nodded yes.

"Is it good?"

She nodded again, but her eyes looked sad and lost. She was only an inch away from me. I could feel her warm womanliness radiating through the cool water and was drawn another sixteenth of an inch closer. Her naked body—even distorted beneath the rippling surface—was perfect, but I was afraid to touch her, afraid the moment would end, afraid she would break into a thousand tiny shards like a porcelain doll. "If you're going to die, I want to die with you," I said, slipping the rolled-up hundred-baht note from between her fingers.

I couldn't keep my senses from devouring every inch of her—her fragrant hair, her sad eyes, her flawless skin, her high cheekbones and full lips, her delicate arms and perfect legs, her firm breasts and taut belly. I wanted to wrap her tiny body up in my long arms and hold her and protect her and make her sadness and loneliness go away. I wanted to make my own sadness and loneliness go away. I wanted my mind to stop reeling. I wanted to *stop* feeling drunk and crazy and afraid—afraid especially that I might be falling in love—except that I was afraid to stop feeling these feelings, afraid that if I stopped I might not feel anything at all. Worst of all, I was frightened that I did not know how to stop even if I wanted to. I kissed Dah on the cheek and said, "I want to do rock too."

I picked up the paper. She clamped her hands around my wrists and said, "Bren-dan—don't. Tom an' I, we have to do. Don' you get sick too—"

"You mean you'd cut off your best friend, Brendie-Bear? Deprive me of my own toot?" Tom took the bill and the packet out of my hands, snorted the rock, and burned the paper. "Believe us, Brendan, you don't wanna start."

"How do *you* know what I want?" I started to say, but he wasn't listening.

Dah had started swimming away from us to the middle of the deep end of the pool and soon Tom and I, her loyal retainers, were swimming after her, solemnly, obediently. Suddenly Tom pulled Dah three feet underwater, catching her completely by surprise. She stayed down a little too long, though, which started to scare me, and when she broke the surface, she was gasping for air. We rushed over to help, but it was a trick—she splashed a mountain of water at both of us, smiling wickedly. Soon mayhem was restored, childlike laughter was again filling the air and all three of us thought we could go on forever taking turns dunking and splashing each other.

"*Shhhh*," whispered Tukada.

We could hear the sound of footsteps on cement. The iron gate creaked open and an intruder appeared in a thin veil of light. Tom and I felt our hearts jump a beat, but before we had time to react, Dah had already swum over to what turned out to be the night manager. They talked awhile in Thai too rapid for Tom or me to follow.

"Give him three dollar," she called back to us softly.

I swam over and fetched the money out of my pants. The night manager was satisfied, as much by the magnified and distorted view he got of Dah's body as by the crisp banknotes. Soon the manager's footsteps had receded into the evening's ambience of chirping cicadas, cackling *jingjoks*, gentle wind, light traffic and the tender lullaby of jet engines being tested a few miles away at the base. The three of us reverted to laughter and childish play that was even sillier than before. When we grew weary, we gathered up the old inner tubes and met together out in the middle of what had become our private lagoon, forming our own little desert island. Tukada kissed her vassals and leaned back luxuriantly.

"This night is so, so wonder-ful," she purred. "Tom and Bren-dan, my two bes' frien' in the whole world—my dearly beloved…. We gazzer togezzer…like the day I get mar-ried to my cap-tain. Santa Cruz was so beau-ti-ful." She closed her eyes and smiled and I could imagine a sunny afternoon in a garden overlooking the Pacific. "So many flower!" she remembered out loud. And I could picture Tukada dressed in white, her gentle features softened further by her veil. The only thing I had trouble picturing was her "captain," and I wondered if what Lek had told me was true about him only being an airman first class.

"My dearly beloved, let us gazzer togezzer tonight…to join in holy mat-ri-mo-nee." She continued, opening her eyes dreamily. "Tom and Bren-dan, will you have zis woman for you' wedded wife?"

"We will."

"Will you love her, honor her, and comfort her even if she get sick again?"

"We will."

"And, forget-ting all ozzer, never butterfly on her for as long as you both still live?"

"We won't," said Tom.

"We won't," I echoed.

"I, Tukada Maneewatana, take you, Tom Whee-lah and Bren-dan Lea-ry, to be my wedded hus-ban', to have and to hold on to you from zis day for-ward, for bet-ter or for worse, for rich or poor, even if you get sick, to love and to care for you, an' never butterfly on you until we die."

She clasped hands with Tom and me, and Tom and I did the same, completing the circle. "I now pronounce us Men and Wife, in the name of the Faz-zer, the Son, and the Buddha. You may kiss the bride."

We tried to pull ourselves close enough together to hug each other, but the ungainly inflatables refused to cooperate. Tom and I managed only to peck her on the cheek before we bounced off in disparate directions, laughing so hard we had to gasp for breath. "An' Dave an' Mole an' Lek an' Sii-da can go to hell!" swore Tukada victoriously.

"To hell with them all!" Tom and I reprised.

We slipped out of our tubes, and when we met again at the side of the pool near the lounge chair that held our beach towels, we grew serious for a moment and took each other's hands once more and held each other together tightly in a circle. For a moment we didn't notice the chlorine burning our eyes and the mosquitos buzzing in our ears. For that fleeting moment we felt that we had made a true, lifelong commitment to each other.

"There is so much love here tonight—I can't believe it really hap-pen. When we have so much love for each other like zis, it feel so good I sink maybe my heart explode." She wove her limbs through and around Tom and me, weaving us into a basket of her happiness. "My Tom and my Brendan," she said softly, giving us each a kiss on the cheek. "I sink maybe zis is the best night of all of my life."

Out of the water, we dressed shyly. On the flight line at the base an F-4 engine was revved up to full throttle, a furious dragon-roar that Tom and Dah and I had long ago learned to ignore.

Stairway to Heaven

Riding back, Tukada again sat behind me, this time with both hands on my chest. "Do you want to make love to me?" she whispered.

I laughed. "Do we have any choice now that we're 'married'?"

When we arrived at Ruam Chon Sawng, the alley was ankle-deep in trash and absolutely stone-dead quiet. At Bungalow #4, we locked our bicycles at the bottom of the stairs and started up, letting Tom lead the way. Dah and I lagged behind, and halfway up, I stopped and pulled her to me and kissed her gently on the mouth. Kissing on the mouth was rare in Thailand in those days, a French practice that had only been performed in the brothels run by the Gauls along the Mekong River until the Americans came. It was still rare and I immediately understood why. If all Thai women parted their lips as warmly and tenderly and invitingly and drew in a man's soul as simply as a bullfrog snatches its evening meal from the sky—I could easily imagine Thailand with the rice crop unplanted, heroin unsmuggled, bribes uncollected, long-distance buses parked meekly by the side of the road. It was too bizarre to think about, and as she continued to kiss me back, sucking out every ounce of self-control and rational thinking ability that I might have once possessed, I concluded unequivocally that kissing was far too dangerous to be practiced by the general Thai public.

"You sure you want to make love to me?" she asked. Her voice sounded like a gentle mountain breeze.

I kissed her again, on the forehead. I ran my lips across her sheer black hair. Her scent turned chlorine to perfume.

"First you have to shave your mus-tache, like I tol' you before."

I could scarcely comprehend. As I rummaged through the back alleys of my memory I began to recall a night that seemed like fifteen years ago when a wonderful hippie massage girl at Niko's by the name of Tukada hinted at limitless joy and pleasure if I would only shave off what I had long thought of unflinchingly as the core of what was left of my identity. I couldn't keep from smiling sardonically when I thought of the commotion I stirred up when I first raised a mustache back at the Pentagon. Careerists simply did not wear facial hair of any description, whether it was technically permitted or not. The Navy and Marine brass acted like they were eating glass when they discovered that under *Air Force* regulations, a pimply-faced enlisted man like me could raise a bush without asking their permission.

I thought how strange it was that during the Civil War you could not be an officer *without* raising a beard. Of course whoever wrote the Air Force regulations got his own perverse revenge, limiting the size of a mustache to precise dimensions that guaranteed its Hitler-like ugliness.

"If you go shave your mus-tache, I come to you. Promise."

I followed her up the stairs like a trusting puppy. She opened the door to the music room, where Tom was already putting on a record, and turned back to me, gazing calmly into my eyes. "It's up to you."

Inside my bedroom the air was hot and stale. I opened the shutters and put the ceiling fan on low, which produced a groaning, complaining sound like an oxcart on its way to market. The room's construction was simple, the roughly finished framing remaining open, allowing the plank walls to breathe while providing extra shelf space in otherwise confined quarters. The screens were an exercise in wishful thinking, filled as they were with random rips and tears. An insect was already buzzing nearby when I knelt down to light a green mosquito coil and set it in an old pie tin on the floor beside my bed. It was a comfortable enough bed, constructed simply of a pine frame that supported thin slats laid side by side. They in turn support-ed three child-sized mattresses that, when placed next to each other, pro-duced the Thais' version of a queen-sized bed. My only other furniture con-sisted of an old card table that held my stereo gear, a small rattan bedside table for my Baby Ben alarm clock, a wicker chair, and a flimsy armoire, which held my modest collection of clothes and toilet articles.

I picked up my shaving kit and went around to the *hong nam*. The bathing room was almost as large as my sleeping quarters, the floor and the first four feet of the walls covered with white tile. There was an Asian-style squatter toilet at one end, a wicked device I sometimes imagined the French invented from a broken bidet when they heard they were being supplanted by Americans. No toilet paper was provided and nobody bothered to steal any from the base. Instead, a spigot opened into a small klong jar that held a plastic dipper. Douching as only the French could enjoy, I thought, but damn if it didn't work. In the corner stood a larger klong jar which held lots of lukecold water and a yellow plastic bowl that we used as a scoop to take our "showers." The water drained out through a hole in the white tile in the corner by the toilet.

I turned on the light and stepped over to the warped, discolored mirror that was nailed to the wall above the sink. Always forgetting how booze and dope made my face look pale and my head misshapen, I scarcely recognized the reflection I was staring at. I took out my manicure scissors and began to trim. Only then did I begin to remember how long it had taken those hairs to grow and how much longer it had taken for them to fill themselves in to what might pass for adult consistency. I cut away the whiskers on the right side first, and I thought of the grunt I had heard about pulling LRRP duty— long-range reconnaissance—up on the Lao-Chinese border who had only grown half a mustache after he heard there was no regulation against it. The rear-echelon brass split a gut every time they saw him back at base camp. Within a few weeks, however, Sergeant Half-Mustache had survived being cut off and surrounded three different times by the Pathet Lao, and thereafter he was absolutely certain that his lopsided lip hair was a lucky talisman. His whole squad began to feel it was their good-luck charm too, and sure enough, shortly after he rotated back to the States, his replacement stepped on a landmine and they had to extract the whole unit.

I felt a brief kick of excitement at the thought of wearing half a bush around the base, especially at the paroxysms of high blood pressure I could give First Sergeant Link and the lunatic assistant base commander, but the faint echo of Dah's voice wafting through the single-ply wallboards gave me a deeper sort of rush. Leaning in close to the mottled surface of the mirror, I snipped away at the last of the whiskers and lathered up.

When I began shaving, however, I suddenly felt ridiculous, filled with second thoughts about taking such desperate action on blind faith. Dah was alone with Tom back in the music room, achingly close to my own room, sharing the same landing, the doors at right angles, practically touching. So many evenings the gang had gathered there to smoke and drink and rap and listen to Tom's stereo, only tonight it was just Tukada, alone. Through the thin walls I could hear her humming sweetly to the Temptations album he was playing. When "Ain't Too Proud to Beg" came on, she knew the words by heart and sang along.

I took the last couple of strokes with my safety razor and rinsed off my face. My head reeled. *I look like a goddamn Young Republican*, I thought. *For crying out loud, I look like my own son!* The baby face I had been trying to hide with the mustache was now utterly exposed, looking ten years younger than young, practically pre-pubescent now that the thin stand of lip whiskers had been cleared away. I had originally hoped for a Hemingway macho look. The mustache had at least given me a sense of stiff-upper-lip British detachment. At times when I leafed through my well-worn volume of Wilfred Owen's war poems, I was struck with how familiar his face looked on the back cover. That World War I infantry officer, with his dignified mustache, could have been a cousin or even a brother, but it was the picture of an older brother with eyes far too weary for a man of twenty-five.

Coming out of the *hong nam* feeling naked and frail, I couldn't help laughing. By raising a scrawny patch of lip whiskers simply to get into a Georgetown club without being carded, I had inadvertently entered a charmed inner circle—when you met a character with a mustache, a wristband, sideburns, or non-Air Force wire-rimmed glasses, you had found a fellow hipster. Instantly we shared a deep and profound bond that could only result from discovering identical loopholes hidden among volumes of Air Force regs. Even for a gung ho MiG-killer like Robin Olds, commander of the 8th Tactical Fighter Wing, a handlebar mustache hinted at unlimited potential as a hell-raiser. Why had Pentagon careerists decided that in my case it was a symbol of defiance? Why had I enjoyed playing along?

My ruminations turned into remorse as I walked barefoot over the splintery deck back to my room. Here I was—after being denied countless automatic promotions, after enduring all varieties of harassment from redneck sergeants and being forced to collect my mail at 2:00 a.m., all over this three-inch patch of individuality that I wore over my scarred upper lip—shaving it off in an instant for Miss Tukada Maneewatana. *How could I so easily turn into a Pavlovian dog, salivating when I hear the faint trace of a female voice? How could my raging hormones so easily deliver a karate kick to the Catholic values—guilt and fear—drummed into me by Father Boyle? Goddamn,* I thought, *this had better be great.*

I slowed down when I passed the music room. Light was streaming from the wide gap under the plank door. Dah's humming stopped. I couldn't keep from pressing my ear within a few inches of the door. "There is so much love in this house tonight," I could hear her murmur. Back in my room,

I stripped down to my boxers and stretched out on my bed, half expectant and half resigned. The ceiling fan groaned, but my attention kept going back to that door. I turned out my light and cracked my door and saw that streaks of light were still leaking out of the music room. And then, with a stab of disappointment, I realized it had grown silent and had stayed that way for several minutes.

I tried to lie down again, but the silence was driving me crazy. I bolted out of bed and tiptoed out of the room. Unable to stop myself, I bent over awkwardly and looked through the keyhole into the music room. In a way the vignette I saw was lovely—Dah was giving Tom a massage, working her hands deep into his back the way she had with me that fateful night long ago at Niko's. "What's zat?" asked Tukada, turning her head toward the keyhole.

I almost fell on my fanny backing away from the door and retreating to my room. Peeking outside through my own keyhole, I saw Tom crack open their door, look around and go back inside. I stretched out on my bed again, but I was unable to relax, afraid I was going to go mad with an aching desire for Tukada and a fierce loathing for myself. At last, staring in darkness at the overhead fan, I was able to force my mind to slow itself down and focus on the steadfast turning of the blade. Finally I began to feel at peace, pleasantly exhausted as I lay there sinking into limbo land. The door opened. Coolly I watched Dah come into the room and undress in silhouette. She pulled down the sheet and sidled up to me. "Hurry," she whispered.

Next door in the music room, Tom flipped the switch to his big Teac tape deck and headed back to his bed-sitting room. The voice of Joni Mitchell began filling Bungalow #4 with one after another of her melancholy ballads.

Dah and I simply touched our cheeks together at first, breathing in each other's scent, before I brushed my lips lightly over hers and kissed her throat and neck. "Oi!" she cried out softly. And then she kissed me back, on my lips, warmly at first and then hungrily. Ripping her nails across my back, she began kissing my chest, and my whole body came alive, charged with an electric intensity by her incredibly satin-smooth Thai skin. And as I slipped off my shorts and slid deep into her, my mind's eye turned my tiny hovel into a galaxy of endless miles of indigo illuminated with a million pinpricks of starlight. A waterfall of silk and velvet coursed over my body, and Dah transformed into a winged goddess who devoured me and at the same time melted to my touch. Rainbow colors exploded inside my head as she continued to shower me with warm kisses. The black velvet galaxy turned pastel, then blood red, then into sunshine.

"Hurry, Bren-dan, hurry." I heard a soft, familiar voice but could not tell where it came from. And then I felt her legs pull tight together underneath, squeezing me, trying to deepen our pleasure. Or was she just trying to rush me? She pressed and squeezed and prodded, and like the one-celled amoeba I had been and still was, I finished quickly and pleasantly and felt warm and drained, relaxed and exhilarated. I closed my eyes again and the inside of my head turned black and quiet and empty. And the emptiness swelled, slowly and inexorably, and consumed me. "*I really don't know love at all,*" sang Joni Mitchell's muffled voice, bleeding through the paper-thin walls.

As I lay there next to Tukada, the cooling breeze from the ceiling fan felt good on my moist skin. I was about to ask her if her if she could spend the night, but before I could speak she climbed out of bed, wrapped herself in a bath towel, and tied it at her side. "You have money for tax-ii, Bren-dan? I don' get check from hus-ban' yet this month."

I was taken aback. Tukada had fooled me. I had confused a brief moment of pleasure for something more. Coming back to earth with a thud, I remembered the two missing hundred-baht notes from the night of Dave and Dah's first visit. Was it possible I had friends who would steal from friends to feed their heroin habit? *Who is this lady? A dream come true? A slightly slicker-than-average bar girl? A thieving scag addict?* "Sure," I finally answered. "Is five dollars okay?" I found a hundred-baht bill and stuffed it in the pocket of her shirt, which hung from a nail on the wall.

"It's not like *that*—"

"I didn't say it was." I tried again to ask her if she was going to stay the night, but Dah was already zipping up her jeans. Silently, she pulled on her shirt, buttoned it up and was soon closing the door behind her, leaving the towel on the floor where she had dropped it.

I felt numb as I crawled back into bed, bone tired but unable to sleep. The stiletto blows of high-heeled shoes sounded on the wooden stairs outside, resonating like pagan drums announcing the arrival of a Polynesian queen. I wasn't positive, but I thought I could make out Lek's voice. A minute later there was no mistaking the sound of Dah and Lek shrieking at each other, footsteps indicating a scuffle, and finally the sound of furious blows. I found my pants in the dark and went out.

Dah was standing at the railing of the porch, her back turned to Lek, saying nothing. Lek clutched her pasteboard suitcase tightly in her arms, guarding the music room door like a cornered animal. "Goddamn whore!" she screamed. "You sell your body just like every other Suzy Wong. You whore just like me—only worse. I *know* what I am!"

Dah did not move or say a thing. Suddenly Lek noticed my clean-shaven face. "And you! Look what she make you do! She make you a *lifer!*"

She dropped her suitcase, ran into the music room, and began beating on Tom's naked chest. He had just come out of the shower and had only a beach towel, the one Lek had given him decorated with the signs of the zodiac, wrapped around his waist. "Lek," he said, "you better leave."

"Leave! I go away so we can stay together, and you sleep with Suzy Wong—after she sleep with your frien'. Look what she make him do! She do the same to you, *same* way. She make you all lifer in her private army. She do to everybody."

She flailed at Tom again. "You don't believe me, do you? You believe Suzy Wong, but you don't believe *me*—after I give you everything."

She started to cry. It embarrassed her so much that she pounded at Tom even harder. "I was never going to tell you dis. But now it don't matter. I tell you everything. In Takhli, long time ago, I have boyfrien' in Thai Army. He give me baby, so we going to mar-ry. Except Suzy Wong come and steal him. Know what she do? Wear see-through blouse, no bra. She do floor show—take off clothes for everybody! Nice?"

"So I take off baby an' almos' die, but den I go to Korat an' meet Mitch an' love Mitch very much, an' with Mitch I keep our baby. *An' she come an' do same thing!* Why you so dumb, Tom? Why you let her do same thing to *you*, huh?"

She slapped his face. Doing it gave her strength to do it again, harder. I had never seen Tom mad, but his face was burning on the outside and from deep within. He grabbed her hand and said, "Don't do it again. I'm warning you—"

She jerked her hand away and hit him in the face, harder yet. Tom could no longer restrain himself, throwing Lek wildly around the room like a rag doll, screaming, "Stop hitting me! We didn't do anything, you jealous bitch!"

She twisted out of his grasp and shoved him with might and fury built up from years of backbreaking labor on her father's rice farm. Tom—almost a foot taller and outweighing her by eighty pounds—was caught off balance and sent crashing into his beloved tape deck, his precious Teac that he loved more than red-rock heroin, the tape deck that was the source of music that was more than music, of music that was manna for his body and soul and far less fickle than any woman. It fell to the floor with a leaden, sickening thud. Tom charged at Lek in a frenzy. I rushed in and held them apart, afraid he was going to kill her.

"I go," she said, collapsing into the pillows of the bamboo sofa and beginning to cry again.

Tom and I retreated to the porch. We got there in time to see a *sahmlaw*'s long shadow, thrown by a distant streetlight, sliding off into the night like water returning to the sea after a wave has broken. Tukada was gone.

Train Ride to Surin, OR:
Going Nowhere Slowly

I let Danielle's stream of letters pile up unopened at Bungalow Ruam Chon Sawng and did a lot of lying around, too unfocused to even look at a magazine or the *Stars and Stripes*. Band rehearsals were an ordeal, and even when we performed at the clubs I was just going through the motions—until at least once a night my mind played a dirty trick on me, convincing me for an instant when I looked out through the gauzy haze of cigarette smoke that it was Tukada I saw coming through the door, dressed to kill after trading in her jeans and work shirt for a tailored silk dress. And always it was a case of mistaken identity, a cruel illusion conjured up in my imagination with the help of cheap Thai booze.

I was too numb to feel crowded by the slow trickle of lifers who were beginning to move in to Ruam Chon Sawng, renting the occasional bungalow vacated by a brother rotating back to the World or one of the hipster potheads turning himself in for detox. According to Lek and Pueng, the beer-bellied lifer types liked Ruam Chon Sawng because it was about the only place left in Ubon where they could still get a four-room bungalow for sixty a month. That left them plenty to send home to their families, and—more important—they had enough left over to keep their *tii-rahks* happy. I could put up with the trickle of lifers, even when the boarded-up storefront next to Mama-sahn's noodle shop reopened as a tailor shop for master sergeants. As long as most of the lifers preferred to stay on base within walking distance of the NCO Club, they were never going to be a major problem in a remote corner of Ubon like Ruam Chon Sawng.

I fell back into my old routine, but I was filled with an unnamable sense of foreboding. Whether I was flying in a hypervigilant state of terror over the Trail with Spectre, working with the band, or sitting around the music room at Ruam Chon Sawng, I also felt an undercurrent of loss. That undercurrent was heightened by the seeming omnipresence of Dave Murray, whom I saw every day in the orderly room at ComDoc, who turned up anywhere the Band of Brothers was playing, and who was a constant presence at Ruam Chon Sawng. I *liked* Dave well enough, but having him around was awkward when I was quietly yearning for Tukada, whose very name was taboo.

Wheeler, Zelinsky, Murray and I decided to celebrate Thanksgiving at the chow hall on base, meeting up with Washington, Shahbazian and a few other Rat Pack enlisted men. Baker, Sachs and a couple more Spectre gunners joined us, and the next thing we knew, Sugie Bear, Ackerman and Rev Golson from the band were squeezing in with us. There was so much good cheer and camaraderie that nobody minded when Murray asked the Reverend to say grace and he accepted. They were serving up something that looked and smelled and tasted an awful lot like a turkey dinner. In fact it was so much like turkey that it left us too drowsy to do any nightclubbing afterward. Instead, the guys living on base went back to their hootches to crash, the guys living off-base headed home, and our inner circle ended up lounging around late into the night at Ruam Chon Sawng solving questions of world war and peace, the creation and destruction of the universe, and the existence and non-existence of God. Dave Murray insisted after his third bong that the universe ended at a brick wall. "Sort of like love," said Zelinsky.

We waited for Dave to say something about Dah, but he didn't take the opening. Zelinsky filled the gaping silence, speculating that the universe was flat and we'd fall off like one of Columbus's galleons when we got to the end and be eaten by intergalactic sea serpents. "God must like a good joke," he smirked. "Why else would he have created the human race?"

Baker insisted this was all a bunch of bullshit, but that if *anybody* was running the show, he had no doubt it was Beelzebub and his right hand man, the Antichrist. "Who else would have taken a bunch of puke, given it the power to walk and talk, and then turned it into pitiful excuses of human beings like you guys?"

Wheeler was more a theological anarchist or a scientific pagan than a Satan-worshipper. "What I've wanted to know ever since eighth grade is *who* lit the fuse that set off the Big Bang? Leary, you haven't been saying much—"

Even though I couldn't move my body, my mind thought it was working just fine. In reality, I was on a thirty-second delay, still ruminating about Dave and Tukada and wondering if their love had indeed hit a brick wall. I had speculated for a microsecond on how wonderful my life would be if it had been *Dave* who had disappeared and it were *Tukada* who did the typing in the orderly room every morning and followed me devotedly from night club to night club when my band was playing and who spent free evenings curled up beside me in the cozy confines of Ruam Chon Sawng and who maybe even slipped on a flight suit and stowed away with me for a sortie or two over the Ho Chi Minh Trail when the moon was full. I had somehow managed to follow the drift of the conversation, though, and tried to probe my fellow philosophers with an even more profound and disturbing question: "If—as Tom implies—it were God who lit the fuse, where did He get the match and how did He get here in the first place?" I half expected Father Boyle to burst through the flimsy door, rap my knuckles with his oak ruler and send me back to catechism class.

"You ever wonder if we're just part of some giant's dream?" Dave asked.

"Or sub-atomic particles in a mad scientist's electron microscope," said Zelinsky.

Lek, who had resigned herself to staying with Tom, poked her head in from time to time, usually declining a hit on the bong but being compassionate enough to bring us cut fruit to stave off our periodic attacks of the munchies. She tended to take a position somewhat similar to Harley's, the only difference being that we made her laugh instead of pissing her off. "What the hell kind of bullshit are you dudes talking about, huh? I think all this dope is making you crazy."

"What's a theological Antichrist?" Dave asked.

I started dropping by Harley's occasionally and was amused to observe how Khun Jim—Jim Scott, the Peace Corps volunteer who had taught English to many of the adorable young shop girls in Ubon—was living happily in the same compound with Baker and Pigpen Sachs, two of the gnarliest purveyors of death in Spectre. I supposed it was appropriately incongruous that his *tii-rahk*, Pye, was one of the hardest drinking females in all of Ubon, while Mali, Harley's *tii-rahk*, was a picture of schoolmarm decorum. When Jim found out I had taught English to Portuguese immigrants before going into the Air Force, he asked if I would be interested in teaching a class for the American University Alumni Association night school that he ran in Ubon. At first I declined, remembering the fiasco in Bristol, Rhode Island, and not wanting to repeat the experience.

When Khun Jim brought it up again a few days later, he explained to me that it would be a small class of professional Thai adults, many of whom worked on the base. I finally started to come around late in November when Rev Golson, lead singer of the Band of Brothers—announced he was on his short-timer countdown, which meant he only had a month to go before he returned home. Given that he was our heart and soul, it was pretty well accepted by all of us that the Reverend's departure meant the Band of Brothers would be disbanding. The following week, sitting around the table eating some of Mali's home cooking, Harley asked me why I hadn't signed up to teach now that the band was breaking up. "You're right," I said and got up from my unfinished dinner to walk back to Jim's converted-rice-barn bungalow. "Is that night-school job still open?"

"We won't start another term until January," he answered.

"Perfect. That's exactly when I'll be packing up my drums for the last time."

The Special Services trip to Big Buddha had been scheduled for the Saturday after we came off base alert, but our little syndicate decided to avoid getting mixed in with a crowd of clueless sightseers and postponed our scouting expedition for a couple of weeks. The Surin Elephant Roundup that Jack Wu had been so excited about fell the following Saturday, on the weekend after Thanksgiving. Jack and I tagged along with Tom, Lek, Larry and Pueng. The train ride out and back was boringly free of bandit attacks, and the festival itself failed to produce a single elephant stampede, to our mild disappointment. The Tourist Authority of Thailand knew how to put on a good show, nevertheless, featuring war elephants re-fighting ancient victories over the Burmese and Kampucheans, elephants gleefully and gracefully kicking around a giant soccer ball, and a single elephant defeating a hundred Thai soldiers at tug-of-war. Jack was enraptured trying out his new super-telephoto lens and monopod, which had come in just in time on the courier flight from Hong Kong.

The Saturday after the festival, our same group plus Sagittarius Smith and Annie Kim, the new lead singer of the Chirping Sparrows—the one who could really sing—took a fleet of *roht tax-iis* north to Wat Pah Mongkol, a forest monastery near the town of Amnat Charoen. Major Horney had to cancel at the last minute due to a cartel "training flight" down to Sydney and over to Hong Kong that somehow involved the duty-free swapping of opals for Sansui radios. At Wat Pah Mongkol we finally saw the star of our bicycle race—what the Issan Thais called *Ph'a Yai*—the Big Buddha. I hadn't known what to expect, and what was awaiting us was both simpler and more elegant than the mosaic tile and gold of the ornate Buddhist temples of Bangkok. This Buddha image was seated outside, serene yet imposing, on a platform decorated with bas-relief columns that seemed almost Grecian. The statue itself was fifteen feet tall, which meant it would have been thirty feet tall if it miraculously decided to stand. The figure was trim and erect in the classic Thai style and was covered with radiant squares of gold leaf. Jack Wu wandered off to get pictures of the Buddha from some fresh angles and soon drifted away photographing the monastery proper. The rest of us, even my antsy American compadres, stood there a moment in awe of the peaceful countenance that smiled down upon us beneficently.

The Buddha's gaze had an especially powerful effect on Pueng and Lek and even the well-traveled Annie, transfiguring them into demure, traditional Asian village girls as they approached the base of the shrine. Childlike, suppliant, they knelt respectfully in front of the Big Buddha, lit sticks of incense, and placed the joss sticks carefully in large, sand-filled ceramic bowls. After a moment of silent prayer and reflection, the three young ladies stood and rejoined us.

Zelinsky finally broke the spell, looking up at the Big Buddha and remarking, "This is how Tom would look if he were wise instead of stoned."

"Maybe *you* would look wise, Zelinsky, if you ever wiped that smirk off your chubby face."

"I afraid Lar-ry too much smart-ass to ever be wise like Buddha," said Pueng, pinching his cheek playfully.

Annie patted Sagittarius Smith on the stomach. "Maybe Smitty can be Laughing Buddha in next life." Sagittarius just grunted and took out a cigar. "Let's go fatten him up right now," Annie said, leading the group back up the wide dirt lane to order lunch at the outdoor *rahn-ahahn* just outside the gate.

I lingered behind, noticing how different it was here from the bustling city temples of Ubon and Bangkok. Part of Wat Pah Mongkol's elegant simplicity came from being a forest monastery situated three hundred yards off the quiet country road that ran from Ubon to Mukdahan, a trading town on the Mekong. Most of the structures were tiny wood-frame huts called *kuti*'s, where the monks lived simply, sleeping on grass mats at night and spending much of their days in deep meditation practicing Noble Silence. The many trees muffled the noise of occasional trucks and buses that passed on Route 212.

I had just started back to rejoin the group when a monk in his early twenties approached me. His head was shaved, as was the custom, and he wore traditional robes that went back to the time of the Golden Age of Athens and in fact looked like a saffron version of a toga Socrates might have worn. "You like Buddha?" he asked politely.

"I don't know much about Buddha. But I like the quiet and the trees and being out in the country. My mother's family lived out in the country back in America. I never get to hear quiet like this back in Ubon—Americans like noise."

"Are you wit' Air Force?"

"I'm afraid so. I'm a combat cameraman—*tahahn akaht tii tai papayon*. And on my nights off, I'm a rock and roll drummer—*chang len glong*. Everywhere I go it's noisy! Noisy airplanes, noisy nightclubs, noisy bungalow."

"City noisy for Thai people too. You should come stay at wat. Just come for visit."

"You know, I might like that, but I don't know the customs. And my Thai isn't very good."

"You can go Wat Pah Niraphai, not too far from Warin, about ten kilomet' from *satahnii rohtfai* where you take train to Bangkok. Two American monk live there."

"Wat Pah Niraphai?"

"Yes. Forest Monastery without Fear—without Danger."

"I could use some of that," I chuckled, taking out my notebook and writing down as close to the sounds as I could come up with in English.

"Let me write for you in Thai so you can show taxi driver." He jotted down what looked like Sanskrit and I thanked him. "You fly in war over Lao?" he asked.

"How did you guess?"

"Every day and every night we see Air Force planes go to Lao. And we have many Issan people come here to pray for cousin, aunt, uncle, who still live in Lao. Many Issan family come from both sides of *Mae Nam Kong*."

"That makes sense. It's two sides of the same river." I looked up to the road and saw that our meal was being served. "I've really enjoyed talking to you, but I'm afraid I must go join my friends for lunch. Would you care to eat with us?"

"Thank you, but monk cannot eat after twelve o'clock. I must go do my meditation now. But if you come back here, it is good for me to practice my English. We don't often have English and American people come to here."

"I'll be back, I promise. I'm sorry, I never got your name."

"Please call me Prah Samrong. And you?"

"Brendan Leary. Just call me Brendan. I look forward to seeing you again, Prah Samrong. Unfortunately, I'm afraid that soon you might be getting too many chances to practice English. We're having a bicycle race from Ubon to Ph'a Yai in February and I think many American soldiers will come to visit before that."

"Very good! Monks don't know too much about bicycle race. We only walk or go in car or bus as passenger. But weather in February is perfect— cool and dry."

I smiled and gave him a respectful *wai*. "Thanks for telling me about the Monastery without Fear."

I wandered off to rejoin my friends, who had ordered a spicy green curry for lunch, topped off with my favorite Thai dessert—mango and sticky rice. On the drive back to Ubon, my stomach pleasantly full, I reflected on how Prah Samrong had a certain intangible poise and pride in his culture that reminded me of Sergeant Prasert. Even the way he wore the intricate folds and wraps of his monk's robes was as impeccable as the way Prasert wore his uniform. I was reminded of how pleased Prasert had been, smiling and telling me how much we would enjoy our trip, when he first heard we were going out to Big Buddha. Alas, I hadn't been thinking about Prasert for long when a ripple of fear and sadness stirred deep in my belly, reminding me that through all the comings and goings of the past month my commitment to Danielle was on shaky ground and that it was my femme fatale, Miss Tukada Maneewatana, who lingered on my mind.

When we got back to Ruam Chon Sawng, Prasert, in uniform, was sitting in the rattan throne chair on our front porch waiting for me. It was the kind of coincidence that didn't seem unusual in Thailand. "Tukada come to see you at Soul Sister," he said, "but Dave always there and she cannot stay."

"Please tell her I think of her," I told him in Thai.

"She will be happy to hear that," he replied, getting up without saying another word and disappearing down the stairs. A moment later I could see him across the alley chatting briefly with the kickboxer and his *tii-rahk* before he continued down the alley toward the gate.

It was around two by the pale light of my Baby Ben when I heard a soft tapping at my door. No sooner had I opened it a crack than Dah slipped in and pushed the door shut behind her. "Prasert tell me he talk to you," she whispered.

I was half asleep, only half able to open my eyes. "He told me you tried to see me. I've been thinking about you a lot. Too much. Hell, I think about you all the time—"

Before I knew it she had stepped into my arms and laid her head against my chest. "I thinking about you too, Bren-dan. *Jing-jing*. But I too tired to fight with Lek and Dave."

It seemed like a dream when she kissed me hungrily and helped me lift my T-shirt over my head. We undressed each other and slid into bed. Once again her skin was smooth and electrifying as we melted into each other's arms and kept on melting until our bodies were one, bathed in a warm glow that lingered on after we finished making love. "I *really* want you to stay tonight."

"I can't, Bren-dan. I afraid to leave my baby alone all night. Housekeeper is only young girl." I rolled over on my side and felt Tukada inch closer, pressing her warm body against my back and sliding her hand around me and resting it on my chest. Before I could awaken from what had to be a dream, we made love again. I wanted to ask her if she could at least stay another hour, but she spoke first. "You have fifty dollar? My mother have problem with my father's pay from Thai Navy. When his ship come to Sattahip, I pay you back, *jing-jing*."

By the time I found my wallet and dug out two five-hundred baht notes, she was dressed. "*Chan kit tung khun mahk*, Bren-dan—I think about *you* all the time." And then she took the bills and slipped quietly out the door.

It didn't seem to be getting any cheerier flying over the Ho Chi Minh Trail, but Tom and I knew the holiday season had arrived at Ubon Royal Thai Air Force Base when we rode past the water tower on our way home one fine day early in December and were greeted by a fifty-foot banner strung up courtesy of the 13th Bomb Group—the Grim Reapers—of a smiling skeleton wearing a red Santa's stocking cap and holding a bloody sickle, wishing all the world a big "Merry X-Mas!" Unfortunately the North Vietnamese 559th Transportation Group refused to get into the holiday spirit. Nothing that lit up along the Ho Chi Minh Trail turned out to be a Christmas tree.

Back at Ubon there must have been *someone* who enjoyed the non-stop Christmas carols from Armed Forces Thailand Network that blared over the base loudspeakers, but it wasn't Tom and me. Somehow, being in the tropics made it doubly irritating. We did manage to have a few laughs Christmas shopping at the Noy Market picking out hand-painted lacquerware for our moms and grandmoms and hill-tribe smoking jackets for our grandfathers. I sent Dad a set of silver wine goblets even though I had never seen him drink anything but beer and whiskey sours. My brother got a handcrafted bronze and silver chess set and my sisters got a couple of ornately costumed hill-tribe dolls. Tom found Lek a sweet little Sony AM-FM radio at the BX. I was having a harder time finding something for Danielle. My concentration was broken every time I saw a young woman with long, silky hair walking through the shadows of the crowded market. I could rarely stop staring until I knew for sure it wasn't Dah. Eventually, after a lot of looking around, I found Danielle a beautiful sarong made of Thai silk—*Perfect!*—and then realized after I mailed it that she would never wear it back in the States and that it had really been perfect for Tukada.

It wasn't until late in the holiday season that Jack Wu was finally able to snap me out of my funk. He rounded up Wheeler, Washington, Shahbazian and me and hurried us over to Zelinsky's cubicle in the editorial trailer in time for the noon news. On the little portable radio we heard Sagittarius Smith's booming voice announce, "Only sixty more days till the Big Buddha Bicycle Race! That's right! The Big Buddha Bicycle Race! You'd better oil up your wheels and start getting in shape today, because there will be cash prizes and the more of you studs who register, the bigger the prizes will be! Stay tuned! More details will be coming every day! This has been Sergeant Sagittarius Smith, your friendly host at the NCO and Airmen's clubs."

"What do you think?" asked Wu.

"That's what I call *bitchin'!*" I replied enthusiastically.

"Isn't it a little early?" Zelinsky asked.

"We figured better a little early than starting too late," I explained. "We want to begin lining up sponsors right away. And we need to visit every squadron commander on the base to get the unit competition thing going. That'll leave us a full month to sign up the individual competitors."

We all agreed it sounded good. "And it's really happening in sixty days?" Tom asked.

"Colonel Grimsley confirmed it with General Gong at Seventh Air Force," Wu replied.

And so the race was officially on. Peddling home that afternoon, I noticed my bike squeaking and groaning in ways I had never bothered to pay attention to. I'd be paying attention now if I wanted to take the run out to Big Buddha seriously. By the time I reached the main gate it had begun raining softly but steadily. I stopped a moment under the roof of the open-air bus stop to put on my poncho. Taking a deep breath, I put my head down and set out again past shivering *sahmlaw* drivers, cozy taxis, a couple of resolute motorbike drivers hiding in a doorway, and on past the already-crumbling stucco shops and bars that wrapped themselves around the American enclave.

Near the corner of Route 66, the two-story Maharaj Palace of Massage looked dark and empty inside. Next door, a truck was gassing up at the Shell Oil station. Weighing in at a good five tons, its cab was painted in a baroque pattern of pinks and yellows and lavenders. The cab interior was done in violet plush with felt balls dangling in the windows. Its bed was made of teak and mahogany, varnished like a millionaire's 1920 Chris Craft, and the entire vehicle was adorned in a plume of chrome. The overall effect was of a combination tin temple, Turkish bath and riverboat on wheels. I was amused seeing how the centuries-old tradition of Thai boat-building had been turned loose here on trucks since World War II, somewhat the way Western carriage makers turned to autos after the First World War. I wondered how the drivers could afford what I computed to be $2.80 a gallon for petrol, ten times what we were paying back in the States. Pushing off onto Route 66, I wondered if cases of black-market Blue Moon cigarettes paid for the extravagance that adorned the metal mastodon. Had the Blue Moons I'd been smoking paid for a chichi ball or two? Was Papa-sahn really the brains behind the slickly packaged reefers that some old mama-sahn went to the trouble of filling by hand and plugging at each end with real tobacco? Were the rumors true that none of the cigarettes stuffed with dope, the bars staffed with bar girls or the massage parlors filled with smiling China dolls would be possible without the approval of the Thai general who served as provincial governor?

I pedaled on toward the center of Ubon, the buildings growing older and darker, reminding me of pictures in *National Geographic* of the sides of buildings in Venice, Italy, that had turned into abstract paintings over the past millennium. The only difference was that in Asia the change was at least ten if not a hundred times faster. The streets were turning crimson from the clay that washed in from the countryside. I ignored the constant spray of mud and rain thrown up by my bike and by the passing trucks, buses and taxis that splattered my poncho. I ignored the stench emitted by the overflowing sewers, no longer amazed at how fast I had adapted to the rancid, acrid aromas that lurked around Ubon. As I pushed on, I found a small degree of pleasure in the drumming of raindrops on my hood. It produced a droning that soothed me like the Pali chanting that emerged in the morning and evening from the mysterious *wats* of Ubon.

I carried my bicycle up the stairs out of the rain. Peeling off my sodden poncho, I hung it up to dry on the wall next to Lek's cooking area at the far end of the balcony. My door was stuck in the humidity, so I had to give it a little kick to get it open. Our shack was so flimsy and perched so precariously on its stilts that the whole place shook. I had left a small stack of snapshots on the exposed 2x4 next to the door, photos that I had taken of Tom, Lek, Larry and Pueng on the night of Loy Kratong, forgetting I had also taken one of Sii-da. The shaking of Bungalow #4 must have knocked a few of the pictures loose, and, as luck would have it, it was Sii-da's face that stared up at me from the pile of pictures on the floor. It had a gauzy, mysterious quality that Tom had liked, saying it made her look introspective and deep. Sii-da disliked it so much she gave it back. Tom and I had laughed about it. Maybe she was from such a primitive part of Laos that she had never seen a photograph of herself before, or perhaps she was a spy whose face had been so cleverly transfigured by plastic surgery that she failed to recognize herself. Or was she already wanting to look like the girls in Lek's movie magazines?

Stepping out of my rain-soaked pants, I regretted trading in my full rain suit for the poncho when rainy season supposedly ended. I set my jungle boots by the door and hoped they'd dry out by morning. Wrapping myself in an oversize bath towel, I walked around to the *hong nam* to clean up. I dipped the plastic bowl into the large earthen cistern time and again, but the red clay clung to my nails and to the cracks and wrinkles in my feet and hands and face. Sii-da was of that same red earth, which sounded poetic to my mind's ear, but it reminded me that in reality I had been forever tainted by her sordid mindlessness. I decided to stop thinking about Sii-da. She had disappeared without a trace, leaving the brothers in Bungalow #3 without a cook or housekeeper. She no longer mattered unless I let her.

Back in my room, I put on a pair of jeans and a hill-tribe smoking jacket that felt warm on a rainy day in cold season. Thoughts of Lek popped into my head. Why hadn't she told me Sii-da was bringing strangers to my bed? Why had Lek tried so hard to sell me on Sii-da as a *tii-rahk*? Had I already become part of her feud with Tukada? I stretched out on my bed, letting out a long sigh. Tukada. I didn't need to stumble upon an old snapshot to bring up her memory. She was a picture I couldn't erase, a song that played over and over inside my head. I was sickened at the thought of being a pawn in an ancient battle between her and Lek. I wanted to stop thinking about it. About Lek and Dah and *tii-rahks* and whores. It was a relief to hear foot-steps outside and the door to Tom's room slam.

It didn't take us long to get a little happy hour going in the music room. Tom lit up his bamboo bong and put on some Hendrix. I took a toke from the bong and chased it down with a gin and tonic. I was going for a Rudyard Kipling touch, a little class for a change, and even managed to throw in a twist of lime. Tom scooped up some red rock and snorted. For him, grass was the chaser, the after-dinner mint. Seeing Tom high now for over a year and a half was starting to get to me. Dave was down the tubes. Hopeless. Tom was heading there. No collapsing at his desk, no trips to the emergency room. Not yet. But he was going for days at a time without getting himself straight. It hadn't affected his easy-going disposition. Yet. But what about that scene at the chow hall a few days earlier when the black dude flipped because Tom had been staring at him? His judgment was going, even though he had been cool enough to defuse the situation, saying, "Yeah, I *was* staring—sorry," and smiling one of his peaceful Buddha-child smiles. But he used to be too cool to get into a scene like that.

"I don't get it," I said. "I'm not getting high tonight."

"Maybe it's a weak batch. It's not like Papa-sahn's stuff is FDA approved."

"I can't stop thinking about the war. And I keep getting bummed out thinking about Lek and Dah—and *their* little war. Which gets me worrying about Dah—and missing her."

"Nothing much we can do about any of that, bro. For us, it'll all be over in a few months. Then back to the World. Back to real life."

"Yeah, but for these people this *is* real life. We came as their saviors and we've defiled them. Couldn't tame the heathens with Bibles in China so we'll use bullets this time. Except if McNamara, the great statistician, had done the math, he might have figured out that bags of rice are cheaper than body bags and bullets. It would have been cheaper to drop 'Bolkswagens' instead of 500-pound bombs, Silver Clouds instead of smart bombs. Instead, we've turned Vietnam and Laos into a desert and turned Thailand into a big brothel."

"Hey, man, don't jump on me. I've just sat at a typewriter for three years and done what I've been told. I don't *want* to know about Nam. We already know it's a bad scene. As far as Thailand—I haven't seen anybody here doing anything at the point of a gun."

"I suspect there's something a little corrupting about an ignorant New Guy fresh out of basic training coming over here and making as much as a Thai doctor. How would you feel if a bunch of Arabs moved into Wappinger's Falls and your sister and all the other girls in town started shacking up with them?"

"I don't have a sister. Thank God."

"And you really believe you're going to go back home and give up red rock overnight. And get happily married and never think about Lek again."

"I'm just a file clerk, man. You're the one who's been seeing the real war. From a distance, maybe. But you know those planes are killing somebody. And you know somebody's hosing you down with triple-A and firing SAMs back at you, really trying to kill you. That's different. I'm in purgatory. You've made it into hell."

"I wasn't thinking about killing and dying. I've been thinking more about what's happening to our souls. In my editing days I thought I'd come home unscathed. College graduate, mature, able to see the big picture. But even you rear-echelon file clerks are going to have a corrosive, addictive memory of Thailand whirling around in the cesspools of your hearts and minds. Maybe we should feel worst of all for the people back in the real world who are going to have to deal with this—with us—and not have a clue what it is they're dealing with."

Tom touched my shoulder. "I think this rain is getting to you, man. You'll feel better tomorrow. There's a warm front coming through. Got it from a reliable source down in Saigon."

Tom was right about the weather. The next night we flew to Steel Tiger East and the triple-A was extra nasty. I didn't have a moment to think about Sii-da, Lek or Tukada—or Danielle back at the University of Redlands.

The Malaysian Princess

Thursday night, the night before Christmas Eve, marked the beginning of Brian Golson's modest farewell tour, but for me it meant something deeper. I didn't know if I'd ever again get to be part of the kind of funky, soulful, glorious music produced by a bass player from Brooklyn, a sax man from New Orleans, a guitar player from California and a singer from North Carolina. I didn't understand why a white drummer from the suburbs of Boston would connect more deeply with these guys than I did with the bands I played with in high school and college, but I did. I had never heard Sam Cooke's "A Change is Gonna Come" before the Reverend performed it at the Soul Sister, not even in rehearsal. The guys didn't figure a drummer needed to rehearse a slow ballad. But later, when I heard recordings by greats like Otis Redding and Solomon Burke and Sam himself, I realized nobody did it better than the Reverend, capturing the yearnings of three hundred years of black history in a three-minute song. It had been a special time and place that brought us together and I knew that didn't happen often, even with professional musicians. But Brother Brian was our heart and soul and the end was near.

We did a final gig that night at the Soul Sister, then packed up our equipment for a final show at the NCO Club on Christmas Eve proper. It was 2:00 a.m. when I got back to Ruam Chon Sawng. Sergeant Prasert, still in uniform, was waiting for me at a table in the shadows of Mama-sahn's empty restaurant. Tonight, though, his uniform was not impeccably starched and pressed. The visor on his dress cap couldn't hide the tiredness in his eyes. "Tukada hear from waitress at Soul Sister that this the last time you' band play there. She go to see you, but she see Tom and Lek and Dave and come see me instead."

"Where is she now?"

"She say for you to meet her at Ubon Hotel. At the downstair bar."

When I got there she was nursing a cup of coffee, sitting in the same booth in back we had sat in the day she told me she wanted to kick her heroin habit. I ordered a coffee for myself and then sat there afraid to open my mouth, afraid of saying something stupid. She looked as tired as Prasert.

"How are you?" I finally asked, feeling like I was talking to a ghost more than a person.

"I'm very confusing," she said. "Dave keep coming to house, tell housegirl he want to see me. I make housegirl lie to Dave, say I not there. I'm confusing because my hus-band write from Korea, say he no want to get divorce, say he want to come here and see baby. But I keep sinking about you. How Prasert say you a good man wis good heart."

"I heard you came to see us play tonight at the Soul Sister."

"I *want* to see you. Jus' to look at you, until all this confusion over. But always Lek or Dave around."

"The band's playing its last gig tomorrow night at the NCO Club. I can leave you a pass at the main gate. Lek won't be there. And I'll get Tom to put Dave on night duty so he won't be there either. I'd really like you to come see us play one last time."

"I want to see you play," she said. "But I want to see you tonight too."

"You want me to come to your house?"

"No, not wis my baby zere. And housegirl and neighbor—too many people to talk gossip."

"Can you come to my place?"

"I afraid of Lek. Last time I come I was too scared. Afraid she see me an' we fight again."

"Why don't we stay here?"

"*Toklong.* You go get room. Come tell me what number and I follow in five minute."

The lobby was still busy with American airmen and Thai bar girls taking elevators to and from the penthouse nightclub. I found an out-of-the-way service elevator to ride to my rendezvous with Tukada. Waiting up in the room with nothing on Thai television but a test pattern, thoughts of Danielle began popping into my head. Depending on how you defined making love, she was the third or fourth American woman I had made love to. She was by far the best, giving herself to me as completely as she knew how. And yet, even with Danielle, there was a kind of Puritan residue that clung to America, something that forced American women to hold themselves back in a way I couldn't quite put into words.

And then I didn't have to put it into words. Tukada was knocking softly.

The moment she stepped inside and closed the door, it was no longer a hotel room that we had entered, it was another realm, a sacred temple not of this earth where she could draw me ever more deeply into her sanctuary of sensuality. The touch of her Thai skin, every movement of her body—as reserved as she appeared in public, she was electrifyingly and perfectly supple and yielding in private.

I gave her a kiss and hungrily she kissed me back. Quickly, we stepped out of our clothes, pulled down the covers and stretched out on the smooth, cool sheets, where we made love fluidly, effortlessly. Lying there afterward I enjoyed the feeling of a gentle pulsing between us and didn't mind when I realized it was the bass from the band upstairs bleeding through to our room, especially when I realized it was pulsing in time to the beating of our hearts. Tukada blew on the perspiration that covered my chest and neck and cheeks and forehead, and it felt wonderfully soothing, cool without being cold, and tender and loving and gentle—touching me with her breath, her spirit.

And once again after we finished making love, I was left in a state of perfect contentment, looking forward to a night with her next to me in bed, not even needing for us to touch, just wanting to feel her body's radiant warmth. We fell asleep for an hour or so, and when we woke up, I asked her, "Can you stay the night?"

Once again the mood was broken by Tukada having to leave. "I have to go home for my baby. You have hundred dollah?"

"What!" I gasped, recalling the time Prasert told me a hundred dollars was what some Issan rice farmers made in a year.

Her face showed no expression. "Always same-same. Hus-ban' no send money. I no have money for cab to get home tonight and for come see you tomorrow at NCO Club. I have to pay housegirl and pay rent for house. This month I need *big money* because I must go see faz-zer. His ship come back from Wietnam, stay in Sattahip only two week. If I go back to America, I afraid I never see him again. If you can help me to see him, I be so sankful—an' I pay you back, *jing-jing.*"

She was a smart girl. It was the payday before Christmas. I pulled a roll of Thai bills out of my pants pocket and carefully peeled off twenty one-hundred-baht notes. Half dressed, she tucked the bills away in the pocket of her denim work shirt and then surprised me by kissing me warmly on the mouth. It was the kind of kiss that lingered pleasantly, but *she* didn't, sliding off the bed and disappearing out the door into the night. I lay there awhile, smitten, and stayed smitten when I took a shower and dressed and took a *sahmlaw* home. Still smitten the next day, I arranged the pass at base security and left it with the Thai guard out at the gate, along with a suitable bribe in U.S. dollars. For the first three sets of Reverend Brian Golson's Christmas Eve Ubon Farewell, I kept a close watch on the double doors in back, looking forward to seeing Tukada. By the time we took a break before our final set I had pretty well lost hope.

It was while we were on that final break that Sagittarius Smith let the band know he had a little something extra in store for the Reverend, a little surprise to give him a proper Ubon sendoff—a "floorshow" by Harley's old friend, Tiger. We had about a minute to decide what key to play "The Stripper" in before we had to get back up on stage, but it wasn't until halfway through the set that Tiger was finally high enough to go on. Sagittarius gave us a little wave of his hand and to the Reverend's amazement, we began playing bump-and-grind music, the cue for Tiger's entrance. Soon she was dancing lasciviously around Brian with nothing much on but her high heels, a feather boa, and a toothy smile. She tried to get the Reverend to dance with her, but he maintained his cool, strumming away gamely on his guitar until she gave up and decided to improvise. She looked at Harley, gave him a dirty look, and turned towards me, staring a moment, vaguely remembering me from her last appearance at the club, and then danced her way over.

Without warning, she took off my brand new Byrds-style, baby-blue sunglasses and tried them on for size before unexpectedly cramming the tiny lenses into a part of her anatomy where the sun would never shine and shades would be forever unnecessary. The airmen applauded and whistled, with a few shouts of "*Right on! Right on!*" sprinkled in. When she put the glasses back on my nose, the crowd went bonkers, giving her a standing ovation. Consummate pro that I was, I kept on drumming through all the distraction, not losing a beat. But while my glasses were off, I panicked that I saw *Dah* standing in back. With the glasses back on and the room in focus, I could see that "Dah" was actually a floor fan. All I could think of *now* was how my nose was going to fall off from some incurable Asian-French scourge and I'd have to walk down the aisle with Danielle wearing a Lee

Marvin-style silver nose. The instant the set was over I ran back stage to the roach-infested dressing room to stick my face under the spigot of the utility sink and scrub desperately with Fels Naptha soap and the hottest water I could stand. For once I was *relieved* that Dah pulled a no-show.

Christmas night fell on a Saturday, which Sagittarius saved for his biggest surprise of all. Somehow he knew the Thai interior minister, who was wrapped up in supporting a leper colony located not too far from Chiang Mai, a picturesque medieval town tucked away in the mountains of northern Thailand. I cursed Tiger and prayed I would never need to check myself in there to live out my days without a nose. Chief Smith had volunteered our services for a charity fundraiser in Bangkok that would earn us a couple of extra days' R&R to spend in the Thai capital and down at Pattaya Beach. And so it was that we postponed Christmas and, mildly hung over, lugged our equipment over to the aeroport for the daily mail run to Bangkok.

The benefit concert was a big success, featuring us and three very good Thai bands from Bangkok. To my amazement, we were the hit of the show. We were invited to an after-party at the minister's villa, hosted by his college-age son and daughter, where I met a lady who spoke impeccable English, wore a long, elegant silk dress and introduced herself to me as a Malaysian princess. Unfortunately, upper class Thais and their upwardly mobile hangers-on insist on serving Johnnie Walker Red to show off their sophistication and wealth. I again disgraced the Leary bloodline by not being able to handle it. I had to puke on my hands and knees into, mercifully, a Western toilet bowl and was pleasantly surprised to find that my Malaysian princess was still waiting serenely and patiently for me when I came back fifteen minutes later. It seemed she adored American cinematographers almost as much as she adored American rock drummers. Inasmuch as she would be attending medical school when she returned to Kuala Lumpur, perhaps it would be a good idea for her to look after me on the cab ride back to my hotel. *This is so cool!* I thought. *Nursed back to health by a Malaysian princess! The hell with Tukada and all her ex-husbands and future husbands! Maybe this war isn't going to turn out so bad after all....*

I had planned to stay on with the guys for a couple extra days in Bangkok before heading down to Pattaya. I was especially looking forward to taking pictures of the Floating Market, the Temple of Dawn, and the Reclining Buddha that Jack Wu had told me so much about. But when I woke up Sunday morning at the Viengtai Hotel, the Malaysian princess, my cash, and all my camera equipment were gone. The only good news was that the freight elevator wasn't running—my drums were still sitting out in the hall. Humiliated, I made up a lame story about having to cover Leo Guttchock's missions while he was back in sick bay, borrowed cab fare from Sugie Bear and took the next flight back to Ubon.

Climbing on board one of Klong Airline's conventional non-Spectre trash-hauling versions of a C-130 that Sunday morning, I knew I was in trouble. I had grown up around airplanes but never got used to the rubbery smell of stale air that hit you when a plane was being opened up for its first trip of the day. It was a little worse in the tropics and the Johnnie Walker still sloshing through my system made it worse still. I prayed I could some-how fall asleep before I started a whole chain reaction of passengers puking on the trip up-country.

The belly of the C-130, like the hold of a tramp steamer, was hot, cramped and dimly lit, even with broad daylight outside. What little light we had seeped in through four portholes high in the compartment. The center of the plane was jammed with pallets of BX whiskey, Camel cigarettes and Sansui stereos from the nose under the flight deck back to the cargo ramp in the tail. My fellow passengers, mostly pale young GIs in starched green fatigues that hadn't yet faded in the tropical sun, walked down the narrow aisles as if they were on their way to their mothers' wakes. They crammed themselves onto the slick red nylon paratroopers' benches that ran down each side of the cabin, propping themselves up on the slippery fabric by wedging their legs against the baggage. Using gym bags and val-packs for pillows and using each other for armrests, the waxy-faced boys did the best they could to make themselves comfortable. I had a little advantage over the others in that my bass drum case, turned sideways, made a perfect coffee table to rest my legs on.

It wasn't like Nam. You couldn't exactly feel sorry for this crop of New Guys. Unlike Danielle's husband, they were all going to make it home from their tour with nothing worse than a dose of clap. It was pilots and Air Commandos like Harley who died where we were going. Other than Lieu-tenant Liscomb and me, you had to volunteer to meet your Maker in the

U.S. Air Force.

I snapped out of my reverie when I heard the loadmaster start to describe the forced-landing procedure. Back in the hung-over present, I tried to pay attention because despite flying the C-130 Hercules day in and day out in the line of duty, despite the assurances of Harley and other professional soldiers I worked with that this was the most indestructible bucket of tin ever to take to the air and despite coming from a family crawling with pilots, I still lacked unshakable faith that God meant for man to fly, even in peacetime. I also wanted to hear those instructions because I had once read an FAA/NTSB-type news report that people who looked over the emergency instruction card in the back pocket of airliner seats actually had a higher survival rate in plane crashes. There was some sort of socio-psychological theory to explain this, but I was still filled with enough of Father Boyle's catechism class to fear this might be proof of God's existence—that He rewarded good boys who followed directions. I especially wanted to hear the loadmasters' instructions now that I could no longer in any sense be considered a good boy, but even if God weren't personally hunting for me, I simply felt that after two and a half months of flying gunships night-in and night-out in the line of duty over the Trail, my luck was about due to run out in the C-130 department.

"One bell means prepare for ditching," said the loadmaster. A massive Allison turboprop engine began to shriek and soon all four were piercing my ears like the banks of speakers that used to shake the clubs on Sunset Strip.

"What did he say?" I screamed to the Fuckin' New Guy, a blubbery baby in uniform sitting next to me. He was one of those pasty-pale guys from the heartland who looked puffed up and over the hill at age twenty. He screamed something back, but it was obvious that neither one of us could hear the other a foot away. Airman Idaho Potato and I each took a waxy pink square of what looked like bubble gum from the assistant loadmaster when he came by. Instinctively, like a mother with her child, I grabbed blubber boy's little square before he could stuff it in his mouth and showed him how to roll it up and soften it in his hands before inserting half in each ear for perfectly fitting earplugs. I tried not to think about the damage that drumming and Spectre missions were doing to my unprotected eardrums night after night.

Sometimes, looking through the porthole of a large ship, the dock can seem to be moving backwards when in fact it is the ship that is ever so slowly getting under way; so it was when that old cargo workhorse started taxiing that we seemed to be sitting at the gate while the whole airport slowly backed up. My stomach lurched, but closing my eyes and curling up in a fetal position seemed to calm it down. By the time we rotated for takeoff I felt like I was in the arms of an overprotective mommy on my first teeter-totter. With the noise level muted to a soft screech and no chance of further conversation, I let the plane rock me slowly into semi-sleep....

"Thirty...thirty," chants Strbik's copilot, the plane banking sharply so the Gatling guns can to do their dirty work. Like a bloated body rising to the surface of a lake, pieces of the scene begin breaking loose from my memory and float into a dream vision that slowly comes to life for me, lit hell-fire-and-brimstone red from dim instruments on board the plane and from flairs and tracers that light up the sky below. The distorted image of a truck appears on the infrared sensor and as I move in with my camera to film the screen, Sach's gun gives off a deafening blast. A garbled, scratchy intercom voice calls "Triple-A... break left!"

The plane twists and drops violently, tracers flashing through the cloud we just vacated as I am hurled against the 40-mm gun mount and then pinned against the exposed ribs of the plane. The roar of the outboard engines dies and my face contorts. "We're gonna crash!" I cried out in my sleep.

"We've landed," said the New Guy, shaking me awake, staring at me with eyes full of fear and pity. We pulled out our earplugs, gathered up our baggage and waited while the passengers behind us started filing out. Finally I was able to push my bass drum back onto the pallet with the rest of my kit and catch up with my old friend, Airman New Guy.

"Do you always shout in your sleep?"

I smiled. "Only since I started flying combat missions on these airborne mausoleums."

"Was that a set of drums on the pallet?"

"Yeah, I'm part of a new program they're trying out over the Ho Chi Minh Trail. I'm supposed to bang on them whenever things get too quiet."

"No kidding?"

I loved kids from Idaho and would have continued the conversation except the terrorist cadre that may or may not have attacked while we were on a high-level Red Alert in November decided to drop back for real while the base was asleep on the Sunday after Christmas. At first we could only hear the muffled sound of a mortar and a few gunshots drifting in from the runway behind us. Moments later, Air Policemen in jeeps and armored personnel carriers careened across the tarmac and screeched to a halt a few feet from where our C-130 and waiting shuttle bus were parked. Not much more than a football field away, the enemy commandoes charged towards the fighter revetments. Automatic-rifle fire opened up. The passengers reacted in varied degrees of confusion. No sooner did my dear friend Airman New Guy and I duck behind the front wheel of the bus than Lieutenant Hill pulled up in the Rat Pack pickup truck, dressed for battle. Grinning from ear to ear, he shouted, "Would you looky here! If it ain't Sergeant Leary—back from Bangkok a week early! We been looking for Guttchock, but you'll do just fine!"

I looked at Airman New Guy and shrugged. "This is what I do when I'm not playing drums." Spitzer pulled me into the jeep, Washington handed me a movie camera, and away we went. "Don't let anybody shoot my drums!" I shouted to the New Guy, who actually gave me a little salute.

The End of the Universe, Part II

Even though the firefight was over almost before it started, I was feeling like a zombie in a B horror flick when we dropped off our film and equipment at ComDoc. I hoped Washington and Spitzer had gotten some good footage because I was certain mine was crap. I was certain because I was still too wasted from my weekend in Bangkok to tell if it was me or the camera that was blurred and shaky. At least Lieutenant Hill had been kind enough to let me gather up my drum kit and gym bag on our way back from the aeroport. By the time I unchained my bicycle and started pedaling out to the main gate, there was nothing I looked forward to more than stretching out and reading an old *American Cinematographer* magazine when I got down to Ruam Chon Sawng. I stopped off at the base post office and was bemused to find a battered package from Danielle waiting for me, along with a smaller one from Mom that had made it unscathed. I stowed them in the wire basket on my handlebar and headed on home.

Tom was sunning himself on the porch when I came up the stairs. "Weren't you and your band supposed to be spending a week down at Pattaya Beach?"

"It's a long story," I replied.

"Give me the *Reader's Digest* version."

"It had something to do with a Malaysian princess of somewhat tarnished repute seducing me at the leper colony benefit concert."

"So what they say is true—"

"What's that?"

"A good Malaysian princess is hard to find."

"If she was a princess. Or Malaysian. Or if she was even a *she*. But enough of this trash! The real reason I came back early is that I couldn't stand the thought of missing Christmas at the Ghetto."

"You're a sick man, Leary."

After a pleasant afternoon reading and napping, all it took was a trip to the *hong nam* and a little cool water splashed on my face for me to feel completely rejuvenated. I even put on a tailored shirt and slacks, trying to catch a little of the holiday spirit. Unfortunately, it went without saying at Bungalow Ruam Chon Sawng that any time you had recovered from too much dope or booze, it was time for friends and neighbors to gather together once again and start you back down the road to perdition.

Tom, Lek, Larry and Pueng had taken a stab at decorating the music room for the holiday season while I was away. Somehow they had scrounged up a scrawny two-foot pine tree but only managed to dress it with a string of popcorn, a few *pictures* of Christmas ornaments cut out of magazines, a string of fake pearls and a pair of clip-on earrings. A couple of Christmas cards from home and from friends on base had been tacked to the walls along with the December Playboy centerfold—a cheerful shot of a voluptuous lass wearing nothing but a Santa cap. They had already gathered in the music room for an end-of-the-day smoke when I came in to join them.

"Why if it isn't Brendan Leary!" said Zelinsky with a warm grin. "Tom said you were back, but we didn't believe him."

"I'm not only back, I bring goodies from home!" It seemed only fitting, in keeping with whatever feeble Christmas spirit we had managed to evoke in the steamy tropics, that I should bring along my CARE Packages. The group got excited when I pulled out a tin of cookies from the battered cardboard box Danielle had sent, but the dented lid should have warned us. When I pried it off we were crushed to see that the cookies inside—a wonderful assortment of macaroons, gingerbread men, and sugar cookies decorated as snowmen and Christmas trees—had themselves been crushed into a cookie salad. The poor condition of the shipment didn't seem to matter, however—within minutes there were only a few crumbs left in the tin. I opened the smaller, thinner box from Mom and discovered a green and red Bugs Bunny tie and semi-matching socks decorated with the Tasmanian Devil playing golf in the snow. Wheeler and Zelinsky laughed and ran back to *their* rooms, where they brought back ties that their mothers had sent. "What the hell do we do with these?" Zelinsky asked.

Pueng had an answer. "The Buddha say if you no wan' gift, then give to somebody who need more."

"Who needs ties and socks in Thailand?" asked Wheeler.

"Let's pass them on to our *sahmlaw* drivers," I suggested.

"What the hell will *they* to do with them?" asked Zelinsky.

"Let's go find out," I said. We wandered down to the main gate in a festive mood and passed out our gifts to four idle drivers. The one who got the socks had no idea what to do with them and decided to turn them into riding gloves, poking holes where his fingers needed to come out. The three drivers who got the ties tried them on as bandannas first, before two of them decided to use them as sporty sashes. No sooner had our four laughing *sahmlaw* drivers pedaled off than Dave Murray and his reclusive friend Mole pulled up in a cab coming from the opposite direction. "Come on up!" Zelinsky called to them. "We're having a Christmas party!"

"Perfect!" said Mole. "We just happened to come bearing holiday cheer— some of Papa-sahn's finest!" Mole spent most of his life working the night shift at the base motor pool or lying around stoned at the bungalow he shared with Dave. He saved a lot of time and money by sleeping in the same grimy, wrinkled fatigues he wore to work, leaving the shirt open to reveal an equally rumpled olive-drab T-shirt.

The brothers were out dancing on the porch at Bungalow #3 when we walked past, and it was only a few minutes before B.J. and Leclerc stopped over to see what was happening, hoping Mole had brought along some fresh toot. He didn't have red rock, but he didn't disappoint, quickly making himself comfortable, pulling out his Zig Zag papers and rolling a couple of joints.

"Hear anything from Dah?" asked Zelinsky. I cringed.

"Heard all kinds of rumors," Dave answered. "Heard she's gone off to see her mom in Korat or maybe she's gone off to see her ex in Korea. I also heard she might be in Sattahip visiting her dad—that his ship's back from Vietnam...."

"Forget about her," Lek said.

"Lek and I help you find somebody better," said Pueng.

"I dunno," said Dave. "Not right now." He took the shorter of the two doobies that were circulating and attached it to his roach clip, put it to his lips and took a deep drag. He held it for what seemed like minutes, finally letting out a steady stream of pungent smoke while he sat there in silence. Listening to Dave, I felt like hell. I wished Lek or Pueng had been more convincing. Luckily Mole filled the silence. "I'm off rock completely," he announced, "especially now that my man Dave is back. We're strictly doing this Burmese ganja that Papa-sahn got in a few days ago."

This sounded great, except there was a problem. When I took a drag on the freshly rolled reefer, there was a nasty bite to it, and I had a strong hunch Papa-sahn was lacing his marijuana with opium.

I hadn't seen Mole in person in months even though he seemed to be having a powerful effect on my life. He still had the gray complexion I remembered and gave the impression of being furry even though the only facial hair he could raise was a wispy mustache. His greasy hair soaked through his greasy San Francisco Giants baseball cap, his one item of clothing that wasn't Air Force issue and which nobody bothered him about, because no self-respecting Air Force officer—not even the lunatic assistant base commander—was willing to give up his drinking time or rack time to snoop around checking up on the grease monkeys working the graveyard shift at the motor pool. Beneath the greasy brim of Mole's baseball cap, his eyes were red and beady, and his runny nose seemed to be sniffing around in several directions at once. "Is this great stuff or what?" he asked.

"Maybe they'll have pot like this when we get to heaven," said B.J.

"The world will come to an end before any of us make it into heaven," Leclerc replied.

B.J. leaned back and lit up the room with his toothy grin. "If I'm smoking weed like this when the Saints come marchin' in, I figure I won't care—I'll be going out in a blaze of Glory!"

"You sure this grass hasn't been cut with something?" I asked.

"No way," said Dave.

Even though I had no trust whatsoever for Dave's judgment, I kept smoking Mole's grass anyway. It was free and I figured Mole owed me. For exactly what, I couldn't say, except I couldn't help blaming him for Dah's running off to the Gulf of Thailand. I felt like a Salvador Dali pocket watch as my body melted into the wall and slid to the floor while swirling clouds engulfed my mind. In a woozy haze I contemplated the world coming to a fiery end. *What hope is there for the human race now that we're capable of Mutually Assured Destruction? What weapon has ever gone unused? Why would nuclear weapons be the exception?*

Lek shook me gently and called out, "Hey Bren-dan, what you sinking 'bout, huh?"

"Nothing," I answered. "B.J. and Leclerc got me thinking about the end of the universe, that's all. How as surely as mountains turn to dust and dust turns into mountains, as surely as deserts become seas and seas become deserts, the earth itself must go through spasms of destruction and rebirth." I heard myself talking without quite knowing what I was saying. "And if that's true with the earth, why not the solar system, galaxies, constellations, the entire universe? Did existence always exist? How will it end? Can it end? Or is existence stuck with itself? "

"Isn't that kind of existential?" smirked Zelinsky.

Dave dropped in from his own private universe. "In the end will chaos rule? Or will modern science come up with all the answers and save us?"

"Could go either way," said Leclerc.

"Build us Utopia," said B.J., his face lighting up again. "Turn the world into a giant shopping mall where we get to live forever, provided we get to smoke Mole's dope back there too. Hell, I'd give up red rock for that. Just be sure to throw in a little pussy."

"I think I'm sick of pussy," Dave mumbled.

"If the universe does end someday, will anybody come to the funeral?" I asked.

"I'll come," said Dave.

"Count me in," said Mole.

"Will its death lead to a rebirth in another time and place and form? Are atheists and existentialists wrong and will the spirits that have inhabited all men survive in some way? Is some new incarnation possible that the human mind is too crude to imagine? Or will it all truly end someday—distant or soon—and existence turn out to be meaningless after all?"

"I sink you making my head hurt," Lek complained.

How was it that I found peace of mind in the gallows humor of an indifferent universe? Why was I no longer frightened at the possibility of all human endeavor ultimately proving to be mere thrashing about in a cold, dark sea that would finally and impersonally drown us all? Was it Mole's opiated smoke, or were the thoughts racing through my mind so powerful that they were lifting my legs off the ground and floating me several feet above the cushions I had been resting on?

Taking a long drag on a bamboo bong that had appeared from somewhere when Mole ran out of Zig Zag papers, I realized I had stopped thinking about Dah, and it felt good. I passed the water pipe back to Tom and contemplated how all these thoughts had taken less than an instant.

I couldn't remember how much I had said out loud and wondered why in repeating my strange riddles to this motley crew of friends, I had not been teased or ignored. I reflected too on how in almost any other time and place in human history I could have laid men's terror bare with free-form thoughts like these and would have been lucky to escape with my life.

"It's very perplexing," I rambled on. "You look around and see a world full of chaos and violence. And yet, to paraphrase Hemingway and the Book of Ecclesiastes, the sun rises every morning and sets every night. Birds sing. Flowers bloom. Sometimes we can improve on nature, sometimes we muck it up. But creation itself will remain out of man's reach for a long time—sort of like Babe Ruth's home run record."

"Yeah, but Harmon Killebrew may catch the Babe in a few years," mumbled Dave.

"Or Hammering Hank," added Leclerc without opening his eyes.

I laughed. "If they beat the record, it won't be by much. But that's not the point! We're talking science and philosophy, not sports. We comfort ourselves by believing that at least some of our best scientific minds are capable of understanding the universe. But maybe the priests of the world are on to something. They're all wet when they think they have the answers. But the Questions! *Where did it all begin? How and why? Where will it all end? Is there any way of avoiding our fate?* The burning of candles and incense in temples and cathedrals—it appalls my atheist-existentialist sensibility, but it's hitting me now that perhaps those rituals tap into the great unknowable mystery of life and existence."

I looked around the room, eager for some of my thoughts to be challenged or expanded upon. To a man and woman, Tom and Lek, Larry and Pueng, Dave, B.J. and Leclerc were all passed out, their heads and limbs akimbo in a bizarre array of contortions. Mole revealed another unnerving quirk: sleeping with his red, beady eyes half open.

Harley and Mali stepped in the door but stopped. "Whoa! What has happened here?"

"Can't you tell?" I asked. "We're having a Christmas party. What the hell are *you* doing back?"

"Pattaya was already gonna be dull without Mali along. When Sugie Bear told me you went back early, I grabbed the next hop out of Don Muang."

Tom was sucking the last of the bowlful of grass from his bong, his eyes still closed. "Brendan's having some kind of hallucination about being the parish priest of the Church of Science."

The laced grass was making me tired and grumpy. "Gertrude Stein talked about Hemingway and his pals being a Lost Generation after World War I, but they weren't half as lost as we are. They were strictly boozers—and at least a few of the women they hung out with in Europe weren't hookers."

"I'm not a hooker," said Lek, "I'm a bar girl."

"And Mali could have been a schoolteacher," I said.

Mali smiled pleasantly, her eyes not giving away how much she did or didn't comprehend beyond recognizing her name.

"Fuck you," Harley grumbled. He repacked the bong with some fresh grass and lit it up. "Whew!" he winced. "This is *nasty.*"

Beyond bone tired, I climbed up on the bamboo sofa and stretched out with my hands behind my head, too lazy to even unzip my low-cut boots. And then I was hit with an attack of the munchies. "I almost forgot—I got a Christmas CARE Package!"

I found Danielle's tin under the bed and pulled it out. I took a few crumbs and passed the rest over to Harley and Mali. "I could sure go for a long, hot bath. Maybe I'll check in to some nice hotel in Bangkok or Pattaya after all."

"If you went to Pattaya Beach right now," Harley said with a smile, "you'd make the whole ocean stink, you're so full of bullshit. Good cookies, by the way."

"Merry Day after Christmas, everybody!" said Zelinsky as he helped Pueng up and headed off for his bedroom. "I can't wait to see how you guys screw up New Year's Eve."

"Thank Congress" (only 54 more days...)

Monday morning I was supposed to meet Washington and Spitzer at the ComDoc editorial trailer to watch dailies of the flight-line firefight. The usual scenery of burning sampans and thatch huts, napalmed truck convoys, and endless miles of cluster bombs spinning down over virgin jungle was playing on the Moviola when I made my subdued entrance. "Hey, Jack," I heard Zelinsky calling to Sergeant Wu, "can you make up a title saying: '25 December 1971—Enemy Monkeys Demoralized by Christmas CBU Attack'?" When Zelinsky noticed me, he cried out, "Why, if it ain't the Shade Man!"

I froze in my tracks, and the trailer broke into a spontaneous standing ovation. "Let's hear it for 'Shade Man' Leary!" shouted Perez. He was soon joined by Shahbazian, who popped out of the repair shop wearing a wicked grin and yelling, "The Shade Man is our main man!"

No sooner had I slinked out amid a chorus of "Shade Man! Shade Man!" than Zelinsky caught up with me and told me that Lieutenant Hill wanted to see me in his office. At the Rat Pack orderly room Tom Wheeler was typing one letter at a time, concentrating more on the acid rock coming though his oversize Pioneer headphones than on his work. Dave Murray was fast asleep at his desk, completely undisturbed when I banged the door shut behind me. Not really expecting an answer, I said hello to Dave and Tom as I walked through to First Sergeant Link's office. He wasn't there and I couldn't find the duty roster to sign in. Lifting up Tom's right earphone, I asked, "Where's Link gone off to now?"

"He's with Guttchock," said Tom with a stoned smile.

"Now there's a scary thought—The Missing Link doing business with Leo Guttchock. And what in hell brought about this meeting of the minds?" I asked.

"Well, Link and Harwell went over to the NCO Club for breakfast, but they got called back. There was some kind of SNAFU over at the ComDoc trailer involving Leo. If you wanna sign in, Murray's using the log for his pillow."

I looked over at Murray, told Tom, "Thanks," and put his headphone back over his ear. I couldn't find a place in the logbook that wasn't covered with Murray's slobber and decided to take one more day off. Moving the logbook must have wakened him up, though. "I thought you were in Bangkok," he mumbled.

"You saw me *last night*," I replied, but he had already lapsed back into his coma. I knocked on Hill's door and stepped in. "You wanted to see me, sir?"

"How were the dailies?" asked the lieutenant.

"They hadn't come out of the soup yet. I'm sure Washington got some good stuff."

"You're too modest, Leary. But what I really wanted to ask you is how's the flying going?"

"I'd prefer shooting 'grip and grins' for the base newsletter. Or editing *Hits of the Week* with Zelinsky."

"Well, I might be able to arrange that for you."

"Very funny, sir. Now, what did you really call me in for?"

"I've got some genuine good news for you, Leary. Looks like you camera guys are finally gonna be replaced by television."

"You're kidding, right, sir?"

"That prototype Colonel Strbik has been flying around the past couple months has passed muster. The first of the new TV birds got in yesterday. The Armed Services Committee likes the 'Cadillac' gunship program so much they're upping the funding. The plan now is for the whole Spectre squadron to be converted by the end of March, nine months ahead of schedule. It looks like it's really happening—they're replacing you cameramen with videotape recorders. With any luck, this oughta give you and Washington a lot of extra time to spend with Wu on the bicycle race. You can count on Captain English and me to give you all the help you need."

I shook the lieutenant's hand, unable to contain a gleeful grin. "Thank you, Lieutenant! I can't thank you enough!"

"Don't thank me. Thank Congress," replied Hill. "Just remember, this is going to be more of a lap-dissolve than a jump-cut. We'll still have missions for you to fly till all the conversions are completed. We're going to be a little short-handed the next two weeks, for instance. But Ron Cooper is finally coming in to handle the F-4 stuff."

"They're getting Cooper off a sound stage?"

"He managed to pick up a dose of malaria at Snake School over in the

Philippines, but the report from the hospital at Clark says he's coming along fine."

I went back to the editorial trailer to find Jamal Washington and Jeff Spitzer, my fellow cameramen. If Hill was on the level, I wanted to take my compadres over to the NCO Club to celebrate. They were nearly finished describing Sunday's scene at the flight line to Zelinsky and Shahbazian when I stepped inside. "A real suicide mission," said Jamal. Spitzer's eyes lit up. "The APs totally kicked their butt!"

Before I could get Washington aside, Zelinsky jumped in. "Brendan, you're too modest—not saying a word about this last night. But don't you get enough combat action when you're on duty? Why the hell didn't you stay in Bangkok?"

I was starting to hate this story. "I ran out of money." I started leafing through the duty roster, trying to tune the others out, but giving the roster only half my attention, it wasn't making much sense.

Zelinsky wasn't going to let up. "Christ, man, I thought you took a couple hundred bucks with you! And I thought they were paying you guys a little something—"

I continued staring at the roster without paying full attention to Zelinsky or the schedule. "We were at the interior minister's mansion after the concert. This beautiful Malaysian chick started laying this rap on me about how she was a princess by a minor wife or some such mumbo jumbo, how she was pre-med at Kuala Lampur University and how much she loved soul music and blues and—this was a little strange—how she wasn't a bar girl, she just loved to dance. I was flattered, but I swear she put something in my drink, because the next thing I knew I was puking all over the interior minister's marble bathroom. I thought it was just good manners that she waited around for me and maybe her pre-med training in bedside manners that she took the taxi back to the hotel with me. Catch was, next morning when I woke up, she was gone, along with my wallet and my cameras. Luckily for the drums, the freight elevator was on the fritz."

"Luck of the Irish," said Shahbazian.

Suddenly my aching eyes about burst. My name popped into focus, practically leaping off the page of the duty roster. "Spitzer! Washington! Did you see this? Why the hell do they have us flying all the Spectre missions? Hill just told me we were being phased out—"

Harwell, our phantom ComDoc supervising director of photography, stepped through the door just in time to overhear my question. As usual, he had on his sweat-soaked flight suit and looked like he hadn't shaved in days. "That would be because you won't be getting phased out for another month or two and you're the only cameramen we have left. Lieutenant Liscomb is handling all the large-format after-action recon photography. They've got me going TDY again down to Tan Son Nhut and Leo Guttchock is going back into sick bay with another jaundice attack. When he came in to fly this morning he was drunk. His eyes had turned yellow and his skin had turned olive drab—and he was mumbling something about how his wife's gonna be picking him up at a train station. Link and I had to ruin a perfectly fine breakfast to run back and take care of the SOB."

"Well if *that* ain't a fine Merry Christmas and a Happy New Year!" I cried. "Here I'm about to take Spitzer and Washington over to the club for a little celebration and damn if Cooper and Guttchock don't keep messing with us!"

Zelinsky gave me another one of his Cheshire-cat smiles that I hated almost as much as Ron Cooper. "Word is, Guttchock's going into alcohol detox for a week after he gets out of sick bay."

Harwell's bloodshot, baggy eyes brightened up as he continued his brief-ing, saying, "In the unlikely event any of you guys are worried about Leo, Captain English has him under control in the ready room. Sergeant Link is helping out."

Washington shot Harwell a look. "Would you mind if we go smack a little sense into him?"

"You'd better hurry," he replied, cracking a little smirk. "English already has an ambulance on its way."

"Let's go get that sucker," said Washington.

I followed Jamal over to the ready room where Guttchock was slumped on the bus seat, reading the *Pacific Stars and Stripes* and humming "Swing Low, Sweet Chariot." First Sergeant Link was standing so alertly at the window watching for the ambulance that his knuckles barely touched the ground. "You know this guy?" he sneered.

"Wish we didn't," answered Washington. "Leo, what's this shit about get-ting drunk again and getting yourself grounded?"

"My wife sent me a story from the L.A. *Times*. Sesh the war's about over.

Sesh there'll only be about 25,000 troops left in Vietnam by the end of the year...down from half a million. Why should I get shot down when the war's as good as done?" Leo was indeed drunk and had successfully poisoned himself again—his skin and eyes were as discolored as Harwell had described them.

"Leo, who's gonna fly if you quit?" I asked.

"Let Spinelli and Nevers fly. They *like* to fly—"

"Spinelli and Nevers are dead," Washington blurted.

"See? That's better. They haven't got anything to lose if they're already dead." He put down the paper. "Because that's the big question now—who's going to be the last to die? My vote is for either Spinelli or Nevers."

"Leo, ain't none of us has to die," said Washington with a touch of exasperation.

"Damn it, Leo, if you don't fly, that means Spitzer, Washington and I gotta fly every night we're not socked in."

"Sorry to miss it, Brendan, old buddy, but the wife's gonna be meeting me at the station. Couldn't disappoint her now, could we, after all she's been through—"

"After all *she's* been through!" Washington laughed in disgust, slapping his knee *Hee-Haw* style.

The medics arrived, English signed off on the paperwork, and we gave Leo a hand out to the waiting ambulance. He started singing a cheerful rendition of "Swing Low, Sweet Chariot" as they drove away.

"Only Fifty-Three More Days!"

Zelinsky and I stopped by the orderly room the next day to round up Wheeler and Murray before heading over to the chow hall for lunch. "Did you hear anything more about Leo Guttchock?" I asked Tom while he finished up some paperwork.

"Yeah. English and Link were on the horn to Tan Son Nhut seeing if we could keep Harwell here."

"Why does that fool Leo drink?" asked Dave, looking up hazily from his typewriter. "It's really messing him up. You'd think with a wife at home, he'd have enough sense to quit."

Tom jumped in. "Looks like you're going to be doing some extra flying, Brendan."

"What's the deal with Ron Cooper?" I asked.

"Nothing you're gonna like," Tom replied sympathetically. "If his malaria doesn't clear up soon, they may be sending him stateside for—"

He was cut off by a familiar voice booming over AFTN Radio. "Only *fifty-three* more days till BBBR-Day!" announced Sagittarius Smith. "That may seem like a long way off to you short-timers, but time's fast running out if you're planning on getting into shape for Ubon's first annual Big Buddha Bicycle Race. Thanks to Indian Joe Enterprises—that's Indian Joe Jewelers, Indian Joe Custom Tailors, Indian Joe Stereo, Indian Joe's New Delhi Restaurant, Indian Joe's Flying Carpet Massage and Indian Joe's all-new and very private Bengal Kitten Gentlemen's Club—and thanks to Sheik Tailors, Niko's and Maharaj Massage, Woodstock Music, the Corsair, the New Playboy, the Soul Sister and the Ubon Hotel, we can already guarantee a one-thousand-dollar Grand Prize and a one-thousand-dollar Unit Prize with at least a hundred dollars each to our top three finishers in the three-speed, ten-speed and custom-modified divisions. The more of you who enter, the higher the prizes go, so hop on your bicycles today and see Major Bill Horney at the 16th Special Operations Squadron for you fly-boys who actually get down to the flight line, Staff Sergeant Jack Wu at the 601st Photo Squadron, or me, Senior Master Sergeant Sagittarius Smith, at the NCO Club. And now back to AFTN music—"

Wu popped in looking very pleased with himself. "What do you think, guys?"

"Smith is making this so exciting I may have to get myself a bike after all," said Zelinsky.

"You're not going to believe this," Wu continued, "but we've got thirty-five hundred dollars in the kitty already from local sponsors. Indian Joe put in five hundred just to promote his gentleman's club. And that's without collecting a cent in entrance fees."

Wu wasn't the only one feeling pleased with himself. "And to think this all started as a picnic outing," I boasted. "Right here at ComDoc!"

"Say," Jack announced, "I still haven't had a chance to show you gentlemen my slides from Chiang Mai—"

"We were just heading out for lunch," said Zelinsky. "Why don't you join us and show 'em to us over at the mess hall?"

"Thanks anyway," Wu laughed. "Gotta check in with Smith over at the NCO Club. Maybe I'll catch you later."

Dave Murray ducked out on us along the way to the enlisted men's dining hall, telling us he had to run a quick errand and asking us to save him a seat. Zelinsky, Wheeler and I had already made our way down a long line of stainless-steel serving pans, filling our plates with chow-hall food, when we spotted Murray joining the back of the line. He seemed a little woozy when he reached our table, but it was nothing out of the ordinary until his face took a nosedive into his dinner plate. Tom pulled him out by his shaggy hair, asking, "Anything wrong?"

"Oh, no," Murray replied. "Jus' the opposite, in fac'. I'm totally getting my act together. Yesterday I signed up for a $3,000 re-enlistment bonus. Last night after I left you guys, I ran into Prasert and found out for sure that Dah is down in Sattahip visiting her father. I'm goin' down tomorrow to straighten things out with her. Captain English jus' okayed a couple days leave for me."

"What the hell did you *re-enlist* for?" Tom asked.

"Well," Murray replied earnestly, "when I got my head straight back there at the hospital, I realized Thailand is probably the only country in the world where I can feed a first class heroin habit on a quarter...."

He went back to sleep before he could finish, still sitting up in his seat. The rest of us dug into our meat and potatoes. "Murray, you're never gonna make master sergeant," warned Zelinsky.

"And you won't be feeding your heroin habit *or* Tukada jack on what they give you in Leavenworth," added Tom, watching Dave's head sink back to the table.

Lek's Cat

I had a cold season cold. Badly congested, weak all over, it seemed like a fine night to turn in early and save my bar-hopping for another day. A brew of cough syrup, Mekong whiskey and Coke with a twist of lime seemed to be sending me to Dreamland, even with Tom and Dave singing along to AFTN Radio, somehow making themselves heard over Tom's Sansui receiver blasting in the next room. *Where's Lek?* I wondered woozily. *Is she working the bars again or did she go back to Korat?* Moments later I couldn't tell if I was groggily awake or dreamily asleep. *Why does her cat look like a rat? Or does she have a pet rat that looks like a cat? Lek's warm kisses on my cheeks and forehead—that's what I need to get me over this fever. Except they are more like little tongue licks…. Why can't I turn my head? And why does her tongue feel like sandpaper? Wait! Is it Lek or her cat? Oh, my God! It's her pet rat! Why can't I turn my head? Why can't I move my arms?*

I woke up, burning with fever, aching all over, nauseous. I got to the *hong nam* just in time to throw up over the back wall, missing the squatter toilet completely. Fortunately, the little hose we used to fill the klong jar stretched out far enough for me to wash up the mess. I was about to crawl back into bed when I was hit with a vicious attack of the runs. This time, at least, I didn't miss my intended target. I crawled back into bed for the third time and figured I'd just nap. *Hot apple pie. Vanilla ice cream. Wing Dings. Pecan Sandies that Mom used to mail me in California. Coconut chocolate chip cookies—Keebler!*

I woke up again, feverish and dry. I smelled barbeque in the distance, but it made me nauseous. I felt the runs coming on, but nothing happened when I squatted this time in the *hong nam*. I reached into the klong jar for a dipper of water and poured it over my head. For a moment I felt cooler as the water dripped down my face and chest. Walking back to my room at the other end of Bungalow #4, I noticed the Ghetto was absolutely quiet, not a soul in sight. By the time I crawled back into bed, the smell of barbeque was going down a little better, making me almost hungry. *Floating like an astronaut in the back of my gunship, deciding that weightless combat photography is the way to go, I check the magazine on my Arriflex, sense that I've already lived through this exact moment, wonder if this is déjà vu or a dream. Wonder if you can have déjà vu in a dream. I don't need headphones to hear over the intercom. We've spotted a truck. No, wait, it's the point truck for a whole convoy. The crew goes into the kill sequence. I focus on infinity, open the f-stop all the way to 1.4, check the cable connection to my weightless belt battery—"Thirty.... Thirty," I hear in an endless loop over my extrasensory intercom, the plane banking and circling. Flares drop, the miniguns, the twenties, the 40-mm Bofors all begin firing. I smell gunpowder, wonder why I never noticed it before.... Major Horney, popcorn nestled between his knees, gazes at a bank of sensors emitting ghostly streams of cathode rays. With the touch of a joystick, the sensor operators line up their targets and Horney selects the clearest image. Strbik steadies the plane and squeezes his trigger finger, destroying the target. "We got us a burner!" Horney yells ecstatically. "Shit hot!" calls Colonel Strbik, "And the hell with what the Pentagon thinks." They burst round after round into the trailing trucks and I can make out drivers getting out and running. One seems to be a girl, running with a lighter gait. A flight of Night Owl F-4s reports in and is cleared for a napalm drop. The countryside is splattered with flaming liquid, steel mills belching in the jungle.*

"Triple-A! Seven O'clock! Hold course! Hold course!" The tailgate explodes, vaporizing the illumination operator. The wiring near the gate begins to spark and more gunpowder stinks up the air. I want to smoke some opium with Captain Rush, the NOD operator, but when I find him his flight suit has been ripped open, flesh blown away down to his chest bone. I want to cry, but it's against regs. I want to go home, but I can't remember which form to fill out. I really wouldn't mind a cigarette. Anything will do. Rush is overdoing it, though. I'm choking. I'm on my hands and knees. My headphones are on now, Colonel Strbik asking in a new endless loop, "You guys got a fire down there? We've got a fire indicator light. Anybody on headsets? You guys got a fire down there?"

I didn't know if I'd wakened up or this was another dream. The room was filled with smoke that seemed to be coming out of my closet. Strange. I opened the bottom doors, and flames seared my face, burning my hair and eyebrows with a stench that made my stomach convulse again. More alarming, I could see out the back of my closet through a smoking hole in the wall and directly into Tom's bed-sitting room, where flames were leaping to the ceiling. I ran around to his room, screaming, "Tom, wake up!"

The door was locked. I kept screaming. My skinny cross-country body coursed with adrenaline. The door didn't have a chance, ripped from its hinges with a single pull. "Tom!" I started to scream again, but the room was devoid of people and engulfed in flames. I was certain the Ghetto was doomed, certain everyone was asleep or gone for the night. But from the alley that had been absolutely quiet moments earlier, streams of neighbors started pouring out of their bungalows, showing up with gourds and baskets and buckets of water. Miraculously, the fire began to die. I didn't get to enjoy our victory, however, because I could see through the hole in the wall that people were now entering *my* room with buckets of water. Running at full speed, I got there in time to find B.J. and Washington standing in the middle of the room, each about to throw ruinously large quantities of H2O across my modest but precious Pioneer stereo. "Whoa!" I called out. "It's okay—the smoke all came from *Tom's* room."

B.J. and Washington hung around with me for several hours scouring Bungalow #4 for any cinders that hadn't been put out. Back in Tom's room I found a burned-out roach lying in a little charcoaled groove on the sideboard of his bed. It was pretty clear from the way the sheets on the bed were scorched that this was where the fire had started. I called to B.J. and Washington, "Come have a look at this."

"Looks like we found our fire bugs," said Jamal. He was not smiling.

We could hear a cab door slamming, followed by the sound of incoherent jabbering coming up the alley. Without saying a word, we went out on the porch to welcome back our prodigal brethren.

"Why if it ain't the Tom and Dave Show!" called B.J. as they approached.

Tom gave me a big grin when he reached the top of the stairs. "What's up, dude? Thought you were sick in bed."

The two sidekicks were totally wasted. "Did we miss a party?" Dave asked.

"You missed a *great* party," said Washington.

"Think it might have been *yours*," I said, handing Tom the roach and gesturing for him to step into his sautéed sleeping quarters.

Tom's eyes nearly came into focus. "I *wondered* what we did with that doobie." He looked sheepishly at B.J., Washington and me. "I'm *really* sorry, guys. I don't even remember firing it up."

"You better think of something better than that to tell Lek when she gets back from Korat," said B.J.

"Jewelry's always good," said Washington. "Don't forget to grovel."

Dave was wandering around doing double and triple takes. "Far out....
Say...Tom...what do you think happened to this room?"

"I think we'd better get to work cleaning it up," said Tom, already rolling
up a couple of Lek's partially burned dresses and tossing them out on the
wet porch.

"I'd like to help you, dude, but my flight to Don Muang leaves at the crack
of dawn."

"Weren't you supposed to go see Tukada *today*?" I asked.

"I *tried*, man, but I missed my flight. Tom and I lost track of the time," he
replied with an sheepish smile.

I loved Dave but tonight I was sick and my body ached. I had gotten tired
of looking into his droopy eyes and seeing no one home. It was a relief when
he meandered off and B.J. and Washington followed him down the stairs.
But long after Dave and the guys left and Tom turned in for the night, I
lay awake, unable to breathe through my stuffed-up nostrils, listening to
the groaning of the ceiling fan, the hizzzing of mosquitos, and the distant
laughter of *sahmlaw* drivers. Somewhere in Bungalow Ruam Chon Sawng
I could hear water dripping very slowly, exactly the speed that could keep
you awake all night.

New Year's Eve was going to be uneventful and that was fine with me. My cough syrup high was all the excitement I wanted or needed. I was trying to write a thank-you note to Danielle but was having a hard time figuring out how to ask her to send more cookies without letting her know that the first batch arrived as a bucket of crumbs. Tom finally talked me into putting down my pen and paper and joining him for a couple of Mekong and Cokes while he, Lek, Larry and Pueng lollygagged around getting ready for the big New Year's party at the New Playboy Club. Once they left, I forced myself to finish up Danielle's letter. I might have felt bad about being remiss lately, except Danielle had gotten busy with school and wasn't writing a lot herself. She seemed to get my drift that I was now doing dangerous, geo-politically sensitive work that I couldn't discuss and that the band had been taking up the rest of my time. I wondered if she had figured out that "geo-politically sensitive" meant "in abject violation of the Geneva Accords by all parties involved," and I wondered if I'd ever get to explain it to her someday. I finished writing her letter, embarrassed at its brevity, and then thought to add an update on the race. "You won't believe this, but we've got everyone from the wheeler-dealer who runs the NCO Club to the base commander backing this thing! We've already raised thousands in sponsor money with a month and a half to go! We might not have been lying after all when we told the base commander we'd get him on the cover of *Life* magazine."

I sealed up Danielle's letter and dashed off an even shorter *"Everything's fine! Thanks for the tie!"* note to my parents. I fixed myself another Mekong and Coke but didn't enjoy it sitting there alone. I knew I needed to get some sleep but dreaded turning in early on a night that was going to be filled with raucous laughter, loud music and bursts of fireworks. I didn't resist when Shahbazian, Perez and Washington dropped by and told me to get dressed.

Before I knew it, we had squeezed into a beat-up Corolla taxi and were headed uptown to Niko's Massage and Turkish Bath. Having Shahbazian along reminded me of our old San Bernardino-Tijuana road trips in my trusty V-Dub, except this joyride took minutes instead of hours and I didn't have to do the driving. "A New Year's scrub and rub!" cried Shahbazian. "Now *that's* the way to start off the year!"

"The Chinese think 1972 is gonna be the Year of the Rat," said Washington. "But we of the 601st know it's gonna be the Year of the—"

"Rat *Pack!*" everybody shouted.

The four of us rolled merrily out of the cab and into Niko's, where we were led to a couple of large, luxurious sofas not far from a picture window of one-way glass where we could peruse the lovely young Thai beauties on display. The last thing any of us needed was another drink, but drinks turned up nonetheless and did seem to help speed us on our way to making our selections. I purposely picked a strong, not-too-pretty masseuse who might actually give my tired body a good working over. Judging from her powerful hands, she must have transplanted plenty of rice shoots in her youth. She took me in an instant from excruciating agony to sublime relaxation and back to a lightning bolt of pain. The overall effect, somehow, was to make me so relaxed that I nearly fell asleep toward the end. When she finished she offered me a hand job. I wasn't really in the mood. It had something to do with the Malaysian princess and a need to find my moral compass again. It also had something to do with guilt about Danielle and confusion about Tukada, my enigmatic lost cause. I was starting to sit up when my strong, plain farm girl asked, "Why you don' like me?"

It was probably just acting, but I didn't have the heart to turn her down. I didn't know how to say that I picked her purposely because she wasn't attractive. Instead, I told her, "I like you just fine. Go ahead. It's been a tough year—let's at least give it a happy ending."

I stretched back out on the massage table, but even though I had spent the past hour in the nude while being bathed and massaged, I suddenly felt *naked*! She went back to work on me with her tube of Brylcreem, but a little dab didn't do me. She tried another dab, a little bigger this time, but nothing was happening. It was probably the five or six Mekong and Cokes—I'd lost count—but try as she might, nothing she did brought anything but a feeling of numbness to that most sensitive part of my body. Even though she had plenty of that Issan water-hauling, rice-planting strength and endurance, she finally gave up and stepped out for a moment, bringing back another girl to help. They were mystified. Apparently nothing like this had ever happened before in the long history of Niko's. They each shot another dab of Brylcreem into their hands and started in again in all possible combinations—one-hand, two-hand, three-hand, *four*-hand. One at a time and both of them together, they struggled with as much energy and concentration as they might have used to fell a tree in a teak forest, but my manhood insisted on acting more like my boyhood. After giving it more than a fair shot, they suddenly packed it in. "*Mai pen rai*," said my masseuse with a little giggle, "It's okay, *na*?"

Her partner smiled at me more sympathetically. "Don' feel bad. You come *ram wong* with us!"

They very sweetly helped me get dressed and led me out like a lost child to the reception area, which had become unexpectedly spacious with all the furniture pushed back. Already most of the massage girls, a few of their Thai boyfriends, and a couple of *sahmlaw* drivers had gathered in a large circle, along with Shahbazian, Perez and Washington. The stereo was playing loudly, alternating between Thai folk tunes and Thai pop, a form of mellow rock that had a Caribbean feel to it. The music inspired the fair young ladies to *ram wong* in a sort of slow-motion samba while their hands glided with the fluid, intricate grace of Polynesian maidens trying to beguile a young warrior-king. Astonishingly, the rough-hewn Thai and Laotian men, their skin bronzed and baked from years working outside in the tropical sun, matched their partners' delicate movements perfectly. For the next couple of hours the girls and the Issan men danced elegantly, a powerful, playful sense of Thai-ness filling the room, while we *farang* made good-natured fools of ourselves, dancing along less than gracefully while drinking far more than any of us needed amidst merry shouts of "*Sawatdii Pii Mai!*" and "*Happy New Year!*"

Just before midnight, Tukada and Dave came in for a New Year's reunion with her former co-workers. Dave was high. Dah wasn't. I was secretly glad when Dave made a brief stab at dancing, barely kept from falling over his own feet, and finally retired with Dah's assistance to one of the sofas pushed into a dark corner. There, he curled up and quickly fell asleep. I caught Dah's eye and she slipped in next to me when she rejoined the circle of dancers. Following her moves, I was pleased to discover I could do a passable *ram wong*, especially for a drummer who had rarely had a chance to dance in the past ten years. "How did Dave find you in Sattahip?" I asked.

"He luck-y. Thailand only have small navy," she replied. After checking to see that Dave was still asleep, she began talking to me just loudly enough to be heard over the music. "I'm worry about Dave. My hus-ban' come soon from Korea, want me an' ba-by go back wis him togezzer."

"I want you to come with me to meet Chaplain Kirkgartner. You've got to promise me."

"I try," she said with the expression of someone who had grown weary of living a life of lies.

Before we had a chance to talk further, Guy Lombardo's Royal Canadians could be heard playing "Auld Lang Syne" over Armed Forces Radio. I kissed Dah quickly, sadly. In the distance I could hear fireworks going off and hoped it wasn't shoulder-mounted rockets, rocket-propelled grenades or mortar rounds being lobbed at the base in some half-baked Thai Communist attempt at another Tet Offensive.

AUA

I worked it out with Spitzer and Washington, trading trips so that I could teach on Monday and Wednesday nights. And so it was that on the first Monday in January 1972 I was able to start teaching at the American University Alumni Association night school. As Khun Jim had promised, most of the class was made up of middle-manager types from firms like the Bank of America and Chase Manhattan that had branches on base or from Thai-Chinese businesses in town catering to GI customers. The students were mostly a mixture of bright, pleasant young men and women in their mid- to late twenties. My one big surprise came when who should walk into class and sit down among my twenty students but *Sergeant Prasert*. There was one more Thai soldier besides Prasert in the class, a leathery master sergeant named Anant, who appeared to be in his late thirties or early forties. He was just back from Vietnam with an artillery unit, friendly enough but tough, someone who had seen combat and, as a career military man, expected to see it again in his part of the world. One younger girl stood out, Miss Pawnsiri, a friend of Sommit and Vrisnei's younger broth-er Chai, who, like them, was Thai-Chinese. A week earlier on one of my black-market record runs from the BX down to Woodstock Music, Som-mit had told me how Pawnsiri and his brother had gone to the Polytechnic High School together and how both of their families had relatives still living in the same village in southern China.

On that first night I was taken in by a Thai custom that was new for me: being invited out for a bite to eat after class by several of my male students. They got to practice their English, asking endless enthusiastic if innocent questions about how long it would take Thailand to catch America in industrial and economic development. For my end of the bargain, I got to eat some of the most delicious food in Thailand, including many Issan specialties that only a local would know to order. I was visiting Woodstock Music after the second of these after-class dinners when Sommit gave me a sphinxlike warning. Showing me the front page of a Chinese-language newspaper from Bangkok, he pointed to a picture of logs floating down a Mekong tributary in southern Laos. "These logs are hollow," he said with a polite smile. "Full of supplies for Viet Cong and Khmer Rouge."

"Very clever," I said. "I've heard rumors about this, but I think we're too busy over the Trail to start blowing up logs. And I don't know if we could see these at night."

"Be careful," he responded. "Even what you just told me could help the enemy. The enemy is very clever. Miss Pawnsiri hears maybe there is a spy in your class. Not for sure. But be careful about everything that you say."

"Thanks for the information," I replied. "Maybe we'll just stay with the textbook for a while."

I was both disappointed and relieved that Prasert didn't join us for our after-class get-togethers. I badly wanted to ask him about Tukada and Dave and if her husband was in Thailand or still in Korea, but I couldn't imagine an answer that would make me feel good. Finally, I couldn't hold out any longer, and, when class ended on the Wednesday of week two, I asked him if he would like to come along. He shyly accepted, and after dinner had been cleared away and the others had left, he stayed behind for a cup of coffee. "How is Dah?"

"Very bad."

"Is she still back with Dave?"

"No, she send him away. Her husband come TDY from Korea to see Dah and their little girl. This man she call her captain is really just an enlisted man like us, but he really *is* her husband, and when he see how bad she is, he want to take her to hospital at base. She look very worried and ask if they can see your friend, Chaplain Kirk-gart-ner. Husband say okay, they go to him first. And when Chaplain Kirk-gart-ner ask Tukada if she still taking heroin with the needle, she lie and say no, she stop. And your friend, Chaplain Kirk-gart-ner, he ask her why she wear navy shirt and he ask her to roll up sleeve. And when he look at her arm he see the mark. He ask, 'What are those?' And she just cry. He ask, 'Do you want to go in the hospital?' And she say, 'No, I can't, I must take care of my baby.'"

"So what happened?"

"Her husband and Chaplain Kirk-gart-ner keep talking to her, and chaplain ask, 'How can you take care of baby if you die from heroin? Isn't it better to stay in hospital?' And her husband say, 'Dah, I can take care of baby while you get better.'"

"So she went through detox like Dave?"

"She stay ten day. And she feel better, promise doctor she never do again. Same thing when chaplain come to visit her—she promise she quit forever. But when she get home, baby is gone. Her husband take baby back with him to Korea. Very bad. She can do nothing."

"Goddamn…. How could he do that to her? She was finally cleaning up her act!" I felt awful for Tukada and awful that a lot of people's good intentions had turned to crap, including my own. "Isn't there *something* she can do?"

"She go see Thai lawyer, but she cannot pay his fee. She go to see lawyer at base and he say she should complain to husband's unit commander. But she doesn't know his unit, only his APO address. She very sad every day, so she go stay with her mother, but her mother still mad about see-ing Dah sniff red-rock heroin. Mother tell her, 'You take heroin, you deserve to lose ba-by!' Now she come back, sit all day in her house, say maybe she and Dave get back togeth-er after all. What do you think about *that*?"

"I think it's a mess. I think we should go have a drink and see what we can figure out. There must be something we can do."

"*Toklong.* Tonight I can use a drink."

"Let me take you to Dah's favorite club," I said, needing some soul music to ease my mind. I hoped it would be quiet on a Wednesday night. The juke box would do just fine.

I hailed a taxi, but when we arrived at the Soul Sister, I could guess from the overflow crowd that Jay and the Ugly Americans were performing. So much for a conversation. I figured Prasert and I could have one quick drink and then go someplace quieter. A long, rousing rendition of "Everyday People," normally one of my favorite tunes, was in progress as we climbed out of the cab. "This is Dah's favorite band," I shouted over the noise to Prasert.

"I thought *your* band was her favorite," he replied politely.

"Okay, her *second* favorite."

The moment we walked through the door I got a bad feeling. Prasert looked uncomfortably at the bar girls and the young Thai women with their American *tii-rahks,* all dressed up, some looking elegant and others flashy and trashy, as we made our way through the club. We found a table near the stage, but instead of enjoying the band, Prasert kept looking around, now focusing on the couples on the dance floor. Without exception, an

American GI was dancing with a Thai female—either his girlfriend or a stranger he was hoping to take home for the night. It was obvious from Prasert's expression that he was sitting on a reservoir of revulsion.

"Brendan!" Marcos called from the stage, "You want to sit in?"

"Not tonight," I replied, waving him off. I looked back at Prasert, concerned about the unhappy expression on his face and hoping that a couple of ideas I had might help him feel better. "Prasert," I said over the din of the club, "I'll go see Captain Kirkgartner tomorrow. There has to be a way he can help. But if he can't help, I have another friend who maybe works for the Air Force secret police. If I have to, I'll go to the base commander, but I promise I will find Dah's husband for you."

I don't think he heard a word. "You know," he said, "these girl make money more than college professor?"

I didn't know what to say to him, but I was reminded of driving in to Hollywood with Tom Wheeler and cruising Sunset Strip shortly before he shipped out for Southeast Asia. There was a long line of Mercedes and BMWs and a few Jaguar convertibles pulling into Carlos and Charlie's, all driven by the sons of Arab oil millionaires—and every one of them had a tanned young California blonde hanging on his arm. Tom and I kept cruising through the crush of traffic and continued on down to Barney's Beanery, where we knew we'd be allowed in without being on somebody's list. "That really pisses me off," Tom had said.

And I remembered saying to him, "I've never seen *anything* piss you off, but I know where you're coming from." When Tom and I got back to our mountain cabin that night, I dumped the contents of my wallet—three dollars in cash and the stub for my $138 monthly paycheck—onto my dresser and headed for the bathroom, where I brushed my teeth and stared long and hard into the mirror at my two-dollar GI haircut.

And for Prasert it had to be worse. Why hadn't it crossed my mind that he might have this reaction? Why was my love for soul music so strong that I hadn't imagined anyone *not* being swept up in it? Why did my joy at cool white dudes and cool black dudes playing music together that could heal America's racial wounds blind me to the fact that this didn't mean a thing in Thailand. GIs and Thai girls holding hands in public did. After a long wait I ordered drinks. When they finally came, Prasert tossed his down. "These are village girl," he said to me through the ruckus of the band playing "Knock on Wood." "These girl grow up wearing sarong. Now they dress like movie star. They make in two week what it take their father all year to earn. I don't like."

"I'm sorry, Prasert. I thought some music might make us feel better. "

"I don't know why Dah like this band. Thai people dance gracefully. This style of dance not graceful."

The band went into "I Wish It Would Rain," a song I hadn't heard them do before. It *was* a graceful song that the crowd was dancing to gracefully, but it was lost on Prasert. A dull, hard gaze came over his eyes. The din of the band was a polite excuse for him not to hear me, even though he wasn't listening to the music, either. He was completely focused on the American men and their Thai women, dancing close together, touching in public in a way that would be scandalous anywhere else in Thailand. The band changed pace again, rousing the audience into a mild frenzy with "Dance to the Music." Prasert ordered another drink and threw that one down too, without pleasure. "Should we call it a night?" I asked.

Without responding, he got up and started winding his way through a crowd that was way too big for a work night. For a split second my heart skipped at the sight of what I thought was Tukada herself. When her mirage walked past me and turned into a nameless face, I felt like I had taken a gulp of lukewarm tap water when I had been expecting champagne. Even though it was after eleven, Prasert and I had to squeeze our way past a steady stream of people who were still coming in. We just got out the door when we ran into Tom, Lek, Larry and Pueng.

"Prasert! Brendan!" they yelled cheerfully, but Prasert was already closing the door to his cab. "I Want to Take You Higher" bled into the street almost as loudly as the band was playing it on stage, and as Prasert's cab drove away, I knew I would never be taking a trip with him to Uttaradit to meet his family and hunt for wild boar.

Tom let the others go on ahead. "What happened to *him*?"

"Remember Carlos and Charlie's in Hollywood?"

He paused a moment before a look of understanding crossed his face. "Where the teetotaler Moslems came to drink and flaunt their petrodollars and flashy American girlfriends?"

"I just made a terrible mistake," I said. Between Prasert and Tukada, I felt lousy.

"Smart" Bombs and Thai Iced Tea

First thing next morning I went to see Kirkgartner, the good-hearted junior chaplain, who seemed to be as disturbed as I was when he heard about Dah's husband and her missing baby. "If you can get me his APO address, I'll start looking into it," he promised.

When I found Jack Wu at the lab, I repeated the story. He gave me an embarrassed smile and replied, "I don't know where all this OSI stuff came from. I've played along with the joke, but if I *was* doing undercover work, I couldn't really be telling you, now, could I?"

"Sorry to bother you, Jack."

"*Mai pen rai*, Brendan. However, I do have a couple of sergeant friends in the Air Police. Let me see what they can find out."

Flying-wise, we had locked into a dry-season routine. Cooper hadn't come in, Guttchock was in alcohol rehab, and Harwell was usually off on TDY, which left Spitzer, Washington and me to do all the flying, mostly with Spectre, who continued night after night to rack up hundreds of enemy truck kills. I continued to find it disturbing that the North Vietnamese Army kept sending convoy after convoy down the Trail, seemingly impervious to the vast quantities of trucks and supplies that ended up annihilated.

Friday afternoon I got a respite from the carnage of burning trucks when Hill and English sent me on a day mission in the back seat of an F-4 over to Savannakhet and Saravan provinces in southern Laos, parts of Steel Tiger where Spectre often operated at night. The region had special importance because it was one of the first places the NVA could complete its end-run around the DMZ and attack the U.S. Marines defending I-Corps. Stopping convoys there also meant keeping them from reaching Cambodia or turning off into South Vietnam at hundreds of places further down the road. According to Hill and English, the brass was confident that this was going to be the day they finally brought down a couple of French bridges that the NVA had been able to repair again and again whenever they had been hit in the past. Spectre could kill trucks but not bridges. The Wolf Pack had just started receiving laser-guided smart bombs that were supposed to do the trick.

Lieutenant Liscomb and I were going out on the same mission, in different planes, him shooting the stills and me doing the motion picture end. We sat together at the pre-flight briefing, where I spotted my old friend Lieutenant Glotfelty and gave him a little nod. I hoped he had gotten all his bad luck out of his system on the training flight he took me on back in September. Liscomb poked me with his elbow and said, "That's my pilot."

"Cool," I lied, figuring this was not a good time to brief Moonbeam about the surprise visit I made with Glotfelty to Maharaj Massage in a skidding F-4 Phantom.

My pilot was a cocky son-of-bitch I nicknamed Lieutenant Asshole. He was enjoying the briefing, even though we would be operating in broad daylight just south of Route 9, the road South Vietnam's finest assault troops followed west into Laos in 1971 when they were routed trying to cut off the Ho Chi Minh Trail at the provincial capital of Sepone. We were briefed that more than a hundred American helicopters had been shot down on that aborted campaign and hundreds more took battle damage, so we were warned to expect more of the same. Lieutenant Asshole couldn't wait to get started. Liscomb and I couldn't help remembering that Nevers and Spinelli were with Larry Burrows near Sepone when their luck ran out. Our first target was just twenty miles south of Route 9 at Muang Phin and less than thirty miles west-southwest of Sepone. That was five minutes in F-4 time.

As we headed down the runway, my heart was pumping hard and it was still pumping hard when we crossed the Mekong into Laos. By the time we started in on our target, a long trestle bridge that crossed the Se Banghiang River at the village of Ban Tat Hai, my stomach was feeling plenty gnarly and I realized there was a good chance some of us were going to die. Much to my surprise, anti-aircraft fire was light even though this was a major western branch of the Ho Chi Minh Trail. If you hated the French or their bridges, it was a beautiful sight watching smart bombs take out span after span of steel span, leaving nothing standing but the pilings.

We got done in time to peel off fifteen miles to the southeast, expecting to watch the second bridge get dropped with similar efficiency. That bridge was located between the villages of Ban Thongatua and Tumlan where the Trail crossed the Huay Phim River, and that was precisely where the NVA decided to spring their trap, letting loose a heavy barrage of 23-mm, 37-mm and 57-mm anti-aircraft fire, with a few rounds from their AK 47's thrown in for good measure. Two flights consisting of a pilot and a wingman went after the triple-A positions they had spotted, quieting them down enough for the rest of us to go after the primary target. With all the noise rattling in my helmet from radio chatter, camera grinding, jet engines roaring and ordnance being expended, I scarcely noticed a little thunk in the Plexiglas canopy. It wasn't until we were leveled out and heading back to Ubon that I spotted a dud 57-mm shell lodged directly in front of the pilot. When we landed, I noticed Lieutenant Asshole had lost a little of the swagger in his step. On the other hand, just being alive added a little spring to mine.

Lieutenant Liscomb and I were debriefed together. The intelligence officers seemed happy to see us and offered us each a Singha, but when Liscomb passed, I did the same. We didn't have much more to tell them than that the bridges blew and we got it on film. They pressed us, but we couldn't tell them anything special about the flak trap because we both pretty much expected a flak trap to be waiting for us anywhere we flew. When they finally turned us loose, Liscomb invited me over to his trailer.

"You're not worried about being hassled for fraternization?" I asked along the way.

"If anybody bugs us, we're planning for the race, remember?"

It was a relief to talk to Liscomb without English or Hill looking over our shoulders. "How long do you think they'll keep you under house arrest?"

"It doesn't matter. It's not as bad as it sounds. Now that I'm flying combat, I get an air-conditioned trailer. They let me work out at the gym, do a little sparring, do a little roadwork on the track. They've even let me have a housegirl. It could have been a lot worse. Colonel Grimsley wanted to court martial me big time, but General Gong back at Seventh Air Force sent word down that ain't gonna happen to an Academy grad. He used to teach there."

I followed Liscomb into the trailer. "This is nice," I said, admiring several large photos of California and Thai landscapes hanging on the walls. "You took these?"

"Sergeant Wu's been nice enough to do the printing."

"This *is* nice, but I don't think I could handle it. I'm afraid I'm hooked on living downtown."

"Maybe I'm lucky in a way. I never got downtown enough to miss it."

I noticed a white marble Buddha image sitting on a little altar next to a jar of sand filled with the stubs of burned-out incense sticks. "What's that?"

"I've gotten back into Zen meditation. This isn't a bad place to practice."

"My friend Tukada took me into a temple here in Ubon a couple months back. She's a troubled soul, but lighting incense and meditating seemed to bring her peace. I'd like to learn more about it, but reading about Zen back in the States always left me scratching my head."

"The books make a lot more sense after you've actually practiced meditation. A good teacher helps. If we end up back in San Bernardino, I'll bring you in to the Zen Center in L.A."

"Sounds like a plan to me, Lieutenant."

The following Monday, when I paid visits to Chaplain Kirkgartner and Jack Wu, I learned that they didn't need an APO address to bring me bad news about Tukada's husband. "We've got a very slick operator here," the chaplain told me. "His unit moved several times in the past year. Right now they're back in Japan, but he's got someone—maybe someone working in the base post office—sending money to Tukada from his old APO at Taegu Air Base in Korea. That's where she thought they were going."

When I found Jack, he gave me a pained expression and reported, "This guy's a bad penny, I'm afraid. My friends tell me he was under investigation when he was stationed here for some black market deals and impersonating an officer. They were ready to arrest him when he came back, but he was on leave, not TDY, and he skipped out early—almost like someone had tipped him off. I don't think you want to get mixed up with this, Brendan."

I decided to ignore Jack and stick with Kirkgartner a little while longer.

That night I taught my first AUA class since taking Prasert on our ill-fated trip to the Soul Sister. It didn't surprise me that his sense of honor would force him to sit out a class, but I was concerned. In addition to being a friend, he had been one of my best students. On a very practical level, I needed him to tell Tukada that Chaplain Kirkgartner might be able to help her get her baby back. I put away my attendance book and started the night's lesson, hoping he might come in late. Holding up my paper-bound textbook, I asked the class to turn to Lesson Three, page 29. "Let's do a substitution drill. Ready? Everybody—repeat: 'The market is to the right.'"

"The market is to the right," the class echoed enthusiastically.

"Good! Now substitute 'left'—"

"The market is to the left," answered most of the class.

"Good! 'The market is to the left.' Substitute 'straight ahead.' Row one."

Row one answered, "The market is straight ahead."

"Good! Substitute 'hotel.' Row four—"

Row four was on the ball, answering, "The hotel is straight ahead."

We continued, generally with the whole class answering at first before I mixed it up. Often it was each half of the class responding next—back and front, right and left—and then each row, sometimes followed by the men or women as a group, and finally as many individual students as I could before coming back to the entire class.

Later in class we practiced the dialogue they had been given for homework. To my surprise, it was Sommit and Vrisnei's friend, the shy Miss Pawnsiri, who volunteered to go first, along with a classmate sitting nearby. "May I ask you something?" Pawnsiri began.

"Go ahead," answered her partner.

"If I want to read a book, but the room is too dark, what should I tell the servant?" There were a few snickers.

"What's your servant's name?"

"Her name is Toy."

"Tell her, 'Turn on the light, Toy.'" There were a few more snickers.

"And when I don't need the light anymore, what do I say to my servant?"

"Tell her, 'You can turn off the light now, Toy.'"

"So it's 'turn on' and 'turn off'?"

"That's right."

I told them they did a good job and could take their seats. By the time class was over, my voice was tiring out as usual, but I before I dismissed them I asked what the laughter had been about during the dialogue. Miss Pawnsiri, who had been so shy for the first couple of weeks, again raised her hand. "Khun Brendan, textbook written in Bangkok. In Issan part of Thailand we don't have servant to turn on-off light."

Her fellow students smiled in agreement. "I'm afraid it's the same for me. When you're a GI by day and a teacher by night, you turn out your own lights and open your own doors." Several people laughed again, and I joined in. "Good night, everybody. See you Wednesday. Good job."

Miss Pawnsiri made a point of saying good night, blushing a little as she did so. My group of bank managers asked if I were joining them for dinner.

I told them I'd be right out, but before he got away, I wanted to speak with Master Sergeant Anant. "Have you heard from Sergeant Prasert?" I asked.

"Sorry, Khun Brendan. I don' know about Prasert. He infantry. I artillery. I never see him except here."

"Thanks," I said to the sergeant as I gathered up my things. To my surprise, Miss Pawnsiri was still waiting in the back of the room and met me at the door.

"My family would like you to come for lunch on Saturday."

"What a pleasant surprise!" I answered. "I would be honored." She gave me directions to her family's compound. It turned out to be located in a neighborhood I was familiar with, near the teachers' college and Phra Sri Hospital at the north end of Ubon, not far from where Tukada lived.

Class was routine Wednesday night, except still no Prasert. Saturday I rode my bike to Miss Pawnsiri's as planned, but I couldn't help taking a detour along the way. The grounds at Tukada's were overgrown, and her abode was dark inside. I knocked a few times and listened, hoping *someone* would come to the door. When no one answered, I took off. Miss Pawnsiri and her younger sister were waiting for me on the corner where their dirt lane turned off of Route 66. I got off my bicycle and walked with them to the house, not much different in style from our bungalows at Ruam Chon Sawng, but four times larger, telling me she came from a family of some substance.

We left our shoes out on the porch, a custom we generally ignored back at the Ghetto. Once inside, she slowed at the first doorway we came to and showed me her family's shrine room, where a low altar held several statuettes of sitting Buddhas, a vase of fresh-cut flowers, sticks of burning incense, and black-and-white photographs of several of her ancestors. She paused a moment and seemed to say a little prayer before she turned away and led me past the kitchen down a hallway to a large living area, where her mother, father and grandmother were sitting comfortably on a large mat with a lovely assortment of home-cooked Thai delicacies waiting for us in the middle. I sat down with them, not quite so comfortably, and *waied* as Miss Pawnsiri introduced us.

She put us at ease by pouring us all some orange Thai-style iced tea, heavily sweetened with condensed milk but delicious in the early afternoon heat. The others began scooping white rice onto their plates and covering it with spoonsful of various types of stir-fried chicken, beef and pork. They topped it off with dollops of condiments that ranged from hot to hotter or fish sauce that added saltiness. Pawnsiri scooped a mound of rice onto my plate and nodded for me to help myself to the other dishes. During the meal I learned a little more about Miss Pawnsiri's family and about the region. Her brother had a government job in Mukdahan, a trading town further north on the Mekong River opposite Savannakhet, Laos. I learned that Savannakhet, like Pakse to the south, was one of a string of lowland towns still under Royalist control and still trading actively with Thailand, critically important for landlocked Laos. When Pawnsiri told me her older sister was a nurse in Bangkok, she added with a smile, "Someday maybe I be nurse in America!"

"Maybe my mom can help you," I suggested. "She used to be a nurse too."

"Very good!" Pawnsiri replied before slipping out to the kitchen to bring in more curry.

We ate wonderfully, maybe too wonderfully. Every time we seemed to be out of a particular dish, Miss Pawnsiri, her mother, or her sprightly grandmother got up to bring in more. Even without being able to follow much of the Issan dialect, I couldn't help noticing the warmth and liveliness of the conversation. And in the midst of this, I couldn't help noticing Miss Pawnsiri's attentiveness—her uncanny ability to anticipate when I needed more spice or another helping or when I wanted to know exactly what was in the local delicacy she was serving me. I couldn't help thinking how she *would* make a good nurse and how different this was from eating back at the Ghetto in terms of a comfortable kind of formality. Even though we were sitting on a large grass mat, we were seated in a circle with the food in the middle where we could easily pass it from one to another, not sprawled out in chairs scattered around a porch. There was none of Lek's earthy laughter or Pueng's bawdy humor and not once did someone interrupt, shouting "Bull shit!" There *was* something they had very much in common, however: a Thai love of enjoying a good meal with friends and family.

I tried to remember what made family get-togethers so uncomfortable for me back home, drawing a blank at first. For one thing, they were rare with Dad often away on layovers. And then I started remembering all the taboos—politics and race and religion and the family skeletons. Even sports and the arts could be touchy if my brother was doing too much drinking or we strayed too far from aviation to something Dad knew nothing about and therefore hated. Maybe I was missing a lot of what was being said, but if Pawnsiri's family was only talking about the weather, they were having a great time doing it. As the afternoon wore on I felt full and content, and I was sure no one else was going hungry either, but the food and the afternoon heat were also tiring me out. My bad Thai and the need for Miss Pawnsiri and her sister to do a lot of translating for me, their parents, and their grandmother tired me out a little more. Afraid of being a bit abrupt and at the same time not wanting to overstay my welcome, I finally said to Miss Pawnsiri, "Thank your family for a wonderful lunch. It's been a lovely afternoon. Unfortunately, I need to get going. We still have a lot of work left to do on the bicycle race to Big Buddha."

She translated for her family, and they laughed, before *waiing* warmly. Her mom and grandmom seemed to have a look of pity in their eyes. I suspected they found the idea of a bicycle race as ridiculous as Lek did, but I *waied* back, smiled and made my way out. Before I got on my bicycle, Miss Pawnsiri said, "I will be singing in Thai nightclub in Det Udom next Saturday. Can you and your friends come?"

"I'd really like to. I used to play in some bands, myself. But the race is so close—I'd better wait till it's over. Will you be singing again in February?"

"Oh, yes," she answered, blushing and smiling shyly. "I'm also busy—with college, but I try to sing almost every weekend. It's not too difficult. We have four girls who take turn, so we only have to sing one hour. Some girls go to other night club, sing more. But for me singing one hour every week is enough."

"In that case, I'll be looking forward to hearing you in a few weeks." She and her sister walked down the lane with me to Route 66. They spoke in rapid Issan Thai that I couldn't keep up with. "*Arai na?*" I asked.

"My sister say you walk beautifully—like a Thai."

"Thanks," I said, glad I was fitting in and a little embarrassed at the same time. As I bicycled home I wondered what the hell it meant to "walk like a Thai." A little further down the road, riding along quietly, I thought of Danielle and recalled how much we used to enjoy the simple meals we cooked and ate together in our mountain cabin.

I stopped by Jim Scott's classroom before school Monday night. According to Jim, Prasert was still registered, but once again he didn't show. Riding home, I decided to give up on Prasert and go directly to Tukada to pass on the information Kirkgartner had given me. This time her housekeeper came to the door, but all she could tell me was that Tukada had gone out that morning and had not said where she was going or when she was coming back. *Fuck them both*, I muttered, *Jack Wu's probably right. And I can't do this by myself.*

"Any sign of Prasert?" Tom asked when I got home.

"Nope. I'm afraid 'Sweet Soul Music' failed to win his heart or mind. So much for being a cultural ambassador. It never occurred to me how much the GI bar scene might piss him off."

"Anything new about Dah's old man taking her baby back to Korea?"

"I've asked Kirkgartner and Wu if there's some way they can help, but it's not real encouraging. The SOB might not even be stationed in Korea. What a mess!"

"I don't think Dave has begun to wrap his head around it."

339

By the end of January my ass was dragging from flying and teaching, but I agreed with Wheeler that with less than a month to go before the race it might be a good idea to start getting into shape. Our intentions were good when we headed out that afternoon, but the minds that lurked within our minds had other ideas, and soon we were back to doing aerobic dope ingestion, far out of town among wide expanses of golden rice fields. Riding our bikes along the country roads in a semi-trancelike state, we failed to notice when the pavement turned to hard-packed clay. We did notice the tropical sun hitting our eyes and decided it was time to head back, picking up the paved road as the outskirts of town came into view. Pedaling swiftly down a pleasant tree-lined *thanon*, we passed several large old Thai residences with a British-colonial feel to them interspersed with other comfortable upper-middle-class homes created, in the Thai style, by connecting a series of teak huts together to make a larger structure. One, with a wide thatch roof shading a series of porches and verandas, had an ornately hand-lettered sign out front announcing it as the parish house of a Dutch Methodist missionary and his wife.

By chance our ride took us by a new, especially impressive structure that I suspected was the American-funded mansion of the provincial governor. "Isn't that the governor's limousine pulling in the front gate up ahead?" I asked Tom.

"Could be," he replied.

We slowed down and caught a glimpse through the wrought-iron fence of the mansion's massive teak front door opening and a uniformed bodyguard stepping out, putting on his American-made, silver-coated sunglasses. The black Mercedes limousine pulled to a stop about twenty feet away and the driver, wearing a similar uniform, got out and stood by at attention. The governor appeared at the door. He was a dirigible of a man, exaggerated in his bearing and much taller than the average Thai. His mistress joined him in the vestibule. She appeared to be little more than a teenager, but she was lavishly dressed in silk and her hair was styled in a Geisha-like chignon.

She pulled the cigar from between his blubbery lips and showered a display of affection on him that would have been considered scandalous in a more public place. He smiled paternally and whispered something obscene in her ear, which ignited a burst of falsetto tittering. He put his cigar back in his mouth and descended the stairs, sauntering pompously toward the waiting car.

Tom pushed off and I followed a bike-length behind. Before we got a hundred yards, though, bursts of automatic-rifle fire broke out around us. Tom reflexively screeched on his brakes, skidding on a patch of gravel and falling. I turned hard to miss him, hit a pothole instead and flew headfirst over the handlebars. No sooner did I land in an ugly heap in the drainage ditch next to the road than a burst of machine-gun fire tore into the shrubbery a foot over my head on the other side of the ditch. I was starting to feel a little discouraged—like you feel in one of those nightmares where you're running like hell but not getting anywhere. At least I hadn't done what hard-as-nails Harley did at Qu Son and crapped my pants. "I thought the friggin' war was supposed to be winding down!"

Tom crawled into the ditch after me. "Maybe this is just Thai politics—although if this were the States I'd say it was a big dope deal gone very, very bad."

Another burst of gunfire ripped into the pavement in front of us. We looked at each other in mounting desperation. I spotted an opening in the vegetation on the embankment behind us. "Come on," I shouted.

We charged three-fourths of the way up the berm when Tom stopped abruptly and ran back down, leaving me exposed. I was frozen in disbelief before I saw that Tom was picking up his bicycle, which was glistening rather brightly in the setting sun. I ran back for mine and, halfway up the hill a second time, a fresh volley of gunfire opened up. Madly we tugged at the bicycles and wrestled with the branches of the hedgerow. Bullets continued to zing past, tearing up the terrain around us. They didn't seem to be aimed *at* us, which offered no comfort whatsoever—we were still trapped in a mish-mash of crossfire and ricochets. At last, we broke through and found suitable cover in a shallow depression a few yards further back. There was just enough underbrush spreading out from the shrubbery to hide our bodies and the bikes, and we were obscured a little more by the shade of a grove of acacia trees. "There's got to be an easier way to train for this fuckin' race," hissed Tom.

"Mark my word, this is the last time I ever start anything early for the rest of my life. We could be sitting by the pool, sipping a bargain-basement Bud—"

Brrrrrrrat! Another volley, far more intense than any of the others, rudely cut off my griping. And then, as abruptly as it began, the firefight stopped. A very silent silence. Finally, an almost comforting buzz of cicadas. "Damn!" I said, remembering to start breathing.

From the governor's compound voices could be heard—men crying for help, cursing, all keyed with staccato bursts of emotion, followed by the faint groaning of the front door opening and the shrieking and wailing of a girl far too young to be a concubine widow. "I really, really, really want to go home right now," Wheeler said to me, "and I don't mean *Ruam Chon Sawng* home!"

The surfer dude was smeared from head to foot with gravel, mud and grass. He was not smiling his Buddha smile. We got to our feet, brushed ourselves off, and started pushing our bikes along in a crouch. A football field away we found another opening in the hedgerow. Crawling through, somehow dragging along our bikes, we froze when we heard the sound of combat boots rushing towards us. Looking up, we came face to face with *Prasert* crashing his way through the thick branches. He was wearing jungle fatigues and carried what might have been an AK 47 and some sort of bulky field radio, but before I could be sure, he turned around and tossed them hard and we could hear whatever they were splash into the muddy klong behind him. When he turned back to face us, we could see that under his bush hat his head was matted with blood from a bullet that had grazed his right temple. "Goddamn!" I whispered loudly. "Which side are you on here?"

"Don' worry—this have nothing to do with you American, this is Thai politics. Can you get me to my sister?" he asked, his eyes darting about cautiously. "Dah know what to do...."

It was dusk when the cab pulled up in front of Dah's villa, two bicycles sticking out of the trunk. Tom paid the driver and went around to unload the bikes. I put Prasert's arm over my shoulder and helped him out. He was wearing sunglasses, had his hat pulled down over his wound, and was singing an old Thai Army drinking song. Nudging the door shut, I smiled at the driver, said a quick good night, and hurried like hell to get Prasert inside the front gate.

Tom and I helped him up the stairs to the veranda and knocked at the door. Nothing happened. We knocked again and waited. I was about to give up when we heard the door open just a crack. It was the housegirl. "Dah *yu thinii mai, khrab*?" I asked her.

"Dah not here, *kha*," she replied.

I stepped closer and swung around so she could see Prasert. "He's hurt," I said, and the girl ran off into the house.

We could hear female voices speaking softly but with urgency, followed by a small commotion of footsteps. Dah unchained the door and let us in. She took off Prasert's hat, studied the wound, and then led us down to the basement, where she helped Prasert stretch out on a bamboo bed next to the bathing room. She disappeared a moment and came back with a wet cloth. While Dah cleaned his wound, Prasert glanced at me and asked, "You not report me?"

"No, we won't report you," I answered. "We're not getting mixed up in Thai politics, right, Tom?"

Tom leaned back against the wall in silence. Prasert tried to explain, "In Bangkok, they say we have parliamentary democracy like England, but that a lie. The Issan is very poor, but we only get to vote for one party, the party already in power. The governor—he not elected, he appointed by a big general in Bangkok. Very corrupt."

Tom followed a few steps behind when Dah and I went upstairs. "You have twenty dollar?" she asked. "Have to take Prasert to Uttaradit. If he stay here, *tamruat* find him for sure."

I handed her five one-hundred-baht notes. "Take a little extra."

"You a good man," she said, putting her arms around my neck and kissing me. She whispered, "I be back tomorrow night, come see you at Ruam Chon."

"Promise me. We need to talk."

"I promise."

"Chaplain Kirkgartner wants to help with your baby."

"Maybe not possible." She picked an envelope off the end table and handed it to me. "Husband was at Taegu Air Base in Korea, but letter I write to him come back. I afraid his unit move to Japan or Okinawa. Or maybe he already out of Air Force, go back States."

"Don't worry, we'll find him." I stuffed the letter in my back pocket and gazed back at her. "Before I go, a serious question. Who is Prasert, really?"

She looked up at me, radiating strength I had never seen in her before. She was going to need it if she were going to look after Prasert right now and someday get her daughter back. "He my half-brother and he my cousin. Hard to explain to *farang*."

First thing the next morning I tried to play it cool, not mentioning Pras-ert when I stopped by Chaplain Kirkgartner's office and showed him Dah's letter. He warned me that this wasn't going to be easy. Even if Tukada's hus-band could be located, he might challenge her fitness as a mother. Kirk-gartner asked me if I was sure she was up to raising her daughter alone. I wasn't sure but I said yes anyway and he told me he'd press on with locating her husband's commander. I wasn't taking any chances, however. I found Jack Wu at the motion picture lab and asked him to pass the Korea APO address along to his Air Police friends. I had just headed over to the Com-Doc camera trailer when Lieutenant Hill and First Sergeant Link pulled up in the Rat Pack jeep and told me to climb in. Tom Wheeler was already sitting in the back seat, looking none too happy. Before I knew it, we had parked in front of the Little Pentagon and were being escorted up the front steps and around the promenade toward Colonel Grimsley's office. "If this is about the complaint on the Commander's Hot Line," I prattled, "I can as-sure you it was a practical joke. We never thought anyone was really putting arsenic in the chow-hall coffee, right, Tom?"

Tom was intent on something else. "That's right, sir," Tom answered glumly. "Whatever he said."

"Seriously, what seems to be the problem, lieutenant?"

"*You're* the problem, once again," replied Link, pushing open the door and leading us into the outer office.

Hill announced himself to the receptionist, then gazed back at us coldly. "Looks like you guys finally hit the big time."

It didn't look good when we stepped inside. Colonel Grimsley sat there imposingly, tapping his pen on the desk and looking like he'd prefer to be in the cockpit of his old F-105. His beady-eyed vice-commander, another full-bird colonel, stood on his right giving us a thorough once-over, sternly looking for dress-code violations. A tough young captain, commander of the Air Police squadron, stood on Grimsley's left with what looked like a high-ranking Thai national police officer standing beside him. Link and Hill reported in, saluting sharply. Tom and I mimicked them as best we could. Grimsley slid a picture to our side of the desk. Snorting more than breathing, he asked, "Either of you know this man?"

My heart sank when I picked up a black-and-white photograph of Prasert. I handed it to Tom, who studied it for a moment in strained silence. The colonel harrumphed impatiently. Tom finally answered, "It's possible that's the brother of a massage girl I know down at Niko's. Unfortunately, it also looks like about a hundred other people I've seen around Thailand in the past year."

Grimsley snatched the photo out of his hand. "Cut the crap, airmen. His unit reported him missing yesterday. Sergeant Prasert Maneewatana. AUA records show he was registered in your night-school class, Leary. The Thai police think he may be connected to the assassination attempt on the governor yesterday."

"Sergeant Prasert is a serious English student. He never talked politics. I hope the governor is okay," I said meekly, glancing at the Thai policeman, noticing how lean and fit he seemed for a man in his forties.

"The governor will recover," said the Thai.

"Thanks in some measure at least to the American-made flak jacket we provided him just last month," the Air Police captain added smugly.

I was afraid to open my mouth and opened it anyway. "If this *is* Sergeant Prasert we're talking about, I think we can clarify his disappearance, sir. You, see, he really has a sister, but she doesn't work at Niko's anymore. She's got a problem—"

"She's been strung out on heroin—off and on—for years, it seems," Tom said. "Her brother came around last night looking for her. Said she was on the needle this time."

I picked up the story. "Pretty good chance that he found her last night and took her home to her family before the police locked her up. She's got a baby to look after—a Thai jail could be a real problem."

I glanced at the Thai police officer, who wasn't about to play his hand.

"And did she ever mention where it is her family lives?' asked Grimsley.

"It might have been Phrae," I replied.

"Or was it Takhli?" Tom added.

"Apparently their father has two wives, possibly sisters, who get along better by living in two different towns in two different provinces," I tried to explain.

Grimsley looked at the police captain, who looked at the Thai officer. "We will investigate," the Thai pronounced solemnly.

"Will that be all, sir?" asked Hill.

"That will be all—for now."

Tom stopped as we reached the door. "Sir? Do they know who attempted to assassinate the governor? Isn't there a chance, if it was VC terrorists or the like, that with the bicycle race and all, they might—"

"The assassination attempt was the work of a renegade opposition party," the Thai officer replied authoritatively. He smiled at Tom's poor grasp of regional politics. "The Viet Cong operate in *South Vietnam*, Airman Wheeler, fighting the South Vietnamese government. There are no *VC* within a hundred and fifty miles of Ubon. The Pathet Lao are trying to bring down the *Laotian* government and North Vietnamese Army units are operating on the Ho Chi Minh Trail, but that is all over a hundred miles away, high in the Annamite Mountains on the other side of the Mekong. I can assure you there are no insurgents operating in Thailand."

"In-tell says the same thing, sir," added the captain.

"Sir, why were we on standby alert then back in November?" Tom asked.

Colonel Grimsley leaned forward, smiling at us paternalistically. "The alert in November? That's just regs—we've got to have one every few months, that's all. Kind of like a fire drill in elementary school."

"But what about the mortar rounds and gunfire out along the perimeter?"

It was a touchy subject for Grimsley. The Air Police captain jumped in. "That was friendly fire, airman. Somebody shot at a palm tree shadow and all hell broke loose."

"It didn't *sound* friendly. Couldn't a saboteur have started it?"

"I'm afraid your imagination has gotten the best of you," said Grimsley.

"We investigated it thoroughly," the captain added.

"But what about the firefight out on the flight line?" I interjected.

"That's still under investigation," said the captain. "They were wearing local peasant's pajamas and had no I.D., but it's looking like a rogue unit of North Vietnamese rangers."

"Well, *that's* a relief," Tom sighed.

When Tom and I got over to the chow hall a little after noon, we spotted Woody Shahbazian and Jack Wu having lunch together and decided to join them. Shahbazian was looking though Wu's slides and prints of an elephant training school in Chiang Mai, at the same time describing a conversation he had just had with Indian Joe downtown. "Far out," he gasped, holding up a little one-slide viewer. "You can see the veins in the trainer's eyeballs. That thousand millimeter lens really gets you in there, doesn't it!"

Wu smiled proudly, happy he had finally found someone who appreciated the greatness of his photography.

"As I was saying," Shahbazian continued, "this dude, Indian Joe, asks me if I can get my hands on a flak jacket. Can you imagine that?"

I was having trouble picking up on the drift of their conversation, but I noticed that at the mention of the word "flak jacket" Tom's face had gone blank. "Hey Brendan," asked Shahbazian, "any of your buddies at Spectre got a flak jacket they can spare? Maybe double up, something like that. Seems this Thai business associate of Indian Joe's is going out of his gourd. He's certain the governor's henchmen are going to wipe him out for being connected to one of the opposition parties. Indian Joe will pay two hundred American dollars for it—just cut me in for a 10% finder's fee."

"I'll see what I can do," I said as I started to eat.

Tom got up and walked out, leaving his tray on the table. "What's with him?" asked Shahbazian.

"He's been a little touchy since we got caught in that crossfire yesterday. Wasn't in his job description as a clerk-typist."

The regular programming on AFTN Radio was interrupted by Sergeant Sagittarius: "Only 24 more days till the Big Buddha Bicycle Race!"

I stopped by the editing room after lunch to see Zelinsky, who was running the latest sync-sound Spectre footage on his Moviola. A giant explosion lit up the screen as an oil truck was destroyed. Colonel Strbik's gravelly voice could be heard on the sound track, shouting, "*Golly, gee-wickers, we've got us a very prodigious BURNER—*"

"*Wow-ee!*" cried Major Horney. "*That's a mind-boggling secondary! And she is still burning very prettily….*"

Wheeler must have been keeping an eye out for me from his desk in the orderly room. Before I had a chance to ask Zelinsky about the latest numbers on the race, Wheeler burst in. There was no Buddha smile. He looked edgy. "Guys, I gotta talk to you."

Zelinsky shut off the Moviola. "Yeah?"

"There's something funny going on—I think you should call off the bicycle race. I wanted to talk to you and Jack Wu at lunch, Brendan, but—"

"You know how much *money* is riding on this right now?" asked Zelinsky. "Between entrance fees and bets, Sagittarius has over five thousand bucks sitting in his safe, and we're just getting started."

I jumped in. "Tom, after all we've been through—the peace marches and the road trips back home and our all-night rap sessions here—how could you bail when we're so close to pulling off our greatest accomplishment, something we can be really proud of?"

"I've got a bad feeling, guys—I think local insurgents and the North Vietnamese regular army might be linking up the way they have in Vietnam and Laos."

Zelinsky laughed. "You've got a *bad feeling*? Come on, Tom! The war's winding down. You think any self-respecting Thais are gonna let a bunch of V fuckin' C go marching through Ubon Province when they can collect a two-hundred-dollar bounty for every one they turn in?"

"It's not the VC, Zelinsky. The Thai colonel explained it to us this morning—the VC are in Nam and the Pathet Lao are in Laos. But he was dead wrong about Thailand. He said there's no insurgency here, but I think the assassination attempt on the governor and the attacks on the base and even the train robberies near Surin are connected."

"The Red Alert was a *false alarm*!" Zelinsky laughed nervously.

"We don't know that for sure. The Viet Cong over in Nam carry away their dead and wounded all the time. And there's no doubt about the day after Christmas. They hit."

"Yeah," I said reassuringly, "and they got wiped out, remember?"

Tom wasn't buying it. "A friend of mine over at In-tell claims there's a whole NVA *division* hanging out in the jungle not ten miles from here, trying to decide whether to kick our asses or slide on down to Cambodia."

Zelinsky switched on the Moviola. The screen lit up with napalm dropped from a flight of Night Hawk F-4s, liquid fire sloshing over the remains of a fifteen-truck convoy. "What the hell does In-tell know? We got two hundred sorties going out of here every twenty-four hours, day and night. You think they're gonna overlook a *full division*?"

"You may be right, but I'm dropping out of the syndicate just the same.

Lek thought this was crazy from the get-go, and I think, as usual, that her street smarts are more dependable than In-tell."

"Tom," I pleaded. "We're doing a great thing here! Why don't you sleep on it?"

Instead of an answer, though, all I got was the tinny sound of the trailer door slamming in my face.

"You think smoking all that grass is making him paranoid?" asked Zelinsky.

"I think that Tom's judgment has been pretty shaky for a while now. What the hell was he thinking getting himself strung out on red rock? And then getting *Tukada* strung out. He's been screwing up big time. I mean, even if he didn't get her started, he sure kept her going."

I wondered if Tukada had gone underground with Prasert or if she was going to keep her promise and come back. If she *was* out of the picture, I couldn't help blaming Tom. Sure, there was plenty of blame to go around—Dave, Mole, drug-dealing Papa-sahns, life, Tukada's ersatz captain, Tukada herself—but I expected more of Tom. Sadly, my anger at Tom was the only anger I could direct at anyone, and I couldn't say anything about any of this to Zelinsky. When it occurred to me that I hadn't answered Zelinsky's question, I told him, "I think you might be right about too much dope. But I'll be goddamned if I let a lovable pothead-turned-heroin-addict talk the rest of the syndicate into canceling what's probably the greatest thing any of us have accomplished in our lives."

I was fired up when I left Zelinsky in the editing trailer, and I felt good climbing on my bike for the ride home, but pedaling along the perimeter road on the way to the main gate I was suddenly overtaken and forced off the road by a jeep that skidded to a halt in front of me. "What the hell!" I screamed.

It was Link, looking plenty unhappy. "Listen up, Leary. And don't try getting your friend Liscomb to dig you out of this pile of shit."

"What the *hell* are you talking about?"

"Word's come down that you're poking around, asking about your *tii-rahks's* husband—or maybe it's her future ex-husband. Doesn't matter. They're both smack-heads. Not nice people. And you're fucking up a major investigation. So clear out, Leary. Nothing good will come of it."

I changed into civvies back at Ruam Chon Sawng and tried to prepare my lesson for AUA, but I was too distracted by thoughts of Tom, Link, Prasert and Tukada and the drama of the past two weeks to concentrate. My heart wasn't in my teaching that night and I wrapped up class early. I hurried home to wait for Tukada, hoping she would keep her promise and knowing she wouldn't. I read for a while but soon got groggy. I took a quick shower to try to freshen up and put on a clean T-shirt and boxer shorts. I tried turning off the light and getting some sleep, but my eyes kept staring at the double and triple shadows circling on the ceiling above the fan. I got up again and pulled on my jeans and a pair of flip-flops. Outside, I unchained my bike, dragged it down the stairs, and rode aimlessly through the empty back streets of Ubon, passing the Siam Hotel and pausing a moment to glance through the gate at the empty swimming pool before continuing downtown to the Ubon Hotel. I wandered inside, almost sleep-walking, sitting for a moment in the downstairs bar, ordering a coffee and then getting up abruptly without finishing it and riding the elevator to the ninth floor. It was hauntingly empty, that limbo time after the respectable citizens of Ubon finished their dinners and before the whores and GIs started rolling in for after-hours imbibing. Climbing back on my bicycle, I rode along the side streets parallel to Route 66, absent-mindedly passing Miss Pawnsiri's family compound and then crossing the highway to Tukada's decaying villa. I parked my bike and walked over to the gate. There wasn't even a candle lit inside. I walked around the house, peering occasionally over the wall, but nothing changed—the house was dark and empty. I rode back home to Ruam Chon Sawng and crawled into bed. I finally fell asleep, but before I did, I knew my chronic exhaustion had grown deeper yet.

I was sitting in the ready room the next day when I heard the phone ring in Homer Harwell's office. A moment later he called me in. "It's Captain Kirkgartner," he said. "He needs to see you right away."

Hurrying over to the chapel, I didn't expect to be hearing anything good. I just didn't want to hear that something awful had happened to Dah. "There's been a development you might find interesting. Regarding your friend Tukada's husband—he's been arrested for possession and distribution of heroin."

"Whoa…it does keep getting messier, doesn't it?" Kirkgartner gave me a little half cringe. "What about her little girl?" I asked.

"I'm trying to track that down."

I ran over to see Tom at the orderly room, but Dave was there when I poked my head in the door. "Tom, I need to talk to you outside."

He followed me out. "Whazzup?"

"Dah's husband's been busted for dealing heroin. Who knows what's happened to her daughter."

"Leary, you gotta back off. Tukada is bad news. This is her problem to sort out, wherever she is. Let Dave worry about it. Or Prasert…or her mom."

"I *can't* back off—"

"Well, you *got* to! Link's on your tail, man. He wants to bust your chops. And for what? Tukada's not worth it, man. She's beautiful to look at, but she's trouble. She's completely messed Dave's head up. But that's to be expected—they're a couple of druggies, unlike yourself. And her husband—apparently he deals *and* dabbles. Listen Leary, there's nowhere you can go but down. Go write Danielle a letter. Forget about Tukada."

"You're full of shit, Tom."

"No, Leary, I'm not. You got involved because Prasert filled your head with a bunch of false hope. But she's a loser, Brendan. She's a complete fucked-up fuckin' loser, and you're going to trash your Ivy League education and your engagement to someone who really loves you—and it'll all be for nothing!"

"Fuck you, Wheeler!" And that was the last we spoke for the next week.

On base and down at Ruam Chon Sawng, Tom sat around for days in sphinxlike silence. It was creeping me out not being able to talk to him, and I couldn't talk to Zelinsky without spilling the beans about cuckolding Dave, which left me little choice but to keep on agreeing when Zelinsky figured that Wheeler's gloom was just grass-induced paranoia. A lingering fear that Wheeler might be completely right—about Ubon's security being iffy and about Tukada being trash—kept me permanently pissed off. Fortunately, my heavy schedule meant that I barely saw him. When our paths did cross, I was too zonked to talk to him about subjects as touchy as Tukada, my star-crossed lover, or the possibility that insurgents could mess up my precious bicycle race. I was zonked because the ComDoc camera department was still understaffed and we were routinely flying three nights in a row now. I didn't want to give up teaching, though, and I didn't want to give up organizing the race, but I was paying a price. One surprising piece of good news in all this was the discovery that as much as I missed the camaraderie of hanging out with my friends at Ruam Chon Sawng, I did not miss the booze and dope.

Any spare minutes I had were now being taken over by the Big Buddha Syndicate. Working under my overall guidance, Jack Wu and Sagittarius Smith drove us in different ways—the square-jawed, starched-and-pressed Wu by being meticulous in planning for any details that the rest of us brought to his attention, and the street-savvy Smith by seeing endless opportunities to expand our operation. I recommended visiting every unit on the base, signing up the unit commander first whenever possible and then working on his men. The motion carried, as did my recommendation that we be on a perpetual hunt for sponsors whenever we were downtown. Wheeler's concerns kept weighing on my mind, but when I brought the subject up with Wu and Smith, they assured me, "Don't worry about it—Intell and the Air Police have it covered."

On the last Monday before the Big Buddha Bicycle Race, we gathered at noon for a syndicate staff meeting in Zelinsky's editing cubicle, just in time to hear the base radio station play Sagittarius's latest pre-recorded announcement. "Only *five* more days till the Big Buddha Bicycle Race! You heard it right—just five more days! For all you unit commanders out there—*fifteen* units have signed up. The 25th Tactical Fighter Squadron just signed on this morning with a team of twenty. Is *your* unit going to let *them* have all the fun?

"For all you individual riders—we now have seven hundred entries! You heard correctly—*seven* hundred! If we can reach the magic thousand, we can guarantee *four* one-thousand-dollar prizes! That's right, four different prizes! We'll have three Blue Ribbons for *individual* winners in the three-speed, ten-speed and unlimited-modified divisions. And the Commander's Award will go to the *unit* with the three best finishers!

"But wait—there's *more*!! This has gotten bigger than just the 8th Tactical Fighter Wing, folks! We've extended invitations to the *Thai* units on base and both Thai fighter squadrons have accepted. You better watch out, guys! My Thai may be a little rusty, but I could have sworn I heard them say they're planning on kicking your butts! But that's not all! *Just today* students from Ubon Teachers' College and the Ubon Polytechnic High School asked to join the party! Why not join them! Don't forget, if we can reach a thousand *entrants*, we'll be paying a thousand *dollars* for Win, six hundred for Place and four hundred for Show in three different divisions—and you'll be giving your unit a shot at being the pride of Ubon Royal Thai Air Force Base and snagging the extra loot that goes with it!"

The announcement finished with the usual list of whom to see in order to sign up. Since we already knew who we were, I turned down the radio and started our meeting. I called on Jack Wu first, who showed us the thousand race numbers he'd had printed and the four thousand little safety pins Major Horney had scrounged up for putting the numbers on the riders' jerseys. "Your hippie friend, Greg Quam, over at the base print shop was terrific, Leary."

"Any project that's got nothing to do with the Air Force—he's a whiz. How's he doing with the programs?"

"He can hold off till Friday night," Wu replied, "so we can drum up sponsors right down to the last possible moment. He did make some proofs, though, which should make it easier to sell ads."

"And how are we doing with the start/finish line?"

"Colonel Grimsley put a call through to Ubon city hall. They'll be putting up a stage and a public address system for us."

I turned my attention to Bill Horney. "Major, that nurse friend of yours came through with flying colors on the safety pins, just like you said she would. And now that she's gotten into the swing of things, would you like to tell the group what else she's promised?"

"She's arranged for two first aid stations staffed by some of her *finest*, funnest nurses, if you get my drift—one at mile fifteen and one at the Big Buddha. And she's got a couple of medics with a jeep who will be on call at the start/finish line."

"Which reminds me, sir, how did the flu situation turn out?"

"Great," he answered. "I put myself under the personal care of Nurse Wozniak after she shot my ass full of penicillin. I knew I'd met my match when she told me *next* time I went downtown without wearing my 'little raincoat' she'd have to personally give me a spanking."

"Whoo-ee!" shouted the Big Buddha Syndicate.

"Way to go, Nurse Wozniak!" shouted Shahbazian.

Horney continued cheerfully, "Thanks to her I've been 'flu' free. Of course it's helped that I've been spending most of my off-duty hours with her over at the Officers' Club. She's been a *big* help getting the last couple of squadron commanders on board—if you get my drift."

I called on Shahbazian, who was next on the agenda. "Field Maintenance has come up with portable toilets to set up near the nurses' stations," he announced. "All I had to give them were a couple of beat-up Nikon cameras."

"Sergeant Washington?"

"I wangled a couple of bullhorns and a starter's pistol from the Air Police in exchange for the chocolate cakes I wangled from the chow hall in exchange for some out-of-date slide film."

I jumped in. "In other words, gentlemen, the logistics are coming together nicely! And now, a word from Sergeant Smith on finances."

"Were you serious about seven hundred entries?" Zelinsky asked.

"Seven hundred and two as I speak," answered the Big Man, puffing proudly on his cigar. "But we're realistically shooting for a thousand. Momentum is picking up. We didn't think the Thais would be interested, with a ten-dollar registration fee, but word's gotten out about the *prize* money. Not only do we have the two Thai Air Force units signed up, I just heard on my way out the door that the teachers' college team and the other team from the polytechnic high school will be bringing in registrations and sponsor money this afternoon. We're looking at possibly *ten thousand dollars* in registrations alone, gentlemen. If you can get out and help Major Horney the next few days with the holdout unit commanders, we could be bringing in another five thousand in Unit Pride sponsorships of the Commander's Award. We're already well over five thousand in outside sponsor money. I think we can spread out downtown with some of those proof programs and bump that number up quite a bit. In fact, this is going so well I'm going to reduce my cut to a regular syndicate share like the rest of you. Instead of deducting expenses, I'm going to handle on-base betting. I'm negotiating with Indian Joe right now for the off-base betting concession. He wants to have windows set up out by the starting line."

"Is this on the up and up?" I heard Washington ask Wu in a hushed voice.

"Don't worry—I'm having the OSI keep an eye on him," Wu whispered back with a glint in his eye.

"What about the T-shirts?" I asked.

"Indian Joe's tailor-shop division is all over it," Smith answered.

"So what kind of money are we looking at?" asked Shahbazian.

Smith beamed. "I'm projecting—if everything goes perfectly—over two thousand dollars for each of you—tax free. Not bad for a few weeks' work in your spare time."

"As far as 'going perfectly,'" I asked, turning to Wu, "How are we doing clearing this with the Thai authorities?"

Wu answered confidently, "Colonel Grimsley visited the provincial governor at his mansion last week—where you'll be happy to know he is convalescing nicely. They figured this might give the general's public image a welcome boost, so the governor's on board. And once he was on board, the district chief for the town of Ubon—the mayor, if you like—fell right in with him. They're both planning on making an appearance at the awards ceremony. Which might explain how easy it was to arrange the stage and sound system."

Sagittarius was getting itchy to get back to his office and his big leather chair. Sounding like one of his own commercials, he exclaimed, "Momentum is building, gentlemen! We might have us an Asian Boston Marathon on our hands!"

The only rain on my parade besides Tom was the letter from Danielle that was waiting when I stopped by the base post office. I had written a week earlier how the race was shaping up better than I ever could have imagined and how, to top it off, I stood to make a sizable pile of money in the process. Maybe I shouldn't have mentioned the cast of characters involved. The charms of Sagittarius Smith and Indian Joe might have been hard to explain to someone halfway around the world. "You sure this isn't a scam?" she asked. "I thought there was still a war going on over there."

Dave's Farewell
(two more days!)

Late Thursday afternoon when I met with Wu and Zelinsky at the editorial trailer, the situation could not have been better. We had amassed over nine hundred registrations, we had twenty of the base's twenty-six units on board, the two Thai units were in, and the teachers' college and the poly-technic high school had brought in fifty more registrations and a list of potential sponsors. Very hush-hush, not wanting to curse our good fortune, Wu handed me the loose-leaf notebook he was using to do the record keep-ing. I looked it over carefully and concluded Wu's figures were correct—the kitty was now over $20,000. It seemed almost too good to be true. For once I had taken the lead in a project that was not a lost cause—and I was going to get paid for my efforts.

The base was buzzing with so much excitement that I was getting caught up in the hype myself and was eager to get in a last little bit of roadwork. There was one dark cloud still lingering on my sunny horizon, however, and before I went out to train, I decided to drop by the orderly room one last time to see if there wasn't something I could do to bring Tom Wheeler back into the fold. Even if he didn't want to rejoin the syndicate, I wanted him to *ride* with me in the race. When I stepped in the door, the first thing I noticed was Dave Murray sprawled out on his desk. It wasn't all that un-usual. What caught my attention was that he was wearing his civvies. "Lifer there is being shipped to Germany," said Tom. He had a bit of the old twin-kle back in his eye. "Seems there was some fine print that got skipped over when he re-enlisted."

Murray managed to sit up. "They didn't mention 'Needs of the Air Force' when I re-upped. Maybe I shoulda read the contract. Oh well," he yawned, "I don't think things're gonna work out with Tukada, anyway. I went to talk to her yesterday, but her housegirl said she was sleeping and that she had been very sick. I told her I was leaving for Germany in just two days, but the housegirl said she had strict orders—no one was to wake Tukada up."

"Maybe she'll feel better tomorrow," I said.

"I'm *leaving* tomorrow!"

"Maybe it's all for the best," Tom said sympathetically.

I felt lousy for Dave and for the rest of our *ménage à quatre*. The trailer suddenly seemed cramped and I wanted to get outside. "How about riding home with me?" I asked Tom.

"I'd better leave my bike here," he replied, helping Murray out of his seat. "Come on, Dave. You're going to spend your last night in Ubon with friends." Tom turned to me. "Are you coming with us?"

"I'd better get a *little* riding in. I'll meet you at the bungalow in an hour."

'Round about midnight, Murray ran out of the Corsair Club and climbed into a *sahmlaw*, blubbering, "Tukada! I've got to see my Tukada!"

By the time Tom and I staggered to the door, surprised that Dave's fifteen-second delay had switched off and ours had surreptitiously switched on, he was heading up the street as fast as an old Laotian could pedal a 175-pound, limp-bodied drunk in a 200-pound carriage. While we squeezed ourselves into another *sahmlaw* waiting nearby, Tom waived his hand and stammered as he tried to think of the Thai words he needed. Finally, as Murray began to disappear around a corner, Tom ignored Thai etiquette, pointing at our fugitive friend with an outstretched finger and commanding the driver, "Follow that *sahmlaw*!"

In the brief chase that followed, Tom and I pumped our bodies in a drunkenly uncoordinated attempt at coaxing more speed out of our old vehicle. Mostly because Dave's driver didn't know he was racing, Tom and I caught up with him shortly before we reached Dah's villa.

As we helped Murray to the gate, Tom told him with feigned sincerity, "*Of course* we want you to say goodbye to her, Dave."

"We also want to make sure you don't get any more wasted than you are," I added, "and end up missing your flight tomorrow, right, Tom?"

The gate seemed to be locked, but I remembered how Prasert once opened it by reaching in through a gap in the slats of the fence. I tried with some difficulty to get my large American hands through the same gap.

"Why is it so quiet?" asked Murray.

"Why am I doing this?" I asked, sweat quickly beading up on my forehead and dripping into my eyes. My hands felt damp and dirty and awkward, but my fumbling finally got the latch to spring open. Stepping inside cautiously, we closed the gate behind us and walked towards the house.

"Man, it's dark," said Tom. "I don't even see a mosquito coil burning in there."

We climbed the stairs to the veranda, which was pitch black under the gently sloping eaves. Dave reached the door first and found it padlocked. There was some sort of sign tacked up which he couldn't read. "What's this?" he asked.

Tom flicked on his cigarette lighter. In Thai and English, it said, "For Lease." He backed away, suddenly sober, muttering bitterly, "If we're lucky, she's in a hospital somewhere recovering from an overdose, because otherwise she's gone who-knows-where with her bastard brother and his *VC friends.*"

"Lucky if she OD'd? You crazy, Wheeler? You crazy?" cried Murray. "And whattaya mean, VC friends?"

I jumped in angrily, my head jumbled in confusion. "Tom, you've gotta snap out of it. The VC are in *Vietnam,* for Christ's sake. Prasert might have been right—Thailand might be a banana republic where people vote with bullets. And Prasert might have been hurt a lot worse than we thought. Could've been a concussion or a skull fracture or who knows what. What would be so strange about closing up the house if she's gonna be away awhile and her kid's been taken to Korea?"

Murray was even more confused. "Whattaya mean Prasert's got a fractured skull?"

"Brendan," Tom said sadly, "I know how you feel about Tukada and Prasert. I love 'em too, man, but the writing's all over the wall that something bad's coming down."

"*What?*" I blurted. "You think she's some sort of Thai Mata Hari and Prasert's a General Giap in training? Get a grip, man." I didn't want to think any more about Tom's speculation and walked down to the gate, where I gazed out forlornly into the distant palm trees silhouetted by the glow of the evening haze. I leaned against the rails, holding them tight, almost wishing they were rosaries, and muttered, "When you think about it, Tom, we don't *know* a damned thing about her *or* Prasert. We just don't know."

"I know one thing, Brendan. I'm more convinced than ever that Lek was right about a bicycle race from a backwater provincial capital out to the middle of the boondocks."

"What are you guys talkin' about, huh?" Murray rambled.

I thought at first I was dreaming. I could have sworn it was the Chirping Sparrows singing in the background, ever so slightly out of key: "This is the dawning of the Age of Sagittarius, the Age of Sagittarius…" *Oh my God*, I thought, *it is his private harem, using our half-baked race as an excuse to sing the praises of Sheik Smith himself! How does a cigar-smoking sumo wrestler with sergeant's stripes pull this off, anyway? Are girls back in Seoul that hard up for work? Or has he memorized every honey-dripping line of every love song Solomon Burke and Sam Cooke ever sang?* The announcer at the base Armed Forces Thailand radio station had gone into some blah-blah-blah stuff about the race, finishing with a rousing: "Only twenty-four more hours until the Big Buddha Bicycle Race!"

Sergeant Wu came in the door at the ComDoc ready room and spotted me lying half-unconscious on the bus seat. "You okay?" he asked.

I sat up, too proud to confess I'd been nodding off a lot lately. "Wheeler and I had a farewell party for our ol' buddy Murray last night. His flight left this morning."

Wu's face brightened. "Well, I've got some great news for you. As of right now, we've got almost a thousand starters. Every unit on base is in. This *is* the Boston Marathon of Southeast Asia! Too bad the war is winding down. Sagittarius didn't even need his adding machine to figure the pot has topped $25,000!"

The phone could be heard ringing in Harwell's office. Ordinarily I might not have noticed, but today it sounded like we were hanging out in the bell tower with the Hunchback of Notre Dame. I tried taking my mind off my hangover by focusing on my greed. "And we've only got to pay out $7,000 in prize money? Christ," I replied, turning my grimace into a smile, "this could be like a re-enlistment bonus without re-enlisting. Looks like our little syndicate will do okay."

We were going to be making a lot of money. It was now a sure thing. The race—my baby—was going to be a big success. And yet my happiness seemed tainted. Maybe it was Danielle's lack of enthusiasm when I wrote her about how our prayers were answered, how the payoff from the syndicate was going to make up for a very paltry GI Bill and pay my way through USC. Maybe it just didn't seem right without Tom and Dave around. Wanting Dave around was *really* messing my head up because I still held onto a strong if pitiful hope that Prasert would bring Dah back to me and we could straighten her out once and for all. But I was also missing Danielle—even though I was finding it incrementally harder to remember exactly who she was. I switched my thoughts back to all the things going *right* with the race, pasted on my happy face, and immediately started to brighten up. "Imagine if one of us can win this thing to boot? Hell—*I* want to win this thing! I think I'll split early today for a final tune-up—and maybe burn off some of last night's hangover. How about taking the jeep and clocking me?"

Before Wu could answer, Homer Harwell, our elusive supervising director of photography, poked his head out of his lair. "Come on in here, Leary. And bring Washington while you're at it."

Jamal Washington and I sat down in front of Harwell's desk. "Bad news for you boys—"

"I'm not a boy," Washington interrupted.

"I'm not flying," I interrupted at the same time.

"You're both filming the race," Harwell continued. "Lieutenant Hill's orders."

Washington and I continued speaking at the same time, asking why the lieutenant always had to give *us* the dirty work.

"Guttchock's brain has gone completely sunny side up. Captain English is having him medevacked out tonight for the Philippines. Seems he's been talking nonstop to himself and his imaginary wife, except now he don't need a drink to do it. We figure maybe Hollyweird'll do him good, if you know what I mean—and the sooner the better."

"I swear, Homer—he and Ron Cooper have dreamt this scheme up together."

"Actually, Leary, you and Washington should be *flattered*, because if Hill's gonna win that *Air Force Now!* Newsclip-of-the-Year Award like you promised him, he's gotta have his best ole boys out there—"

"*Men*," said Washington.

"Why doesn't *he* cover it then?" I protested.

Harwell grinned. "He's *directing*, Leary. A project this big needs leadership. He's already decided to give Lieutenant Liscomb a chance to redeem himself—he'll be doing helicopter shots from a Jolly Green. We got Sliviak coming over from Danang. The rumor he'd been shot down turned out to be exaggerated. It was just a crash landing. Anyway, he'll do a parachute jump from Liscomb's Jolly Green to kick things off, then come back out in an F-4 re-con bird to do some of his patented upside-down flybys. Hill and Liscomb think it'll be a great way to film the finish."

"What are *you* going to be doing, Homer?" asked Washington with a little edge in his voice.

"Lieutenant Hill wants me and Lutz staying with *him*, doing sync-sound interview stuff."

"Frank Lutz, my favorite sound elf? How'd you get him up here from Tan Son Nhut?" I asked.

"Liscomb promised to set it up with Captain Sherry over at Danang, and he did—Lutz'll be coming in with Sliviak. Wu has volunteered to do some extra camera coverage at the start and finish. Spitzer started to cry—*really* cry—about all the time he had spent customizing his bike, so we're gonna let him ride, on the condition that he's gonna do some prime helmet cam stuff for us. He'll pass off his footage to Zelinsky and Shahbazian along the way. Shahbazian's offered the use of his shiny red Fiat to drive VIPs around, but we're gonna take advantage of its speed during the race and use him as a courier. He and Zelinsky will also be using it to hightail it up to the Big Buddha and get some nice wide idiot-proof shots of the leaders making the turn. Maybe get some funny stuff of the stragglers too."

Washington had been figuring on helping out Sagittarius with registration and then going back to sleep while the rest of us fools were out breaking a sweat. "With all this great coverage, what do you need *us* for?"

"You're gonna be the *A*-Team. You've got the pickup at your disposal so you can focus on the leaders and any good dogfights you see developing. You'll have room to take Leary's bike along, set up with a camera mount or two, and we're giving you an extra helmet camera. You're getting a blimped Arri BL for recording some sync-sound footage, a Nagra recorder with a shotgun mike, and a couple of Arri St's for grabbing handheld shots. You're also getting the high sticks, the baby sticks and the high-hat, so you can get any camera angle that pops into your heads. And we've even mounted a sheet of plywood on the roof of the cab for you—the way Cecil B. DeMille used to do it—for some running shots."

"You know, you're making this sound kind of fun," Washington conceded, cracking a gritty smile. "Been shooting night ops on the Trail for so long, this'll be like R&R."

Hill poked his head in the door. "You boys do this right," he said, "and there might even be a Bronze Star in it for you!"

Across the river at Papa-sahn's that night, a bright sliver of moon was rising in the black sky. The clouds were thin, cutting across the heavens like scimitars. The air was chilly, cold enough for jackets along the river. As Papa-sahn told Harley and me weeks later, the Big Buddha Bicycle Race had turned out to be unexpectedly bad for business. There was only a single longboat crossing the Mae Nam Mun that night, nearly empty, not filled with the usual platoons of wise-cracking GIs hopping unsteadily to the rickety ladder and stumbling across the weathered planks to shore. Sitting with Papa-sahn on his porch as he told his story, I feigned sympathy, but it was one of the customers that Papa-sahn *did* have that night whom I was interested in.

Beyond the dockside storehouse filled with kegs of Thai, Laotian and Burmese grass, in one of the back rooms reserved for Ubon's most wretched, Tukada Maneewatana was curled up in her cubicle. With a little help from some of Papa-sahn's finest Khon Kaen weed to stir my imagination, I could picture her touching her full, soft Liv Ullman lips to the gently curving mouthpiece of her opium pipe. I could hear the water burbling as she drew on the pipe, filling her supple body with an intoxicating cloud. I could imagine her thinking hazily of Tom and Dave and Prasert and hoped that she thought of me. I could imagine her recalling how she once carried her baby on her hip and held the hand of her "captain" who was really an airman first class, walking through the park near Sausalito where the fog floating under the Golden Gate Bridge turned San Francisco into an island fairy tale kingdom. I could imagine her seeing her father and mother bathing in the copper sunset at the headwaters of the River Mun beneath the shadows of the ancient Khmer ruins at Pimai when she was a little girl, before her father left his drought-plagued rice farm to join the Thai Navy. I could imagine her mind drifting like the river itself, meandering gently through the Korat Plain past the ancient moats of Nakhon Ratchasima, past countless villages, past Surin and Ubon and on to the Mother River Kong itself.

I remembered how Tukada once told me about her captain's mother—how when the baby was born, she had smiled too broadly, her face seeming as though it would crack open like dry Issan clay and how back in Thailand after Dah had given up on California, her own mother looked at the baby for the first time and turned away. And I remembered the story of her daughter, when she was first old enough to walk and talk, looking into a mirror and crying *"farang"* while, outside, little children were running through the dusty village laughing at the scrawny dog that barked and chased after them. Tukada had told me about her own childhood when her family was poor but life was simple and how she used to sing with the rest of the village women in the fields outside Ban Ang Hin as they harvested the rice. I imagined her as a scrawny teenage girl watching the candles float beneath a canopy of stars on the swollen rivers and ponds and streams that nourished her village, making the rice harvest possible, on Loy Kratong Day, a day of thanks and night of atonement. According to Papa-sahn she sang the Loy Kratong song over and over on the night before the Big Buddha Bicycle Race, the same song Lek and Pueng and Sii-da had sung for us in Ubon the night we floated our candles on the River Mun a few months earlier—

> *When we've floated our krathongs,*
> *we ask the girls to dance ramwong;*
> *ramwong on Loy Kratong Day,*
> *ramwong on Loy Kratong Day!*
> *Good deeds will bring us happiness,*
> *Good deeds will bring us happiness!*

Papa-sahn said Tukada looked very tired on the night before the race. I could picture her trying to put the pipe aside, trying to push it toward some nameless, toothless skeleton in the next cubicle but giving up because she had grown too weak. I could see her curled up like a sickly kitten, like the orphans she used to feed, trying to keep herself warm until, still shivering, she finally fell asleep.

19 February 1972
The Start/Finish Line

Just after sunup on the day of the race, Jamal Washington and I were loading our camera gear into the back of the Rat Pack pickup. The morning haze that blanketed Ubon had not burned off, and I found myself fretting over details of the race that were now out of my control and in the hands of the likes of Woody Shahbazian, Sagittarius Smith and Indian Joe. At least Jack Wu was staying mobile and keeping an eye on them. I turned my attention back to the camera equipment, testing the batteries and light meters, and was comforted to see that Washington was doing the same.

Chuck Sliviak, the cameraman from Danang, and Frank Lutz, his Lilliputian soundman, had just walked over from the base transit quarters and were working nearby, sorting out which of their equipment to take down to the flight line in the big, boxy delivery van and which Lutz was going to keep with him while he recorded sound for Billy Hill. It had been almost a year since I had last seen Lutz back in California. I knew Sliviak by reputation from my editing days. Any time I got his footage to cut, it was good, really good, and now I could see why. Along with Sliviak's personal Arri BL and his lighter Arri St, they had found a Tyler mount, the latest thing in aerial photography, gathering dust in a back room at Tan Son Nhut and brought it along for Rick Liscomb to use to smooth out the shots from the helicopter. None of the guys at Tan Son Nhut had figured out how to use it in the year it sat there, but Sliviak, a reformed car thief, had assured Liscomb it would be a piece of cake swapping out one of the door guns on the Jolly Green for the camera mount. Built like a fireplug and chain-smoking Chesterfields, Sliviak was the toughest little non-Irishman ever to come off the streets of South Boston. He was originally going to wear a helmet camera for his parachute jump, but he handed it to me instead, explaining that he had brought along a chest-mounted camera brace he had made in the welding shop at Danang. "I had to remind him that I haven't been to jump school," said Lutz, "or he would have had them build one of those contraptions for me too."

Lieutenant Liscomb picked up Sliviak's chest brace, looked it over, and broke into a wide grin. "Damn, Sliviak, if you aren't *still* the bitchingest director of photography in the entire U.S. Air Force!"

It was just about time to head for the start/finish line. Washington and I threw the last couple of camera cases into the pickup and slammed the tailgate shut. Sliviak fired up the equipment van and headed down to the flight line with Liscomb riding shotgun. Hill had wandered off to the ready room a little earlier to have a cup of coffee with Link and Harwell, leaving his jeep parked in front of the orderly room. Lutz was heading over to the jeep to load up his sound gear when I called out, "Hey, Frank! You didn't forget Hill's San Miguel, did you?"

"Link's already taken it off my hands. It's in that meat locker where you store all your film, in a couple of Eastman Kodak cartons labeled 'EXPOSED FILM—DO NOT X-RAY!'"

"Speaking of beer," I said, "let me buy you one over at the NCO Club after the race—or is it *your* turn?"

"If I'm gonna be with your boss all day it doesn't matter whose turn it is—*you're* buying!"

I heard the sound of bike tires crackling through the gravel behind me, and damn if it wasn't Tom Wheeler pulling in. "Why if it isn't the High Priest of Paranoia himself!" I cried. "I thought you were staying home today."

"How could I stay home knowing that our old drinking buddy, Frank Lutz, had come in all the way from Tan Son Nhut?"

"You must have heard he's promised to buy the first round after the race," I said.

"Like hell," Lutz said. "I only signed on for this mission because Liscomb promised us a free week of R&R at Pattaya Beach."

"That'll be a little hard to pull off given that he's still under house arrest," said Wheeler.

"The conniving bastard!" chuckled Lutz out of the corner of his mouth. He and Wheeler laughed and gave each other a vigorous handshake. "Well, at least we'll always have Tijuana, Tom—nobody can take *that* away from us."

Wheeler turned to me. "I still think you and your Big Buddha Syndicate and the whole damn base, for that matter, have gone out of your minds," he said. "Lek and Pueng used to agree with me—until they found out there's *betting* involved. Now they're in line to play the daily double over at Indian Joe's window at the start/finish line. Truth is, they're the ones who dragged me out of bed this morning and sent me down here, jabbering about how I couldn't let you go out shooting all by your lonesome, and that did get me thinking how you could probably use a driver—"

I was about to give him the keys when I got an idea. "You can drive later. Right now we've got something even better—you're going to wear Sliviak's helmet camera and ride your bike at the start of the race. Should be a bitchin' POV shot. And it'll give us some protection footage in case anything goes wrong with Spitzer's camera. We'll leave the camera mounts on my bike in case we want to use them later."

Downtown, the city park across the street from the Ubon Hotel had been turned into a staging area that was just around the corner from the start/finish line on Route 66. Over at the starting area, near the stage, long lines of GIs and local Thais were lined up at the betting windows Indian Joe had set up. Sagittarius had livened things up by getting the Chirping Sparrows in mini-skirts to help out Indian Joe's Sikh nephews taking wagers. Out in the street, huge signs hung above the competitors dividing them into three groups. The five- and ten-speed racing bikes lined up first, followed by the wildly modified bicycles of the Customized Unlimited division, with the slower one- and three-speed contingent taking up the rear. The mass of spectators was so thick that it took me a moment to realize that the two grinning fools who were waving and yelling at us as we drove by were Lek and Pueng. The scene was so ablaze with color from sponsors' advertisements and banners from every unit on base that Woody Shahbazian's shiny red Fiat convertible was hardly noticeable pulling up to the front of the stage with Jack Wu, Sagittarius Smith and Indian Joe perched on the trunk, waving to the crowd. Wu hopped off first, making his way to the podium where red, white and blue Thai and American flags and bunting fluttered around him. Wu, a solidly built professional soldier, was dwarfed by Smith and Indian Joe when they joined him. He did a quick mike check and gave an excited "Welcome to the First Annual Big Buddha Bicycle Race!" After waiting for the applause to die down, he began announcing starting instructions followed by information on rest stops, repair stations and first aid facilities set up along the way.

Indian Joe translated into Thai, Hindi, and Mandarin and then went into overdrive, nudging Wu aside with a friendly smile. "It has been a great honor for Indian Joe Enterprises to be an original sponsor of The Big Buddha Bicycle Race! Indian Joe Jewelers, Indian Joe Custom Tailors, Indian Joe Stereo, Indian

Joe's New Delhi Restaurant, Indian Joe's Flying Carpet Massage and Indian Joe's exclusive Bengal Kitten Gentlemen's Club all look forward to your continued business. But enough about *me*, Indian Joe. We also need to thank the other Ubon business people who had the foresight to make this such a day we will never forget: Sheik Tailors, Niko's Massage and the Maharaj Palace of Massage, Woodstock Music, the Corsair Club, the New Playboy, the Soul Sister, and the Ubon Hotel with its breathtaking ninth-floor Top of the World Restaurant."

Sagittarius Smith stepped in to continue in English. "In the weeks to come, you can keep right on supporting our sponsors by dining and drinking at Ubon's other fine hotel restaurants and bars. What better way to cap off a perfect day than by meeting your friends for dinner and drinks at the Siam, the Pathumtana, or the Sri Issan hotels? And for any of you GIs who have spent time in Japan and have had a *yen* for *sukiyaki* lately, don't forget the newly remodeled Hotel Tokyo. For the latest in Shaw Brothers action flicks and Thai tear-jerkers your *tii-rahks* will adore, don't forget Ubon's air-conditioned movie palaces, the Chalerm Seen Theatre and the Ubon Cinema."

Smith took a breath, waiting for Indian Joe to do the translations, and then continued, "Today's winners can deposit their cash prizes with another of our sponsors: Thai Farmers Bank, the Bank of Ayutthaya, Bank of America or Chase Manhattan. They also accept paychecks! And don't forget our newest sponsors: Raja Jewelers, Imperial Tailors, Ubon Bowl, Thai Airways, Toklong Tours, the Ubon National Museum, the Catholic Church of Ubon, the Post-telegraph Office of Ubon and the Phra Maha Pho Hospital—which does *not* want to be seeing any of you today! And if you find yourself getting hungry or thirsty later on, don't forget Tippy's Pizza, the Golden Palm, the Carlton, and Sabol Thong restaurants, and, of course, our good friends at the Jaguar, the Sampan, the Club Miami and the all-new Lolita!"

Indian Joe did some more translating before Sagittarius stepped in to make one last pitch: "You might be having trouble remembering the names of today's many generous sponsors, but *don't worry*—we've got all those names printed out for you in our handsome four-color souvenir programs! Don't forget to take one home! Or better yet, they're on the back of our souvenir T-shirts, on sale next to the stage, so you'll have a permanent reminder of the best places to do business in Ubon."

"And speaking of doing business in Ubon," added Indian Joe, "wear your race number or bring your program to any of our sponsors this weekend and get your Big Buddha Bicycle Race specials!"

Wheeler was trying out his helmet camera, riding slowly through the teeming mass of men and bicycles. Lek and Pueng didn't need a bullhorn or a microphone to be heard screaming, "Tom Whee-lah, you a bitchin' dude!"

Washington and I alternately shot from inside and outside the truck and up on the reinforced roof, taking turns driving when we had to. We spotted Hill's jeep, moving a little erratically as it approached us through the thick crowd. Hill sat up front gesticulating wildly, directing up a storm, while Link chauffeured and Harwell operated the Rat Pack's newest, quietest Arri BL. Frank Lutz was hanging on by his toes, one arm wrapped around the roll-bar, trying to operate the Nagra recorder slung over his shoulder with one hand while holding a shotgun mike with the other. They were all wearing red silk shorts and white singlets that exposed far too much of their pale arms and knobby knees. "In case we get in somebody's shot," Hill explained.

"You owe me a second beer!" shouted Lutz as we headed off in opposite directions.

Further towards the front of the ten-speed area we saw my old friend, Lieutenant Glotfelty, my unlucky F-4 pilot who acquitted himself a few months later knocking out the bridges at Ban Tat Hai and Tumlan. From behind, five Thai groups, hard and lean, pushed to the starting line. Three of the groups—one from the teachers' college, one from the polytechnic high school and one from the National Police—waived and smiled broadly to the applauding crowd. The fourth and fifth, from the two token A-37 squadrons at the base, did not. The A-37 pilots were especially hard and especially pissed at having to fly modified sissy trainers into combat at an F-4 base that was home to the Wolf Pack and the U.S. Air Force's most swaggering ace, veteran of three wars, Colonel Robin Olds. This was their chance for revenge.

We headed over to a spot near the one- and three-speed section where we saw that the Spectre contingent had rendezvoused. Harley Baker had just pulled up in a crew van whose seats had been removed so it could be filled with spare bicycle wheels, assorted spare parts and a couple of extra bicycles. "Whoa!" I exclaimed. "What's all *that* shit?"

"Spectre's gonna *win* this sucker," he sneered.

I recognized Major Horney at the center of the group, but looking around I sensed that a few people were missing. "Where's Pigpen?" I asked.

"Putting some finishing touches on his custom-special," said Baker.

"And where's Captain Rush?"

There was a long silence. Finally Horney answered, "He's been sent TDY up to Nakhon Phanom to fly goddamn C-119 gunships until he gets his head straightened out."

"I thought you and Colonel Strbik didn't mind him doing a little pot."

"Yeah, but Della Rippa *did*—especially when he saw Strbik quoted in *Newsweek* saying that the men in his unit who smoked dope only did so in moderation. He and Rush went out on the same flight."

"I thought we gave those obsolete twin-engine flying turds to the South Vietnamese," said Washington.

"They gave them back," Horney replied.

"And where's everybody's favorite pilot, Captain Rooker?" I asked. "I thought he signed up."

"Didn't you hear?" answered Baker. "He was pulled out of the cockpit by the Air Police and led away in handcuffs the day before yesterday. Can you believe that shit? The best damned pilot in the unit! The *superpilot* who could take out a truck with a single bullet and land one of these four-engine turkeys on a single engine! And he was nearly put under house arrest, except that was his problem—the *tii-rahk* he brought back from Bangkok to live with him turned out to be a *katoy*—a potential Miss Universe if only the field were open to boys."

"You're shitting me!"

"Nope. He's up at NKP with Strbik and Rush. He was too good a pilot to completely kick out of the Air Force, but everyone around here is creeeeeeped out."

"It's creeping me out," said Washington, breaking out in a cold sweat.

"And you know what he kept repeating while they marched his ass across the tarmac?" Baker asked. "'It was an accident! It was an accident!'"

"Some accident," Washington mumbled.

Tom Wheeler pedaled up, smiling happily, and while we loaded up his bike and stowed the helmet cam, we were passed by some very cool customized bikes on their way to the middle group of starters. Spitzer made the Rat Pack proud, riding a chopped Schwinn that wouldn't have looked out of place with Dennis Hopper and Peter Fonda in *Easy Rider* and gamely wearing the second of our helmet cameras. Pigpen Sachs, wearing a Spectre T-shirt that said "You can run, but you'll only die tired," rode an even more elaborate Schwinn, covered with a streamlined fiberglass body. It was amazing—even Mole showed up on a kid's bicycle rigged with a huge sail, apparently unafraid to expose his squinty eyes and sallow skin to the harsh glare of the tropical sun. "This is big!" I shouted to Wheeler and Washington.

"This is big!" echoed Tom, climbing behind the wheel and starting up the truck.

"This is WAY BIG!" Washington shouted from the rooftop camera platform. And then, only half-believing, I thought I recognized Dave Murray circling around on something out of a Charlie Chaplin movie—one of those old-time penny-farthing two-wheelers with a ridiculously large five-foot front wheel.

"Missed my flight," he called over to us when Wheeler pulled up alongside him. "Should I line up with the one-speeds or the custom-specials?"

"You just come out of a time capsule or what?" asked Washington. "That thing's only got but one speed."

"In that case, I'm gonna kick butt—this thing'll do forty on a straightaway."

"Who sold you that bill of goods?" I asked.

"Indian Joe—who else?" he answered and headed off for the rear group of bicycles.

Back at the staging area, Wheeler stopped the truck. "Catch that," he shouted, pointing out Colonel Grimsley, the base commander himself, who was sitting in a four-wheeler wearing a gold silk basketball uniform, several sizes too small for him, and a green translucent visor. Washington climbed down from the roof and set up the Arri BL on the high sticks in front of the colonel. I connected the sync cable and announced, "Sound rolling."

I heard the BL beep and Washington call out, "Speed."

"Colonel Grimsley," I asked, "what will you do if President Nixon drops in for a surprise visit?"

"General Gong called me from Seventh Air Force. Nixon's advance men hated the Ubon Hotel. It's five-stars or nothing for those assholes. That damned Kissinger wouldn't know a good bicycle race if it bit him in the butt."

"Cut," called Washington.

Colonel "Grouchy Bear" Della Rippa, the Spectre commander, pulled up in a four-wheeler identical to Grimsley's, not looking grouchy at all. "Rolling camera!" called Washington. I pointed the mike at Della Rippa.

"What do you think, boys? We had the welding shop fasten a pair of bikes together for each of us. We've got a little side-bet going between Headquarters Squadron and the 16th SOS." With a grin and a big thumbs-up, Grimsley and Della Rippa rode off. We kept the sound and camera rolling as they disappeared into the crowd of cyclists heading for their starting positions.

It was amazing. With the morning haze burned away, it was turning out to be the most glorious day I had spent in Thailand. The sky was turquoise-blue. Billowing clouds cushioned the sun's rays. Tom loved the helmet camera so much that he insisted we let him use it *and* the two cameras mounted on my bike to film the start. We pulled my bike off the truck, reloaded the helmet cam and set the shutters on all three cameras. Tom tested the three start switches and off he rode.

Washington drove and I cleared away the crowd so that he could maneuver the truck into the best possible position to film the start of the race. I climbed up on the reinforced roof to make sure we got it right, and, when I looked around me, felt like Custer at Little Big Horn, only in the most *positive* sense of being surrounded by *happy* Indians and of this tribe being *my* tribe that I had gathered together personally—not for further death and destruction, but for the glory of all the shades of humanity that surrounded me, from the local Thais to the entire motley crew of Anglo-Americans, Irish-Americans, Afro-Americans, Scandinavian-Americans and Greek, Italian, Polish, Hungarian, Armenian, Korean, Cuban, Mexican, Samoan, Baptist, Jewish, Catholic, Hindu and every other variety of American who had crawled out of bed early that day to go on a Saturday morning bicycle race. More than anything, we had caught the Thai spirit and gathered in the glory of *sanuknicity*—fun!—and we were going to make a pile of money doing it!

Washington and I set up two cameras and slowly panned across the vast aggregation of cyclists, spectators and hucksters. Jamal was as amazed as I was at what our little syndicate had assembled. "You ought to be very proud of yourself, my man! This is your baby!"

And I was proud. Below us were competitors from every unit on base, with their banners waving. We zoomed in our lenses to full telephoto and began picking them out—the headquarters squadrons of the 8th Combat Support Group and the 8th Tactical Fighter Wing; the 25th, 433rd, 435th and 497th Tactical Fighter squadrons; the 16th Special Operations Squadron ("Spectre"); the 13th Bomb Group (the "Grim Reapers"); and their support units, the 8th Field Maintenance, 8th Avionics Maintenance, 8th Supply, 8th Tactical Dispensary, 8th Security Police, 8th Civil Engineering, 8th Special Services, 8th Transportation, and the 408th Munitions squadrons. A bunch of tenant units were there too, detachments of weather, tactical control, communications, aerial port, air rescue, air postal and special investigation squadrons, Blind Bat operations, and our own little Rat Pack of a photo squadron.

It was finally sinking in—all twenty-six American units from the base were represented, along with the five Thai teams. Jack Wu joined us up on the plywood camera platform and brought us up to date. "We've reached eleven hundred entrants!" he beamed. "Your friend Quam kept the print shop humming all night!" Pulling us into a huddle, he continued discreetly, "It's looking like the syndicate's share will be *three* thousand apiece!"

"No shit!" laughed Washington.

"I better go get to my camera position," Wu said before he climbed down and disappeared into the crowd.

"Leary, what are you going to do with all that money?" asked Washington.

"It seems too good to be true—I'm gonna be able to pay off my lawyer bills and still put enough money away to pick up a master's degree. What about you?"

"This could buy a lot of bullets for my Black Panther chapter back in Newark," said Jamal with a wink that failed to clue me in whether or not he was kidding, a wink that got me wondering what "Jamal" meant in Arabic. "Too bad about Tom dropping out of the syndicate," he said. "Maybe we should cut him in for a half share—like the bat boy on a World Series team."

"Don't worry about Tom. He was doing dope deals in elementary school that had a bigger payout than this. When he finally got busted, he talked the judge into letting him join the Air Force, and now he's sending grass home in sniffing-dog-proof envelopes. It's only a little at a time, but he's building a couple of nest eggs with an old girlfriend and an old business partner."

"Smart guy," Washington replied, "not putting all his nest eggs in one basket."

Across the River—the Rooster Crows

Legend had it in Issan Thailand that certain highly advanced monks possessed the ability to go into a deep trance and travel freely in time and space. Papa-sahn's Khon Kaen grass gave me the same ability, letting me travel back to the morning of the bicycle race and float invisibly across the River Mun, along his dock, and through his compound. I watched unnoticed as a rooster crowed at the rising sun and strutted through Papa-sahn's yard pecking at its feed. Out on the road, the wooden bells on the water buffalo rang low and clear as they lumbered through the morning mist on their way to the rice fields. In the back room that Papa-sahn reserved for Ubon's most wretched, I could see Tukada's body still curled up in her cubicle, perfectly motionless, her lips still touching the mouthpiece of her pipe. Nothing burned in the bowl, however, and her lips were stuck together, the corners of her mouth encrusted with dry saliva. Her eyes were dusted with sleep, motionless but not quite closed. A single thread of morning sunlight crept across the plank floor, finally striking Dah's unfocused eye, and I could hear her singing to herself, barely moving her lips:

> *When we've floated our krathongs,*
> *we ask the girls to dance ramwong;*
> *ramwong on Loy Kratong Day,*
> *ramwong on Loy Kratong Day!*
> *Good deeds will bring us happiness,*
> *Good deeds will bring us happiness!*

She blinked, looking confused for a moment, and then, as her eyes grew clear and her face grew calm, she seemed to remember something vaguely important. Stiffly she rolled over on her hands and knees and gingerly pulled herself up, unsteady as a newborn colt. Drawing a deep breath, she made her way through Papa-sahn's dilapidated cluster of bungalows and across the porch to the gate that led down to the rickety wooden dock. Papa-sahn was waiting for her.

"*Sabaidii ru, khrab*?" he asked her with his fake smile that was hard to tell from a true smile. "You okay? You sleep so quiet I think maybe you die."

"Not yet, uncle."

"Where you go?" asked Papa-sahn.

"I come here to die, Papa-sahn, but I forget something."

"You owe me five hundred baht."

"Later, uncle. I must go hire motorbike right away. Please wake up the boat driver. I really must go right now, quickly."

Jamal Washington and I were perched alertly on the roof of the camera truck. Washington, the more experienced cameraman, would take the tight shots and I would shoot the high-angle master. We liked the idea of working side by side with so much uncontrolled action about to explode before our eyes. Working together we could relax and stay alert, double-checking our meter readings as the sun moved in and out of the clouds and at the same time giving each other an extra pair of eyes to pick up something unexpected that was worth photographing or an extra pair of hands if a camera malfunctioned or a battery died. We could see Tom Wheeler astride my bike on the other side of the starting line chatting with Lek and Pueng, who were now joined by Mali. He was too far away for us to change any of the settings on his cameras, but we weren't worried—we had made a pretty good estimate of average conditions and taped down the f-stops. He spotted us on the roof of the truck and gave us a big thumbs up, which we reciprocated, before he put on his helmet camera. Lek kissed him on the cheek and he pushed off, wedging his way into the starting phalanx. A giant HH-3E "Jolly Green" helicopter from the 38th Air Rescue Squadron hovered overhead, twenty-two hundred feet above the starting line. Lieutenant Liscomb stood by, ready to film with his Tyler mount in the side door. Chuck Sliviak was standing by to make his parachute jump out the rear, the signal to Sagittarius Smith for the race to begin.

Everything was looking splendid until we saw Billy Hill's jeep approaching, honking its way a little too quickly through the crowd. First Sergeant Link screeched to a dusty halt that left Harwell and Lutz scrambling to hang on to their equipment. Hill had had an inspiration—the kind he imagined he would have again someday when he was directing action pictures in Hollywood—and decided to have me pull my camera down and set it up at street level next to the starting line for a tight shot that would give him interesting blurs streaking by in the foreground while a compressed mass of racers blasted through the frame further back. He wanted Washington to drive a hundred feet up the road to get my old high-angle master shot from the rooftop there. I kept a Nagra recorder with me and rigged up a microphone held down by a couple of sandbags so that I could record some sync-sound huffing and puffing of cyclists scrambling out of the gate. The new camera positions would have been brilliant if Hill had thought of them half an hour earlier, but now, suddenly, I had a much more difficult shot to execute while worrying about turning on the Nagra and monitoring the sound level. I tried to get Lek or Pueng or Mali's attention to help out with the sound—just turning it on and off for me would have been great—but they were off at Indian Joe's betting windows placing some last-minute wagers and I was now lost from their view. I glanced at my watch and saw that we had a minute to go. Still fumbling to get the audio recorder hooked up and my lens refocused, I heard Hill call out to me, "All set?"

"Ready, sir!" I replied as I hurriedly double-checked my sound and camera settings.

He called Lieutenant Liscomb on his walkie-talkie. "All set up there?"

"Ready here!" answered Liscomb. "This is going to be *bitchin'*!"

My right eye was glued to the viewfinder, focused on a tight group of cyclists about to burst across the starting line. By opening my left eye, I could monitor Smith up on stage on the opposite side of the street cocking his starter's pistol and slowly lifting it over his head, watching for Sliviak's parachute jump. "Wu," commanded Hill over his megaphone, "take your position!"

Jack Wu grabbed a small World War II—vintage spring-wound Bell and Howell Filmo movie camera and hopped into the pit that Billy Hill had ordered dug for him in front of the starting line, determined to get his John-Ford-cowboy-movie stampede shot for the lieutenant. Perez and Price, his lab techs, covered him with a sheet of Plexiglas borrowed from the 601st latrine, anchored it with a couple more sandbags and ran for the sidelines. Perez made the sign of the cross. Price looked worried that this might be the last he ever saw of his boss. Meanwhile, Shahbazian revved up the engine to his Fiat pace car. Zelinsky was kneeling backwards in the seat next to him, looking intently through the viewfinder of a camera mounted on a baby tripod and pointed back at the racers. Liscomb's voice crackled over the field radio, announcing, "*Heeere's* Chucky!"

A dot fell out of the back of the Jolly Green and spread beautifully into a silken parachute, inspiring a loud cheer from the crowd. My heart was racing. "Man, this is great!" I shouted to a smiling Washington.

"The greatest thing since Pinky Lee, Muhammad Ali and sliced bread!" Jamal shouted back.

Billy Hill picked up his bullhorn and commanded a little too loudly, "Roll cameras!"

Even Homer Harwell—the Rat Pack's supervising director of photography and granite-faced veteran of 150 combat missions—had gotten caught up in the excitement, reaching into the front seat, grabbing Hill's walkie-talkie, and barking, "Roll helicopter camera and any other cameras in the sound of my voice!"

Sagittarius Smith squeezed the trigger, the gun sounded, and the mad dash to Big Buddha had begun. And mysteriously, wonderfully, with the sound of that gun, I suddenly felt calm and lucid, my hands steady and my eyes sharp. We kept filming for several minutes as wave after wave of bicycles rolled past us—until Wheeler turned back, threw my borrowed bike into the truck, took off his helmet, and checked that Washington had his tripod legs securely chained down to the plywood on the roof. They picked me up and we started hopscotching to new camera positions further down the road, covering the progress of the race from a variety of angles, some moving and some standing still, all the while taking advantage of a landscape full of rice paddies, wooded hills, and rain-carved ridges that beneath the azure sky and white clouds looked like a painted backdrop. We captured a fair share of collisions and spills, starting with Mole's sail bike taking him airborne over the side of the road and wrapping him and a couple of bystanders up in parachute cloth and bailing wire. We also followed a couple of neck and neck duels between some of the more evenly matched competitors from the Thai and American fighter squadrons. The Thais were tough, but the Americans rose to the challenge, at least in the beginning. We stopped briefly to flirt with the nurses at the mile fifteen first aid station, asking them to say a few words to the folks at home. Washington connected the sync cable to my camera, handed the mike to a cute blond nurse lieutenant, and rolled sound. "Welcome to the very first Big Buddha Bicycle Race," she said with a big, embarrassed grin. "Hopefully it will be my last."

Lieutenant Liscomb's Jolly Green thundered by overhead, followed moments later by Sliviak's inverted F-4 shrieking past in the opposite direction at what seemed like no more than fifty feet off the deck. We tossed down some water from the little paper cups at the aid station and reluctantly bid the nurses goodbye. It was time to drive on up to Big Buddha to get set up for the turn at the halfway mark.

When we got there, the highway outside the monastery was crowded with spectators. The normally quiet outdoor *rahn-ahahns* were so busy serving up steaming food and cool drinks that there was plenty of overflow business for Indian Joe and several other restaurateurs from town who had also set up food stalls. Indian Joe had figured correctly that there would be plenty of Thais eager to keep betting even after the race had started, some wagering on leaders at the halfway mark and others updating their bets on the eventual winners. The auxiliary betting windows he had set up were located discreetly across the street from the monastery entrance.

Sagittarius Smith had used his local Thai connections to get permission from the abbot of the Big Buddha Forest Monastery to use the dirt road and parking area inside the gate for the cyclists to make their turn, which gave them a chance to take in an inspiring view of the Big Buddha itself looking down on them as they rode past. Smith and Wu had worked it out with the Air Police commander to use one of the Special Services tour buses to bring out a squad of Air Policemen dressed as civilians to set up the orange cones that directed the contestants back towards Ubon. "They're also on standby," Wu had told me, "to do security work."

Waiting for us in front of the Special Services bus was Jack Wu himself, with his precious Nikon hanging from his neck and the banged-up Filmo movie camera cradled carefully in his right hand. Wu rushed over, covered with dust but smiling proudly, and handed me the movie camera. "The stampede shot should be great if the camera didn't jam. I wanted to get the same shot out here but nobody brought a pickaxe, so Hill wants me to shoot some stills instead. There he is!" said Wu, pointing out Hill's jeep pulling up to Zelinsky and Shahbazian, who had arrived early in Woody's Fiat convertible after picking up a couple of rolls of film along the way that Spitzer had shot with his helmet camera and doing some fast traveling shots themselves of the lead bikers.

Hill was at the top of his game, working out a variety of camera positions for Harwell, Washington and me that he could cut together dynamically in post-production while at the same time giving Zelinsky, our faithful editor, and Shahbazian, our camera repair technician, high and low wide-angle master shots that were impossible to mess up—as long as they remembered to turn on the cameras in the heat of battle. Washington and I gave each other a low five when we saw that everyone was set up and ready to go in time to film the arrival of the lead racers. Above us we saw Liscomb's Jolly Green move into position to get a bird's-eye view of the turn from directly overhead. He called down to Hill on the field radio, "Just heard from Sliviak's pilot that they're heading south along Route 66. They should overfly the lead riders just as they peel off into the monastery."

Their timing was perfect. As the F-4 roared past, we rolled cameras and filmed at least a hundred bicycles making the turn, led now by the Thai groups who had somehow, somewhere learned Tour de France racing techniques of drafting for each other and rotating the lead cyclist so that the whole team stayed fresh. Spitzer from ComDoc and Sachs from Spectre were holding their own on sheer guts and pride, ignoring flying gravel and dust as they sped past us. When Hill signaled for us to head back to town, Washington and I loaded up our equipment and climbed back into the cab, telling Wheeler we'd return later if we saw any interesting stragglers on our way home to the start/finish line. We slammed the doors shut, Wheeler put the truck in gear, and we pulled out on the highway towards Ubon.

Rattling down the road, Tom let out a hint of a smile. "Gotta admit, I'm kinda sorry not to be racing." I lit up a number and passed it over to Washington, who took a drag and offered it to Wheeler. "No thanks," said Tom. "This is one trip where I'm keeping my faculties intact."

"In that case," Washington asked, "now that your faculties are lucid, maybe you can tell us why there were thousands of Thais at the starting line this morning and another thousand out at Big Buddha if there was going to be trouble?"

"Weed can make you a little paranoid," Tom replied apologetically.

"Now what I *do* wonder is why there weren't a few more locals racing," laughed Jamal. "I mean, it's not like they've got a shortage of bicycles in this town."

"They probably figure it's more *sanuk* to do the betting and let the *farang* do the dirty work," I replied.

"Why sweat when you can bet!" said Washington, laughing a little harder as we zoomed happily down Route 66.

We filmed another series of vignettes on the return leg, including a shot of Colonel Grimsley, who was standing next to his quadricyclicular contraption holding one of the wheels, now bent, in his hand. We could have stopped, but when we took a vote, it turned out we preferred to rush back to the nurses at the first aid station. We pulled in with both cameras rolling and after shooting way more footage than Hill could ever use, promised to make our subjects famous when we got to Hollywood, to which they were both intrigued and derisive. When we asked for their addresses so we could stay in touch, the pretty one we had interviewed earlier scribbled something down and handed it to me. Back on the road, I opened it up and read, "In your dreams."

"That's cold," said Jamal, and we rode along for a while without talking.

By the time we rounded a bend in a small range of hills about ten miles north of town, we had passed most of the racers, one by one and in clusters. The truck was noisy, but a sound leaked through that caught my attention the way silence can tell a mother something is wrong with her baby. "Slow down, Tom. I thought I heard an AK."

We pulled off the road and shut down the engine. Nothing. A couple of bicyclists flew past, tossing a little more gravel and dust at us. And then I heard it again, for sure. A loud, pounding *brrrrat! Bat!*

"Let's go!" I shouted.

Wheeler shoved it into gear and floored the accelerator. Halfway around the next bend he slammed on the brakes. Shahbazian and Zelinsky were bearing down on us from the opposite direction, weaving erratically and then swerving off onto a dirt side road that led to a wooded patch on one side and a wide stretch of rice fields on the other. Shahbazian aimed for the trees and came to a grinding, dusty halt. Wheeler waited a moment and then drove in after them. We found Shahbazian and Zelinsky sitting in the Fiat, stunned. Several bullet holes had pierced the hood and the engine was giving off a mixture of steam and smoke. The windshield was shattered and their faces were bleeding in tiny rivulets. "The fuckers shot my Spyder," said Woody in a disbelieving monotone.

We got them out of the car and sat them down on the other side of the road on the bank of a rice paddy, out of harm's way. I was glad we did, because right about then the Fiat started to burn. At first it was little lizard tongues of fire that licked at the hood, but soon the whole chassis was engulfed. "Those fuckers killed my car!" said Woody in a louder monotone.

"What's going on?" Zelinsky asked.

"Wait here while we find out," I told them with as much authority as I could muster. Wheeler maneuvered the truck back onto the highway and sped off. At the straightaway at the bottom of the hill we spotted a group of the fastest ten-speed cyclists in a bloody heap on the hard asphalt. Two of the Thais had made it through, driving their legs furiously, pushing the bikes to what looked like thirty miles an hour, but even they, the lucky ones, were trailing blood. They wove so erratically we couldn't tell if they were purposely taking evasive action or if they were weakened by their wounds. Spitzer and his chopper ten-speed lay a little closer to us than the rest, and next to Spitzer was Pigpen Sachs's bike, its fiberglass shell shattered. Tom braked hard and swung the truck in a screeching, dusty one-eighty, ready to high-tail it back to Big Buddha and the Air Police plainclothesmen. Washington told him to hold up, he thought he'd spotted Sachs over in the grass trying to move. And sure enough, Sachs crawled to his feet and began staggering in our direction. Jamal and I leaped out of the truck, crouched down, and started running towards him, but before we got more than a few steps, Sachs was taken down by AK 47s firing from several positions along the ridge on the other side of the highway. We were driven back by a second volley, just out of range, just a little too far away to be accurate, but these shooters were *not* on a suicide mission. They'd learned from the disaster at the flight line and had spread themselves out enough to triangulate on a target while at the same time hiding themselves well from anyone wanting to return fire. Tom shoved the truck back into gear and sped away as soon as Washington and I grabbed hold of the tail gate and jumped onto the rear bumper. When the truck came to a halt behind a cluster of parasol trees, Washington and I climbed down. Jamal reached into the bed of the pickup and pulled out a .38 caliber Smith & Weston from his gadget bag.

"Where the hell'd you get that?" I asked, catching my breath.

"The equipment guy at Spectre let me borrow it for the weekend."

"It's Murray!" Tom shouted, pointing to a small figure coming up the road from the other direction on his penny-farthing two-wheeler.

Washington fired two shots with his pistol while Tom and I screamed in vain. A burst of AK 47 fire threw Murray off his bicycle and splayed him onto the asphalt in a rumpled heap, at the same time sending the giant front wheel of his bicycle flying through the air in a slow arc. "Goddamn!" shouted Washington, looking back in the opposite direction. "Here comes more fuckin' bicycles!"

We managed to flag down the next cluster of bikes before the snipers could get any more shots off and told the riders to head back to Big Buddha. "Stop *everybody!*" Jamal ordered as they rode away.

"You've gotta go get help!" I yelled to Tom.

"I saw a field radio back at the first aid station," he replied. "Come on, let's go!"

I reached into the cab for the Arri BL I had left sitting on the front seat. "I'm staying here to film the action."

"And I'm staying behind to keep an eye on Leary," added Washington.

"I'm out of here!" answered Wheeler, who barely gave me time to grab my camera before he gunned the engine and took off in a cloud of gravel and dust. I spun out of the way and glanced at Jamal, who nodded towards the hills. For the first time in my young life, I was *glad* I had been flying combat. I was still maintaining my high from the start of the race, too pumped with adrenaline to be scared. After working in pitch black while bouncing around in a thirty-degree bank at ten thousand feet, filming something lit by sunshine instead of napalm was going to be a piece of cake. Without saying a word, I stuck the camera on my shoulder and started up a ridge to the right of where most of the shooting was coming from. Washington pushed ahead of me, saying, "You shoot the pictures, I'll shoot the Bad Guys."

I might have smiled if my teeth hadn't been rattled by a ground-shaking explosion. We turned and saw our pickup fishtailing up the road, a scorched crater splitting the asphalt in its wake. I couldn't tell if it had been a mortar or a rocket-propelled grenade, but my adrenaline high suddenly took a nosedive. "Maybe we should pack up and come back later. These guys are fuckin' serious."

"These guys are *very* fuckin' serious," said Jamal, his eyes open wide, darting around quickly in several directions. We reached a point about three-fourths of the way to the top of the ridge and began looking for a spot that would give us cover and still let us film the action when the Air Police showed up. "This might be a little more challenging for the APs than mopping up out on a runway," he whispered. "No guard towers. The Bad Guys have the high ground."

I couldn't answer. I was too busy trying to get a meter reading, check my belt battery, check the cable connections and make sure there was still film left in the four-hundred-foot magazine. Now *nothing* was happening. Even the cicadas were taking a siesta. Not a *jingjok* in sight. It was *too* silent. And we were too damned exposed next to a sheer wall of limestone. Washington pointed, I nodded in agreement, and we made our way down through some elephant grass toward a small cut in the hill, only to discover we couldn't see a thing when we reached the depression. We started climbing again through thick shrubbery and bamboo before coming out in a clearing at the top of the embankment, once again finding ourselves completely exposed. Washington dropped to the ground and pulled me down with him, wrenching the heavy camera off my shoulder and into my eye socket. He indicated with a quick twitch of his head the direction I should look.

And there he was. One of the serious Bad Guys about a hundred feet ahead, talking over a field radio, just enough below us to have kept him from hearing our clumsy footsteps. Jamal started crawling toward him, armed only with his .38, the kind of small-caliber pistol Harley used to call a peashooter. I put my eye back into the viewfinder and zoomed in tight, rolling through my focus. The Bad Guy gunman began to turn towards me and I said a little prayer of thanks that I had the blimped, silent Arri BL with me instead of the lighter but noisier 16St. Keeping my left eye open to figure out where Washington was positioning himself, I started rolling. The tiny beep for synchronizing audio to film—so miniscule I long ago learned to ignore it—might as well have been a temple gong. The Bad Guy spotted me and then spotted Jamal. The rotation of the mirrored shutter caused the image to flicker and darken so that, when the sniper shouldered his AK 47, I wasn't sure at first why I seemed to recognize him. It wasn't until he took direct aim at Jamal that I figured it out—it was Prasert, back from the dead or back from Phitsanulok or wherever the hell Tukada had taken him, his head wound hidden by a bandanna. "Don't shoot!" I cried. "It's Brendan and Jamal!"

Prasert's face loomed large in my viewfinder, his eyes dull and hard. I was certain he was about to shoot me—he could have done it easily—but instead he took his eye out of the sight and turned to the side. "Prasert! *Mai dai! Yut!*" called a woman's voice. I panned over to see Tukada, looking frail and haggard, trying frantically to run toward him, instead repeatedly stumbling and twice falling to her knees. When she reached him, she grabbed the muzzle of Prasert's AK 47 and yanked it away. And then I didn't understand what I was hearing or seeing while I peered with tunnel vision through the flickering shutter of my camera. Above me and around me the ground shook, rocks and dirt swirled and my body was pounded with the thud-thud-thudding of powerful rotor blades, suddenly joined by a short, nasty dragon-hiss of mini-gun fire. Tukada's back ripped open, splattering into a vapor of flesh and bone, pieces of a Mona Lisa masterpiece knifed by an invisible madman. Several members of Prasert's cadre appeared out of the brush behind her and returned a withering fusillade of automatic-rifle and rocket-propelled-grenade fire, enough to drive back the chopper. Somehow Prasert was still standing even though he had been shot in his shoulder, arm, and leg. His bandanna was gone, blood running across his forehead and down his face. Ignoring Tukada as she clutched his leg and crumbled at his feet, Prasert squeezed off his own burst of return fire into the distance behind me and then coolly turned back, staring down my lens, his jaw set. "Oh, mama!" I cried. Prasert's barrel flashed, my lens shattered, and my world went black.

When I woke up, I thought I saw God Himself gazing down at me. It wasn't until my eyes cleared and the world began to come into focus that I realized it was Moonbeam Liscomb. Even though he was kneeling, he seemed tall, looking down with his sweet, comforting Sam Cooke smile as we headed back to base on board his Jolly Green, the wind blowing in wildly through the open side doors. He studied my face carefully for a moment, seemed satisfied, and gave my shoulder a reassuring squeeze before he made his way past the door gunner towards the cockpit.

I noticed my head was pounding, but my attention quickly shifted to the warm, limp mannequin I was holding in my arms, the bleeding body of Tukada Maneewatana, "Baby Doll," the object of half a dozen men's futile dreams and misguided devotion. I pulled myself up and managed to cradle her head in my lap as I looked into deep, liquid, sad brown eyes that asked a question I couldn't answer. They slowly closed and I prayed for a brief moment that she would die quickly and find eternal peace from a life that had already been too harsh, too full of false hope, too full of loss and confusion. She made a soft crackling sound as if trying to clear her throat in her sleep, and an old, shameful dream I once had of stabbing my baby sister, Mary Elizabeth, the most cheerful, lovable, imperturbable baby in the world, came rushing at me and through me. I lost all feeling in my hands and forearms, revisiting the most horrible part of the nightmare—I had watched helplessly as my hands moved of their own volition, stabbing Mary Elizabeth over and over. Now I was filled with loathing and remorse that *I* had been the one who inflicted this dreadful wound on Tukada.

Why were false memories crushing me with false guilt? Wasn't I just the cameraman, the observer, the photojournalist, the fly on the wall, an idea man for the syndicate? Didn't I love her and try to save her? I remembered now—crawling even as my cheekbone throbbed and blood oozed from the side of my head, crawling past the crouching form of Jamal Washington, crawling over rocks and thorns and the red clay dust of Issan Thailand to reach the sniper and his half-sister, my friends who had been enemies. Prasert had taken a head shot from one of the sharpshooters traveling on Jack Wu's tour bus and was down, barely moving, his eyes staring at me in shock. I ignored him, instead turning Tukada over on her stomach on the grassy knoll above Route 66 the day the Big Buddha Bicycle Race ended in a river of blood, and it became again the dream of my sister, my hands stained with crimson that would never wash away. I touched the bloody shreds of her navy work shirt, wanting to cover the gaping wounds in her back, but the denim wouldn't stretch. She was still breathing, but in a rasping, shallow gurgling that meant her lungs were failing her. "Washington!" I called, looking around in the smoke and dust. "You okay? Where's Tom? We need the truck—we gotta get back to the base pronto!"

The late-morning sun was beating down harshly, turning my sweat into burning acid. I felt ever fainter watching Tukada hemorrhage, and, helplessly trying to help, I numbly pulled off my T-shirt, desperately wanting to stop the bleeding. Folding it into a compress, I tried as best I could to bandage her wounds, ugly pockmarks of pink human meat spilling out of a person I loved. And in the midst of being convulsed with a wave of nausea, I had a vision that Lieutenant Liscomb's Jolly Green was coming down from the heavens to save us, but the miracle ended when real bullets from the surviving members of Prasert's cadre began slamming into the fuselage and cockpit and the auxiliary fuel tanks. It made a violent dive to the right and escaped, leaving us behind.

Wu's Air Police sharpshooters scrambled further up the hill behind us in a confusion of smoke and dust and guns firing and bullets ricocheting and cut down the last remnants of Prasert's band. Moonbeam's helicopter made a third pass and finally landed in an even bigger confusion of dust and flying rocks and whirling blades. Standing in the doorway as I approached, he knelt down and tried to take hold of Tukada, the baby doll I now could barely carry. With a rush of forgotten strength, I handed her up to Liscomb and tried to climb on board myself, but the Jolly Green had started lifting off. I had used up whatever strength I had carrying Tukada and now my sweaty fingers were losing their grip. Before I could decide whether to let go or try to hang on, Liscomb reached back with his powerful boxing-champion hand and pulled me inside by my belt loop, dropping me with a thump. The vibrating of the helicopter floor rocked me into a woozy sleep, and somehow, while I was fading in and out, Tukada instinctively inched her body close to mine.

Her eyes were dull as they opened. "Bren-dan—are we going home?"

I kissed her once-silky hair, now disheveled and caked with blood. "As soon as you get out of the hospital," I answered, remembering how little time we had spent together, how it had all seemed like a dream, yet how it had all seemed like the prelude to something soft and tender that might last a lifetime.

"Can we get mar-ried and go Sa-dates?"

"Yes," I lied.

"What happen to Prasert?"

Another white lie couldn't hurt. "They're taking him to the hospital near your house."

She looked worried. "Everyone who die today have very bad kamma. Everyone who have violent death have difficult re-birth."

"Innocent victims too? That doesn't seem fair."

"It mean you still have bad kamma from previous life. I worry about my kamma. I afraid I have much bad kamma from last life and I afraid I keep making more."

"Not today. You saved a lot of lives. When we get your daughter back, we can have a good life together. You can be a good mother and do many good deeds for your family and friends. We can make offerings to the monks—"

"I sink I'm hurt bad, Bren-dan. Something inside of me bro-ken."

"You're gonna make it. Lieutenant Liscomb's with us. He's gonna make sure you get Dr. Lioci. He's the best damn surgeon in the Seventh Air Force."

"When I get out of hos-pi-tal, you promise we go Sa-dates?

"As soon as you're strong enough, if that's what you want. Or I can stay here and teach English. We don't have to decide that right now, do we?"

"No," she replied, her sad face serene as we hit an updraft and she was jolted with a wave of pain. "Bren-dan?"

"Yes?"

"Can we go see Gran' Canyon?"

"In our magic purple paisley bus." My eyes sparkled, my face lighting up with a gentle laugh. For a moment I could picture the freshly painted van parked at the North Rim. For a moment I believed my own bullshit. And for a fleeting moment I saw a smile on her flawless, stoic face.

"It's so beauti-ful," she said as she drifted off to sleep. Her eyes were closed when she called a little later, "Bren-dan...it's okay you shoot me. You don' know."

"Shsh, shsh. It wasn't me. We were caught in a crossfire. You were trying to help. I was just making a movie—*tai papayon taunan*—about a goddamn bicycle race. But you don't have to talk about it right now. You should rest till we get to the emergency room."

But she couldn't rest. Her eyes opened again. "I sor-ry, Bren-dan. I so sor-ry I come too late. I sink Prasert jus' talk big to his frien' when he say bicycle race a 'soft tar-get.' Everysing Liberation Front do end up a mess. I don' understan'—he *like* you and Tom and Lar-ry and Dave. You his *frien'*. I so sorry, Bren-dan. Wis baby gone, I cannot sink straight. I smoke opium. I so ashame." She stiffened when another wave of pain pierced her body, then relaxed and sank peacefully into my arms. Her eyelids were only halfway opened, her pupils glassy and unfocussed. "Bren-dan—you are a good *farang*, not like all the oz-zer."

"Shush, goddamnit, and get some rest." And this time, for the first time in all the months I had known her, she did what I begged, letting her eyelids shut, taking my hand in hers and squeezing like a baby. "That's a good girl."

She was still alive when we landed and got her onto a stretcher and into the ambulance that took us to the base hospital. Liscomb rode shotgun and told the driver to step on it. I climbed in with Tukada. "Brendan?" she called softly, not opening her eyes this time. "Promise you not ever leave me?"

"Of course I'll never leave you."

"You're the finest man I ever know."

"I love you, Dah."

"I love you too. You promise you never leave, Bren-dan?"

"Never."

Shortly before we reached the hospital I told Lieutenant Liscomb we could slow down. Dah was gone for the last time.

It was not until Dr. Lioci had officially pronounced her dead and instructed an orderly to notify the proper authorities that Wozniak, the head nurse, called him over and lifted the bandage that was covering my right temple. When a few red droplets hit my surgical gown, I was reminded that it was not just Dah's blood smeared across my chest and arms and encrusted in my pants. "It doesn't look like you were shot, Leary, but they turned your camera into a ball of shrapnel when they hit it." The good doctor helped me onto a gurney. "I'll have a better picture when we finish cleaning the fragments out of your hands and scalp and get some X-rays. One thing's certain, though—a couple of inches to your left and you wouldn't be with us. You're a lucky guy."

I wasn't feeling lucky. I wasn't feeling a thing, even if my face and hands were starting to throb. All I wanted was to sleep. I wanted this dream to be over. I felt cursed and I wanted the curse lifted. I felt guilty for the massacre and I hadn't fired a shot. I felt doomed by a blood sacrifice that bound me to Tukada across the dimensions of life and death. Once again, I wanted to go home; only now I sensed that I would never leave. As they were wheeling me out of triage, Liscomb told me that Wheeler's truck had just pulled in with the bodies of Murray, Sachs and Spitzer. They had also brought in Shahbazian and Zelinsky, who needed some patching up. Wheeler and Washington had gotten through the day without a scratch.

That night, lying in my bed, I could hear a steady rumble through the thin walls of the prefab base hospital as Spectre bird after Spectre bird rolled down the runway and headed off for Laos. Nixon and Kissinger were on their way to China, but the war went on, and now that Sachs was dead, it had gotten a little more personal for the 16th Special Operations Squadron. His death would be avenged a hundred times over. And then a hundred times more.

The End

Glossary

There is no direct transliteration of Thai—a tonal language with 44 consonants and 21 vowels—into English. The following, however, should give English-speaking readers a sense of its sounds and rhythms.

Frequently occurring vowels:
> /**ai**/ = /y/ as in my; /**ae**/ = /ay/ as in say; /**ao**/ = /ow/ as in wow; /**aw**/ = /aw/ as in saw; /**ii**/ = /ee/ as in see; /**oh**/ = /oa/ as in oat; /**u**/=/oo/ as in shoot.

Frequently occurring consonants:
> *Except for the /**Th**/ in Thailand, the aspirated /**t**/ will be written as such, and the unaspirated* **t** *and* **d** *will both be written as /**d**/. The aspirated /**p**/ will be written as such, and the unaspirated* **p** *and* **b** *will be written as /**b**/. Finally, /**kh**/ = /k/; /**k**/ = /g/.*

ampuhr—district

Ajahn—form of address for professor, master, senior monk

ao—want, have

arai na?—what? what was that again?

Arri(flex) BL—blimped 16mm movie camera, good for filming interviews

Arri(flex) St—handheld 16mm movie camera, noisy but good for combat photography

ARVN—Army of the Republic of Vietnam (pro-American South Vietnamese soldiers)

baht—unit of Thai currency, traded twenty to the dollar in early '70s

bai tiao—go out for fun

bai tura—go out on business

BDA—bomb damage assessment

Bolex—relatively cheap 16mm amateur movie camera

BX—Base Exchange, on-base department store for GIs only, source of tax-free imported goods like whiskey and cigarettes traded on the black market downtown *chang len glong*—drummer (lit. "expert at playing drum")

CO—conscientious objector

CBPO—Consolidated Base Personnel Office

DMZ—Demilitarized Zone dividing North and South Vietnam

FAA/NTSB—Federal Aviation Administration / National Transportation Safety Board

farang—foreigner of European descent

GI—slang for American soldier, especially enlisted man (from WWII-era "Government Issue")

G's—abbreviation for g-force, the gravitational force felt in flight while accelerating or banking

hong nam—bathroom (lit. "water room")

jing—real

jing-jing—really

jingjok—small household lizard, normally harmless

Jolly Green—large-capacity Sikorsky HH-3E rescue helicopter

katoy—transvestite

kha—polite way for female to end sentence (akin to "sir" or "madam," see *khrab*)

khaojai mai?—do you understand?

khaopaht gung—fried rice with shrimp

khii mao—(adj) stinking drunk

khrab—polite way for male to end sentence (akin to "sir" or "madam," see *kha*)

Khun—Mr./Mrs./Miss

kuti—small hut where monk resides

LRRP (pronounced "LURP")—long range reconnaissance patrol, or member of said team

Mae Nam Kong—Mekong River

Mae Nam Mun—Mun River

mahk—much/very

mai—no, not; at end of sentence, makes it a question (e.g. "You're ready, no?)

mai pen rai—idiomatic "no problem"/ "no sweat"

na?/!—sometimes meaningless syllable added for emphasis/ there!

nuat—massage

NCO—non-commissioned officer

NCOIC—non-commissioned officer in charge

NVA—North Vietnamese Army (highly trained regular soldiers)

OTS—Officer Training School (Air Force)

Prah—form of address for monk

prohd pud chah-chah noy—please speak a little slower

Puff ("The Magic Dragon")—AC-47 gunship, first in series of converted cargo planes that led to the AC-119 Stinger and the AC-130 Spectre, the only one with four engines

pud—speak

pu-ying—girl/woman

rahn-ahahn—restaurant

ru?—short-form question word meaning "or not?"

roht—vehicle, as in rohtfai (train), roht meh (bus), roht tax-ii (taxi cab)

ROTC—Reserve Officers' Training Corps, trains college student to become US military officers

RTAFB—Royal Thai Air Force Base

sabaidii—all right!/? (Lao/Northeast Thai greeting)

SAC—Strategic Air Command; USAF unit flying B-52s capable of delivering nuclear warheads

sahmlaw—bicycle-powered rickshaw (lit. "three wheels")

sahp—to know

sanuk—festive

sapparoht—pineapple

satahnii rohtfai—railroad station

sawatdii—hello/goodbye

Slick—UH-1, or Huey, transport helicopter without protruding armaments

tahahn akaht tii tai papayon—air force cameraman

tamruat—police

TDY—Temporary Duty Assignment

tii—to/at/that

tii-rahk—informally, girl or boyfriend; GI/bargirl slang: to live together (lit. "loved one")

triple-A (or AAA)—Anti-Aircraft Artillery

Tukada—char. name, literally: doll

USAF—United States Air Force

VC—Viet Cong (insurgents operating in South Vietnam)

wai—prayer-like gesture of greeting or respect

yindii tii dai rujak—pleased to meet you

yu—reside, stay

yut—stop

Acknowledgments

The Big Buddha Bicycle Race is a work of fiction. Poetic license has been taken. But I would like to thank the following writers and teachers for whatever cultural and historical authenticity this book contains: Jack Kornfield, whose writing and teaching opened many doors for me, Ajahn Buddhadasa, Ajahn Chah, Dean Barrett, Capt Thomas D. Boettcher, Joe Cummings, Alan Dawson, Dieter Dengler, Col David Hackworth, Jane Hamilton-Merritt, John Hinds, Yupa Holzner, Stanley Karnow, Lutz Lehman, Alfred W. McCoy, Gen Bruce Palmer, Jr., Christopher Robbins, Richard A. Ruth, Denis Segaller, William Shawcross, Wallace Terry, Col Gerald H. Turley, Bill Weir, and Col Henry Zeybel. And the following publishers: Aerospace Publishing, Amaravati Publications, Arnow Press, Insight Guides, The International Labor Organization, Lonely Planet, Military Press, Moon Handbooks, Shambala Publications, and the World Fellowship of Buddhists. And finally, the many Buddhist laypeople in Thailand, the US and England, whose generosity has made possible the publication of countless books, in English and Thai, available for free only at Buddhist monasteries in those countries.

And I would especially like to thank the following people who directly supported me on this undertaking: MSgt Larry Tener (USAF, ret.), a big-hearted warrior and friend forever; Susan Craig, for her continued encouragement; Ajahn Jayasaro; Ajahn Pasanno; Ajahn Sumedho; Ajahn Thanissaro; Bhikkhu Nirodho; Charles Agar; Capt John Harkin (USAir, ret.); Gordon Kappel; Francis Kirby; Dorothy Little; Capt Bob Mueller, (USAir, ret.); my brother Murph; LtCol Chris O'Grady (USAF, Ret.); Samai and Lumpian Pengjam; Jeanne Rosenberg; Harry Spring; Jay and Nittaya Uhley; former Air Force Captain Duke Underwood, Shinzen Young; Susan Walsh; Joe Rumbaugh and Tong at Asia Vehicle Rental in Vientiane, Laos; my high school English teacher, Rudy Spik, who pored over the first draft; Professor Irwin Blacker and editor Caitlin Alexander for challenging me to dig deep and make this a better book; Ken Silverman for getting me back on my bicycle; Rebecca Weldon and Writers Without Borders in Chiang Mai, Thailand; Professor Michael Fitzgerald for his close reading; Trasvin Jittidecharak, my publisher, and Joel Akins, my editor, at Silkworm Books; and finally, my wife and best friend, Nancy, for her insight, humor, and unwavering support.

About the Author

Terence A. Harkin earned a BA in English-American Literature from Brown University while spending weekends touring New England with rock bands that opened for The Yardbirds, the Shirelles, the Critters and Jimi Hendrix. His play, *Resurrection*, produced during his senior year, was a winner of the Production Workshop Playwriting Contest. He won a CBS Fellowship for his screenwriting while completing an MFA at the University of Southern California and went on to spend twenty-five years as a Hollywood cameraman. His credits include *The Goodbye Girl*, teen cult favorite *The Legend of Billie Jean, Quincy, Designing Women, Seinfeld, Tracy Ullman, MASH*, and the mini-series of *From Here to Eternity*. *The Big Buddha Bicycle Race* and its sequel, *In the Year of the Rabbit*, are set in Ubon, Thailand, where he served with AAVS Detachment 3 during the Vietnam War. He is currently at work on a third novel, *Tinseltown Two-Step*, set in L.A. and Chiang Mai.

For further information, readers can contact Terence A. Harkin at his Web address: http://www.tharkin.net.

Made in the USA
Middletown, DE
19 July 2017